Kevin Curran grew up in Balbriggan, County Dublin. He has a Masters Degree in Anglo-Irish Literature from University College Dublin. *Beatsploitation* is his first book. He teaches in Dublin.

First published in 2013 by
Liberties Press
140 Terenure Road North | Terenure | Dublin 6W
Tel: +353 (1) 405 5701
www.libertiespress.com | info@libertiespress.com

Trade enquiries to Gill & Macmillan Distribution
Hume Avenue | Park West | Dublin 12
T: +353 (1) 500 9534 | F: +353 (1) 500 9595 | E: sales@gillmacmillan.ie

Distributed in the UK by
Turnaround Publisher Services
Unit 3 | Olympia Trading Estate | Coburg Road | London N22 6TZ
T: +44 (0) 20 8829 3000 | E: orders@turnaround-uk.com

Distributed in the United States by
Dufour Editions | PO Box 7 | Chester Springs | Pennsylvania 19425

ISBN: 978-1-907593-74-1
2 4 6 8 10 9 7 5 3 1

A CIP record for this title is available from the British Library.

Cover design by Philip Farmer

The publishers gratefully acknowledge
financial assistance from the Arts Council.

BEATSPLOITATION

Kevin Curran

For my parents, John and Una Curran. Thank you.

September.

On the third note, the low C after the high G and E, I've sat down, opened the Mac and started it up. The three notes from the bell cut me off from everything, signal the end of my working day. Chairs scraping off tables and kids shouting aren't my problem. Even though I'm in my class I'm not a teacher. I'm loading up the songs Steve sent and I'm a musician.

Some student comes up and stands over my desk and goes, 'D'ye hear about Jake Ryan sir?'

I stare at the screen and go, 'No, why?' Humouring him cause the internet's slow.

'He's gone to the Community College.'

'Good lad,' I say.

'He has,' he goes on, despite my reaction. 'His ma says this place's a kip and it's nothing like they said it would be, so he's gone to the CC and he's repeatin second year and he's gonna do nets for them. He's captain of the Ireland Under Fifteens now too sir. That's cat on you.' He laughs and leaves and the room is empty.

I shake off his words and put on my big ear-muffler headphones. Steve's been going on about the songs all day in his texts. The new vacuum of the headphones relaxes instantly and I look up at the paper balls, toppled chairs, discarded essays, with a new, almost magic detachment. Dull shadows pass outside in the corridor. They ramble to their lockers, home. The pulled blinds that hide me, silhouette them. There's the usual rumble as they go and I ignore it since it's not in my room.

A shadow at the door behind makes me look up. A face, lips moving and I tear my headphones off and through the blaring music go, '*What?*'

'Sorry Robert,' a little timid voice goes, some young sub, more eyes than face behind thick frames, 'can you give me a hand inside?'

I'm fooled by her calm tone and let out a heavy breath and say, 'Okay. Where?'

She leaves without answering. She's waiting for me outside and I see there's a mill-up in the room across the corridor. A crowd is gathering, jumping and clawing to get a glimpse. I look at her and she smiles an apology and I think, *Nice one, thanks for the heads-up.* On the surface it seems like I've a choice, but the moment bystanders see me on the scene, my reputation depends on getting in there.

What reputation? I'm about to turn away, hide out, ignore it all but Lauren comes around the corner and sees me so I pretend I'm just closing my door and I plough through the cheerers, the noise rising with my arrival, and land into the chaos in the classroom. There's about four or five lads on top of each other, chairs and tables thrown all over the place, schoolbags all over the floor. I size up the situation quickly. The majority of the rumble are lads trying to break it up. I wade in and lean over the collapsing group to try and get between them and get to the two lads battering each other. I somehow muscle in and make myself known, thinking – stupidly – if they see me they'll stop. They don't even flinch and keep on wrestling with each other. I can hear their breathing, the heavy gulps and grunts with each dig.

'Break it up!' I shout into the noise. Somehow I manage to get between them. A face finally appears. It's John. Kembo. He manages a few short, powerful digs into the white lad's head. There's blood smeared on white skin. Me and another helper grab John, big beast of a fella, all tensed up, and pull him back off the other lad. As we do this either he, or me, or someone else, trips on some bags and we all pile backwards, falling against the wall.

We fumble around on the floor and I scramble to my feet to save any sliver of dignity in case Lauren's still there. I look up past the smiles and open mouths to see the other lad being pushed out the door before another teacher arrives. Eamon, a big six-foot-two old-school head, shouts orders and tries to get a handle on things. The helpers scarper from the room and I close out the stares, slam the door. I turn and see John towering over me.

'Outta the w-w-way, sir, please,' he shouts.

There's a new silence in the room. The cheers've been muted out-side. I'm shaking, riddled with adrenaline. So's he. He's fuming, breathing all heavy, his chest lifting and falling like mad.

'Get back, John,' I say, my hands raised. 'Calm down.'

We're both caught up in the chaos of it all.

He goes to grab the door handle, his bottom teeth, his top lip, his breathing whistling through the gap, spit coming and going.

'He-he called me a nigger s-s-sir an-an he took my box sir. He called me a nigger.'

'Box?' I'm saying and he tries to get past by grabbing my shoulder. I hold my ground and grip the door handle. But it won't keep him for long.

'Get back John,' I say, trying to sound menacing, 'you're not going out there.'

'He called me a n-nigger, sir, he took my box. I-I just wanted to like show the class my box. I'm gonna kill him sir,' he says, his voice pitchy, like he's gonna cry. Before I can answer him he heaves at my arm. His massive hands seize me and I brace myself and hold on to the door with my left hand and clock him one with my right. Instinct or fear, or both, I dunno, makes me do it. A short circular swing, down over his eyebrow, scraping down to the cheek. His spit is warm on my hand and he jolts back just as stunned as me, his breathing stopped, his mouth gaping. His eyes are massive and his chest still. He looks confused, like he's thinking of what to do with me. Something sad's about to be spoken but he stops and lunges for the handle. I flinch, the adrenaline soured into fear, and let the door go. He reefs it open and runs.

The cheers are weak when he emerges and I fall back shaking against the wall. This pain appears in my hand. It looks like it's starting to swell up. My knuckles are red. My legs are about to give way. My collar is soaked, my armpits sticky. I feel like fainting. And then I see her, cowering in the corner, little sniffles. That sub. Those glasses, the teeth taking over her face. She's trying to say something, but she can't stop sniffling.

'You didn't see that,' I say through deep breaths.

'B . . . b . . . but,' she tries to answer.

'You didn't see that,' I say, a new steadiness returned.

'But you just . . .'

'Where were you when it started?' I shout, cutting her off. 'Huh?'

'I – I had to go, I had to go to the toilet.'

'So you left the room with a full class still in it?'

'I – I had to. . .'

'Do you think that'll go down well with the principal?'

She shakes her head.

'Exactly. You caused this. You didn't see what just happened there and you were in the room when it started and I heard the noise and came in to help. Okay?'

She pulls up some snots.

'Okay?'

'Okay,' she whispers and heaves a portable stereo cassette player yoke from under a table. It's like something I had when I was twelve.

'They were fighting over this,' she says.

I peer at the piece of junk, say, 'Give it to me,' and hold out my hand for her to bring it across the room.

I take it from her and tell her to pull herself together. She rubs her eyes and I say, 'Don't worry, I'll deal with the principal. It wasn't your fault.'

'Thanks,' she whimpers, and I open the door for her and go, 'Don't mention it.'

*

Everything. The gollier green sea; the rolling telephone wires hypno-tising me as the train rocks down the coast; the stone that hits the window but doesn't smash it; the long grass coming through cracks in an unfinished road on one of those estates; the rubbish dumped over the ditches onto the sides of the tracks; the bedpan that is the new stadium spied between rooftops; the one lonely crane; the empty, half-complete office blocks; the slivers of silver all merging into just two parallel rail lines; the traffic on the quays; the Mediterranean heat from the backs of busses as they pass me on Wexford Street; the fruit and veg stalls being folded up; the early neon sizzling like a fly catcher across the road; the smell of incense inside the door; the dark-ness of Anseo; the small glow from tea lights; the chequered floor; the growing list of books on the new shelf; the smell of bleach when someone goes into the jacks; the cool touch of the pint; the dull clink of glass on glass when we say a muted 'cheers'; the slightly metallic taste of an early evening beer; everything keeps my mind from it until I follow Steve out onto Camden Street for his smoke and he notices the bruise and goes, 'What happened yer hand?'

'Nothing,' I say, 'just knocking the kids around in school, ye know.'

Steve looks at me through the smoke, narrows his eyes like he's judging me, big concerned face on him and I grin, finally, as if I'm joking and he shakes his head with a rueful smile and says, 'Ye had me there man. Either that or ye've had another fight with Mono.'

Mono's the guitarist. Steve's the bass player in the band. My band. Our band. The Terrors.

'Nah – just knocked it off something,' I say and Steve puts out the smoke and we head back in.

We sup away at our pints on the torn couch beside the jacks. Steve says nothing for a while. Doesn't even ask why I wanted a pint. He stares across at the bar where the new barwoman is doing her thing. After a while of this, when I've properly settled and melted back into the seat, relaxed and forgotten all about school again, Steve asks for the time.

I check my phone. 'Half-six. Why?'

He nods to himself and goes, 'We would've been finished our sound check by now.'

I tell him not to start.

'I'm just sayin,' he goes, all innocent.

'Well don't,' I say. 'I've had enough from Mono. And I'll tell you what I told him: it would've been a wasted trip.'

'No trip to play in London is a waste.'

I don't have the energy. Really don't. But I'm compelled to fight my corner.

'C'mon Steve. London on a Thursday in some random back hole boozer isn't gonna make us. I'm barely two weeks back and yis were lookin for me to take time off for an unpaid gig for some lad we've never heard of. It's ridiculous.'

'It's not.'

'It is. Forking out for our own flights and accommodation. Not even guaranteed anything from the door. Do you have any idea how much it costs to carry four keyboards on a plane?'

'We woulda chipped in Rob, if you'd have even entertained the idea,' he says, lifting his pint, looking like he's not being swayed by my argument. I tut and blow a breath and wave him away.

'No yis wouldn't,' I say, real low, cause I don't wanna argue.

I take a gulp of my pint, start tracing my finger down the side of it, 'I saved us a wasted journey – a fortune – and I'm the one who gets it in the neck.'

Steve shakes his head, 'Ye don't know that,' he says, relaxed now too, 'we don't know. The promoter told Mono there was a chance there could've been A&R there. He said A&R always go to those gigs.'

I wave him and his holy grail of A&R in London away.

'Barry said it'd be a good move . . .'

I laugh, almost spit out my pint. The cheek. I picture Barry, our 'contact' with a Major Label in the UK, with his big serious head, rubbing his big, serious, important chin, considering what Steve said to him.

'Would ye go away outta that,' I say, drink the last of my drink, glance to the bar, smell the incense. 'Barry will say anything to sound like he knows what he's talking about.'

'He does know what he's talking about,' Steve says, holding up his hand to the barwoman and asking for the same again and gathering up the empty glasses, the ripped bar mats, the remains of the Bacon

Fries. Dinner. I'm a bit locked. Don't have the energy.

'Look,' I say, 'London was a con. We'll have another chance. A proper chance. There's no point going over there just to say we went over there and play to a sound engineer and the barman. It'll have to be a proper gig to get me over there, Steve. And I'll be the first on the flight. I can guarantee you that. That's the end of it.'

Our pints arrive. Steve smiles and goes, 'Grassy-ass,' and she puts her hands on her hips, all impressed, and goes, 'De nada.' She turns and when she gets to the bar glances back, still smiling.

Steve goes and asks the question I was half dreading he'd ask, 'How's school anyway?'

'Ah,' I say, mulling over how to respond, 'just needed a pint. Feel like I'm after wastin two years of me life with all this teachin lark.'

'That bad?'

'I'm after getting myself in a bit of bother.'

'Yeah?' he says, a fake disinterest. 'How serious?'

'I'll know tomorrow. Don't wanna talk about it.'

He whistles and holds up his pint, 'Maybe ye shudda taken the days off and gone to London after all.'

'Not a hope,' I say. 'Then I'd definitely be outta the job.'

'Well, cheers anyway,' he goes and we clink glasses. It's nice to be here with him, as a friend, now that all the band talk's been put aside.

'This is me last though,' I say after we take our sups. 'Big day tomorrow. Don't wanna be stinkin of booze.'

'Course, yeah, course,' Steve says and waves to the bar and goes, 'Kay passeh?' and all of a sudden we're having shots on the house and the Spaniard's sitting with us, nestling into Steve and we're going across the road for late drinks and I'm swaying at the toilet mirror, still in my shirt and jumper from school and I'm taking my bag and coat from the cloakroom, checking my phone for the first time in ages, seeing eight missed calls from Jen, waiting on the traffic lights, stumbling around the corner and knocking the jackets off the hanger in the hall, slamming the door behind me and slumping onto the bed, landing on Jen's leg, hearing Jen moaning in my ear, 'It's two o'clock Rob, where were you? I've been calling you,' and I'm listening, but sleeping, getting comfortable outside the sheets with my clothes still on.

★

I've been in bits all day, hiding in my room, shoving mints in my mouth and shrugging off the incident if students ask me what I know about it. I'm just waiting for the knock, sweating out the worry. Every class has been given a fake test to keep them busy for when the knock comes. I'm not surprised, but still spooked, when it finally arrives. Last class. This time yesterday I think.

The principal sticks his head in.

'Can I eh . . .' he says.

Eyes rise from their work.

'Me?'

He nods. No emotion.

There's a hush of whispers.

'Just need you for a while,' he says when I come outside. 'Issues with more of the NN's again,' and his eyes flick to the ceiling and he sighs. The sound of scandal starts up behind me. He looks down at his feet.

'Okay, em, if you can . . .'

He nods for me to follow.

He walks ahead and I can see deep blue patches on his pale blue shirt. We don't speak. The corridors are so quiet I can hear his slacks swish. He walks with his hands turned out and flapping, the knuckles near scraping the floor, the bandy leg stroll of a farmer in his fields. I try to calm my breathing. Compose myself. He disappears into his office. I see legs, jeans and tracksuit bottoms and dirty runners.

The principal settles behind his desk, facing John and his mother. John's older brother sits facing me on the opposite side of the room. We've met before.

'Mr Lynch, this is the student's mother, and brother.'

I don't greet them or shake their hands or acknowledge we've already met. I just nod.

'Take a seat, please.'

I sit and wait for it: *Kembo has made an allegation.*

Kembo is John. Kembo is his African name. John is his school name. The name he picked to try and ensure he didn't stick out.

The sub is there too. She's hidden, nearly melting into the pale wall, lurking behind the big potted plant. My legs are fidgety. I cross them and cover them with my hands. I see the bruise on my right hand, cover it quickly with the left.

'Now, em,' the principal says, his fingers entwined before his rubbery nose. He stretches his lips and his whole face warps as he savours the atmosphere of fear.

'Now, we had an issue yesterday with this student.'

John stares ahead at the principal. His right side faces me, but I can see a lump, bruising of sorts, on his left side. It's hard to tell with the dark skin. His left eye looks bloodshot. The brother glares across to me, silent and emotionless. He's hard to read.

'What we believe has happened is that there's been a very aggressive altercation with another third-year student yesterday. Now, what we hear is that the other student had to visit the doctor . . .'

'H-he started . . .'

'Enuff!' John's older brother shouts.

The principal wipes his mouth and nods to John's brother.

'Okay,' the principal says. His voice, although not rising and not quite angry, becomes more intense. 'What we don't need from the likes of *you*, is more lip. Just button it, okay?' It's a deep type of whisper that suppresses something.

'Sorry sir,' the brother says.

'Now, we've spoken to the other boy, and we've spoken with students in class at the time.' He stops, a beat, and looks to the sub, extra gravity given to the situation. 'And I've spoken with Ms Faherty.' The principal's eyes rest on me. John's eyes meet mine too. Nothing though. The radiator hums into action. A clock ticks. John's eyes flicker like he's got something caught in them.

'We have a clear picture of what went on,' the principal goes. 'We know what has been alleged, by both students, and what has been clarified. The other student is not going to press charges. His father does not want to make a fuss. Ultimately, what we are left with here are injuries and actions and racist taunting that cannot, and will not be tolerated, in this school, on our premises or in our classrooms. Now, there will be changes. And after considering everything, all options open to us, we realise *you* need to realise that in this school, in *this* community, you need to adhere to *our* rules. And if you don't adhere there are repercussions – so – as of today you will be excluded for seven days.'

'B-but sir . . .'

His brother nudges him, grips his arm. He stops his protest. The sub keeps her eyes on the ground.

'What do you have to say to Mr Lynch?' the principal says.

John turns to me slowly, his whole body shifting with his head, like his neck is stiff or something. I'm still unsure of what's going on.

My mouth is dry. My chest feels tight. All eyes are on me. I feel like I should say something to defend myself. Launch a pre-emptive attack. And then John speaks, whispers.

'I-I'm sorry, sir.'

Silence. My heartbeat. The sub looks up, her brow creased.

'For what, young man?' the principal whispers, like some daytime TV host, emotional but probing.

'F-for knockin you o-o-on the ground, sir.'

'And will it happen again?'

'No, sir.'

I'm so surprised I nearly forget to accept his apology. The trigger is cocked, but not pulled. I wonder can they see my whole body exhale.

His eyes burn into me, without judgement, no sense of the lie we share.

'That's okay John. Let's just forget about it,' I say.

The principal gets to his feet.

'Thank you, Mr Lynch. That'll be all for now.'

I look to John one last time and try to read his mind, see what's happening in his head. I stand up. The mother remains mute. The room wobbles. I'm spent.

'Thanks John,' I say and the principal nods in appreciation.

As I go I hear the principal start up again, 'This sort of behaviour makes a positive asylum letter quite difficult . . .' and I'm drifting down the corridor, smiling, sweating, confused, but so relieved I could dance. It's not the relief of keeping my job; it's the buzz of getting away with murder.

★

Jen's got a bored look on her face when she meets me at the entrance to the club with my synthesiser. It's just a little thing that you plug into a digital keyboard. I left it in our apartment. The lads are round the back getting their gear from the van. The driver keeps on hassling us cause we're running an hour late and he has another pick-up. He tells us he'll be back at twelve and to be ready.

Jen gives me the synth and I kiss her and say thanks, but then realise something's missing.

'The plug?'

'What plug?'

'Ah, Jen – I told ye – the plug was beside the bed.'

She frowns, shrugs.

'I forgot.'

'Ah, Jen.'

'I forgot, I'm sorry – what more do ye want?'

'Can you get it?'

She throws her head back and goes, 'For real?'

I kiss her forehead.

'I'm sorry, just ye know I need it, babe. I'd go myself but I've to help the lads get the gear in.'

She turns away, without a word, her head shaking, and she calls me from across the road and starts to say something but I can't hear cause the Luas glides past, scraping and screeching between us.

Denise – one of these 'Band-Aids', hangers-on like – arrives off the Luas.

'Hey you,' she beams, jumping in to kiss me on the cheek. The noise moves off and Jen is still there, looking on from a distance. I move away from Denise. Her extreme pleasantness, fake happiness, always puts me on guard. Denise sees Jen looking on.

'Hi Jen,' she says, waving with her fingers. You can tell Jen thinks about joining us, thinks better of it, and moves off.

'What you doin here on a school night Bob?' Denise says and fondles my sleeve.

'Playin.'

'Playing?' she says, laughing. 'Very funny – this is an up-and-coming showcase. You lads played this last year.'

I shrug it off.

'. . . and the year before, remember? It was on in August then, not September – and we all went back to the party in Kieran's and it was mental and you, didn't you end up havin a blow-out with him? What was that all about?'

She just won't shut up

The lads arrive under the old orange street lamp, finally, with their soft cases and bags of leads. She squints, like she's short-sighted or something.

'So you guys really are playin. The Terrors,' she says and looks into an imaginary space where she sees our name up in lights. Her hand draws across the air, 'Up-and-coming since 1981,' and she giggles. 'What time yis on?'

'Eleven,' one of the lads says.

'Eleven, shame, Ali are on in the other room – sorry guys. They're massive right now.' And she leaves, taking the worn steps down into the club.

'She's still thick about that gig we got over her band years ago, isn't she?' the drummer says and brushes by me with his snare and cymbal bag.

'Yeah,' I shrug.

'Get the synth?' Mono asks.

'Yeah, but Jen forgot the plug.'

'Bob,' he says, anger in his voice, 'we're on in half an hour – Barry's gonna be here.'

'Barry's always here,' I say, dismissing the buzz of having A&R at our gig, and point at his guitar case, 'Sure you forget your spare strings.'

'So what? We can play without spare guitar strings, we can't play the new song without the synth . . .'

'We can play without the guitar full stop.'

His brow creases – he stares hard.

'What's that meant to mean?' He steps toward me.

'Forget it. Just forget it Mono.'

I turn and take the steps down to the venue. Punters squeeze by going up, peering into the orange darkness.

Mono takes a hold of my shoulder as we go down.

'What's that supposed to mean, Bob?'

'Nothing. I'm joking.'

A bouncer comes between us.

'You're blockin the way lads,' and puts out his hand to display the rest of the stairs.

There's a huge crowd. The one venue, for this weekend only, has split itself into five different stages. The space can't accommodate it. The crowd is just too big. I can barely squeeze my keyboards in the door and then we have to get everything ready in a side hall – in everyone's way as they go to the toilet. This 'Dublin's up-and-coming' festival is becoming more popular every year. I should know; we've played it the last four. Our stage is a lot quieter than the previous years. The place isn't empty – just not rammed like it should be. Like it used to be.

We don't give the assembled crowd opportunity to clap or shout.

We've been burned too many times by horrible, embarrassing silences between songs. After one song ends I start another up with a few sounds from my synths. But through my sounds, past lights, through the dry ice, and the odd dancer at the crest of the stage, I can see gaps, and people queuing to go next door to see Ali. There's a lump in my throat. I get that suffocating feeling.

Jen's at the back of the room, arms folded, just standing there like she'd rather be somewhere else. She's on her own. Cut off from the punters swaying and nodding and tapping their feet around her.

The gig goes alright. Not great, but not brutal. We put our gear into the soft cases beside the stairs to the toilets. Barry, A&R from a major label, comes over to Derek, our singer.

'That was great,' I hear him shout over the noise of another band starting up, 'really great.' Derek nods in appreciation, wearily.

'Really great,' Barry says again. He's rigid, real self-conscious of the fact that our destiny is in his hands, distant but still 'our mate'. He's a fan, but a businessman, too old to be trendy, too young to be suited.

I join them.

'Alright Barry,' I say.

'Ah, Bob Terror,' he says, shakes my hand, 'great gig, great gig.'

'Any word on that recording session?' I say, just to cut out the back-slapping and get straight to it. He smiles an uncomfortable smile and looks to Derek, then Mono, who has joined us.

'Don't worry Barry,' Mono says, hand on his shoulder. 'I'll e-mail you about it Monday.'

But we've e-mailed and e-mailed.

'I'm just askin – we're waitin. We'll record, pay for another EP ourselves if you tell us . . .'

'There's no need to do that,' he says.

'But there is. Time's passin us by. I dunno if you've noticed, but we're not the most popular band in the city anymore . . .'

'But you're still the best.'

I shake my head.

'The best according to you, Barry.'

Mono's hand flickers between the noise and the smoke and the lights. It goes from Barry's shoulder to mine.

'The best according to Barry is enough for us, isn't it Derek?' he says.

Derek nods.

'Defo.'

'Whatever,' I say, and turn to finish packing my stuff.

Barry steps around me and goes to the back of the venue to fold his arms and look all serious analysing other bands.

'Well?' I say.

'Well what? There's no need to be like that with him, Bob. He'll come good,' Mono says.

'Yeah, yeah. One session he's paid for – one – and we're still sittin on our hands.'

'We won't be though. Have some faith.'

'We will,' I insist, 'it's nonsense. How many bands has he ever signed?'

Mono turns away.

'How many?' I shout.

He doesn't say anything. We all know it's none. We know he's been in the job for four years, has worked with a few bands and hasn't got one of them signed to his major label bosses in the UK.

'We're hittin our heads against a brick wall,' I finish as he walks off. 'We're bouncin our heads,' I say to Derek who's standing over me as I zip up my bag. He just shrugs.

Jen saunters into our space.

'Are you ready yet?' she goes.

'Gimme a second,' I say.

She grimaces, stops moving, blows out a breath.

'You've been ages already. This is worse than last year.'

I give her an apologetic kiss, a peck, and she nods a hello to Derek and ghosts through to the toilets.

I struggle out with my gear and walk, weighed down with everything, over the shining samurai steel of the curving Luas lines. Jen's with me.

'What a waste of time,' I say.

Jen links arms with me and gives me a brief hug and says, 'The same as last year. It's always the same.' We get split up, lost between the rickshaws and the oncoming, outgoing, leery crowds from the down-market meet-market, nurse – and Gardaí – cardholding 'Discothèque', before finding each other again and making our slow retreat to the apartment.

★

The grass on the field beside the gym has been cut. And I'm dying with hay fever – and a hangover. Kids are kitted out, running everywhere, kicking the three balls I've brought out for them. It's chaos. I take a gulp from my bottled water and Solpadeine.

Cars take the soft slope to freedom at the bottom end of the field, where the school gate is. The drivers, teachers all going home, wave sympathetically, as if to say 'god love ye' or 'fool'. But in fairness the games, if we do well, gimme the chance of a few half days. Anything that gets me out of the classroom is a bonus.

I blow the whistle and roar.

'Right, c'mon in, c'mon in.' Four o'clock. I'll be on the ten past five train.

They saunter over, big men in little men's bodies, all aching to be taken seriously. Two balls drop from the sky into the group. I take them and grab the third from a small lad.

'Okay lads, listen up.'

They huddle around. A good few of them look down at me.

'This is an Under Sixteen Junior Cup team. Junior. So if you're under sixteen and you're a senior, in transition year, goodbye.'

There are some groans. Not a cloud in the sky. It's roasting.

'So transition years, sorry, but that's the rules.'

General noise and complaints, curses, lads throwing their arms and fists downward as if they're punching an imaginary face below them.

'I'm sorry lads, but if ye can find another teacher to do the senior teams – you can play.'

'Why don't you?' someone shouts.

Cause I couldn't be bothered.

'Cause I can't get classes off for matches for two teams. It's hard enough for one.'

A handful of them traipse away, deflated, towards their kit bags, the weight of the world on their shoulders.

I gulp my Solpadeine and water.

'Okay, the rest of ye. How many we got?'

I count them. Twenty-eight. Should be twenty-nine but for our keeper, Jake Ryan, defecting to the other school in the town. Regardless, ten will have to go.

'Right lads,' I say, 'yis all know about Jake goin to the Community College – so we need a keeper. Who wants to do nets?'

A lull. Eyes drop to boots and feet kick the grass. Everyone's a striker. Nothing.

'We need a keeper lads – first game's in October.'

A gentle tap on my shoulder makes me turn. I look up to see John staring down. The bump is gone and his eye's no longer red. I feel happy, relieved really, now the proof of my dig has disappeared. I can't be blamed, found out anymore. I'm in the clear. Of course, the other student got the blame, or accolades, around the school, but still, I like being safer than safe. John breathes on me. He smiles a big Cheshire cat smile, grinning wider than wide.

People snigger. Him. We haven't spoken since the fight. I've thought about him though.

'So you're back from suspension.'

'Uh-huh,' he goes.

'Okay, you can try out, for sure – but you'll need gloves.'

'Why I need gloves?'

''Cause I said so.'

'But, I-I don't have gloves.'

'It's not an issue now but you'll need gloves.'

'I d-don't need gloves.'

He holds up his massive hands. Giggles.

'Yes you do. Boots?'

'Nah-hah,' he says shaking his head, kicking his basketball trainers, big tongue, open laces.

Sniggers. Three-quarter-length shorts and a loose basketball top.

'Why don't you try out for the basketball team?'

'They, they threw me o-off it sir.'

More sniggers.

'Right, doesn't matter for now. C'mon, get in there. Okay, twenty-nine. Two teams of eleven and subs. I'll bring you on and off.

Squad list will be on my classroom door tomorrow morning.'

I divide them up, give them bibs and blow the whistle. There's way too many. They swarm. Some shine immediately. John makes some great saves. He's brave. Huge. Head and shoulders above everyone. The others are afraid of him.

'W-when can I come out sir?' he shouts across the pitch to me.

'Out?'

'Yeah, like, I wanna be there.' He points at the group of outfield players swarming after the ball.

'Later,' I shout back. 'Later.'

A dark mass appears from behind the gym before breaking off into three silhouettes. Big pale green faces come into focus the closer they get. It's the Droogs. They're young lads. They pass by John's goal and I can see them throwing stuff at him. But I'm in the middle of the pitch, surrounded by players. I look over racing heads. John runs after the group and swings a kick at them. He just misses and they run off giving him gestures and laughing. While John walks back the ball ripples his net. There's a groan from his team.

'What?' John roars into the field, throwing his arms up. No one answers back. He looks to me. I blow the whistle.

'That's n-not fair!' he shouts. 'I wasn't even in goal – them lads w-were callin me names. Th-that's not fair.'

'You gotta ignore them John,' I call back. Everyone's looking on. The Droogs have gone out the gate.

'They were callin me n-names sir, th-th-that's not fair.'

'You wanna play, you have to stay in nets.'

He shakes his head and folds his arms and glares at me. A seagull flutters in and picks at the leftovers of a chicken fillet roll near the peno spot. John toes the ball out from the net, flicks it back and then lumbers toward it and drives it out. He just whacks it. It's a daisy cutter that takes the seagull off-guard. The seagull's smashed. A short squawk and it flops onto the grass. The ball stops dead. One of the second years sneaks over to the bird and toes it.

'Eh, I think he's after killin ih,' he says.

Nervous laughter's suppressed around the pitch. John steps forward.

'Bird killer – John killed a bird!'

'Bird killer! Bird killer!'

His eyes expand and his big bottom lip turns inside out, nearly dropping off his face. He strides over and looks down at it. A gang of jerseys surround the scene. John's face is calm.

'Cuchulain,' someone jokes, quietly, but loud enough to be heard. A wave of laughter washes over them.

'Stop that,' I shout, but no one's listening.

John turns away and grabs his bag from beside the pitch and leaves, the group still laughing. I catch up with him.

'Ih-ih-it was an accident,' he says, his head down. His cheeks are glistening. I hear a sniffle as we breeze over the long grass near the school gates.

'I-I didn't mean ih. Why'd you haveta put me a-away from them all anyway. I didn't mean ih.'

'I know you didn't John, c'mon back.' Cuchulain.

He strives on out the gate and I turn to see the jerseys and bibs still standing over the bird.

'Right – lift it. We'll get the caretaker to get rid of it. Twenty minutes left. Let's go. It was an accident, leave it, let's go,' I say and blow the whistle.

We play another twenty minutes. A few more catch my eye.

John's name is the first one down on the squad list. He doesn't come in the next day to see it.

*

All the way from the school to the apartment, the forty minutes on the train from the suburbs to the city, my headache increases. It's like the farther away I get from the school, the closer I get to the apartment and that Friday evening, weekend freedom buzz, the more intense this sick feeling gets. I swear it's my classroom. The lack of windows, a clean oxygen supply. Granted, the school's newish, just about five years old I think, but the population explosion in the town meant the building filled up quicker than expected and what was a large room in the centre of the school had to be literally split in two and a partition, a thin, rickety wooden yoke, was placed in the middle. The principal wouldn't entertain the idea of sending an overflow of kids to our neighbours, and competition for students, the Community College; so two cramped classrooms were put where one large one once was.

A few other teachers and me share this space. At least they have windows on their side of the partition, windows that open out into fresh air. My windows open out into a corridor. Not just any corridor, but a corridor where kids' lockers are. The air in my room stagnates and then the germs outside in the corridor seep in my top windows too. I don't stand a chance. And so ye have it – I feel brutal. The only positive about this partition mess is Lauren. She's next door a lot. We can hear everything that goes on in each other's classes so we have this weird kinda honest relationship. We're good neighbours. I like talking to her. It helps that she's beautiful too, I suppose.

Anyway, I'm flat out on the couch back in the apartment after work, just sprawled there, too sick to eat, or too weak to get up and eat, or maybe too weak with the hunger to get up, and I'm taking a gulp here and a gulp there of my Solpadeine and water when Jen comes in.

She's concerned of course, and she leaves her bag and jacket on the table by the window and comes over and places her soft hand, cool, on my forehead.

'Wow,' she says, her eyes given an extra intensity with the make-up she wears for work, 'you're really hot. You look so pale,' and she leans in and kisses my forehead. When she draws away I see her cleavage, but I'm too sick to be interested, and I look at her standing there, her tight little skirt and the high heels and I go, 'You look great.' She flashes an eyebrow, like she's weary or something, and goes, 'You really *are* sick,' and we giggle and she moves out of shot into the kitchen.

'Have you eaten?' she calls in.

'Not since lunch,' I say, a croak in my voice for extra effect. Milking it. Why not?

'You must be starving – I'll make my lasagne. That'll cure you.'

It's Friday evening so I'm surprised she's going to all the hassle of her lasagne. She normally makes it at the start of the week to do us a few days. But for some reason there's a pep in her step. She whistles as she goes and comes in and checks my forehead the odd time and kisses my cheek and when the time comes she turns on some soap or another. She sits down at my feet and rubs my leg but keeps on getting up to make some more noise and do some more preparing out of sight. I see her shadow flitter across the coffee table.

My hunger pains go and after my third Solpadeine the headache softens and before I know it, just as it's getting dark outside and the smell of her lasagne is filling the apartment, the headache's gone. I don't tell her it's gone though. She'd only think I was making it up. When she arrives beside me with our plates, I make a big deal of sitting up and leaning down to the coffee table.

'This is nice,' she says just as she's about to eat. I look at her. She smiles and rubs my leg, 'Not you being sick – just this. Not rushing around or running off anywhere. It's nice to have a night in, save some cash, isn't it?'

I mumble something, pretending to be restricted in my response by a full mouth.

We eat in relative silence. Jen's attention is drawn to the television and I interrupt her the odd time with a 'this is lovely,' and 'mmhh,' just to let her know I appreciate her and to keep her happy cause I know she won't be later.

When we're both finished I take the plates up and bring them into the kitchen. Jen protests, but moving slowly, like I'm improving, I say it's alright, it's the least I can do. I even wash the plates and the knives and forks, and ease out of the room, unnoticed, and go to the bathroom.

She laughs through her nose, quietly, a confused look on her face when I come back in. Fresh and showered. I'm standing behind the couch, between the hall and the living room.

'Why'd ye get changed?' she says, and she must see the remains of the steam floating around the hall cause she goes, 'And showered?'

'I'm feeling better,' I say.

'And?' she says, the smile disappearing.

'And, ye know, I've got tickets for the gig in Tripod tonight. The lads are going too.'

She stands up, hands on hips, her head at an angle.

'It's, it's half-nine Rob. That gig'll be over.'

'It's a late one. They're not on til eleven.'

She blows out a long steady breath, points to the kitchen, says nothing, looks to the couch, kinda peers into it like she's gonna find the sick me lying there.

'I thought we were gonna have a night in. I just made you . . .'

'I know Jen,' I say, 'but you knew the gig was on.'

'But I came home to find you sick. If you're sick I presume you're staying in.'

'Well, I'm better now so I'm going out. C'mon, don't make a big deal of this. Ye knew I was goin.'

She waves me away, dismisses me, mad face on her, 'Go – go on. Go. Go to your gig. Stagger in tomorrow morning at stupid o'clock and be sick for real then for the day. Waste your weekend – our weekend. I don't care.'

She shakes her head and turns and sits back into the couch.

'Don't be like that,' I say.

She turns the television up.

'I'll be back early enough, I promise.'

I think she snorts, scoffs, but she keeps her head still, the lack of movement indicating how angry she is.

It's bright when I ease in beside her. The room's spinning, but a steady serene joy. I check my watch. It's a quarter past seven. Jen mumbles something and I go, 'Sshh,' real soft and snuggle up beside her, content and exhausted, delighted to be back.

'What time is it?' she whispers, half asleep.

'Three.'

She mumbles something and goes, 'Thanks Rob.'

I rub her arm softly and whisper, 'No problem Jen. I love you.'

I can tell from her breathing she's asleep when I say it.

★

The school goes quiet only a few minutes after the last bell. Students hang about for a bit, at their lockers or just messing around, but then they clear out – no fight keeps them entertained. The teachers leave just as quick. Silence, and the distant hum of the cleaners hoovering. Everything is empty and still and at ease; the corridors, every room, the court outside the main entrance, the pitch beside the gym, the long grass and ditch the students clear before going on the bounce, the half-built estate at the back of the school the students hide out in when on the bounce. Everywhere is silent. Silence, slow, still silence. I need the silence, especially when it's on a day I'm rehearsing. We rehearse til about ten at night. I hang around for the ten past five train. Gets me into rehearsals around six. I'm normally there before everyone else. Ready to go before everyone else.

A rustling announces his arrival before he bursts in. The door flies open and hits the wall, shakes the room. The boom is loud. His bag is trailing from his shoulder like an inconvenience. He stands in the middle of the room looking around. A sudden air of disinterest settles over him with a sigh. His fingers expand and contract over his afro.

'H-how long will I-I be here?'

'Nice to see you too, John.'

He doesn't reply. I look at my watch. It's four.

'Five.'

His eyes rest on me, nearly closed, in his lazy way.

'Five?' he says, half singing the word. 'Why'm I like, even here? C'mon sir, that's unfair.' He slumps and drums a rolled-up A3 sheet off his leg.

'Yes John, five.'

'Can I use your computer?'

I shake my head. He's getting too used to these evening detentions. He sits down and flops back, his bag on the table in front of me. The bag is falling apart. Tippex names and DJs and rap crews – DJ Kembo and 'Da Brig Boyz'.

'Well, w-what'll I do?'

He puts his feet up on a seat. Staples are holding the leather to the sole. There are white gaps where his socks can be seen.

'What have I told you about feet on the seats?'

He notices what I notice and silently eases them down.

I root around my desk for my headphones. The area is overflowing with books and uncorrected copies.

'John,' I say, real serious, 'stop that noise,' and I point a vague finger at the rolled-up piece of paper he's drumming off the table.

'Wh-why you like tha sir?' he goes, 'Just gimme my box back sir, an like, I won't be like, makin noise or nothing.'

Our eyes meet and I immediately think of that punch, and the fact that he's said nothing about it. Our secret.

'You said you'd behave last week and you're here again. I'm your tutor – so if you're here, I'm here. I have to be here. And I'm getting sick of it John. D'ye think I like havin you here? You-are-a-pain-John.'

He scrunches up his face, shakes his head, all thick.

'Th-tha-that's racist sir.'

'No. If I said you were a black pain, now that'd be racist. But you're just a pain.'

The rolled-up piece of paper is like a baton. He holds it steady over his shoulder like he's gonna whack it down on the table. I find the headphones hidden behind a stack of books. I put them round my neck.

'When you're not a pain – you'll get your *boombox*, alright?'

He does this backwards kiss thing; his lips pucker like he's gonna kiss the air – but he sucks in and makes this weird kinda dissatisfied tut.

'It's not my fault you're here, John.'

I pull up the jack from the headphones. Open up my Mac. He

doesn't say anything. His eyes look to some blank spot behind me, big serious face on him. I want a response though. To hear him admit it's his fault he's here.

'It's not my fault John. It's yours. The boombox is gone cause you brought it into school and . . .'

'Ih-ih wasn't my fault – my-my mp3 . . .' His voice goes deep, but loud.

'I-don't-care-about . . .'

'My mp3 was thingy – was, ih goh broken sir.'

'I-don't-care.'

'An-an-an I had no like, no other music thingy sir. I just wanted to show people. Ih wasn't my fault sir.'

'I-don't-care.'

My voice remains calm, measured, without judgement or emotion. But still he goes on.

'I need my box sir, please.' His tone has changed. He sounds upset.

'I don't care John. You'll get the boombox thing when you behave – and this week, again, even after another talk from the principal, you didn't behave.'

He hits the paper baton off the table, eyes wide, his chest drawing up like he's holding something in.

'He's a racist.'

I let out a little laugh.

'Yes John, the principal's a racist. I'm a racist. Everyone's a racist.'

'But he is!' he pleads.

'I don't care. What I care about is you turning up here at four and sitting in front of me for an hour for misbehaving in art.'

He sits up straight, his big cat's eyes narrowed, the baton pointing at me.

'B-b-but they – they were slaggin me sir. They're racist. Th-they are always callin me names. I – I – I'm gonna make a complaint.'

'Okay – but you, John – *you* threw paint at them. *You* reacted to them.'

'Them' are two of the three that hound him. The Droogs. They're three local lads who are singularly weak but new men when they're together. One's in transition year, another in third and the other in second year. Wild.

'Well, didn't you react to them? What have I said about reacting to them? Write down what they say and give it to me or the year head or the principal. We'll do something.'

He scoffs, 'But they never do. I-I tell you like, I tell you all the time and, and you do nothing.'

He hits the baton off the table again. I begin to root around, search for a book.

'That's because you seem to cause more trouble than the others do. Be smart about it.'

I tap my temple.

He takes a breath.

'I'm gonna kill them.'

'No you won't.'

'Yeah I will.'

He laughs. I smile. He holds up his hands, 'Don't blame me. They ask for it.'

We smile together. He knows I know he's joking. For now.

I lay the book I was looking for in front of him. Ignore his baton.

'Okay,' I say, taking hold of my headphones, just about to place them over my ears, 'read the third story – quietly – and I'll ask ye a few questions afterwards.'

He pretends to be annoyed but he can't suppress a smile. It's better than writing lines and he knows it.

'Ah-sops fah-bulls?'

'That's the book title.' I place the headphones over my ears, everything goes dull, distant, calm, 'Story three,' I hear my voice say, '"The Boy Who Cried Wolf".' I point at the page and just as I plug my jack into the side of the Mac I hear him go, 'Oh my days,' and he pouts his lips and runs his hand furiously over his little spongy afro and starts to read.

The song starts up and I'm cut-off from the school, just a spectator to this lad in front of me crouched over reading a book with his rolled-up paper baton disarmed and moving under the words, slowly and deliberately.

October.

We always leave the gear set up over three evenings. The rehearsal studios are a home from home. We pay an hourly rate, but the owners let us keep everything as it is over the three days since packing away and starting up again, getting the sound and all that, is such a pain. If we weren't able to do it we'd try to find somewhere else. They need the business; we need the space.

There's something fresh about coming in to the empty room every evening, all the gear waiting for us, like our outside lives were just a break and what we do in here is important – our reality. Our departure and return wipes the board clean every time. There's hope when I return, for something that will lift us beyond what we are.

We've had our gear up for two days this week already. Barry, the A&R lad, is coming down to hear some of our new stuff. He said he'd be down at eight. We've rehearsed our new songs to death. Tweaked and tweaked and agonised over them for the last two days. Four songs, over and over. I wonder sometimes if we're mad and we're deluding ourselves, if we've put all our faith in Barry to get over the fact that we know, deep down, no one else would be interested, has even shown an interest. Barry's a convenient scapegoat when all this goes belly up.

Outside the air is fresh. Autumn air, faint breath, wafting up into the backstreet. Mono smokes beside me. It's dark. The long evenings have slunk away behind the smog. The cobblestones shine in the weak orange light.

'So what ye think he'll think?' Mono says, exhaling through the last of his words, his eyes closed.

I shrug, 'Does it matter? You know what I think.'

'Course it matters. He's a major label. Ye can't just shrug off a major label. It's the dream.'

'I hear ye Mono. But c'mon, what's he done? Can you really see him doin anything for us? He's keeping his finger in all the pies. He doesn't need us like we need him. He knows that.'

Mono flicks his cigarette away. The red neon bounces on the cobbles.

'If yer not into it, why ye botherin Bob?'

I can feel his anger rising. The frustration of realising I'm right.

'Not into it? What's all this then?' I say, spreading my hands wide. 'I'm traipsin in from Balbriggan, every week, before any of yis turn up. You just saunter in at seven, when ye can be here at five. Don't tell me I'm not into it. I'm just not into *him*. I was – three years ago Mono – when he promised us the world, when we were new. You know as well as I do the scene has changed.'

Mono listens but doesn't hear what I'm saying. He hasn't looked around him, taken in what's happening with other bands. He's so swept up in the prestige that comes with major label interest he's lost touch with what made us a good band from the start: we were a breath of fresh air. That air has gone stale.

When Barry arrives he settles quickly and leans against the wall, his arms folded, his bag still on his shoulder, his long black trench coat folded over an amp. A strategically placed lamp soothes the room from the corner. My eyes adjust to our atmospheric darkness.

His reaction is muted. Sometimes you can tell he's getting into it when his head starts nodding and his jaw clenches. On the flip side, you can also see the interest drain from him when he's not really into it. He says nothing between songs. Just listens and waits. Waits for us to finish before he speaks.

His reaction wouldn't alarm me but for the fact that I can remember the last, and only showcase we did for him before. It was about two or three years ago. He brought along a famous producer. We thought we'd made it. Everyone was told of our visitors; everyone who'd listen. A major label coming to watch you rehearse is something special. Unique. A glimpse of greater things.

We were so nervous. But separately. Secretly. We didn't want to let each other know how big a deal we thought it was. We were meant to be cool about it. Shrug off the importance of it if anyone asked.

We played our four strongest songs and Barry and the producer leaned against the wall with a pen and paper and scribbled away. It was surreal to be rehearsing in that dark place to an audience of two.

They tapped their feet against the wall, one leg planted like flamingos. Their heads nodded and they drummed their fingers on their arms. They even smiled at each other once. After our fourth song they filled the silence with these tiny claps. Ridiculously feeble noises in the soundproofed room. What a sound.

We were confident. Beaming. They couldn't choose the best two, they said. Song one and two were really strong, they said. The producer, a little stumpy lad with glasses and a thick Dundalk accent commented on the technical aspects of the song structures. I wished he'd stop talking. The more I heard of his accent the further he moved from the rock-star producer legend I had concocted in my mind. In fairness though, his credits were mad.

After a few days Barry got back to us with a week of dates for recording, all paid for courtesy of London. We got the days off work and took a holiday off Upper Baggott Street, on the canal.

Naïve and caught up in the whole process, we didn't cop what was happening. While we drank tea and played computer games in the lounge the producer huddled over his mixing desk and cut and pasted, and cut and cut and by the time we heard how he had 'handled' our songs we were too afraid of his reputation to offer our own opinions and criticisms. The recordings were technically perfect, but not ours anymore. He had put more of a stamp on it than we had. We should have seen it coming. What made us us, our dirty unpolished noise, was squeezed out by the clean, defined, synthetic perfection of the market.

Barry didn't call for a few weeks after that, and when, for the fourth or fifth time of asking, he finally admitted he hadn't played it to London, we stopped hoping.

Back in the low-lit room and I know before he says it, what Barry's gonna say. The others must feel it too. If we're honest with ourselves we'll say the new songs aren't up to it. They'll never be recorded. We finish and the sound dies away. The buzz from Derek's microphone gently hums under the silence. I turn the PA down. Everything's still.

'Good, good,' Barry says, shifting from one foot to the other, his arms still folded.

Silence.

Mono's guitar amp crackles. He puts it on mute.

'There's some good stuff there,' he says after an uncomfortable wait. 'I liked the last one. That was more like it.'

We stand and listen. Watch as he tries to wriggle out of it.

'The last song definitely had something alright. You see they're looking for something with a real killer hook. Something that sells.'

He might as well leave now.

'Sells,' I say under my breath and shake my head. The atmosphere changes.

'They're into all that melodic guitar stuff now, all acoustic guitars and floppy fringes and cardigans or mad American kinda stuff.'

I snigger.

'Well that's us finished,' I say. No one laughs. Derek's jaw tightens and he sits back on the spare amp.

'I wouldn't say that, Rob,' Barry says. 'Just keep pluggin away – keep doin what yer doin – something will break for yis . . . I presume you lads haven't just left the demo with me, there must be a few other labels interested too.'

Silence.

'Did the last demo we paid for go to any other labels?'

Steve gets up off his amp and shifts the bass on his shoulder, 'Course, yeah, yeah,' he says, lying. All of our eggs have been put in the one major label basket.

'Well, at least that's something,' Barry says, massaging his chin. He's looking for angles to get him out of here without having to guarantee any cash.

'I'll see what I can do about another recording session. But like I said, it won't be easy.'

He's never said that before.

'So when'll we know?' I say.

His shoulders twitch, 'I'll get onto London and get back to yis. Just keep doin what yer doin – if I can do anything down my end I will, if I can't I'll try and make waves for yis somewhere else. I really like you guys. Just keep plugging away.'

This is what being dumped must feel like. No second base. A short little development deal, a bit of cash to work with and then you're finished. It's not you, it's me.

The others stay quiet and Barry shifts his bag on his shoulder and takes a look around and says his goodbyes and he'll be in touch and all that, but when he's gone we know he won't call us again. We jumped the gun. Got ahead of ourselves with the development deal. We've developed into nothing only disappointment.

Our silence is horrible. I'm gutted. Even though I saw it coming, I'm still gutted. He made it as clear as he could without crushing us.

'So what do yis reckon?' Mono says.

'What do ye think,' I answer back, not looking up from the black and white keys.

'It's not all that bad,' he says, shifting the strap on his shoulder. He clicks off mute and the room crackles. I move out from behind my keyboards and lift my coat.

'Where ye goin?' he says.

I look to the others. They stand still.

'The pub.'

'But it's only half eight. You heard what Barry said. Just one song.'

'What Barry said . . . what Barry said. Get a grip will ye. Just listen to yerself. Barry said he doesn't want to know us.'

Mono moves toward the door. His guitar strings rattle and the amp echoes and then screeches.

'Barry said we're nearly there. Just one cracker of a tune will get us in the door. We've gotta work on it.'

'Well I'm not.' The others say nothing. 'Not tonight lads, my head's wrecked. He's heard all we've made over the last three years – if we were gonna have that *one* song we would've written it by now.'

Mono stands at the door. His guitar is like a gun over his shoulder.

'Get outta the way Mono.'

I make to get by. His guitar knocks off the door.

'We're stayin Bob.'

I shake my head and look to the lads for support. I can't breathe. It's so stuffy and dark. I feel trapped.

'Come on lads.'

Derek finally speaks. Then Steve. They both just tell me to relax. The drummer stays quiet behind his cymbals. I warn Mono, but he doesn't listen. I shoulder him out of the way, and he staggers onto his amp, an electric whip-crack of tubes being rumbled and I'm out the door and he's shouting after me. The noise of other bands knocking their heads against a brick wall swallows up his rant.

★

I eat lunch in my room. It gives me a chance to listen to a new album or some track we've put down. Sometimes I get visitors, students taking a wrong turn, checking why my lights are on. I run them off. Roar – no, shout at them, get them out quick. But now and then John's three tormentors come in. I call them the Droogs. They like this, but don't get it.

They storm in when they get bored; always the three of them, always together, the weirdest looking gang of misfits. None of them would dare call in on their own. I see them sometimes if I stand at my door and look out. One or two of them could be out sick or on the bounce, or suspended. Cuts the group down, exposes its inner workings. Weakens them. They're a different monster when not a trio.

Only one room is available for kids who stay in for lunch and that's on the other side of the building. So when the three of them burst in I jump a little, missing the sound, just noticing the door. They've been hiding in the toilets they say, kicking in the cubicle doors and trying to break the sinks, cracking the mirrors. What they do, or at least what they tell me they do, seems to get more sensational every time. I don't make a scene. Never make a scene. Don't know why. Maybe it's cause it's too much like hard work to be disciplined – to discipline. I dunno. Or maybe it's cause they're kids. They're not doing any harm – not flaunting it anyway. It's a hidden thing. It's their violence and it's contained. I can let that slide.

Together, as ever, they pant. Colm, Taidgh and Andrew. I don't teach Colm. I did last year when he used to hide down the back of class. Every month that passes though, it's getting harder for Colm to hide anywhere. He's sprouting, shedding his baby fat. He came in to me a small crazy-eyed mess, big chubby cheeks and sweaty forehead. He's taller than me now, more relaxed, and cunning. Mad. But there's something sad about him too. When he goes quiet I wonder what he's thinking. Is he really that character, the second name that's been made infamous by his father, his uncles, his aunties that he tries so hard to be, live up to?

Taidgh is only a second year. He looks older than the other two. Spots and bad skin have ruined his face. A blemished mismatch of reds and pinks and scarred purples. His cheeks hold a constant render as if he's been caught doing something he shouldn't have. You'd think this affliction would mean he'd hide. The exact opposite. He's wired. Always wired. Like something's driving him on. His eyes are deranged. Disturbing. There's a disconnect there. The world he sees, if his eyes are anything to go by, is not the real world. He lives on an alternate planet with this wide stretched grin that meets everyone, all the time, when grins aren't even warranted. I don't teach him. Thankfully.

Then there's Andrew. The weak one. The weakest one. Little skinny face, front teeth and pointed nose, small beady eyes and stud earrings. He's nearly seventeen but still hanging round with second and third years. Even though he's in transition year, he should be doing his

Leaving Cert. Regardless, he's the youngest looking of the Droogs. He's a law unto himself. Comes and goes as he pleases. His da can't control him, though he can still do no wrong in his eyes. The attendance officer used to call, but he can't do anything now cause of his age. The year head doesn't want to deal with him either. And then I have him, little timid head up the front of English class, meek and embarrassed amongst his peers.

'Alright sir,' Andrew says, transformed with his crew in tow.

'Alright lads.'

'Do I have you today sir?'

He knows he does.

'Yeah, last class.'

'Great, I'm gonna wreck your head in it.'

'No you won't, Andrew.'

'Yeah I will – and I'm gonna wreck Kembo's head when I see him too. We got him today already.'

'You wanna seen it sir,' Taidgh adds. 'Me and Colm turned his bag inside out at lunch – he went nuts. Mr Tolan had to call out for help.'

'Yeah?' I'm surprised I haven't heard anything.

'Yeah it was classic.'

'Who arrived?'

'No one. They were all at a meeting or something,' Colm says and gets comfortable on a table and gulps from a cheap can of coke.

I should run them, tell them to clear off; but they normally do anyway after a few minutes if I just play along, listen and pretend to be outraged at what they say. I'm still unsure if they're seeing how far they can push me before I snap. Am I another piece of entertainment, like John? Am I disappointing them by not reacting? I look at my phone.

'Right lads, get goin. I've work to do.'

'No,' Taidgh says, smile sliced across his face. He stands tall and still and then slumps and deflates and laughs.

'Only jokin sir, legend.'

They make to move.

'Leave John alone lads. He's gonna blow soon.'

'I know,' Colm says, 'can't wait.' And they shake and giggle. Colm gets braver.

'If he goes near me sir I'll bate him.' He looks for his audience. 'I'll smash him so I will.'

'No you won't, Colm.'

'Yeah he will,' Taidgh says. 'We'll all bate him. He thinks he owns the place. We're gonna destroy him if he keeps on annoyin us.' He punches his hand theatrically, biting his tongue and grunting. Colm's laugh is too loud to be real.

'But *you* annoy *him* lads.'

'So wha?' Andrew says and looks to the lads. 'He deserves it. He thinks he's so great on the football team now and he can't even afford gear.' They throw their heads back and giggle.

'Enough of that now lads,' I say, 'that's not right.'

Colm lobs his can into the bin.

'I hate him too,' he says.

'We all hate him sir,' Taidgh says and I spy his eyes, all bloodshot and sleepy. He grunts and sniffles.

'Why, why do yis hate him? What's he done to you? Sure, you're not even in his class, Taidgh.'

'He annoys us sir,' Andrew says. 'An he thinks he's great when he's with all the black crews and they don't even like him.'

'Yeah, he's a head-wrecker, we're gonna smash him.'

'Leave him alone lads. I'm warning yis. I'll tell the principal.'

'So wha. He's afraid of us too,' Colm says. 'I bang the wall whenever he stops me and he always gets freaked and tells me to move on.'

They won't change. I'll have to work on John instead. Convince him he's better off ignoring them and rising above it all.

'See ye sir,' and they're gone and I turn back to my Mac.

Loud knocks on my window and vague shadows on the blinds show them passing. I hear a teacher shout, 'What are you lads doin in here?' and the urgent rush and pounding of runners sweeps by and they're gone and a teacher's shadow ghosts past the window, playing their game; being played at their game.

★

We're in Laser DVD on George's Street trying to decide what to rent. I've brought two music documentaries to Jen's attention but she's dismissed them with a look.

'But you used to like all these,' I whisper, in close cause the place's packed and you wanna give off the veneer of relationship bliss – you know – the happy couple who always enjoy the banter when deciding what to get.

'Ten years ago,' she whispers back through her best fake smile, 'when we were still in school.'

Someone brushes by that we know and we both nod and wave a quick, friendly hello.

'But what about that thing we saw a few years ago in the IFI – the documentary about that band from New York?'

'That was for your birthday – it was just to keep you happy.' She takes the DVDs and scans the back and presses her lips together and tuts.

'They're all the same Rob. You know it better than I do – band get together, slog away, have their moment of glory and break up with old friends becoming enemies. It's you guys in a nutshell.'

'We're still together.'

She looks around, makes sure no one's listening, or watching. 'Just.'

'That's not fair. It's not about the glory anyway. It's about friends having some fun. Working together.'

'Really?' she says, fake surprise. 'Having fun burning through your spare cash for rehearsals, taxis, recordings? And you guys seem to be having so much fun these days too.'

I snap the DVDs from her and plant them in the comedy section.

'Okay then – you pick.'

George's Street hits us the moment we emerge into it. Yellow signs for taxis, stalled and scanning desperately for a pick up, colour the road. We're just about to move off when this figure glances up as it passes and tries to scatter. But our eyes meet, quickly, unintentionally, and through the darkness, and the fog of our breath, I see it's him and he sees it's me and we're both forced, cause of the eye contact, to acknowledge each other.

'Steve,' I go, all delighted to see him.

'Ah Rob, my man,' he says and puts out his hand.

I hit him with a quick, 'Where ye off to?' and straight away – you can tell it catches him off guard – he blurts out the truth.

'Meetin Mono for a pint.'

It's out there. He's sorry he said it. You can tell. Jen squeezes my hand.

'Yeah?' I go.

'Just a few, ye know? Was tryin to ring ye but couldn't get through.'

'My phone's knackered.' Lie.

'Oh, explains it so. Here, ye joinin us?'

I look to Jen. She smiles this pleasant smile like she doesn't mind what I do. I look back to Steve. Haven't seen or heard from him since I walked out of that rehearsal.

'Nah, not tonight my man. Cheers for the shout anyway. Here, when we rehearsin next?'

Steve waffles on for a second about rehearsals and the band and we move off, finally, awkwardly, saying we'll see each other next week for practice. We're delighted to get away from each other.

'Friends having some fun?' Jen goes after a few strides of silence. 'Having fun without you by the looks of things.'

I don't respond. I'm not really listening. Paying attention.

So we're sitting there on the couch, in the dark, the screen flickering a mad light show all over the room and Jen's all happy and holding my hand and nibbling away at her popcorn. Some romantic comedy is on. I'm not watching. I'm in the pub with Steve and Mono. I'm listening to what they're saying about the band, more importantly, what they're saying about me. I'm running through all the rock and roll documentaries I've ever seen, all the band stories, autobiographies I've read, and I'm thinking about our journey.

Jen laughs at something and I laugh with her. It's half eleven on a Friday night. I could still make an appearance. Jen shifts about on the couch and draws her legs up and puts them on my lap.

'That's not uncomfortable, is it?'

'No,' I smile, 'not at all.'

She turns back to the DVD, big content smile, and I'm facing the screen but looking somewhere different, trying to see another story.

★

The bus is warm and sweaty. I'd love to open a window and let some air in but most of the kids are wet, their clothes, tracksuits and jerseys soaked through. Hair normally spiked, massaged into strict attention, is shiny and flat on foreheads. No one thought of bringing a towel. You'd expect them to be subdued. But they're wired, buzzing. There's loads of music blaring from their phones. They've won their first game. We've won our first game. We kept a clean sheet. Well, John kept a clean sheet. The slap of the ball off his hands on some of the saves made people wince. He had no gloves. He was immense. Everyone was impressed.

John sits up the front of the bus, across from me and away from the banter and mayhem down the back. There's no one in the seat directly behind us. We're the only ones facing forward. He's humming a tune to himself and drumming a beat on his leg. The rest of them are turned to the back row and the nonsense that's going on there.

'Enjoy yourself?'

'Yeah. It was greah. Shudda brought a towel. But it was greah.'

'You shudda brought gloves, never mind a towel. You can't play without them anymore. The ref won't let you.'

He just mumbles so I try to cheer him up by going, 'Do you play for a team John? You should ye know.'

'I do sir,' he says, 'the school team.' He smiles proudly at his new revelation and turns to look out the window, into the condensation and the streaks of water. The noise from the back row rises.

'S-s-sir,' he says after a while, still looking out the window.

'Yeah.'

He grimaces as he struggles with a question. His lips pout and he turns to me.

'Wh-why do I haveta wear the grey jersey?'

51

'I don't get ye.'

The bus bounces on a pothole. Loud cheers fill the back.

'The top I w-wear. Wh-why do I haveta wear it? Everyone else like, wears the purple an white jerseys.'

More cheers down the back. I stand up and peer down at them. I spot someone standing on the seat and give a roar.

I return to John. His eyes are open wide, waiting on my reply.

'Cause yer the keeper John – you have to wear a different colour jersey.'

He tuts and shrugs and frowns as if I've disappointed him. He looks again to the window and goes, 'Then I don't wanna be a keeper.'

'Ye see John, you're different from the rest cause you can handle the ball – the referee needs to see who's the keeper so you have to wear a different colour jersey. Yer made to be a keeper. It's the most important position.'

'Oh,' he says, letting my words wash over him. It's a slow acknowledgement that lasts until his breath dies away. He falls back into his seat, sighing slightly, and runs his fingers down the glass. The raindrops shoot across the pane and split into separate strands. Water surges forward in the rubber grooves at the bottom of the window.

Sometime later he says, 'Sir?' and I turn to him, getting tired of his calling, but giving him a chance since he played so well.

He continues to look out the window. Silence.

'Em, nothing,' he says, shaking his head.

I know there's something, but don't respond or press him and turn back to my own thoughts. Then, again, it comes.

'Sir?'

And again I turn and say, 'Yes, John,' and this time he does go on.

'Me mama doesn't like me playin football an stuff.'

Never saw this coming.

'And . . .'

'Sh-she thinks I'm just doin it to miss class like, and sh-she says I don't even, like I'm no good so I should stay in school an, an not miss class cause it'd be bad for stuff. So – so this is like, sh-she doesn't know like. I can't play after this.'

I blow out a short breath to give myself some time. I can't lose him too. We'd be finished without him. All the potential half days would be gone. I need those breaks.

'Ye know what I was thinking,' I say.

'Mmmhh?' he says, still looking out the window.

'Captain, don't we need a captain.'

He comes away from the middle distance and turns his head to me, lifting it up as if to say *go on.*

'How would ye feel if I made you captain?'

His cheeks lift. His eyes smile.

'Yeah. You'd never not be part of the team then would ye? And yer ma couldn't say you weren't any good then, could she?'

His bottom lip comes out and he shrugs. The bus growls and lumbers around a corner.

'Go up for the toss, and lead the team and everything.'

'Serious?'

'Yeah.'

'Would I get my thingy, my picture in the paper an stuff?'

'If we do well, yeah, defo.'

He nods to himself as if it's sorted.

I call them from the front of the bus, over the laughing and the engine, the wind and the rain. The driver turns the radio down.

'Lads,' I say, 'well done today. Great game. Great game.'

They cheer.

'Right. I've decided on a captain.'

A few of them jump up and offer their services. The others laugh.

'Okay, sit down. I thought our defence was brilliant today – the whole back four and the keeper.'

'The black four . . .' Abdel shouts and they all burst out laughing. John appears beside me.

'Don't say that. Th-th-that's stupid.'

'But it isn't,' Abdel says, shaking his head. 'Me and John an Nifemi an Jordi are all black – we're the black four.' More laughter.

'Wha abou me?' JJ says, his white face popping up from behind a headrest. 'I'm not black and I'm a defender.'

'The *back* four were excellent,' I say, ignoring it, 'and I thought John in particular was excellent and led by example – so he's our new captain.'

The windscreen wiper squeals as it crosses over. Brows go deep and there's mutters; a Mexican wave of disgruntled tuts spread from the back seat up. Whispers and secret looks follow. The engine struggles up a hill and I make to say something but John goes, 'Ih-if I'm your captain we'll win – an we'll beat the Community College.'

A voice, hidden behind a headrest goes, 'That's g-g-great,' and little sniggers swallow up the joke.

'Enough,' I shout and go, 'so for the next game – John's captain. Okay?' Mumbles. 'Okay?' More mumbles. I leave it at that.

They leave the bus quietly, the buzz of winning drained away. I pat each of them on the shoulder as they go and say, 'Well done'. They don't respond. Their mess, crisps and cans mixed with brown water and feet marks, remain.

John is waiting for me at the school gates, his bag over his head, sheltering from the rain. He puts out his hand.

'Let me take one of your bags sir,' he says.

'No way John. You've done enough today. Go on home – go on. You'll get soaked.'

The last thing I want's a hug or something. Can't be too careful.

He shakes his head, the bag swaying from side to side, and takes the footballs. I shift the bag with all of the bibs and cones on my shoulder and we walk away from the gate, down the slope, past the misty pitch beside the containers and into the empty school. I ask him to leave the bag inside the main door and shake his hand and say thanks and well done and move away from him. He nods, a new seriousness on his face, the water dripping from his nose. He stretches his lips and looks into the distance, just like on the bus, makes to move, stops and then moves toward me. He looks troubled.

'Go on ye mad thing,' I say, making light of the new awkwardness.

He doesn't move.

'Everything okay?'

His kit bag is his school bag. It drips on the tiles when he spins it.

'Do ye want me to pass something on to the guidance counsellor?'

I hope he doesn't. I wanna catch my train. He looks at me, finally, with a new determination. I think of that punch.

'Can you write . . .'

'Course I can write.'

He smiles and chuckles to himself, 'No, can you write me a letter?'

'A letter?'

'A letter.'

'Okay, cool. For what?'

'My mama w-w-wants me to get a letter from the school and stuff like, to say that I'm a good s-student. I need it like. We need ih like, to show we're like doin well.'

'A letter. Cool.'

'For immigration like. They need proof an stuff. Is that okay Sir?'

'No problem. Good man.'

I pat his shoulder and feel his damp jacket. I think of the two of us at the door. His face.

'Thanks sir.'

Still there's no mention of it. Will there ever be? I wonder if he's holding it over me, for a time when I say no to him, a time that could've been today.

He opens the door and puts the school bag over his head but then takes it away and strolls out into the rain, easily, as if the clouds have disappeared and the gloom has been lifted.

★

I get to thinking about things. As poxy as it sounds, stupid and all, music's always – regardless of the band – been a kind of journey for me. A road of sorts. The road is signposted by the albums I've discovered, the bands I've loved, the friends I've met, the clothes I've worn, the drugs I've taken, the gigs I've gone to. I was always so mad about whatever type of music I got into, I tended to get caught up in the journey and just went wherever an album's inspiration, or influences or contemporaries, took me. I used to be naïve enough to think what I listened to was the only thing worth listening to, the only road worth travelling. Like a bypass shooting over a back-water town, I used to scoff down at the little roads below, have the confidence to dismiss the tiny secondary routes, short cuts, other genres, as pathetic.

When I joined a band, I copped quick enough that my friends would have to travel with me, and me with them; hitting side barri-ers, widening my road, widening theirs, them making more space for me, me adding new music for them. A band meant my road became a joint effort, like getting funding from the EU or something.

Expanding my travel space always came natural to me though. My road is an extension of who I am at this very moment. I used to be able to look back, tell where I've been through my music, scope out my landscape, and look forward with what excited me and know I was going somewhere, somewhere dynamic; ploughing new individual pathways to break across new sonic territory, discover new soundscapes, create new scenes.

If you're into music your road always grows. It's the nature of the beast I suppose. If you're in a band you just hope the members all go in the same direction. My journey moves forward. My road grows. It's constructed in front of me, shooting off wherever the influences take me. But it's always natural, an unconscious type of thing. Not rushed or contrived or built out of necessity. I've never experienced a road that's come out of necessity. I'd say it doesn't feel right. Doesn't wear well.

But the road I've been blindly following has brought me here, to this point. To this weird kind of juncture, where for once I can't read the signs or suss out the musical landscape or trust my instincts. I'm lost. Even when I look back I can't work out how exactly I got here, to this stale, paranoid place.

★

Even though I grew up in this town, I don't know it anymore. The train station is a three minute walk from the school – I know, I've timed it. My eyes only see the ticket machine, the beach behind the station, the path from the station, the road beside the school, SuperValu across the road from the school, and the big wooden hoarding, remnants of once-started, still-not-finished 'summer works' that hide the school from the town like a dirty secret.

There's a problem with walking though. The entrance beside the pitch, the entrance all the cars take, the students walk through, is the only entrance. The problem with this entrance is that it's on the opposite side of the school to the train station. So I have this key, to unlock a mad thick padlock, hooked onto a heavy chain, which is hooked onto a bolt that is set deep in the wooden hoarding enclosing the front of this side of the school.

Everything, according to my da, if not boarded up, is changing or has changed in the town. But I don't see any of this change around the beach.

'I suppose,' he says, peering up past me, making sure the road is clear before he pulls out, 'the beach seems grand in passing, son. I mean, to the untrained eye.'

I'm in the passenger seat of me da's car. Giving him a hand with something.

'Well, the lighthouse and the harbour look good. They've been done up, haven't they?'

The train station backs up onto the beach. Looks out across the sand, out to the sea, and if I stare hard enough, I can see my parents' estate, on a hill, up and away from the lighthouse and the harbour.

'The beach is the face of the town, son,' he says. We're moving now. 'They've got to keep that tidy. They should do something about the knackers drinking down there though. It's not safe.'

'Yeah?' I try to sound interested.

'It's not right,' he says, don't think he even heard my question. 'Knackers. Scumbags. The whole lot o' them.' He shakes his head, indicates, changes gear. 'I mean gone's the time meself and your mother used walk along the promenade and down into the sand,

and sure, there's gangs of young lads now.'

'Yeah?'

He nods, a rueful nod, his lips pressed.

'But sure it's that end of the town, son. You must see it yerself. They can't build where we are – thank god – cause of the beach and all that, the cliffs, although Eddie Byrne says they've tried for planning permission for the sailor's cottages and whatnot. But they won't get that. Too much corrosion and weather damage to the cliffs. But, by Jesus, they've built everywhere they could – and they're still building where they can down your end.'

'My end?'

He grimaces, as if I've asked a silly question. Never had any patience.

'Your end – the opposite end – your school end. Have ye not gone for a walkabout up there? Have ye no interest? Jesus, it's like Beirut.'

'Really?' I say, just so he doesn't think I'm not interested. He looks at me out the side of his eyes, 'Sure why would ye care, you live in *town*, this place means nothing to ye. All ye did was get reared here. Sure what's the town ye grew up in to the likes of you. But let me tell ye son, it's a sad day the day ye forget where ye grew up – d'ye hear me? Don't forget where ye grew up, where your family's from, where ye teach, where yer childhood friends live, where your parents' friends live, and drink.'

I sigh and feel embarrassed for something I can't quite put my finger on. It feels like I've one of those redners I could never get rid of when I was a teenager. Shame and anger with something elusive. Fair play da. Been a while.

'I don't forget where I'm from. Sure how could I?' I say. 'How far away is Hopper's house from here da? I've got to get a train.'

We've passed the station. It's half four.

'I suppose the train's costing ye too,' he goes, ignoring the question. 'I don't see why ye can't live here in town, the community, be part of it son. How's the town meant to hold itself together if there's no sense of community anymore?'

He stares ahead, at the road, but into it too, into some other place I can't see. He glances at me and frowns like he's battling with something. His eyebrows dig deep, 'Just, son, pride. All I'm askin is ye take some pride in your work – where ye work, and where yer from. Don't forget you're representing your parents, son, when ye work up there.'

'Why ye sayin this da?' I say, losing patience. 'What've ye heard?'

We stop at traffic lights. The air coming from the heaters, clearing the windscreen, blows between us.

'I'm just sayin. People do be sayin things too, ye know.'

I shake my head. I don't know.

'People say things, son. Ye know this place as well as I do. Ye fart at the church and they have ye soilin yer pants again the story reaches the canal.'

'And?'

He breathes a heavy sigh, indicates and we move onto the main street, the old main street; the 'For Let' signs and the African hairdressers – two in a row – the 'Afro Caribbean' restaurant above the boarded-up pub me and Jen met in, the dry-cleaners where the IRA had their headquarters in 1920 when Lawless and Gibbons were stabbed to death by the tans, two Cash for Gold joints facing each other across the main road – one-stop-shops for all the thieves in the area – the shell of a Tesco, waiting on a new shopping centre to be completed up the far end of the town – a mall of the future – before it closes. We pass the school, the hoarding, the door, my main-street entrance, and keep on going. We pass the council estate on our right, the cop shop on our left, into an estate I used to drink in when I was sixteen. But we're on a new road, a big major road type thing, and the estate I used to drink in, the fields we'd hide the booze in, are gone and we're driving on, heading towards what looks like a new town. What I once knew ends after the first roundabout and what were once fields are vast estates. We drive through the narrow streets, like old medieval village paths or something, and I begin to see the new town my da's been talking about, complaining about. A playground, houses with no gardens. No garden walls to chat over, no porches, no space. Just doors and cars up on kerbs. Where once there must've been white paint shining from the buildings, there's a yellowy type of grime. That's what you get when you have tenants, not owners. They're never going to go out and paint something that's not theirs. The people on the path, at the doors, in the green Puntos passing us, are mostly foreign – mostly black.

We keep driving. My father just lets me take it all in. It's too much. Not the spectacle, but the buildings. There's a cramped kind of feeling as if the houses were thrown up, on top of each other, dumped there, just so they didn't have to go somewhere else and deface a nicer town. After a few more turns and a few more groans from my da, we reach what must be the centre of this new collection of roads.

A pub, a supermarket, a Chinese, dry-cleaners, café, pizza joint, chippers, newsagents, beauty salon and a hairdressers. It's not like a new town up here. It *is* a new town up here. Free and independent of the place where I grew up.

'Ye see son,' my da says, finally coming out of his silence, 'this is what we're up against now.'

I don't know who the 'we' is and who they're 'up against'. I just nod.

'Don't forget where ye come from.'

'I won't da. I don't.'

'That end of the town,' he says and nods back, to his left, back to where we've come from, 'remember your own.'

'My what?'

He sniffles, checks his sides and moves off, 'Yer own. Remember who to look out for in the school. People talk. Again you've done something for someone, there'll be two that'll be sayin you did something against them and be bad mouthin ye to those that'll listen.'

'Who's sayin what da?' I go, wishing he'd just get to the point. But that's how he works.

He speaks while his head slowly shakes, 'Just people,' he says, 'don't forget where yer from – that's all. People down our end talk, son.'

'Talk about what?'

'This end.'

'This end?'

He nods to a black man passing by.

'Oh,' I say.

'Just, look after yer own,' he says and turns on the radio to some drive-time show and we leave the unnecessary turns and long-winded tour and return to the main street.

We arrive at Hopper's house and I see the ladder lying in the long grass of his front garden and hope we can get this done quickly; loaded, tied up and be ready to go in five. My trains in fifteen minutes.

'Isn't it well for some,' Hopper says nodding at me, but talking to my da. 'I wish I had the free time our lad has here.'

'I see you're off today Hopper,' I say and my da looks at me all annoyed. Hopper hasn't worked in years.

'How's he getting on below?' Hopper says, obviously talking about me, but facing my da, as if he's the expert. They exchange a sly glance. The question is loaded with some other meaning I'm obviously not clued in on.

'Grand,' my da says and then, from the porch, a figure comes out, still and subdued.

'Ah, Andrew,' my da says. 'Jesus, you're getting bigger every time I see you. What year ye in now?'

'Transition,' I say.

My da looks at me and smiles, 'Don't tell me you have this monster, Andrew, have ye?'

Andrew nods a bashful nod. 'English,' he says. It's weird seeing him without his two cronies: The Droogs.

'Oh, he has him alright,' Hopper says, lifting up the ladder. 'My Andrew could tell ye some stories. Hates the place – but sure – the goings on up there I wouldn't blame him.'

And there's that look again, from Hopper to my da to Andrew. An unspoken look of acknowledgement, as if I'm missing out on something, not part of the gang. In fairness though, I'm glad. Whatever gang they're in, I don't want to be part of it.

Andrew brushes past me into the garden, where himself, Hopper and me da pick up the ladder and bring it to the trailer at the back of me da's car.

'D'ye need a hand?' I shout after them, wondering why I was even brought.

My da struggles with the ladder but looks up briefly and says, 'No son, you stay there and watch us. Sure Andrew is here to help, thank God.' So I stand there like a tool and watch while they work away without me.

'You playin ball at all?' my da goes to Andrew.

'No,' Andrew says, all eyes on the ladder, 'couldn't even make the school team and they were short a goalkeeper an all. They've all sorts playin for them now, even captain.'

'Yeah?' my da goes and looks to me. There it is. I'm about to say, 'You're too old for the team, Andrew,' but don't bother. I know the conversation's not about him.

November.

Lauren's there, leaning into me, squeezed up tight cause one of our locked colleagues is trying to dance on the couch to one of these conveyor belt club anthems. The strobe from the dance floor makes him look almost graceful. I'm breathing in that smell I always smell when she comes into my room and messes with her hair. But there's a new ingredient added that kind of takes away from the usual pure tone.

'So,' she says, the straw mangled at the top from all her biting and chewing between her smiles and playful slaps, little hiccups, 'what *do* you do when you escape from the school? I bet you go home to a wife and kids.'

It's the Smirnoff Ice on her breath. The combination of dry ice and perfume mixes there too.

'What do I do when I leave school? Let me see. I get the train into town.'

She laughs and slaps my thigh.

When she speaks, shouts in my ear, the drink wafts over my face. Her breath is warm and pleasant. She's so close I can feel the heat from her legs, thighs, her skirt hiked up, and her arms – no cardigan tonight. Bit of a view. There's a looseness to her. A look in her eyes I haven't seen before. Normally she's at the back of class at her door or a voice teaching on the other side of the partition. All the way back in school. But there's a new determination about her tonight.

'But really,' she says, settling down again, trying a serious sober face, 'what you into?'

'What are you into?'

She shrugs, 'The visual arts. Culture. Music. Anything that challenges me. Can change me.'

'I'm bored already,' I say.

She smiles and I take a sup from my pint. Some fool has placed us under the speakers and the music's wrecking my head. Modern pop – part of the great swindle to rob us of our self-esteem; insisting how we need to be unhappy with who we are and what we have, since 1991.

'Well?' she says.

I give in. 'Music. Music comes first and last. It's everything.'

'What kind of music?'

'All sorts. You wouldn't be into any of it.'

She shakes her head and tuts and goes, 'I hate when people say that. You don't even know what I'm into – how do you know what I would and wouldn't like?'

I name a band – an obscure one – to impress her.

She counters immediately with, 'Saw them March last year in the Olympia when they were touring their second album.'

'You were there? I was there too,' I say, surprised. 'It was a Tuesday night. I was in bits all day Wednesday.'

Her eyes expand, like she can't believe it, 'So was I. I nearly got sick in class. I was so hung-over.'

'Me too,' I say and we laugh at the revelation.

She flicks her hair behind her shoulders. She nods to me, thinking, no doubt, about our shared story. The lights from the dance floor flash across her face. Some mascara is smeared on the corner of her eye and there's little clumps of it on her eyelashes. She looks so different. There's a lull and we look across the table at the others from work – some lads, mostly women, drinking and throwing their heads back and laughing like some mad opera singers. Their mouths are so wide and deranged we can see the fillings blackening their back teeth. I shake my head in disgust and look around the table at the fake chandeliers, the oversized mirrors and pretend marble. The grandeur of it all.

'Have you ever been here before?' I say to get us started up again. She shakes her head as she sucks on a straw.

Some other teacher comes over and bores me with her problems. Just when I think she's said all she can say and she can shake her head and sway all she can sway – she starts off on another rant, slurring her problems all over my face. If Lauren wasn't beside us I'd shout in her face, 'I'm not interested.' But I behave. Lauren fidgets. Her head tilts all the way back to drink her drink and she bumps into me.

'You know what Gemma,' I say, putting my hand on her arm, 'it's Friday night, we're out, enjoying drinks, let's just relax and not talk shop – please – you're boring me.'

She swallows the words she's about to speak with a hurt gulp and tries a meek smile and moves away, finally, muttering something as she turns.

'Thought she'd never leave,' I whisper to Lauren.

She edges closer.

'Sorry?'

'I said I thought she'd never leave.'

She nudges me and grins a guilty grin.

'That's mean.'

'But true. I wanna hear about your cultural pursuits, not some boring classroom sob story.'

She waves her hand, 'No, no, no. You're not turning this on me. I asked you first. You tell me.'

'I told ye. Music. That's it.'

'What, like gigs?'

'Yeah.'

'Do you play anything?'

I nod.

'You in a band?'

I nod again. She does this thing with her eyebrows, like she's impressed, and goes, 'The plot thickens. What do you play?'

I do a mime on the table of playing the keyboards.

'Oh, we have our very own Elton John on the staff,' and she starts to sing one of his tunes while I protest, 'No – not piano. Keyboards. Synths and stuff.'

'You mustn't play around the city if I haven't seen you,' she says.

'Why'd ye say that?'

'Cause I go to loads of gigs.'

'Maybe you haven't been looking hard enough.'

That smile again, the flick of her hair.

There's so much sub on the speakers it's making the fibre cone distort. She shouts questions into my ear like what we're called and I give her the band bio and tell her about the old development deal, interest from the major label and the frustration at seeing everything turn stale and falter.

'So you're just gonna pack it in?' she goes, staring at me.

'It seems the right thing to do, ye know?'

She continues to stare until finally, she grimaces and goes, 'Do you know anything about music? Art? It's when it gets to the lowest point, hardest, when the artist gets desperate, that's when it gets interesting.'

'I know, I know – but maybe enough's enough. Maybe I should grow up – I'm not a teenager anymore.'

She looks stunned.

'Wow – how noble of you. If you knew anything about music – bands, Rob – you'd know loads that made their mark late in their careers when everything was at its lowest ebb.'

'At least they had careers.'

The music's so loud I really have to concentrate on what she's saying.

She shrugs, 'You sound like you've made up your mind. But art shouldn't be about age, or growing up. That's what makes it art. That's what makes an artist. It's about the love of the form. Do you love music?'

'Course, yeah.'

'Do your friends in the band?'

'Suppose.'

'Well then, make it work,' she shouts, those big eyes staring into me, all excited. 'At least try instead of just giving up. That's such a wimpy thing to do.'

She's drunk. Too drunk. Too honest. Too loose.

'You're not a wimp, are ye Rob?'

'No, course not.'

'Well then, play. The sound of you guys intrigues me – I wanna see you in action now.'

A scream of laughter pulls us out of our bubble, the flickering lights, the reflections, the speakers re-appear and there's another drunk teacher stood between us, shaking, all excited.

'I love this song! I love this song!' she squeals, doing mini-hops on the spot. 'C'mon Lauren, dance with me,' she says, 'c'mon, I wanna dance.'

Your one tugs at Lauren's shoulder and pulls her off her seat. As Lauren goes she looks back and I go, 'Art and culture?' and point to the speakers. The light catches her frame and she smiles an apology. I wish she was beside me still. I flap away her shrug and do a stupid grin and feel like a goofy teenager.

She does shots on the dance-floor and gets so drunk she can barely stand. One of the older teachers puts her in a taxi.

Everything's so quiet you can hear cars pass outside when I come in. The television casts wild shadows over the front room. It's on mute. All the lights are off except for the kitchen one which frames Jen in a neat square of yellow while she sleeps on the couch. Estate agents' brochures are open on the coffee table, on her stomach and there's a calculator on the floor. She looks so peaceful. Happy. Beautiful. I stand over her and just watch her sleep for a few minutes. Just look at her. I listen to the soft sound of her breath, the gentle snore as the air eases out. It's almost like her breathing is the soothing voice of a hypnotist bringing me back, calming me down, returning me to myself after some out of body, heightened state of excitement. I make to touch her forehead, move her hair away from her face, but stop short. I turn for the bedroom and leave her be. She'd only want to ask me questions about the night if she woke up.

★

Right, so I'm doing a class on Jay-Z and Alex Turner with my transition years. They're doing their Leaving in two years so I've a bit of scope to do some doss classes – do what they wanna do, or at least let them believe they're doing what they wanna do. Some *South Bank Show* or BBC documentary on Jay-Z has perked up my interest in him. I'm eager to see what's made his music so popular and his reputation so fierce. And then Alex Turner is just quality, so getting opinions on why the Arctic Monkeys are so popular will be useful too. There's something fresh about Turner's lyrics. The Arctic Monkeys are the real deal, and all the kids – the downloaders – love them.

Besides, I don't see the point in busting my head against a brick wall trying to decode someone's expression of beauty written through some irrelevant form they've no time for. Literature should expand minds, not numb them.

With this in mind, I've got the lyrics for 'Riot Van' on one side of the sheet, and three quarters of the lyrics for '99 Problems' on the other side. Twenty-six copies have been handed out. I've blacked out the swear words and all the 'niggas' just in case Jay-Z's words get into the wrong hands outside class. I don't wanna be done for pedalling filth or being a racist, of all things.

But of course the first thing they say is, 'Why'd ye get rid of the swear words sir?' and, 'Dat's stoopid – we know what the words you've scribbled over are,' and they start laughing and reading out the sentences with the blacked out words and filling in the gaps them-selves, so there's ten 'niggas' being shouted all over the room – and the rest.

I settle them down and tell them why I chose the two artists: 'Some of you lads asked me to.' They don't twig I'm lying. A few voic-es say 'yeah' and things go quiet and I get going. Any insight into what's new now will help me get some ideas. The Terrors are out of touch with new trends and styles. What we think is cutting edge they probably see as ancient. Things move so fast now. A&R know this. I need to know what can make us fresh again.

'We'll start with the lyrics for "Riot Van",' I say and there's murmers from Jordan and Ayub and Tunde.

'Why the white man have to go first?' one of them says. I laugh it off – they do too. But there's always that undertone, even if it's just a stupid remark, changing the dynamics of the group. The laughter dies out. The silence is loaded with twenty-odd minds concentrating on the question.

We fly through Alex Turner's lyrics and I play the song on the Mac through these little speakers. The sound's soaked up by all the bodies. The song is a typical indie guitar one – boring. The lyrics are straight-forward and insightful though, as one of the kids says: 'They're just havin a few cans an the cops stop them.' So I move on to Jay-Z, the black marks sticking out like brail on the page, and read the first two verses. I'm lost on some of the words.

'Zapitoes? Am I pronouncing that right? What are they?'

Ciaran puts his hand up, '*Zapatos*. Zap-A-Toes, sir,' he shouts over the banter. 'He has holes in his *zapatos*. Shoes.'

I nod.

'Cool. Thanks.'

Something else isn't clear either though.

'And GAT patrol?'

Shoulders shrug.

'What's this sir,' Ayub says, 'who's meant to be teaching who?' If what he said wasn't so uncomfortably true I'd nail him, but I play it cool and laugh with the rest of the class like he's being ridiculous. Andrew though, the Droog, doesn't laugh. He's up the front, the seat beside him empty, yawning and shaking his head.

I need to get to the point.

'So what's the thing that makes Jay-Z so popular? What makes him stand out from the crowd out there?'

Most of them are talking amongst themselves, ignoring me, making their own jokes.

'Race,' Geoff says, his seat leaning back against the wall, swinging with the arrogance of youth, thinking he knows everything, 'the way he talks about the problem of race in contemporary American society.'

'Fair enough,' I say, 'but how?'

'Well,' Geoff says, like a professor or something, with his West-Brit accent, 'Jay-Z asks the policeman is it because he's black that he's been stopped. So they're thinking about the colour of their skin.'

'Okay.'

The noise dips.

'And,' he says, a smug smile appearing with the silence and respect his answer is getting, 'Alex Turner's song is just about being smart with the police.'

'Is this what differentiates them from the rest? Why people like them?' I say, opening up the question to the class. 'Is it the lyrics that makes people see something special in them?'

If it is the lyrics, the Terrors are knackered. Derek's words are always vague and general. Not precise and true. I need insights here.

'That's stoopid,' Ayub says, pulling away from the sheet. He turns into the class for an audience, big Punch and Judy smile on him, 'We don't listen to them for their lyrics. This sheet is only like, half it.'

'Yeah,' Jordan says, his voice rising above the mumbles and laughter, 'the lyrics are just a bih of it sir. You gotta hear the beats.' The way he says 'the beats' is like the word itself gives him some sort of satisfaction.

'The beats?'

'Yeah man – his beats an all are why we love him – not jus the lyrics.'

Beats.

'The beats, right,' I say and let the idea take hold, see the possibilities of something new. But the lyrics were all they talked about on that show about Jay-Z the other day. 'Jay-Z's lyrics,' the presenter had said, 'encompass a wide array of cultural references, from the pop-culture post-modern pastiches, so espoused by the avant-garde visionary Andy Warhol, to dispossessed American Youth's own images gleaned from the ghettoes of underprivileged urban societies.' The beats never came into it. Same with Turner; *The Guardian* had English Lit people reading his lyrics and worrying how 'Such a succinctly written and well-structured narrative form was achieved by a working-class youth from the impoverished steelworks city of Sheffield.' Lyrics, and poverty, were the secret to their success surely.

'Play the song sir,' Jordan says, scratching his afro. The class buzzes.

I load the song on YouTube and get them to settle down. No voice has come through the partition so I presume – hope – no one's not in there now.

Jay-Z's voice is strong, perfectly formed on the speakers, no music to block it out and then – wham, the guitar and beats explode. Heads start to dip and nod, like those dogs in the back windows of cars – and they're all facing me at the top of the class, and I feel like I'm on stage. I start to get into it. Everyone's smiling and I think about turning it down but don't bother. I'm the DJ. It sounds fantastic. I get the buzz they get off it, and I realise, they're right; the lyrics are only half the battle. The power and the swagger of the beats and the sounds are it. So simple – but effective. Quality. If you put a four-four, damp eighties' rhythm behind Jay-Z's lyrics the song would fall apart. I can't believe I've never thought of us in this way. The simple off beat and the repetitive guitar chords are massive and purposeful. So simple. Fresh and raw and savage. The opposite to what the Terrors have become. The heads nod back in surreal acknowledgement.

Over and over it rumbles, over and over – simplicity, just raw power, beats and attitude. The Terrors have the attitude. We just never had the beats.

Jordan smiles, like the rest of the class, and there's a stunned, weird kind of silence when it ends.

'Beats,' Jordan says, his head nodding and his mouth stretched as far as it can go. 'Ye see sir – Jay-Z got the beats.'

There's nodded 'yeahs' and 'quality' from the class, some trying to sound as American and black as possible. In the middle of all this posturing there's a whisper. I hear Ciaran saying something to Tunde about Kembo and beats. He's leaning back in his chair, facing away from me.

'What's that?' I say, talking over the crowd. Ciaran looks at me and sits up like he's done something wrong.

'Nothin.'

'No, go on, what'd ye say?'

Conversations are in action all over the room. No one's listening in.

'Wha?'

'You said something about Kembo.'

Tunde sits up and booms: 'Ah yeah, sir, his beats are deadly.'

'John Pereira?' I say, making sure we're talking about the same Kembo.

'Yeah,' Ciaran nods.

'Ah sir, his beats are wicked,' Jordan says, smiling that smile, stretching out that word 'beats' like it's a fine piece of steak and he's chewing and savouring it, like it's the most satisfying thing he's ever tasted.

'John Pereira?'

'Yeah sir. He does beats for like, loadsa crews and loadsa lads are startin to ask him now like Deyz Boyz, Balbrigz Boyz Crew.'

Andrew's head lifts and he leans back into the conversation, his eyes wide and alert, his chin raised to take it all in.

'He's a genius on the drums and keyboards an all,' Tunde adds.

They nod to me and I call over the noise to everyone, 'Okay, well done. We'll relax now for the last,' I check my phone, 'fifteen minutes of class.' I turn to Tunde and Jordan and say, quietly, 'so tell me bout these beats John does.'

*

Mono has called in a favour from one of his mates; he's a lighting engineer who owns loads of fancy LED lights – big mad strips of things that are usually only used at massive gigs, monster venues. We've got four – and a strobe and a few other bits and pieces. We're aiming to impress. We're going to blow their minds. The Terrors are going to terrorise. I can't wait. It's just a shame Lauren can't make it.

Backstage is weirdly quiet. Everyone keeps on looking at their phones and shaking their legs, beating a rhythm on their thighs and knees. There's some mad dirty electronic house being played out front, past the door. Low and menacing. You can feel the tension and the buzz, that sickening kind of feeling of wanting to just get out there and let everything go.

'So who's said they're gonna turn up tonight anyway?' I say, to no one in particular, just to break the silence.

'Eh – all the lads are coming anyway – and a few of the lads from 'Ali' said they'd be down. Fair few heads in fairness,' Steve says.

'No, I meant labels or management. Did they get back to us?'

'Yeah,' Mono says, exhaling and peering through the blue of his second-hand smoke, 'Brian from A-Plus Management's coming, and

Bren from Universal is gonna be here – and Stef from First Born Is Dead Records said he'd be here.'

'Nice,' I say, nodding, impressed.

'This is gonna be whopper,' Steve says, 'this is our return lads. Put Barry and all that major label stuff outta our minds. To hell with them. We've got a few bloggers here too. It's gonna be whopper.'

The songs out front seem to drag. Crowd noise fluctuates, giving an uneven dip and rise to the DJ's tunes. We peek out the side door, looking from the back of the stage into the venue and the dance floor. Lights flash across the front of the stage and then out into the void. But there's no void. Bodies and heads, packed together, face the stage, drinks in hand, all smiles. Lights flash across them and I look over their heads and I see the area at the bar's even jammers.

'It's packed,' I shout back to the lads, 'packed!' Dry ice spurts out at random intervals, covering the stage in a misty kind of cape, gliding out and surrounding the crowd. The drums, guitar, bass and keyboards and all my synths are still, like props on a film set or something, just waiting for the actors to come out and begin the scene. Little green and red digits pulse evenly on the floor, electricity flowing through them all. Guitar pedals, keyboard plug-boards, synth sockets, bass tuners, amp mute buttons, distortion buttons, everything's pulsing, just waiting to be pushed to its live limits. I'm mad to get out there and play. Blow them away.

The massive LED lights and strobe lie in a sort of slumber, waiting to be unleashed on the unsuspecting crowd and the tiny venue. The owner of the club had asked us what we were doing with all the lights when we'd first carried them in in their massive steel coffins.

'Puttin on a show,' Mono had said proudly.

'In this place? I'm taking the electricity bill outta yer fee,' he'd replied and we'd all laughed.

The music stops and the whole venue goes black and the crowd begins to cheer. Tiny white lights from camera phones appear and sway and flash. I ghost across the stage, through the smoke, side-stepping all the throbbing lights, and peer into my synth, my eyes adjusting to the new darkness, to make sure all my settings are correct and I'm ready to go. The others wait for me to start up my sounds before they come on. If I wasn't in the moment, part of the action, in this little bubble, I'd think it was like a scene from *Spinal Tap*.

My sounds warm the room; fuzzy distorted electronic synths begin to arrive and become gradually louder, more intense. The low end takes hold and our waiting pints ripple at the front of the stage. The speakers vibrate the room and shake my eyes. The synth moves through some notes, alone, without any flourishes from other instruments, and I start up a slow pulsing electronic arpeggio and I hear the drummer do a little roll on his ride and the click of sticks, crossed over and counting, one, two, three, four and we all crash in, everything together, like a perfect wave of electronic, dirty filthy noise and knock the punters off their feet. I can hear what I think are cheers and whoops. The lights blind me and cover us from the front of the stage. These are only the little spare things the lighting engineer brought. The LEDs and strobe aren't even on yet. The crowd are lit in red, then green, red then green. My keys change colour, then the black keys cast confusing, shifting shadows across and down their white counterparts. Red and green colour them on the first song, and through the smoke I can see heads, nodding and dipping together, really getting into it.

'We are the Terrors,' Derek shouts into the mic as our first song ends and I start up some sounds to fill the gap while Mono and Steve tune up. Again the sticks and again we burst in together. This time the keys are red and blue and purple – and then a blinding, white strobe flashes, two real quick flickers, and my keys are a luminous mash-up of greens, purples, reds, and the faces in the crowd do mad eyes and their jaws drop as they feel the first surge of the LEDs' warm breath and again the strobe flashes like an electric storm down through them – and again – and then the sound's sucked somewhere, my plastic keys are being pressed but not responding and the whole room is plunged into an incredibly dense black and the drums, and only the drums, damp naked things, pound on alone for, like, a milisecond or something in the new shocking silence. The drums are horrible naked things. Weak and exposed. Just nothing. And in that moment we are nothing. I am nothing. What we've created has come to nothing. Nothing. And the absoluteness of it. Strip back all the bravado of our sounds, the blips, the synths, the oscillators and arpeggiators, the fuzzy bass and the distorted guitars, the vocals swamped in reverb and the flashing lights, and we're nothing but the drummer's naked beats whimpering out from an old rusty drum kit in the darkness. It's a horrible revelation. A horrible revelation.

The power's gone.

Murmurs and rough jeers rise. A torch appears from the back of the crowd and slices its way through green-headed silhouettes. A glowing 'exit' sign over the backstage door is the only other source of light. The torch is like a lightsaber as it cuts a path through the crowd and appears at the side of the stage, to my left, where it wobbles over a sign: Caution High Voltage. The noise from the crowd is rising, the jeers getting sharper.

'What's goin on?' Mono shouts over my shoulder.

'The strobe just blew the whole circuit board,' the lighting engineer says, the torch on his face like he's telling a horror story. 'Someone plugged it into the wrong port and it's after blowing everything.'

I don't say anything. I just shake my head, turn off all my stuff and retreat silently, over the dark shadows of the plugs and pedals, through the dead dry ice and flop into a seat backstage, forty minutes earlier than I thought I would. I kick a bag and sit, sick with the humiliation and think: this wasn't the dream. This wasn't what I had in mind when we started out in a back room with one keyboard and Derek and Steve throwing ideas my way about synths and guitars mashing together to make something no one had heard before. This isn't the dream. This is the nightmare.

'This can't go on lads,' I say when they've all arrived.

No one looks up.

'We can't keep on like this. We need to change lads. We need something new if we're gonna be serious about this anymore.'

No one responds.

The hours pass and we're all at a house party; smoke and sweat and laughter fill the air and I'm in a corner trying to convince Steve the ways we need to change. His eyes are nearly closed and you can tell he's finding it hard to hear me with all the background noise.

'We're not stale,' he's saying, 'we're grand – we're grand.'

I'm shaking my head, tapping his knee, trying to hold his attention, 'We're not grand Steve, we need something new man. A new sound – something to blow them all away.'

'We do though, we do blow them away.'

'Yeah, but not like we used to. It's not happening anymore.'

I grab a can from the floor before some randomer staggers back and falls into me. I hold him up and push him back into the crowd.

'We could do something with our beats,' I'm saying, 'like add a bit of edge – like hip hop beats, ye know?'

His head drops back, all lazy, against the wall, his eyes closed, his mouth in a messy smile, his tongue over his bottom lip. He draws his head up straight and manages to focus his wired eyes on me.

'Hip hop beats?'

He makes this noise.

'Our lad, there's no way . . .' and he looks over to Mono and waves for him to join us.

'It's just an idea Steve,' I'm saying, trying that bit harder to convince him before Mono arrives, 'it's just, ye know, something new. Just tryin to bring something fresh to our sound.'

His lips dip.

Mono arrives over us, his face warped and lazy, swaying with a can in one hand and a smoke in the other.

'Get a load of this,' Steve says.

Mono raises his chin.

'I was just telling Steve about my idea.'

'Oh yeah?' Mono goes.

'I'm just gonna put some beats like, hip hop beats together on me Mac and bring them to rehearsals.'

'We have beats. We have a drummer,' Mono says.

'I know, I know. But they're just straightforward drums. I'm talking big, heavy hip hop beats.'

'So,' he goes.

'So, I'm just sayin – I'd like to add something new to our sound. We could do with it.'

Mono looks annoyed, 'Barry said we're one song away. One good song away. One good song away and he reckons we could get signed. Just one song. And you wanna start messin with us now?'

'No, don't be—'

'Maybe,' Steve interrupts, 'maybe it won't be such a bad thing. Just for rehearsals.'

'Exactly,' I go, 'it's just an idea, something new to try out.'

Mono dismisses me with a sneer, a snort, and turns to go.

'What's yer problem?' I go. 'Ye afraid of upsetting Barry?'

'Get a grip.'

'Well, what's the story then Mono? It's just an idea.'

'Beats,' he says, like the word itself is ridiculous.

'Yeah, beats.'

'Forget it.'

'No,' I say, thick now.

'Here lads,' Steve goes, 'leave it. It's just an idea.'

'Who are you,' I go to Mono, 'tellin me to forget it? If I wanna get them, I'll get them.'

'No ye won't. Ye won't be able to get them together for starters.'

I stand up.

'Yeah I will.'

He laughs at me again.

'Ye won't. Ye can barely manage your synth. Hip hop, our lad. Get a grip.'

'I'll do what I want with my band.'

He goes chest to chest with me.

'Your band?'

'My band.'

Steve sticks an arm between us and goes, 'lads, lads.'

'You're not gonna stop me Mono.'

It's a matter of principle now. It was just an idea, now it's for real.

Mono shoves me, his can spraying everywhere, the ash from his smoke sparking up. People around us get wet and go 'woah', and Steve's still trying to get wedged between us and I push back and we fall, Mono going backwards, and smash into two girls. There's screams. A fist flies outta somewhere and catches me on the chin and I swing blindly and smash something, someone, on something hard.

People get in and separate us and I'm going, 'I'm doin the beats –
I'm doin the beats,' and Mono's shaking his head, blood stained on his
teeth as he smiles.

'Relax man,' Steve's going, 'relax. You're fighting over nothing.
They're just beats man.'

But Mono knows, like I know, there's more at stake than just
beats.

★

This musical road goes way back. The first signpost I can remember
is Michael Jackson. It's a repeat of some sort of that moonwalk on
Motown Celebrates Twenty-Five Years. There's the *Thriller* album –
big mad vinyl sleeve – and then *Off the Wall*. Presents from a friend of
my da's. Everything's blank up until brief flashes of my da's Talking
Heads albums, Rory Gallagher, Dire Straits, Thin Lizzy, Led
Zeppelin and all that. Then there's my ma's Fleetwood Mac. That's
the beginning.

My brother appears with some pop and R&B and soul lite.
Embarrassing stuff. Around this time I get an old guitar from my
granda, big dirty rusty strings that smell of copper and I'm being sent
around the corner with a pound or something for guitar lessons in
some aul lad's kitchen. Three other young lads are there already when
I come in. I must be around ten or eleven. One of the lads is called
Mono. Another lad is called Steve. Forget the other lad's name. So
we're sitting around in a semicircle and the aul lad is teaching us
'She'll Be Coming Round the Mountain' and other tunes I've never
heard. Uninspiring stuff for a ten-year-old. Anytime he gets us to play
the chord sequences together he has to stop us and take my guitar and
tune it up again, and again, and again. The other three are sniggering

away into the necks of their polished guitars while the teacher lad is blowing dust off my machine heads and stretching the strings, literally huffing as he does, and telling me to sit this one out.

We're outside the aul lad's house after one of the sessions, all going home and little Mono and Steve call me over.

'That's a cool guitar,' Steve goes.

'Thanks,' I say, looking at their guitar cases and then to my thing without a cover.

'Where'd ye get it?' Mono goes, rubbing his finger down the strings, 'the dump?' and they fall into themselves laughing and Mono goes on, 'Why don't ye bring a tennis racket next time – be better than that.'

I'm at home practising – busting my fingers cause the action of the strings is so far off the fret board it's not right. Where most guitars are a centimetre, at most, off the fret board, my old thing feels like the strings are inches from it.

I'm sick of the laughing and the looks from yer man when my guitar is clanging and wobbling between all the other notes. It gets to the point where I'm doing laps of the estate for an hour, keeping the pound, wondering what else I could learn.

Some other songs create flickers of interest in learning the guitar again, but I'm still doing circles of the estate, floating between dreams, genres, ambitions and styles; still trying to find my niche, my music, my main road.

I feel like that kid again. Lost, out in the cold, unsure of where to go, what to do with myself. I'm all over the place. There's a pull to somewhere completely different now. It feels like a puncture is dragging me left when all the signs say no left turn. I should go straight. The band's going straight. But hip hop and the beats that come with it seem to be edging me off-centre, off this road. Not cause

I'm interested in the music, but cause I'm interested in what these beats can do for the Terrors. A necessity in a way. Something new for the sake of something new.

I can't write them, the beats. Just don't know how. My drum machine sounds too small, and sure all it does is variations on the four-four disco type beat. Our drummer fills out the rest with his indie rhythms. Old hat.

John Pereira. Kembo. He can do the beats. He can make the difference.

This type of road doesn't feel right though. It could have too many unseen hazards. Could be a landscape I can't navigate. Could put an end to all this road talk and put me in a ditch, cursing the fact I should've just stayed where I was and quit all my wanderings.

★

The first time John came on my radar properly was last November. He was only in second year; he was big for his age and getting a reputation for trouble. I was called into a meeting with his guardians cause I was his tutor.

I sat there with the year-head and talked about John's behaviour. John's older brother, a tall, red-eyed intense mountain, translated everything into Portuguese for his mother. She was a big woman with a rough handshake. Everything was calm enough until some line from the year-head made the brother explode. His harsh dialect boomed around the office. I jumped a little. He translated again, this time pointing from me to John. Words flew from his mouth – angry daggers, no doubt damning the lad. As the words reached their pitch I saw the brother begin to move forward in his seat, spit begin to fly from his lips. The mother, her eyes growing wider, wider, her chin drawing up high, as if she was stopping her jaw from literally falling off, sniffled. Just after she said something herself back to the brother in Portuguese, a simple short sentence like, 'You're joking,' or, 'My god,' a tear escaped the corner of her eye.

The tear was unavoidable – huge. She knew it was there – I knew it was there, the brother knew it was there, everyone knew it was there. That little tear sucked the sound out of the room like a deep breath and then boom – she jumped to her feet and lifted her chair and started to shake it, prod it, into John. I sprung up between them. The year-head stayed seated. I reached up high for the seat and tried to parry it to the ground.

'He go back Angola, he go back Angola – you go back Angola,' she shouted, her grip loosening on the chair. I palmed it away softly. She remained standing, pointing, shouting. Energy drained from her voice, desperation coloured her whimpers.

'He go back Angola. How we stay if he no behave? How we stay?' She finished in her language to him. I eased her to her seat. The brother remained silent. Observing.

Sniffles filled the room and then the brother stepped up. He sucked in a deep breath and cracked his knuckles. He faced me and stared as if he was looking for an answer to some question in my eyes. With a suddenness no one was expecting he turned, his pink tongue sandwiched between his massive teeth, and clattered John, one damp smack, on the back of his downturned head. And just as quick as the first one, another landed, and another. A small grunt escaped the brother's lips with every heave. John let out a weak whimper after every connection but didn't defend himself. The brother turned back to me, smiling sadly, his palms displaying what he had just done.

'Hit him,' he pleaded, 'why don't you hit him? I give permission.'

He raised his palm, like he was showing me how to actually achieve what he was asking. I stepped forward.

'Not here.'

He let it drop.

'Why don't you hit him? I give permission.'

He looked to John, his bottom teeth digging into his top lip and said, 'Understand? Don't you understand?' and boomed something in his language and turned back to me with, 'Hit him. He must behave. He must. The family must make no trouble. Hit him.'

'We can't. We don't do that here.'

'But I give permission.'

I turned for the year-head's support. He looked shocked. The brother grabbed at John's hood to lift him and said something I didn't understand.

'Never again,' he said, and opened the door. 'Not again, sir.'

He pushed his little brother out, 'Never again.'

As they left I saw John was crying, so was his mother – but defiantly, her chin raised. I moved off after them and walked down the empty corridor to my classroom.

*

Me and Jen are in Dunnes on George's Street, getting bits and pieces for the week when I get a text from Lauren. It's Saturday and I'm surprised to hear from her outside school time.

'What you think?' Jen says before I get a chance to read the text. She's holding up a two-for-one offer on these microwave dinners. Beef and potato with gravy and turkey and ham. I look at the text before I can respond.

Hey wot u up 2 2nite? she asks.

'Rob?' Jen goes. 'Do you want one of these, cause I'm not cooking tonight.'

I look at the dinners, look at my phone and go, 'Are you not going out tonight with the girls?'

She shakes her head like she doesn't understand. She lets the dinners, her hands, drop to the side of her hips.

'We're staying in tonight. I'm staying in tonight. I told you – I wanna go through the application forms with you.'

I type back, *Nuthin much.Wot u up 2?*

For some reason we don't go straight to the checkout. Jen strolls around, opening up the freezers, weighing things in her hands. I say nothing, tag along on her wanderlust. She picks up a set of cups with love hearts on them and holds them out to me.

'These are lovely, aren't they?'

I can't believe she's asking me to have an opinion on cups. I go, 'Whatever,' and she tuts and says, 'you could at least show an interest.'

'An interest in cups?'

'Yeah – I like them.'

'Well I don't – ye happy?'

She rolls her eyes and places them back on the stand and storms off to another aisle.

We leave with the microwave dinners and Jen gets herself a bottle of wine. I don't bother with beers. Don't feel like beers. We walk up George's Street, not saying much, just looking around us. Lauren texts again and says she's going for dinner in a place off Wexford Street with her friends and then going to a gig.

Cool.Wot band? I ask.

We get to Wexford Street and Jen goes into a newsagents. I wait outside.

Another text arrives.

Interested?U shud b.These guys r real deal.Dey b goin 4 years.Not goin 2 giv up.U shud take a leaf.

A leaf? I go.

Out of der book:)

I hav :)

I surprise myself with the smiley face. Never use them. They're ridiculous. But she makes me do these things, feel this way. Like a kid again I suppose.

U not givin up? she texts.

No.

Cool.Can't wait 2 c u guys.

Jen comes out of the shop with this big smile and we hold hands and cross at the lights. Synge Street is quiet when we turn onto it from Wexford Street. Lights in the upper rooms of the houses, warm and yellow with bookshelves and plants and framed paintings, catch my attention. The people I spy inside as we make our way to the apartment seem different from me, us. They seem settled and happy, accepting of their lot and easy with it. I picture myself in those homes sometimes, sitting on a big velvet easy chair, drinking some wine or brandy, flicking through a leather-bound book, listening to some jazz, thinking of ways to spend my fortune, standing up to greet my wife as she comes through the door with a prawn salad. But she never comes through the door. She never shows her face. I always presumed it'd be Jen coming into the room. Presumed. But never actually saw her – visualised her. Don't know why.

Our gate creaks – the landlord needs to oil it – and we go down the steps to our basement apartment. It's cold and dark when we come in. The living-room light is too bright. I got an eighty-watt bulb when I should've got a forty. We normally keep it off anyway, let the light from the kitchen set the mood along with the television. Jen wants it on tonight though, the living-room light, cause we've to fill out these forms.

She lays all the forms and application deal things in front of us on the coffee table. My phone goes again with another text and I put my face in my hands and go, 'Ah Jen, I'm not in the mood for this. I need a drink.'

She smiles and disappears into the kitchen and comes back out holding a can of beer.

'Ta-da!' she says.

She leans down and kisses me.

'I *knew* you'd want a drink, so I got you six.'

I take the can from her and she hands me a pen and sits down beside me and separates all the forms in a weirdly jolly manner. I put the phone on silent and do my best cheers with her and survey the neatly arranged mess. Block capitals and black pens, dates of birth and marital status. My phone vibrates with another text. Jen nestles into me and tells me it's nearly over. I don't believe her. It's just beginning. Some Saturday night. She smiles a kind of embarrassed smile as if she knows exactly what I'm thinking.

'This is killing me,' I say.

She rubs my leg, 'Don't worry, I'll make it worth your while.'

I sigh and rub her leg in return and continue on writing in my block capitals while my mind aches to see what's in the text, what that band Lauren's going to see are actually like, if they're any good, like us or nothing like us, using a drum machine – or horror of horrors – using beats. Because someone, somewhere is gonna do it; use hip hop massive beats with electronic sounds and indie guitars. It will happen, and it'll be huge.

'Don't forget,' Jen goes, still with that smile like she knows I'm at breaking point, 'block capitals. Sorry.'

And in it drops. The statement my mind was concocting for some time without telling me. Big black pen, block capitals: I DON'T WANT TO BE HERE.

But maybe I do. Maybe I just don't wanna be dealing with this now, while I feel like I'm sitting on something that could change my life, change the band's life. Or maybe I'm just afraid to follow through with what the repercussions of acting on this new announcement will be. Maybe it'd be easier to stay quiet and work around it than be loud and work through it. Either way, I keep on writing, filling in the forms and wishing I was around the corner seeing that band, bumping into Lauren and having a good time.

★

He's boring me to tears with all his 'W-w-when is our next match sir?' and, 'W-w-what do you know about Angola?' and, 'D-do you know anyone from A-Africa?' lark. He was walking down the corridor with the year-head going to evening detention when I called after them and said I'd take him. So John's slouching in front of me with a rolled-up piece of A3 paper drumming a rhythm on the table, waffling. After a few minutes of ignoring his questions I take my headphones off.

'John,' I say, looking him straight in the eye, 'please close your mouth. You're bothering me.'

His bag rustles and he decides to take out a refill pad. Staples hold the edge of the bag together. It smells of damp socks. I fold over my laptop and see him combing his hair with one of those afro-comb things.

'John,' I say, 'get a grip and put that away or I'll take it from you.'

He looks at me all serious, intense, like he's thinking about taking the chance, like he did in September, but lets himself smile and waves away the problem. The comb is still in his hand.

'I said put it away. Remember your boombox?'

'Wha? I'm just like,' and he sucks in and does that thing between his lips like a backwards kiss.

He starts to drum with the rolled-up paper again, a bass drum, while his left hand acts as a snare – keeping time with finger taps. He looks at my headphones.

'W-w-wha you listenin to sir?'

I let the question linger, the silence rise, like he's crossed into prohibited territory.

'Some hip hop,' I say, pretending to be lost in a copy. He giggles and slaps the table.

'Ah man – y-you don't listen to hip hop.'

I keep my head down.

'Why wouldn't I? Sure what's it to you anyway.'

'Nuthin.'

'Good.'

I flick the copy pages and randomly tick words and scribbles, sentences without full stops or capitals. Casual.

'I love the beats,' I say, 'no one can write them like Jay-Z and Public Enemy. Sampling is such a joke.'

I glance up for a reaction. The line's out there, dangling between us, waiting for his ego to snatch at it and get snared. But he nods to himself and slides back on the chair. The rolled-up piece of paper unravels and he holds it at both ends and spins it. His chin digs into a football scarf. He's folded the scarf inside his shirt like a cravat or something. The paper turns. He's mulling over it. I let him mull and scribble random red marks on the pages.

'They're superstars, those lads,' I say, 'imagine being as good as them.'

He drops the paper and sits up straight, his elbows perfectly planted on the edge of the table, his arms spread out in front of him. Both
hands, all fingers, drum on the table and he looks like a young Stevie
Wonder, but much taller. His eyes blink their heavy blinks.

Another copy page turns and still no reaction so I say, real low like,
almost to myself, 'Seriously talented those lads.'

'Miss H-Holmes called me in for music class, for the choir,' he
says, finally, 'cause Taiwo was playin the keyboard for them and he's
left.'

'How interesting,' I say through a yawn.

'Taiwo,' he says, 'so I replaced playin the keyboard for them.'

'Wow – you must be so proud,' I answer again, deadpan.

He plays an invisible keyboard on the desk and nods, 'And sh-she
heard me playin and sh-she just said I should do a solo.'

'Really?' I say, pretending to be impressed, 'a whole solo.' I mouth
the word 'wow'.

We're not talking about what I'd intended, but I humour him.

'Ye must have a flair for music.'

He shrugs and drags at the scarf with his chin.

'I-I-I think I'm okay. I-I don't know what other people think but
sh-she, she says I'm great.' There's a gap and he blinks into the distance and he lifts his shoulders, shifts on the seat and slumps back, his
hands behind his head, 'An, like, other crews are like, comin to me
now too. Ih-ih-it's greah.'

This is going nowhere.

'So music's your thing. That's a shock. I thought you were goin to
be a football star.'

He nods, his chin lifted, proud.

'You can be a rap star too I suppose.'

His lips squirm.

'Most of those others,' he nods to an imaginary crowd, 'they askin me bout music yeah? And me like, yeah, I like ih, but they all love hip hop and rap and all.'

'What kinda rap and hip hop?'

'R&B.'

Blood from a stone.

'What kind of R&B?'

'R&B's just R&B, sir. I'm not like, into it that much. I mostly listen to gospel.'

I didn't see that coming.

'Gospel?' I try not to sound surprised and wonder if those students were having me on the other week. 'John's a genius,' one of them had said. Gospel? Genius? Doesn't make sense.

'Gospel,' I say again, almost to myself, just to hear it out in the open.

'Rap-gospel sir.'

'There's no such thing.'

'Mmhh-mmhh, there is,' he mumbles and rolls and unrolls the paper.

The silence is long.

'Actually sir,' he says, raising his chin again slowly and purposefully, 'all the hip hop songs and rock songs that are played these days comes from gospel songs. Gospel music like.'

'No it's not.'

'Ih-it is. Its origin is literally gospel. Like rock comes from gospel,' he holds out his piece of rolled-up paper and taps it once on the table, 'and hip hop,' two taps, 'and raggae,' tap, 'and rave,' two taps, 'and dub,' tap, 'and ska,' two taps, 'and gansta rap,' tap, 'and crunk,' two taps, 'and funk,' tap, 'and soul,' two taps. A smile begins to creep proudly up the side of his face as he tries to battle with himself to keep up the rhythm, 'And ghetto house,' tap, 'and house,' two taps, 'and grime,' tap, 'and raga,' two taps, 'and jazz,' tap, 'and blues,' two taps. He keeps on going, letting all his knowledge flow. All I had to do was ask. 'And hyphy,' tap, 'and East Coast rap,' two taps, 'and w—'

'Alright, alright,' I say, my hands held up in submission to his ency-clopaedic knowledge. Genius?

He rubs his hand over his head and says, big smile, white teeth like ivory piano keys, 'My days – th-that's like the longest I've gone for. I musta got like twenty or something.'

I laugh. All music enthusiasts are geeks. I see a bit of myself in him.

'I dunno John. That was a lot.'

'Well, that kinda stuff, ih-its origin is from gospel. It's since they took over and had so many big hits with everything else everyone actually forget where they came from, and they think like, that some-body just made it like that. But it didn't. They don't know, but I do, yeah?'

I suppose I'm learning. So I keep quiet.

'I mean there's lots of gospel songs that don't sound like gospel songs.'

His bottom lip turns inside out.

'Such as?' I ask to keep him talking. Tire him out on the subject.

He blows out a breath.

'I don't think y-you'd know any sir.'

His hands flop onto the desk and he yawns, like he's suddenly bored.

'Can I go now?'

I pretend to check my phone.

'Not yet.'

He tuts and folds his arms.

I'm saying, 'But what about the rhythm of the songs?' just as the year-head appears at the side of my desk and clears his throat.

'Well?' the year-head goes, 'did he behave?'

I cover my mouth with my hand and whisper, 'Unfortunately, no.'

The year-head tuts and says, 'Right, that's it – go home for now Kembo. But if you misbehave again I'll bring you in for detention again, only it will be with me, or the principal next time.'

'It's okay,' I whisper, 'I'm getting somewhere with him. I'll take him. Any sign of bad behaviour – even a sniff, send him here. We've got to be hard on him.'

The year-head nods an impressed nod and pats my shoulder and says, 'That's the spirit.'

John gets up and walks out the door and says, 'See ye later sir,' without looking back.

The year head leaves and I'm zipping up my bag about to shoot off when a knock sounds. It's from the bottom of the room, at the door between my room and the spare one. Lauren peeps her head in.

'Working late?' I say, freaked she might've heard me through the partition, but dying to strike up a conversation all the same.

'Yeah. Correcting second year exams.' She pauses and smiles. 'I heard you talking . . .'

Here it comes.

She twirls her hair around a finger. That smell. Something's missing. Smirnoff Ice.

'Yeah?' I say, casual like.

'God, Rob, you're so good with him. You show such an interest,' she gushes, 'just such a nice thing to do.'

I hide the laughter.

'Thanks,' I say, pretending to be all bashful, like it's part of my job and I enjoy the warm feeling I get connecting with the kids, 'he's a good kid really. Just misunderstood.' Priceless. She kind of frowns, as if to say, 'aahh, that's beautiful.'

'Well it's really great Rob. Really great.'

'Thanks,' I say.

She nods, embarrassed, and retreats, the door clicking shut between us. No mention of the band or the texts she sent, the smiley faces, nothing. I make to go in to her but see the time and go for the train to rehearsals instead.

December.

My breath smokes up in the not-quite-there darkness. I check the time and take my headphones off and hear the crows in the trees and the hum of traffic in the distance; the calm before the storm. I drag at my scarf with my chin and stamp my feet. The soil's nearly frozen, the grass still wet, glowing in the weird light from the school lamps, and I'm standing there like a tool doing the whole 'I'm on guard' thing.

A few kids trickle out the side entrance, see me, stop, tut, shake their heads and turn for the main gate. Then the bell's three notes go and the rest of them escape out the door like you'd see the mess ooze from a burst sewage pipe. They're society's problem for the next forty-eight hours. Our babysitting is over for the weekend.

The Droogs – who else – appear amongst the crowd. At first I look harder to make sure I'm not mistaken, but then I realise they've someone else with them. Whereas the crowd float towards the gate – away from me – the Droogs, and John, seep, heads down, lost in serious conversation, over to me. John stands there smiling, looking for my recognition for his new friends. The Droogs sniffle and smile too, look over my shoulder and chug out streams of smoke. I'm confused by the extra member in their group. There's gonna be trouble.

'Wha ye doin here sir?' Colm says.

'I'm on guard.'

'Where's Peter?' Peter's the principal, their principal.

'Mr Shields to you. He's away, so I'm on watch today.'

They giggle. Taidgh steps forward, into my space. 'You'll let us out this way, won't ye sir.'

'No.'

'Why not?' Andrew says. 'Yer da wouldn't be impressed. I might haveta tell him.'

I ignore his threat and deal with the first part, tell him what I've been told: the ditch is out of bounds. 'There've been complaints from the neighbours beside the estate. They say there's all sorts of vandalism being done to the empty houses.'

'We're not doin it, or are ye accusing us of something?'

I don't respond. Just shrug.

Other kids slow down as they exit the side door. They're gathering, watching to see if the ditch escape route is open.

'Right lads,' I say, changing my tone, widening my arms, like I'm a fishing trawler gonna scoop them up, 'move.'

We're nearly nose to nose. I stare at John.

'You heard me Kembo, move.'

He does the backwards kiss, looks thick, tries his luck and doesn't budge, so I say 'move' a bit sterner. Andrew turns to him and they slap hands, half hand-shake and mumble something and he finally retreats.

'So he's your friend now?' I say once he's gone.

'What's it to you?' Taidgh goes.

I shrug, hold up my hands like I don't care – cause I don't – and say, 'Fair enough. Right, you lads, move.'

The crowd is getting bigger a few yards behind them. John's figure slumps away over the pitch. Colm stares at me for a few seconds. I tighten my fist.

'Okay sir,' he says, turns and walks away. I let my fist unravel.

The other two follow Colm and I look to my iPod. One second, a second, I take my eyes off them and suddenly they're running at me, screaming, laughing, shouting, flying, and before I've time to respond they've gone by.

There's cheers from the small black mass that've stopped to watch. My pride at stake, I turn and run. The grass – knee-length – slaps off my legs and dampens my trousers. The silhouettes are in line, but apart, until they converge at a drop in the long grass, and suddenly they're gone. I'm only a few seconds behind them. But for me, although still technically in the school grounds, just on the outskirts, I've no idea where I am, what I'm getting into. I stand at the cusp of something. There's a mucky looking slope – more a steep drop – of about ten feet, a worn escape route beaten out by the feet and bikes of the Droogs and others. At the bottom of the slope is the ditch, and at the far side, only visible because of the weak light from the school lamps, is another slope up – and then access, I presume, to the ghost estate they've been destroying.

Without thinking, just hearing their taunts and laughter, seeing the trail of their breath disintegrating at the top of the far slope, I shoot down, and with the force of the run down, propel myself through the ditch and up the other side, like I'm on a rollercoaster, and appear, past the bushes and empty branches, into a weird, still kind of nearly darkness.

Mad vertical and horizontal black lines outline the empty estate. Orange lamps, from estates with electricity, give a depressing second-hand light to the deserted place. Different silhouettes give the impression of buildings. The windows, reflections inside the boxes of black, show slivers of moons. Every window is cracked and shattered. Destroyed.

I crunch over bits of rocks and bricks. Big cement tubes lie on top of each other, lined up, waiting to go, never to be used. Cavity blocks are toppled and broken. The ground is murky, and dangerous. The empty houses, scaffolding clinging on to some of them, stand depressed and suffocating. Plastic sheets, white and see-through look-ing things, catch the glare of the moon and snap back into the empty windows and doors. My breath snakes away.

'Ro-bert,' a high-pitched voice calls and there's giggles and what sounds like scuffling.

Small stones bounce and crack onto the gravel and concrete near me. Another, then another. More giggles. If I knew where they were I'd destroy them. I grab a stone and lob it at one of the houses. A window shatters, a massive crack, but doesn't break.

'Come on out,' I shout, 'you're not gonna be able to hide here all day.'

Another stone bounces, a thud off a block, and bobbles over to my feet.

'We're not on school pro-perty,' the high voice mocks. It sounds like Andrew. Brave man in the shadows.

Little scurrying noises, like rats, sound behind me and I turn to see another group of silhouettes scatter clear of the ditch and away into the estate.

'Hey,' I shout after them and retreat. But the shadows are gone, laughing at me as they go. At least I can save face and turn away from the Droogs. I pretend to be stopping others from taking the shortcut. More stones rattle through branches near me. I shout, 'Hey, stay away from there,' to the darkness; but the Droogs won't be able to tell this, and then I say, 'Hey, come back here,' as if I'm running after another group and I brace myself and shoot down the slope and up into the safety of the school grounds. Safe back on civilised territory; protected by the thinnest of threads and, hopefully, looking like I wasn't scared. There'll be other times. I look to see if their silhouettes emerge now that I'm gone, but the estate is dark and still, and only a whisper, high-pitched, I dunno, might even be the wind, sails across the ditch and I think it taunts, 'Ro-bert, Ro-bert,' but I can't tell so I turn my back and return to the school.

★

The waiter notices the silence when he comes over to take our order. He smiles awkwardly and asks if we want any drinks. We laugh at his strange Chinese accent when he leaves. At least that's something. But the laughter seeps away into unease as Jen's smile fades with the return to her menu.

'We could've gone to Diamond Burger,' she says, kind of whispering so the couple a few tables away can't hear.

'Yeah, but I wanted to treat you.'

Her head shakes and she looks up from the menu, deadpan and says, 'You can treat me all you want at Christmas, or my birthday, Rob. This is just our anniversary.'

'Just?' I say, trying to keep things under wraps, these thoughts I've been having, the unease I've been feeling. I've thrown myself into ourselves to get by, get through this. Be normal. Try and remember what normal was with us. Go along with things. See if this passes.

'You know what I mean.' She stops and holds out her hand to the right of the little tea-light candle. I hold her hand and feel the soft warmth from her palm, her fingers, 'We've other priorities Rob, you know that.'

I nod and bite my bottom lip.

'I just wanted to—'

'I know. I love you.'

She leans forward. We kiss softly, but briefly.

The first time we went for dinner was in a Chinese back home. It was a week after we'd met properly at a Terrors gig. We weren't the Terrors then though, we were the Scenemakers and we were supporting one of those bands that are huge in Ireland, but unknown anywhere else in the world and have to tour every horrible back-hole in the country to try and make a living. We were the lucky support act the week they came to our back-hole.

We were all sixteen or seventeen. Still in school. Jen was going to the convent. I knew about her. Had seen her around, at a distance in the chipper or around the square. She was beautiful. She had a quality about her, a calmness that made her seem older. I was young, looked younger. Playing support to the band meant I could get into the pub and be part of that whole buzz. Jen liked this I think. At the time she was kind of seeing someone from the year above mine. But he couldn't get into the pub that night. No ID. She could. She always could. Bit of lipstick and make-up and you'd swear she was in her twenties. This used to blow my mind. Me, baby faced, going out with her. Jen.

The other band wouldn't let us play on their stage, so we had to play on a piece of plywood on top of a load of crates. We played downstairs in the pub. The place was packed when we went on. Derek had to nearly duck cause the roof was so low. We looked ridiculous when I think about it. No one thought so then. We got away with it I suppose. We played our covers. We thought we were the bomb in the early days. The primary roads were becoming one motorway, one musical journey.

Near the end of our set, drips of liquid, water or sweat or something started to fall from the ceiling onto my keys. Once or twice my fingers slipped and I played a bum note or two. This wrecked my head. Mono wasn't happy and made sure I knew it by the way he glared across at me. We were his band then. He was the guitarist. We were playing guitar music.

As soon as we finished our set Jen was there, smiling down at me in my low stool. I remember she said something like, 'I didn't know you were in the Scenemakers,' and I said something stupid back like, 'Am I?' and we laughed and I checked if Mono or Steve were looking but loads of other people, other musicians and stuff, were around them, shaking their hands, patting their backs.

Cause it was so hot packing up and I couldn't really breathe with all the bodies, I went outside for some air. The beer garden was freezing. Almost the moment I stepped outside and closed the door behind me I made to turn back and get a drink. I'd only got a t-shirt on and I was drenched in sweat. A voice called from the emergency stairs at the second floor. I peered up to see Jen leaning over the metal railing, waving down at me. 'There you are,' she said, 'I thought you'd left.'

I remember the rattle as she came down the stairs in her high heels. The louder the noise got the sicker I felt. She was different to the others. There was a spark, I dunno, something different about the way she spoke to me that made me believe she was special. She came over and we began to talk. My teeth were chattering and I had goose bumps, but I hid it well, held tight to my arms, clenched my jaw. We were on our own and laughing and just messing and I didn't want to be disturbed. The DJ was playing The Stone Roses' 'Ten-Storey Love Song' and Derek popped his head out and called me inside, saying the singer from the other band wanted to talk with us.

I went inside as quick as I could. The singer was a skinny wreck of an aul lad, sitting back, nearly lost on a couch in the 'green room' upstairs in the pub. He said something about us being 'rapid bud' and we'd all looked at each other and smiled and gushed, 'nice one, nice one,' and the lads' girlfriends giggled, and then beside me I felt a hand take hold of mine, a soft, slender, warm hand and I looked around and Jen was smiling there. She stayed back to help me pack up my gear, which is saying something; but I got the impression she loved the whole buzz of being in the pub late and being treated differently to the other punters. I dunno.

Jen is moaning to me about some lad in work who still wears his football jerseys to the office on 'Casual Friday'.

'I mean,' she says, making a face, 'we know he had trials for some football teams, Villa and Spurs or something, but does he really have to wear the smelly jerseys into work to remind us? It's unhygienic.'

'Give him a break,' I say, 'let him do what he wants. You girls, when you get together must talk some amount of—'

'Sense, Rob, we talk sense.'

'But it's not a big deal is it? I mean, it's grand.'

'It's pathetic Rob, that's what it is. It's pathetic. Living on former glories. He's an administrator, not some Beckham or whatever.'

I try to hold it in, but it just comes.

'Right,' I say, whispering, 'I get it. Like I'm a teacher and not a rock star and I should try to stop pretending to be one?'

She looks at me, wide-eyed. She overplays the shock.

'Now that's just paranoia.'

I don't respond. She puts down her knife and looks at me sheepishly, 'Now that you say it though,' she goes, 'maybe it is time.'

'Time for what?'

'You don't know?' she says.

'No I don't.'

She takes a deep breath and whispers, 'If you don't know, well then I don't know.'

I don't bother challenging her. I leave it and think instead of what the signpost must've read when I heard 'Ten-Storey Love Song' pulse through the doors into the beer garden while I shivered and chattered and began to fall for a seventeen-year-old beauty ten years ago.

★

I'm a few hundred yards out of the school, the big padlock probably still swinging on the chain, when I realise I've left my computer charger behind. I skip back across the road. The rain flitters past headlights, gusting like silver flecks as I take my keys out and fiddle around in the dark for the right one.

To open the padlock you have to put your arm through a small hole in the wooden barrier; once through you have to grab a heavy-duty chain, yank it up, and try, blindly, to manoeuvre the lock around so you can fit the key in. You see, the wooden barrier is about three metres tall. Impossible to get over. It's not working. I'm running late and I boot the door and curse under my breath. The music is distracting me so I reef the earphones out and compose myself, and try again.

The rain pounding against the wood is heavy, insistent, and then the cars, and their horns and the puddles being destroyed, add to the sense of frustration. Chaos. As I struggle with the lock, the water seeps all the way down my spine, under my shirtsleeves and down my arms. My breath starts to gush between my bottom teeth and I feel like just forgetting the charger.

The noise of a door slamming – glass breaking – rises above the clatter of steel chain against wood and I stop messing for a second.

But it's gone. I look up into the rain – feel it beat my face – to see if I can locate the sound. But there's nothing. I continue, and finally the simplest of clicks – a little ping – and the bolt gives way and the chain unravels, rattles, and I pull my arm out of the hole and yank the door open.

Only one light, a dim emergency thing, colours this end of the school. The light, weak and all as it is, highlights the puddles at my feet, then trails away to muck and gravel, then loose bricks, leftovers, and directly to the source, to what is normally an empty space beside the prefabs about ten, fifteen metres away.

There's a shadow there at first, a shape, then a figure; the orange light catches the quick spurts of breath surrounding it. The figure stays still in the rain, almost waiting on me to act. I'm about to say something, move to close the wooden panel, take the chain, when the shape, I dunno, all of a sudden takes this as a sign to sprint towards me. I must jump a little cause I let my keys slip and in the slipping I try to catch them – take my eyes off the shape – and keys caught, look up to see John nearly barge into me. He skids to a halt, his mouth gaping, his eyes massive and scared, face soaked, bag in hand. He glances over his shoulder and looks to the door, chest rising, breath smoking, nostrils flaring. He just waits – doesn't flinch or say anything, so I step aside, easily, orange raindrops between us, let the chain go and let the door swing open. The whoosh of cars fills the space and he looks over his shoulder once more and without a word escapes.

A slight click, a tiny knock, and the lock closes and I put my head down, shoulders hunched to escape the rain, and go towards the main building to get my plug. When I get there Joe the caretaker shouts down the corridor, 'You after coming past the prefabs?'

'Yeah,' I go.

'See anyone down there?'

'No. Why?'

'Ah, nothing. Just the alarm's acting up again.'

I keep my head down, my eyes like slits, traipsing back outta the school, facing into the gusts. I think I spot broken glass outside the prefabs but don't bother with a second look. It's only when I get out of the place, cross the road and approach the train station that I finally stop and start considering going back to Joe. If I was to turn back, I could play all innocent and be the hero. But that'd mean I'd miss the train, miss rehearsals. I take one step toward the school, stop, brush the water from my face, think about it, take out my keys, look at them and think, do I really wanna be on the scene? Be a witness? Point a finger? Is it worth the hassle? If no one saw me there, I wasn't there. The chime goes in the distance and I think I can hear, 'Please stand back behind the yellow line,' so I continue running away from the school and finally, arriving at the train, feel like I've made the right choice. I begin to laugh, a schoolboy's giggle, and take the steps over the track and arrive just before the green button stops flashing. I step into the horrible bright lights and sit down and smile away to myself as the train moves off. I'm weirdly excited. If John was up to something, I'm his accessory. His getaway man. Now I have something on him.

★

The old guitar clangs as I pull this little forty-nine key Casio keyboard from out behind it in the attic. I plug it in, set a 4/4 disco beat, and find those euphoric chords from the house music I've been listening to. Ultra-Sonic, Scooter, 4th Dimension. I just play the chords over and over and over again. My ma's roaring from downstairs, 'What you doing up there?' and I'm shouting down, 'Nothing,' because this time the embarrassing early stages of development will be confined to my room.

What seems like a main road only turns out to be a little grassy Mohawk country yoke, a short hard-house beat fuelled detour from where I was meant to be. Fifteen I think. Not Guns N' Roses or the whole Nirvana thing. Missed that. It's Blur and Oasis. Oasis first though. My brother's mate from school gives me *Definitely Maybe* and I can remember sitting in the box room listening hard cause everyone else was beginning to. I get the chord progressions from guitar books in town and, hidden away upstairs in the box room, translate them into piano chords. Organ chords. String chords.

I'm allowed queue overnight on O'Connell Street for Oasis tickets but only if my older brother accompanies me. We're relaxed at about half-twelve that night sitting on the steps of the GPO in the thick of things, the queue loose and snaking round the corner. But the cops start to stand us up and push us all together – move us off O'Connell Street and compress us into a neatly packed mess inside barriers on Henry Street. It's one o'clock. The music store doesn't open until eight. I'm fifteen, small and my bro's not much bigger, and we're wedged together – standing between these smelly parka jackets, denim jackets with circle British colour patches, weird severe fringe haircuts. I remember being on my tippy-toes, peering over a shoulder to see a clock above a jewellers. The hands wouldn't move until you looked away. It was a horrible, dripping wait.

We're so close when the store opens we can see the lights come on above the doors and the people, big smiles on their faces, come out with their tickets. We edge closer, half-step by half-step until yards, literally yards from the door a voice goes up, 'Sorry folks – sold out. If you're not in the immediate queue inside the barriers before the shop, go home.' Of course we're not in that semi-circle. I boot the steel barrier that's keeping us in line and see two lads from school run by. I dunno, I'm so tired, angry, euphoric, disappointed, I let a roar at them like I know them and go, 'Lads – where yis goin?' They stop running and the taller lad – long Oasis hair – comes over like he recognises me too and goes, 'We're gonna hop the barrier.' My brother tries to hold me back and says he's gonna tell ma, but I escape and sprint with my two new buddies toward the semi-circle of barriers around the shop. We clear them easily, but the waiting crowd, the hemmed in sheep, start to bleat.

We're hauled back over the barriers and pinned against a wall by three big mad coppers. We're barred from Henry Street for life, they say, and we're escorted onto O'Connell Street and we laugh ourselves silly walking for the early morning train back to Balbriggan.

It's only when we're on the train that the tall lad stops flattening his hair over his ears and introduces himself as Mono. The other lad is Steve.

'I thought I recognised yis alright,' I say, 'we learnt guitar in Fran Farrell's years ago.'

They look at each other and shrug.

'Don't remember that,' Mono goes.

'Me neither, our lad,' Steve says.

'Ah, it's cool, I wouldn't remember me either,' I say and we laugh.

'Do ye still play?' Steve asks.

My time arrives. The secret I've kept in the box room is about to be revealed. I try to hide the quiver in my voice.

'Guitar? No. No, gave that up.'

'Shame,' Mono says, 'cause we're startin a band.'

'I play keyboards.'

It's the first time I've ever put myself out there, into that place where you can be ridiculed for something you are. It's my first true act of bravery. I remember it like I remember my first kiss. It changed my life.

'Yeah?' Steve goes, his tired face perked up, 'deadly.'

Mono shakes his head.

'Nah.'

'What ye listen to? What can ye play?' Steve says, ignoring his mate.

'I love Blur – can play all their stuff. And Oasis of course. Can do all their stuff on keyboard.'

'Deadly. What about it Mono?' Steve goes.

Mono looks out the window to the fields flying past. His face looks pained and he brushes his fringe down, flattens the top of his head.

'I dunno. We're gonna be a guitar band. Rock and roll.'

'Oasis use keyboards live – and on their album,' I say.

'They do Mono, I saw that too.'

He turns to me and shrugs and looks to Steve for unspoken advice and whatever way Steve looks back, Mono turns to me and goes, 'Fair enough. You wanna join my band?'

I nearly forget to respond. I'm stunned.

'Yeah, deadly. What yis called?'

'Don't know, no name yet,' Mono says, fixing his hair, patting it down over the ears again. 'I'm workin on it. Haven't got a drummer yet either, but sure, we'll get one.'

'Deadly,' I say and after a pause go, 'what about 'Modern Shades'?'

Mono looks confused.

'For what?'

'A band name.'

Steve whispers the name again and goes, 'Deadly.'

Mono holds up his hands, says, 'Woah there. It's my band. I'm the guitarist. I'll come up with a name.'

He does, some months and copy covers later.

My secondary road, from nowhere, zips way off track and somehow, on a Saturday morning, tired and buzzing, becomes part of a collective motorway.

★

Ever since some DJ played one of our early major label 'Development Deal' demos on this new indie radio station, I've listened to his show every morning on the way to the train station and then from the train to work. You see, I missed it the first time. Heard it on the podcast of course, but sure, it's not the same. Like having a microwaved Big Mac or something. Yeah, it's grand, but you know it was better the first time round.

So from half seven, the moment I close the door behind me and meet the trees on Synge Street, to Camden Street, the early morning, packed busses staring down as I go, Wexford Street and her morning-after shame of black sacks and cardboard boxes, Stephen's Green, meeting faces heading into the centre, me going against the crowd, exiting right, slicing the edge off College Green, rounding that college, past the broken glamour of The Screen cinema, by the back of the Social Welfare where I claimed for a few months and by Mulligans, onto Tara Street, always giving some time to the advertising hoardings to see if any good gigs are coming up, and then into the station, I listen to that DJ talk absolute garbage just for the chance to hear a song I could hear whenever I want on my iPod. The radio reception holds until about twenty minutes on the train and a good bit outside the city. The white noise kicks in then. No matter how I try to manoeuvre the iPod, the radio station always gives way to the nothingness of green hills and sloping telephone wires with this grey white-noised mess. I lose contact with hope, and settle for the last ten minutes in silence. Horrible contemplation. It's like the white noise is there to turn me off, let me know my life back in town is gone for the next few hours, out of reach, and I'm Mr Lynch again, that stranger who knows nothing about dreams or ambition, knows nothing about the person that gets on the train in the hope of hearing a song he's heard a million times before, just for the chance of hearing it once more.

There's an impromptu meeting called as soon as I get into the staff room. I worry if it's to do with me. There's a buzz about the place. I retreat to the back of the room and sit beside one of the soon-to-be retirees; a transfer from a school which lost numbers. The retiree snorts and rubs his moustache with a disturbing manic kind of vigour.

'What's all this nonsense then, hey?' he says, not caring if he's heard, agitation in his voice, resentment at being disturbed from his Monday morning ritual of sausage rolls and black coffee.

'Okay,' the principal says and the photocopier, as if it knows it's the only thing left making noise, winds down and the chug-chugging of wasted paper ceases. The whispers disappear.

'As some of you may have heard, around five on Friday evening, by the back of the school, near the back gate, em, the prefabs, we had a break in.'

There's the usual murmurs.

'Do ye hear this?' the old teacher whispers to me.

'Was there anything of worth taken?' the actress beside the photocopier pipes in.

'Bits and pieces. Food from the presses and the fridge . . .'

'Do ye hear this?' the whisper continues, getting increasingly agitated. There's spit or something on his moustache. I just shake my head to keep him happy. 'Bloody savages.'

' . . . some toilet roll, from the storeroom. It's shocking but no surprise.'

The tuts and headshaking, large eyes and pursed lips are mandatory.

'This is what happens,' the moustache continues, 'when the lunatics take over the asylum.'

People notice his voice spike and look at us as if we're disrespecting the serious tone of the room. I want to move seats.

'They broke the washing machine of all things. Looking for clothes it seems.'

Horrified gasps punctuate his sentence. He lifts his hands to soothe them.

'Damn bloody savages,' the moustache spits.

'Luckily enough all we had in it were some soccer jerseys . . .'

'This is what happens,' the moustache continues, old tired thing, grey and brown bristles, like a brush.

' . . . so, Mr Lynch, if you could . . .'

And the whole room swishes to me and the moustache doesn't notice and keeps on whispering, 'You know who it was, don't you?'

' . . . if you could just go through this bag, Robert, see if any of your jerseys are missing.'

'Do we have any idea who may have done this?' the actress asks.

'It was the blacks of course,' the moustache hisses quietly in my ear, his breath catching the lobe, kind of warm, too close.

Joe the caretaker appears into the room, like a magician's assistant, my kit bag over his shoulder. The whole room watches as he spots me down the back and makes his way over.

'Do you know, son, what you get when you mix black and white?' the moustache.

There's hushed intakes of breath, anticipation, whispers and heads shaking.

'No?' Warm breath, smell of death. 'Grey. You get grey.'

The caretaker's nearly there. I pull away from the bristles and stand up, take the kit bag.

'Everything there?' the principal says before I even open the thing up. I rummage while the whispers continue. Do they suspect something? I don't need to look. I don't need to count the jerseys. There's loads of purple and white. But no grey. The grey goalkeeper's jersey.

'It's okay,' I say, look up, big pretend relieved smile, 'nothing's missing.'

I zip up the bag immediately in case someone else checks.

'Okay,' the principal goes, clapping his hands to focus eyes back on him, 'that's everything then. We'll have to get keys cut for the gate though. We can't have students using it.'

The retiree giggles and goes, 'I'm outta here fella while I can. But you're gonna have to stay.' He chuckles to himself and grunts for the whole room to hear and the principal stops talking and waits for him to leave. All eyes look to him, then to me, with distaste. He knocks off a few people as he goes, others moving to sidestep his toxic cynicism. He brushes by the principal without excusing himself.

The eyes keep going from him to me, like I'm involved in the madness, like it's my fault for talking to him, like I'm his understudy. But I'm nothing like him, I want to say, he's a cynic. He's finished. I've still got hope. I've got my sights set beyond this white-noised nowhere land.

I don't though. Say anything. I just sit there, still, and keep to myself.

★

The echo of a speedily interrupted guitar chord floats to an abrupt stop the moment I enter.

'Jayse,' I say, failing to hide my surprise, 'very cosy. Wasn't expecting to see you lads here so early.'

Steve looks up with a face that says 'caught rotten'. His bass is on his lap, in his hands. Mono's hidden behind him, on another amp with an acoustic guitar on his lap. An acoustic guitar?

I take off my jacket and drop it beside my bag and continue as I normally would. Don't wanna let them know that I know they're up to something.

I ease the faders up on the PA. The noise from my four keyboards is like a compressed electronic sizzling. I press a key and a fat synth sound squelches out. It's so loud you can hear the snare drum rattle. I get a glimpse of Mono's face; his hair sways from side to side. He looks up through his fringe and glares. A dead, emotionless stare. I hold the stare.

'So what yis up to?' I say, still not flinching; our unspoken challenge.

Mono frowns.

'Just goin through things on the acoustic guitar.'

'Yeah?'

Steve coughs. 'Mono has a few bits of lyrics and ideas he wanted to run past me.'

'Ideas. Yeah?'

'Yeah.'

I move my stare casually from Mono to Steve and smile, like I'm grand.

'That's cool. We're all open to ideas. Aren't we Mono?' I say.

'Sure. I've some acoustic stuff I wanted to run by Steve, that's all.'

Run by him? Who's he to have ideas run by him? Who's in charge of this band?

'Cool,' I say, and step out from behind the keyboards, out towards them. They're in my shadow. 'Go on then,' I continue, 'gissa listen.'

Mono smiles and moves his hair out of his eyes and pulls a face, 'Nah man. If I'm gonna play it for ye I want it to be right.'

I laugh at him, at how ridiculous he's being. We're friends. Best friends. He knows this. We rehearse. We jam. We mess around here.

'Well, what kind of stuff is it?'

Mono turns to Steve and Steve opens his mouth and says, 'Kinda guitar stuff – folky songs like.'

Mono strums a distracted chord. It sounds pathetic on his acoustic guitar. Flaccid.

'Folk's not really us though, is it?'

'What's not us?' Steve says.

'That,' I say, nodding at the acoustic, the sound.

'Why not?' Mono pipes in. 'Sure you're thinking of bringin in new beats – hip hop beats, Bob. I'm just tryin to think outside the box too.'

'I know, but . . .'

'I'm tryin to do what you're doin. Move with things. Push us in new directions.'

'Yeah, but . . .'

'We were just thinking,' Steve says before Mono says, 'I thought I'd take us in the other direction. Start to push our sound into new areas. Try some new angles. You got me thinking there the other day. You're right. We need something new. We should all be tryin for new things, running new things past each other.'

'But folk? Really? You're windin me up.'

'Ye could say the same about hip hop,' Mono says, kind of hurt looking, angry in a way. 'And anyway,' he goes on, 'it's not just folk. It's protest music.'

Get a grip, I feel like saying. Protest songs? Ye haven't even cast a vote in yer life and ye wanna start writing protest songs about the state of the nation. Ye don't even know who's in charge of the kip let alone who's making the decisions on how much you should be taxed, how much your rent will be, how much your electricity will be. Protest songs have to be about something. You've gotta know what that something is. Protest songs? Who's gonna listen to a bunch of wimps moan about the government? Folk music is dead. Vinyl is dead. Free love is dead. The revolutions are dead. The hippies are dead. They're now called spongers Mono. Spongers. Get a grip. Protest music. Jesus.

Steve plugs in his bass to break the static silence. Mono gives him the daggers.

'Just listen will ye Rob. C'mon Mono, we'll show him what we've got so far.'

Mono shakes his head.

'C'mon,' Steve repeats, more insistent, before looking up to our drummer coming in the door.

'Alright lads,' the drummer says, all smiles, oblivious to the septic atmosphere in the room.

'You're early too,' I say.

He looks at his watch, 'No I'm not. I'm late. Mono said to be here for five.' He looks at the lads and mouths a sorry. He squeezes in behind his drums and sits down and asks what we're doing.

'Folk music,' I say, expecting him to choke. He doesn't react, just shrugs his shoulders and says, 'Cool.' Drummers.

I turn to Mono to force the point. 'Well Mono,' I say, smiling my best smile, 'lets have some of this protest music.'

Steve looks at me like he can't work me out.

'C'mon Mono. Plug in yer acoustic there and let's hear it,' I say.

'It's not ready,' he says, his teeth clenched.

'That's not a problem. That's what we're here for isn't it? Practise. Jam. Rehearse. C'mon.'

'Derek's not here.'

'Ah, come on Mono, stop making excuses.'

'What about your beats Bob, let's hear some of them,' Mono says.

'My beats will come in good time. We're here now, the acoustic's here. Lets see what we can do. Can the band not rehearse this new folk sound?'

Mono looks at Steve and stands up as if it pains him. He takes a lead and gently places it into his guitar and slowly puts the strap over his shoulder.

After a few minutes it's obvious it's not working. The drummer's playing a boring beat, even throwing in some rim shots. Rim shots. I never thought the day would come when the Terrors would do the whole rim-shots thing. I tut, but it's lost under the noise of the instruments.

The music stops and Mono blows his fringe out of his eyes and shakes his head at me.

We continue on. But my sounds are all wrong. Mono and Steve keep stealing glances and then looking at the keyboards, not at me, but the keyboards, as if looking at them will change what I'm doing. The noise ends.

'And can ye try a different sound maybe?' Mono says.

'The synth is good though,' I say, giving him a bit of his own protest medicine.

Steve shakes his head and says, real quick, 'No, no, no,' and turns up his bass and flicks the gain pedal with his right foot and plays a mad dirty bass line. 'Let's just rehearse,' he shouts over his noise.

The drummer starts to pound on the drums, big smile on his face. I tap some digits and get a filthy synth and find the right chords and play along.

Mono pulls his guitar off his shoulders and fires it to the ground. The clang warps the PA speakers for a few seconds before it dies out. He shouts something but I can't hear him over the noise. He storms out of the room and slams the door, a gust of wind following him. I shrug to Steve as if to say, 'What's all that about?' and the noise continues, the feeble echo of the acoustic guitar fading out, humming under our power.

★

Two other young lads, first years, are sitting in the middle of the room, tutting because it's Christmas week and I've got them in for evening detention. John barges through the door. He's looking round the room and biting his bottom lip, all on edge, and says, 'Mr O'Dowd says you wanna see me. W-wha you want sir, cause I'm like, late for something.' That football scarf, the local League of Ireland team colours, is his cravat inside the school jumper.

'Sit down John,' I say.

'No.'

He does his backwards kiss thing and says, 'Na-hah. Ih-it's Christmas. I ain't doin no detention.'

The silence. The challenge.

I let the first years hold their breath for that bit longer.

'Hear about the robbery in the prefabs?' I whisper, flicking through a copy. John's head lifts as if he's trying to catch an echo of what I've said. His body stiffens and he holds his chin up, silently defiant. I nod to the table, his seat in front, 'You not hear about it? Washing machine an all broken into.'

I savour the moment before John decides to move and the first years' jaws drop.

John sways over to the desk in front of me and slides into a chair, silently, stubbornly.

I tell the first years to get lost and they jump up and leg it out the door. John stares ahead, seething.

'Wh-why you say tha in-in front of them for?'

'Say what?'

'About thingy. The prefabs.'

'What about it?'

'Nothin.'

'Exactly John. Nothing. No jerseys are missing. Nothing happened.'

'Oh,' he says, drawing the sound out like his anger is being deflated. A new calmness comes over him. His lips twitch, his body moves forward, stops, thinks better of it, his brow creases and he retreats under his football scarf to think.

'Now, I hear you've some songs on your USB key that you brought in for music class.'

He sits up, his bottom lip turns inside out and he goes, 'H-how you know tha? She won't allow anyway. I didn't even get to sh-show it her cause, cause she threw me out of choir practice for like, nothing.'

'It's a real shame you were thrown out cause Miss Holmes told me you were getting on well. She was planning on using one of your songs for the choir until you called her a racist. And ye cracked the window of her classroom door when you slammed it.'

'It was the wind,' he whispers, deflated, 'the wind broke it. A big wind.'

His breath comes heavily through his nose. His head has slowed swaying, as if it's a calming measure or something. An index finger from each hand taps the table each time his face reaches the full angle of sway, like a silent metronome. This action continues for some seconds. I watch his nostril flare, become smaller.

'It's a real shame Miss Holmes didn't get to hear your stuff, John.'

He shrugs.

'I mean, ye know, she can be very influential around here. The choir play the National Concert Hall every January.'

His mouth opens, but nothing comes, again, still nothing, until, 'But we have loadsa games in January sir, don't we? C-cause you, you said all the pitches were in bits like, cause of de rain an all. I w-won't have time to do both and m-my mama won't let me take time, a load of time off school sir, cause sh-she says I gotta keep a good school record for the immigration and stuff.'

'Right,' I answer, thinking fast, 'but eh, the Concert Hall gigs are in the evenings I think.'

'Sorry sir – I – I got gospel practice like, nearly every day, m-my mama won't let me miss gospel practice.'

'But it probably won't even be on the same day.'

'B-b-but it could be,' he says, struggling hard with the b, trying to force it out, eyes closed, mind focused.

I sit forward and open up my Mac.

'Let's not get bogged down in all this nonsense now, John. C'mon,' I say, scrolling around the desktop looking for my music program, 'relax, let's just see what you brought to Miss Holmes so I can pass it on to her.'

He slumps back in his seat and crosses his arms, eyes closed again,

'Nah-hah, no way sir.' The backwards kiss, the long blink, 'Basically I go two times a week to gospel, three times if I want, and, and if it's Miss Holmes's choir, or like gospel practice,' he stops, looks up and giggles to himself, his chin digging into the scarf, 'man, I'm goin to gospel practice every time, cause she's a racist.'

He slaps the table and breaths out, expelling the last of his laugh.

'But Miss Holmes isn't a racist.'

'You don't know her sir,' he pleads and stares into me. To get him back on track I say, 'C'mon now, if ye don't do well for other subjects I mightn't be able to play you on the school team.'

His face scrunches up and he shifts around on the seat and rubs his chin.

'That's not right sir.'

I pretend to be struggling with my conscience.

'I don't know John. The rules are the rules. Mr Shields is the principal . . .'

'He's stoopid.'

'Mr Shields, your *principal*, has said if students don't perform academically they can't take half days for football.'

A tut and a sigh fill the silence. He's thinking about it.

'So what ye say John – I really need you in nets for the next few games.'

A shrug and he leans back and yawns. Nothing.

'We're after getting a bye into the semi-finals, the other team couldn't play, so one more win and we're in a final.'

His eyes open wide.

'Really sir?'

'Yeah really.'

The seat creaks when he sits forward, his hands spread out on the table.

'And you'd be leading the team out as captain in a big stadium, imagine. And we'll have a new blue keeper jersey – just like the school jumper,' I say, catching his eyes, lowering my voice to a hushed whisper. 'And half the school will probably be allowed come, all in their blue jumpers, and loads of teachers too and they'll all be chanting your name and saying "God, I never knew John Pereira was such a great footballer," or "What a great student," or "What a great person," or "What a great hero."'

His voice is a tiny whisper, an echo. 'A hero.'

'The town's hero.'

Hoovering starts up in another room and I let him set the scene in his head, project whatever images he wants to project in his mind, let him play them out.

'But of course, if you can't then this whole situation is over. Nothing.'

The plain hard truth. Projector off, fade to black.

My words sit with him for a long time. I just flick through a book and wait.

'C-could my mama come, like?' he whispers, his chin deep under his scarf, his eyes on the desk.

'Come where?' I say, looking at him like I don't know what he's on about.

'To the game, the final sir, if-if we play it an all.'

Bingo.

'Mmmhh, don't know John. But she'd defo be allowed go to the National Concert Hall. The final would be in the papers too. Imagine your family name in print.'

The moment I mention the press his head lifts and he looks at me with a smile. He wants to know if I'm joking and I tell him no, the press would be there.

'Would they like – definitely like, take a picture of me?'

'I don't see why not. You're the captain. Why?'

'Cause my mama wants like, me in the papers an stuff, like, ye know, to show wha a good student I am, yeah. Show the family, like, takin part in stuff in the town.'

'Course, yeah, course you'd get your picture in the paper. I can guarantee it if we win.'

He fidgets around in his pocket and pulls out his USB key. It makes a clicking sound when he lays it on the table. I don't reach for it immediately. Let it lie there, like it doesn't matter, like I don't notice.

'So eh, what songs you got there anyway?'

'Just like one piano song, kinda like, gospel, no music, just piano and then one hip hop thing I'm doin for one of the new crews in the town. But th-that's not for Miss Holmes.'

'Cool,' I say.

His lips squirm, 'Eh, it's okay.'

'Will we have a listen?'

'How?' he says and puts his hand back on the USB.

'You said you do all your stuff on the program called Reason right?'

'Mmhh-mmhh,' he mumbles, nodding slowly, wary.

'Well I have it on my Mac.'

His brow dips. The confusion turns into amusement and his lips part and his teeth show.

'Ah man,' he laughs, 'that's funny. You – you have Reason?'

A breath of disbelief is spat out and he laughs at me. I shrug and say, 'What? What's so funny?' and he says, 'Sir, sir, wh-what you doin with *Reason* on your computer? Do you not like just use Microsoft Word an stuff?'

I wave away his laugh and just say, 'A friend gave it to me.'

He looks down at his hands and repeats, 'A friend,' and giggles again.

'Yeah a friend. Now quit laughing and give me the USB so I can have a listen.'

'B-b-but why?' His face is all sad now, his bottom lip falling, and he looks like a kid all of a sudden, and I remember he is a kid. Still only fifteen.

'B-but why you wanna listen to it sir? Miss Holmes, sh-she just wants to hear it. She teaches music, you teach English.'

'Yeah, well, we'll just check. Why all the questions?' I take a breath, remember who's in charge, who needs to act like he's in charge, in control of this situation.

'Enough. Just give it here.'

I load the first song and play it. It's terrible. Just a cheap sounding piano with straightforward minor chords. A typical teenager's naïve idea of emotional music. D minor, A minor, C, F. The song finally finishes. There's a silence, like he's holding his breath. I don't feel like saying anything. I'm actually disappointed. I was hoping for so much more.

'Okay,' I say, just to say something, 'I'm sure Miss Holmes will love that.'

And I load up the next one, the hip hop one I presume. Don't hold out much hope.

But the beat is massive, even on the little Mac speakers; a big fat bottom-end boom, an off-beat, one boom, then two booms, and the snare is like no snare I've ever heard and there's a weird riff, a real tight sounding repetitive synth that plays out, about four or five notes over two bars, just over and over. There's so much space for other things. Other instruments. And then, from no-where, this squelching synth appears, a reverse note thing, like you're whipping the attack up with every note, done to three different notes, so you're like laying down your basic chord for two bars and on the third bar your higher chord and on the fourth bar your even higher chord, all with the original riff playing throughout. It ends.

'Wow,' I say.

He smiles and drums on the table, but then goes all serious, 'You think they gonna like ih?'

'Who?'

'The new crew. The D . . .'

'Oh course, course. Actually. Wait a second. You giving this away? I'd keep this to myself, John. It's great, but you can't just give it away.'

'I'm not sir. Like, I-I already have another song ready like, an we traded, yeah.'

'For cash?'

His face scrunches up. 'No. Not cash. For other stuff.'

'And you're gonna give them this?'

'Mmhh-mmhh.'

'Hold off.'

'Huh?'

'If you trade with everyone that wants to use your beats they won't be worth anything soon.'

His face is all lines and dipped eyebrows.

'Don't give your stuff away. That's all.'

'I'm not.'

'No, listen John. The easier it is for them to use your beats the cheaper they'll be. Hold off. Build up a few tracks. Tell them you're still getting them together and watch what happens.'

'Wha-what'll happen sir?'

'They'll go mad for them. Give you anything you want. And then loads of crews will want them. It's the illusion of value John. Be smart. Make them *really* want your beats – don't just trade them whenever they want.'

His lips dip, his head nods. He doesn't say anything for a few seconds.

'So like, ih-if I don't give them beats like, now, yeah, then later they'll be worth more and loadsa people will want them?'

'Exactly.'

He flops back on the seat and blows out a breath, big smile and goes, 'Cool. Thanks sir. You're right cause like,' he drums on the table, 'I've been spending ages on them an I haven't had a chance like, to work properly on them cause my mama . . .'

'Cool,' I say and grab my big headphones and listen to it again in proper stereo sound.

Even though I have the huge headphones on John continues talking. I can't hear a thing with all the sounds. His lips keep on moving and his hands are gesturing and he's drumming on a pretend kit and I just nod and smile back to him and say, 'Yeah, yeah.'

'Okay,' I say, delighted, elated, 'you can go now. Good lad.'

I'm surprised he doesn't move. Just sits there. Still.

'Go on, good lad.'

'B-but my USB.'

'I'll give it to her.'

He checks his phone.

'Sir, ih-it's like ten to five, sh-she got in her car at four, I-I saw her go, sh-she's gone home, I'll give it her tomorrow sir.'

'No, I'll hold onto it.'

'But,' he shifts, stretches his lips, sits forward, panic in his eyes, 'ih-it's my brother's, he-he, he'll kill me sir if he doesn't have it, th-there's loads of his stuff on ih an he needs it.'

He makes to take it out from the Mac. I put out my hand to stop him. We look at each other. There's no hint of what's going on between us. I tell him to go to the staff room and check if Miss Holmes is definitely gone. I hope she is.

I pull the track from his key as soon as he leaves the room and drop it onto my desktop. Just as he arrives back, silently sneaking up on me, the song finishes transferring onto my computer and the Mac, the volume still up and the headphones out, pings to announce 'done'.

John looks at the computer and asks, 'What's that noise?'

'Nothing,' I say, 'nothing. Good lad. I take it she's not there.' I eject the USB and place it in his hand. His hand's real rough, too rough for a young lad.

'Go on home now.'

As he leaves I shout after him. He turns and stops, and raises his head.

'Got any more hip hop?' I say, standing at the classroom door.

'Wha? Like my beats n stuff?'

I laugh it off.

'Yeah, course.'

'Mmhh, a few other ideas an stuff,' he says, 'why?'

'Just wondering is all. I'd love to hear more in the new year.'

He shrugs and says, 'Okay.'

'And John,' I call again.

'Yeah?'

'Don't forget to keep them for yourself. The less there is of something, the more valuable it becomes. And stay fit over Christmas. Remember, two games and you'll be a hero and you'll get your picture in the paper.'

A big smile, the wide grin, the cat's eyes light up his face.

'See ye,' I say.

He waves a distracted hand as if his mind has already gone somewhere magical and he turns and floats out the door and I turn back into my room and plug the headphones in for one more listen before I run for the train.

★

We're sitting in a corner of the lounge, out of the way, my ma, my da, Jen and me. I'm stuck in beside an old upright piano. Ma sits back and moves her bag off her lap. The light, a low orange from the lamps with the felt covers and little dangly things, shines above watercolour paintings of the town. The fairy lights, winking in the corner on the tree, are kind to everyone's faces. Soft.

'This is nice,' my ma says.

'Lovely Bernie,' Jen replies and we wait for the young lad to come over and take our orders.

Our drinks arrive and my da pays and everyone takes a sip and says cheers and happy Christmas and all that lark. My ma adds on to the end of all the salutes a thank you to Jen for coming out on Stephen's day.

'Not at all,' Jen says, smiling a real kind of depreciating smile, 'it's lovely to see you. It's great to be invited out.'

The lounge is full of old couples and spinsters and bachelors. The spinsters are in their groups, together, in twos and threes. They look like they're conspiring over their drinks, sharing the town's secrets in their little knitting groups. When they're not looking inwards around their tables they're surveying the pub for faces to recognise so they can be reminded of a bit of gossip or scandal that's eluded them.

Jen and ma look out into the bar and my ma spots someone and makes a big face, a surprised look, like she's just remembered something, and she turns into Jen and whispers and then Jen says, 'Really?' and looks to me and calls me away from the football match on the TV in the distance and asks me did I hear about my old school friend who bought a house with his girlfriend. My ma nods in the direction of the lad's father. Jen talks about how they're the same age as us, the two that bought the house, and how they were able to buy even though the girlfriend's out of work for months. The way she says 'months' doesn't sit well. It carries something. Anger. Despair. I just shrug it off and take a sup from my pint.

Ma continues on, 'When you see more people from your class Rob, those not even in jobs like your own, getting settled, getting mortgages, getting,' ma stops and takes Jen's hand, 'engaged.' They smile an embarrassed smile. I tut and shake my head. Not a hope. 'And,' my ma says when she's composed herself, 'havin kids too. Does it not make ye think?' She stops, turns her glass, bites her lip. She looks pained. 'Melanie Baxter had a child last month, Rob.'

'Heard that alright,' Jen says, 'a boy.'

My da joins in late about the bargain prices of houses in the Laragh. I'm so bored, so bored, I could literally shout something just to liven up the pub, flip open the piano and start smashing down some out-of-tune chords.

Someone needs to put an end to all this nonsense.

'Don't worry, we won't be going near the Laragh.'

'But why not Rob?' my ma says, the smile gone.

'The blacks of course,' my da blurts.

'Robert,' my ma says, annoyed, slapping da's knee and looking around the tables to make sure no one heard anything.

'No, don't be silly Robert,' Jen says to my da, 'we're looking closer to the city, or just outside it. Not as far away as here.'

'And what's wrong with here might I ask?' my da says, annoyed, his eyes resting on me. I just shrug.

'Didn't yis grow up here for god's sake, the two of yis.' His voice becomes a bit strained and he goes on, 'Now, granted, the far end of the town, the Laragh and all that are not ideal. But to start yis off there's plenty down our end.'

Jen breathes heavily and slumps a little and looks at me. When she does this the other two follow her lead. Everyone's staring at me. So I just say, 'What?' to make them say what they all wanna say.

'Are you saving?' my da says, his tone an accusation, not a question.

'Course.'

Jen looks to my ma and then back to me, without judgement, or an expression. A blank face. She doesn't need to say anything. They understand.

'Are you really saving, Rob?' my ma then asks. She looks to Jen, 'Is he saving at all, Jen?'

I don't believe what I'm seeing, hearing.

Jen squirms, for a second, one tiny second before she says, 'It's hard, what with the costs of the band an all.'

My da kind of explodes, chokes on his Guinness, 'Ah would ye ever,' he gets caught up in the swallow, the things he wants to say. 'The band,' he finally adds, 'the band. Give it a rest, son. For jaysus' sake. Are ye not finished with that yet?'

My ma's face is kind of pained, like she doesn't want to put the boot in. My da takes a gulp of the Guinness, a long satisfying pause and launches into me again, 'And you're still wasting money on it?'

'I'm not wasting money,' I say, loud, and lower my voice so the spinsters can't hear, 'I'm not wasting money. You keep on saying I'm wasting money. It's something I love and it may well pay back.'

My da tuts and looks away shaking his head. The other two don't believe me either. I can see it in them. 'I'm not,' I repeat, trying, for some reason, to make them believe. I don't know why I bother.

'Get real son,' my da says, and I think I see Jen, in the corner of my eye, nod – almost certain it's a nod – in agreement. I look at her, stare. But my da pulls me back with, 'You said the band would be two years, son. Time to get real – get in the real world.'

When I think the abuse is over my da turns to Jen and says, 'Does he ever put money away?'

I look at Jen and can't believe it when she says, 'Sometimes.' Sometimes. Unbelievable.

'Rob,' my ma moans, quiet, like I've disappointed her.

I look around the table; shocked my Stephen's Day has come to this.

'You should get your act together, son,' my da says, 'what are ye playin at making poor Jen wait around on ye.'

'He's not that bad,' Jen says and smiles to me and reaches out for my hand, but I pull away and say, 'Here, I've had enough of this. I'm going.'

My ma frowns, but then goes back smiling and says, 'C'mon Rob, don't be like that.'

I get up and grab my jacket.

'I knew the lecture would come sooner or later. I'm getting a train home.'

'But there's no trains on Stephen's Day,' Jen says.

'Then I'm getting a taxi.'

'Into town?' my da goes, annoyed now.

'Yeah,' I say.

'But Rob,' Jen pleads, half off her seat, 'that'll cost a fortune.'

'I don't care.'

'Well I do,' she says, standing now, 'that's more money wasted.'

Old men's fingers stop midway down the pint, eyes turn to us from all corners of the lounge.

I get a taxi at the rank up from the pub. Jen waits outside the door and I ask her if she's coming. She shakes her head and gets in beside me in the back, but looks out her window.

'This is a joke,' she whispers, 'we'll have to come back for our bags tomorrow – and the fare, I'm not payin – you can. It's gonna cost a fortune to get into town.'

I tut and face her, whispering now, anger scraping the bottom of every word. Surely the driver can hear.

'Who cares?' I say, 'it's always money with you. Money. Always money.'

The driver looks in the rear view mirror.

'Because we need it Rob, don't you get it. We need it.'

'But we don't. Not now. We don't need to be watching what we spend all the time, worrying about it all-the-time.'

'We do if we want a house.'

Taxi drivers must hear everything. Know everything.

'The prices,' she says, containing it to a whisper, 'are never going to be lower – don't you get it? We can get one for two thirds, nearly half of what Brenda or Michelle or James and Ann-Marie got for theirs.'

'But we're not in a race,' I shout and the driver looks in the rear-view mirror again. I stare at her, but she won't turn to meet me.

'It's not a race Rob, just a way of living, living together, with pride, so we're not left behind.'

I'm bamboozled.

'Left where?'

Absolute gibberish.

She looks at me.

'Where?' she whispers. But it's not a question, more a surprised echo.

'Yeah, where.'

She blows out a breath of frustration, 'You really don't get it.'

'Get what?'

'Exactly. God, you're such a . . .'

The hum of the car on the motorway fills my ears. I let it play. After a while I turn to her and say, 'Such a what?'

'What?'

'You said I'm such a something. So what?'

'Nothing.'

'No, go on. Say it.'

She turns away from me and looks outside, her dark reflection warping up the slanted window into the empty blackness behind the barriers at the side of the motorway. I imagine the car rumbling, dum, dum, dum, on the cat's eyes and the car skidding, flipping, the two of us in the back clashing heads, cracking our necks, fracturing our skulls, our bones snapping, bodies tearing, hearts breaking. We're flipping and spinning into the blackness, the nothingness and just lying there, moaning together, in bits, broken, while other cars fly by, oblivious to our collision.

'Loser,' she says, her breath, the word, fogging up that face on the window.

January.

On a guitar amp, an old Marshall I think, is where I'm sitting checking my phone. The screen wobbles and blinds for a second. Five missed calls from Jen. I wonder where she is. Half three. Her night club will no doubt be closed and her work mates will have long got their Nitelink. She talks to me about wasting money and she pays twenty quid into some stupid club, and then there's the cost of drink. I got sixteen Bavaria. Sixteen euro. No entrance fee. I don't ring her back. She's asleep. If she's not asleep she'd probably wanna come over. But she'd ruin the buzz. She's not on the buzz at all at all. Wouldn't be.

Some bird's dancing all sexy – that bump n' grind thing over in the corner of the room. It's more a hall, or large function room, than room. Not a room as in small apartment room, more Georgian Dublin drawing room, entertaining quarters. She's the best-looking bird in the place, and all the lads know it. They circle, discreetly, moving their heads like pigeons, grooving, trying to catch her eye so they have permission to dance in her circle.

I think of Lauren.

All of a sudden I'm in a skinny-jeaned jungle. Everywhere I look I'm surrounded by these twigs wrapped in elastic, skin-tight jeans.

Can't see a thing beyond them. It's packed. Where was I? Lauren. Send her a quick text. *Happy nu yr.* Ask her if she's around town to come over. She'd be seriously impressed by this. This party. Me in the thick of things. Great craic. Deadly party.

The speakers are massive. Part of the PA the band used. No rickety little iPod dock for this party, the sound distorting if you wanna get any sort of volume. No, no. This is the real deal. Whopper start to the new year.

Now and then the skinny jeans sway, like they're caught in the wind, or disappear completely, and what is an Amazon jungle, thick with trees, becomes a sparse forest. But after a while the jeans are back and it's packed again. I notice people are coming and going. I get to my feet and ask Steve where they're all off to. He just nods to the room next door.

It makes sense. Every party needs a panic room. When the music gets too much, the noise and the bodies too overbearing, those heads who wanna sit back and draw out their lines and practise their disappearing acts always break away from the crowd for their own selfish reasons. But I suppose, different highs need different scaffolds.

I pop my head in. The room's packed, loads of birds, green faces reflecting back the mood. Mono and Derek and the drummer are cramped together on a couch at the back wall. Mono sees me first. Doesn't say anything, just raises his glass to me like yer man from *Clockwork Orange* with his moloko, looking out past his fringe.

'Robbie,' Derek says, happier than happy, more alert than awake, 'where were ye? Get over here,' and he pats the arm of the couch, little dust clouds under the lamp, and I move past strangers, over legs and knees. A few deadly birds are there across from the lads. But in this light, at this time, on their high, at the peak before the inevitable plunge, even they look a bit haggard, sickly.

Me and Derek are having great craic. Everyone's laughing and smiling, laughing and smiling, but secretly, thinking no one's looking, the drummer grimaces, gets a little sick in his mouth, swallows, meets my stare, exchanges a weird, lost kind of look and then comes out from behind Conor and shouts something silly, just a random phrase and starts doing an impression of some little-known actor.

Mono doesn't say a word to me, but from nowhere – when I lift my head from the table – he goes, 'Real shame there's no hip hop on next door, wha?' and laughs to the room. A lot of them don't get the joke and just smile back lazily. Sarcasm is a foreign concept in this state, at this time.

When the music next door disappears and the green room dips into embarrassed, naked whispers and the table clears and there's cheers outside, I stand up, and try to escape unseen. But there's all knees and elbows at angles, two or three tuts – tired, obnoxious things. I get out and breathe easy.

The front room's half empty. It's late. Bout five. Must've been in there for ages. Thomo is packing away his vinyl so I put out my hand and stop him and ask him where he's off to.

'Ah man, home. Knackered.'

He must see I'm disappointed cause he goes, 'Ye can hook up your iPod to the decks there if ye want.' I reef out my iPod, put the lead in and flick round and round, find the letter J, turn up the volume and stand back. *'If you're havin girl problems I feel bad for you son, I got ninety-nine problems . . .'* and boom, the room's shaking, the PA's pounding and I throw my hand up and shout, 'Come on!' and think of the song vibrating through the walls, right down Mono's throat.

People tap their feet and nod their heads and salute. About halfway through the track I begin to worry – a DJ's dilemma – what to play next. Mono appears beside me with an iPod in his hand.

One of those massive sixty-four gig ones. He pushes past me, and moves to my left and we're both at the decks now, like Daft Punk or something, up to our waists in technology, sharing the responsibilities.

'Whatchye doin?' I shout, leaning into him.

He continues with the wires and the iPod.

'Turnin this garbage off,' he shouts back out the side of his mouth, still concentrating on the wires. Last few bars. Guitar chord still repeating. Running outta time.

'But it's goin down great – open yer eyes man,' I shout.

He does a 'ppff' and shakes his head, 'Good lad, yeah. You're off yer rocker.'

The fader's pitched all the way over to my side, and as my song comes to an end, he finds it and moves it, gently, to the left. There's this crackly hum, like a vinyl record, and you can tell he's put on an old song, and I think, good lad – your timing's all wrong, you're meant to cue the next song so that it starts as soon as the previous one ends. But I say nothing. Just let him feel the excruciating silence of his missed cue. The most horrible silence is better than any criticism I can mock him with. And then the guitar lick pings and his song plods in, loud and pitchy on the speakers. I circle my iPod, search for a counter argument. Two or three fools cheer and give Mono the thumbs-up. Some bird comes over and shouts, disco-mouth coating the corners of her lips, 'I love this song – woo!' and Mono turns to me, all smug and raises his eyebrows as if to say, 'beat that'.

Some dopes in the corner come over to the desk and pretend to be playing guitar and sing along, '*you don't need the weatherman to know which way the wind blows,*' and Mono sings back to them and I prepare to take over for my next tune. Mono's hand is still on the fader. I cue my song. He looks at me, his eyes all bloodshot, his bottom teeth, his jaw dropping off his face, digging into his neck, as if he doesn't know what's goin on.

'The fader man.'

'The wha?'

I just tap his hand. His brow dips.

'Your hand Mono.'

I go face to face with him.

'Wha?'

I'm ready to push him, just push him back against the wall. I was on the decks first after all.

'I said your-hand-is-on-the-fader.'

'So wha,' he shouts back, big dirty smile sliding up the side of his face. I shove him. He edges back, just a little stumble. People are still dancing. His hand leaves the fader, the song drops out and I manage to press play and flick the fader over and the voice, right on time – no embarrassing, unprofessional emptiness – goes, *'yo man, there's a lot of brothers out there flakin and perpatratin but scared to kick reality, so what you want me to do . . . do,'* and the beat kicks in and the repetitive note goes *a-weee* round and round the room. Everyone cheers. Everyone. My hand stays on the fader, the other hand salutes the dancers. Get in there. Two-one to me.

Derek and the drummer and Steve come from the green room. The front room's packed now. Really packed. And kicking. I'm on fire. Mono's still beside me, flickin through his yoke, the screen lighting up his face, his tongue between his teeth. Regardless, I line up my next track. What a party. What a start to the new year.

Derek's not dancing though. Neither are Steve or the drummer. They look like someone's after putting them on an awful downer. Don't see how. The place's kicking.

From nowhere, a shove, a push, knocks me against the decks, a lead or something comes loose and the music stops for a second. Faces turn, people stop dancing and I put the volume fader back up. The music continues. I turn round to Mono and push him in the chest, square up to him. Don't know if anyone notices. The song just keeps on going, the high-pitched *a-weee*, the James Browne sample, the saxophones, the beat. Mono raises his chin, egging me on. He's loving it.

'Go on,' he taunts, waiting to be clocked. And I'm this close. This close to deckin him. But the music changes. Dips. The soft lull of *wow-wow-wows*, flows through the room. It's a complete transformation from the heavy duty beats of NWA. It shocks me. Changes the whole vibe. Takes the nastiness out of the air. And there's moans and groans. Derek's hand is on the iPod and he shouts, 'Go on,' to the strangers, 'go on, if ye don't like it, go home.'

And that's just what I do. After his rant at the crowd he makes faces at me and whinges about the hip hop and fighting with Mono and ruining the buzz. He's not having a bar of it. The room's real quiet now, people staring and the music's real soft, so I do. I go home. Leave them to their comedown.

I cross over the room, pull apart the velvet curtains, still dark out, and just as I go, say, 'This party sucks,' and slam the door and laugh to myself while I take the trip back up to reality before slipping near the top and cracking my knee off a metal step. A quick glance down. No one saw me. Great party. Shame Mono ruined it.

★

The whistle goes. I can just about hear it through the howl of the wind and the mad gusts of rain, sheets of the stuff, like literally sheets of the stuff, pouring down on us. The lads' bodies slump, deflate. They stagger over to the sideline, moaning, one of them crying – no joke, crying – his bottom lip shivering, his hands in his sleeves and he goes, 'Why we gotta play extra time sir, please, call it off sir, please.' Little Brian. They call him Rico. Means something in Spanish. 'I'm not playin',' he continues, the water dripping from his nose, 'I can't feel me toes sir, I'm not playin.'

I stare at them. Someone's missing.

'Where's John?'

A whimper goes, 'Who?' and I shout at them, on them, 'Pereira. Where's Pereira?' and a shivering sleeve with little pink fingers points over to the far goal. John's stood in the middle of the goalposts, throwing a ball up in the air and catching it with his new luminous green gloves. He's in his new light-blue goalkeeper jersey too, oblivious to the horror show weather around him. I grab the little lad Brian by the scruff of his collar. 'See that?' I roar, pointing for all the players to see. 'See him over there? You'll bloody-well play, and you'll bloody-well win this match, cause if he can come from the scorchin deserts of Africa and get on with things, you,' I let go of him and grab another random jersey, 'and you,' let him go, look at them all, 'yis can all get out there and play in the rain. What are yis – the Igbo tribe? Afraid of a bit of rain? If yis don't get out there and . . .' The other manager gestures to me from the middle of the pitch. 'Wait there,' I shout.

It's getting late, the manager says, and he tells me he's got to get to the other side of the city and there'll be traffic and buses to catch home and stuff like that. I look over his shoulder. His team are cowering together like a frozen bunch of penguins, snivelling and shivering too. Babies. So the ref comes over and shrugs, 'Fine by me, once it's okay with the two of yous. Penalties it is.' And we flick a coin and I choose the bottom net cause I know it's a foot smaller than the top net. The away team don't know that. Their keeper's tiny. John's massive.

The other manager shakes my hand and says, 'Good luck. Penalties are a lottery son.' No they're not, I think, not when ye know the numbers. I'm about to move off when I spot Neil's da sheltering behind a ditch, on the opposite sideline, looking on. He's hunching from the rain. I feel bad for a second cause I never put his son on; he's our sub-goalie. I'm not being stubborn. Just ambitious. I want a day off for the final and I want to win. I'll only do that with John. Behind him, just as I turn I see another three figures, young lads, go behind the ditch and disappear into the ghost estate. Kids on the bounce. Not my problem. I call the team in and give them some speech-waffle about ambition and glory.

John saves two weak enough penalties. We blem one over. Little Brian. Swear he did it on purpose. Doesn't matter. John saves the last one and we go through to the final. He jumps up after making the save and throws his hands in the air and cheers and waits for the team join on him. No one goes near him. Most sprint away towards the dressing room. The fools. They'll have to wait for me to open it up. John's beaming when I come over to shake his hand. His new gloves are still on and they're covered in muck.

'Well done,' I say.

He nods a bashful kind of nod and says, 'Thanks sir, d-do you think my mama can come to the final? An – an will there be like, newspapers and stuff there?'

I pat his back and say, 'We'll see, we'll see. Now give the subs a help with the nets and I'll think about letting yer ma come.' He nods and says, 'Thanks sir, thanks sir,' and runs off to the top goals.

The teams, surprisingly, aren't waiting for me when I get to the dressing rooms. They're already togging out. Apart from the rain bouncing off the steel roof, inside is quiet, everyone concentrating on getting outta the jerseys and shorts and socks and getting home. I ask one of the lads how they got in. He says the door was open. I check my pockets. Find the keys. I never locked up.

I'm in the middle of giving my big winning manager's speech, all the nonsense about team spirit and fight and what we can achieve with honesty of effort and hard work when John roars, I mean absolutely roars, 'WHERE'S MY BAG? WHERE'S MY BAG?'

The whole room stops moving, shocked. You can hear the rain and the team next door talking and laughing. John darts around flinging other lads' bags all over the place, searching for his stuff. Everyone's too scared to give out to him.

'Hold on John,' I say, edging away from the centre of the room, 'what's wrong?'

He goes mad, licking his lips, squeezing his gloves, his head pinging all over the place. 'S-someone, someone h-h-has taken my bag – my bag is gone sir.' I try to relax him, tell him it must be here somewhere. But it's not. I should've closed the shutters.

No one stays back to help look. No one. John's still sitting in his jersey and tracksuit bottoms and boots when I come back in after one final check in the other room, but the team's bolted. The snap of studs on the wooden floor, once just a random sound, has become a nervous, constant drilling. A little bit crazy.

'Stop that for a second John,' I say. But he doesn't stop, or look up to acknowledge me.

'John,' I shout, trying to get his attention. The rain is heavy on the cheap and easy clubhouse. We're surrounded by the chaos of noise. His boots, the rain.

'John,' I shout, 'look at me and stop that noise.'

His head turns up from the floor, his eyes remaining closed, his boots still drilling.

'Look at me John.'

His eyes open slowly. They're all bloodshot. Red things.

'John,' I say, trying to take him out of his trance, 'look, I'll find your bag. It can't have just disappeared. Let me have a look around again.'

His head dips to the floor, lost between his shoulders, 'J-just when I thought like,' he whispers and his words die away.

The bag's gone. I have no option but to tell him to go home as is, in his jersey and boots and all.

He stands in the doorway, arms on each side of the frame, looking out into the rain. The grey of January lies before him. He looks up into the sky as if he's trying to find something. His chin draws out and he breathes deep, his chest expanding in the wet jersey. Tears begin to slide down his cheeks and still he keeps his head high. I leave him be, wait, afraid what he'll do if I disturb him.

'My brother sir,' he sniffs, talking just loud enough to be heard over the rain, 'he – he's gonna kill me, cause I, like, I-I took his runners and-an he said like, if-if I take anything of his again,' he sniffles twice and continues, 'anything he'll kill me and, and he said he'd take his computer and like not leh me have it, put a password an stuff on ih. I-I need the computer for my-my music and he's gonna . . .' He stops and sucks in some air and lets it stream out white. I nearly say something, give out to him for wearing his brother's runners to be cool, but stop, he's upset enough. I wanna get home.

'Wh-who took ih sir? Like, why?'

'I dunno John.'

'Ih-it's not fair. He will, he is gonna kill me,' he continues, still looking out into the rain, 'kill me.'

'It won't be that bad,' I say. He turns and looks at me wide-eyed.

'You wanna bet sir. You-you don't know sir. Like, you don't know what my brother is like,' and he steps softly from the container entrance into the murky light and I can only hear the rain and the muck squelching as he walks away.

★

Those junkies are hanging around Tara Street station. They're always there. They never beg, just slope together, unaware of who or what's happening around them. Always at the corner of Tara Street station, about or around the advertising hoardings at the side of that pub.

The traffic light across the road is counting down, 21, 20, 19 and I wait for the lights to go green. I turn and look at the hoardings, *JCDecaux*, and see if there's any decent gigs on over the next few weeks. Never anything decent in January. Everyone's broke. End of the month, end of every month is the best time to play a gig. Payday. First good gigs will be at the end of February. Always are. The gloom and depression and all that will have lifted. We need a good gig for February. End of February. New songs too. New us. New band. New Terrors.

Some local bands are on the posters on the advertising boards. Big investment. Costs a fortune to pay for that kind of publicity. The internet. Forums. Social networking sites. Odd free music magazine. That's how we used to do it. It's been a while though since we were up there. You're a big band when you're up there. Black and white means you've some cash. Third colour – serious cash. Four colours or more means the band aren't paying for it themselves; they've someone funding the publicity. We had four colours on our poster once. When it was up. Must be over two years ago now.

The countdown for the green man continues, 15, 14, 13 and I see myself, fresh, new to the job, bouncing off the train, skipping down the steps, floating past the junkies, and Mono's waiting for me at the station and it's summer and we're two years younger. I scrunch up my face or something cause he kind of shrinks into himself, as if I've embarrassed him by meeting him, when really he's the one waiting for me. I've never been met off the train before. Feels a bit mad, special.

'Here to hold my hand?' I say.

He punches me on the arm and says, 'Good lad.' I think the sun's shining. Feels like it was. It was definitely bright. No jacket. Maybe just a shirt. Strong shadows from the bridge. Change of t-shirt in my bag.

'I just wanted to see it,' he says.

'Have ye not seen it already?' I say, cutting him off.

He struggles to respond, explain himself. But we're in the height of things. All the parties, all the rehearsals, all the gigs. He doesn't need to. We're brothers in a way. The way we live with each other, live in each other's pockets.

The red numbers keep on moving down 10, 9, 8.

We were so open with each other. So open. Naïve. Full of it. Full of, full of something. Something good. I dunno.

'I wanted to see your face when you see it,' he finally says. And we turn our backs on the traffic lights, the green man, back towards Tara station. We don't care. We're not crossing. We're facing into the oncoming crowd flowing outta the station. Faces on them. Tutting and shaking their heads at us, thinking we're saps. Sure, we don't care. We've a reason for turning into you. Facing you. We're full of confidence. We're young. We're in a band. A deadly band, and a major label is into us. Investing in us. Has paid to fund the advertising for our gig. Look. Over four colours. Creating a buzz. Creating a future for ourselves far away from this road, this traffic, these people.

Mono looks at me as I take our poster in. *The Terrors and special guests, April 30th, The Decca Club. Doors 11.30pm.* Four colours. Our name, our logo, our faces. That pose – five white boys who take their music seriously – look how they frown.

5, 4, 3.

'Quality,' I say, smile, look to Mono. He's still peering up at it like it's a cinema screen playing out our future success. He grabs my shoulder, kinda puts his arm round me and goes, 'Yeeow!' real loud, doesn't care, and all of a sudden he's real excited and clapping his hands and the green man's back and he says, 'C'mon man, can't wait to rehearse – I've an idea I really wanna show ye,' and we bounce across the road. Don't know. Think we stop and look back from the other side just to see how it looks from there.

2, 1, walk.

It's different now. Two years is a long time. A lot can happen. It's darker, the evenings shorter in January. I don't wanna hear any of his ideas any more. I cross the road with the rest of the crowd, facing the way they're all facing. But when I get across I stop and turn and try to look back at the hoarding. Can't see much. But I'm not really looking there. I'm trying to see back to that time I suppose. That's the height of it right there. The tip, the top, and without knowing it, we're sliding down from there and that top is getting harder and harder to remember.

He texted me loads of times after we stood looking at the poster. It would just be a description of a place in the city or a location and the words 'deadly buzz' would follow it. He was letting me know where else he'd seen our posters.

Don't get texts like that anymore. There's no posters. Don't get texts regardless of posters.

★

I'm in the long grass behind the gym, away from the football pitch looking for match balls. My jeans are getting soaked and my shoes are sinking into the mud. The subs were meant to get any balls that went over or wide during the penalty shootout a few days ago. We're two balls short and it's raining, and everyone's gone home and it's getting dark and I'm losing patience. I'd be happy if I found one.

I stop moving, rub the rain from my face and look back at the goals. Try and work out what the trajectory of the misses might've been. I follow a ball in my mind, see it leave the peno spot, fly over the bar, get to the zenith of its flight and see it drop, add on a few feet for the bounce or miscellaneous power, wind, anything, and my eyes rest on an area just before the ditch into the ghost estate. I make to move over, to the ditch, get on the worn mucky path and as I go spot something bright – not bright – colourful, blue or grey, hanging from a branch on the far side of the ditch.

The closer I get the clearer it becomes. It's a basketball jersey; one of those light sleeveless things with the small holes for sweat. It's huge. I know immediately who owns it.

The rain makes insistent noises on the branches and I can hear nothing other than the drops on the bark and my breathing. Past the rain and the cement tubes and the metal grids and all the mess, I see something else, another piece of clothing hanging off some scaffolding in front of one of those empty houses. It's like there's been breadcrumbs left out. For me? Or him? I go across, dodge the rubble and the puddles and take a limp pair of three-quarter-length shorts off the low bar. The front door of the house behind the scaffold is open. Pieces of glass from the door and bits of plastic from the frame are all over the ground. I dunno, I'm so far in, out of my comfort zone, I'm buzzed, intrigued, so I push the door over and move on.

Inside the house is a weird place to be. This real heightened sense of my surroundings comes over me, like I'm trespassing or something. But no one lives here; no one lives anywhere on the estate. It's so cold and quiet out of the rain; just the raindrops pestering the plastic sheeting on the scaffold. The stairs ahead are cracked and falling apart. No banister. The hall leads into the darkness of the kitchen; a shallow shade of grey makes the shape of a window. Mucky footprints are dried into the concrete floor leading off into the front room. Like a detective I follow them and see my own damp prints appear beside the other ones, giving away my presence.

The front room is dark cause of the plastic sheeting on the windows and on the scaffolding outside. My eyes adjust to the bad light and I see crates lined up against the wall and crushed cans of beer and empty flagon bottles beside them. Above a gap where the fireplace should be there's a spray-painted message: *Da Droogz Boyz Crew.* Things get colder, more intense, my neck stiffer, my arms and hands tighter. Spray paint cans, Deli-Burger wrappers, Rizlas and fag-ends make a small trail to the middle of the floor where there's the cold, whispy remains of a little bonfire. But it was a fire that didn't catch on properly cause not everything's destroyed. The charred remains of a huge Nike runner – gotta be John's – lie melted and black beside half a school bag, the tippexed words *Brig Boyz* and *DJ Johnbo* just about legible on the side.

A loud snap sounds off the window and at first I think it's a rock and listen for '*Rob-ert, Rob-ert,*' but see it's only the plastic sheeting catching the wind.

I give the fire a boot, scatter the ashes and bits of runner and bag everywhere. A big puff of dirt fills the room, stains my jeans, scars the floor. A noise comes from upstairs, like a thump, someone falling and I hold my breath, go rigid and peer into the scorched ceiling. A crack on the window again. I look to the words on the wall and, like I've been in a trance and just woke up, gaze around and realise where I am, who's little bonfire I've destroyed. I've picked up breadcrumbs I wasn't meant to pick up. They weren't left for me. I let the jersey and the three-quarter-length shorts slap onto the ground and ease out, crunch over the glass and into the half darkness and the rain.

It's harder to see the puddles. I go into one or two. A stone bobbles to a rest beside me when I stop; I wonder if I kicked it or if it was thrown. The wind whistles through the cement tubes with a low, hollow moan and I think I can hear '*Rob-ert, Rob-ert*' coming from the house. I don't turn around. I'm freaked.

The messing in the school has lost its playfulness. Their friendship was a farce. They're not as innocent as I once thought, as harmless as I'd once hoped. Their violence has moved out of the school. I'm waking up to them, seeing what they're capable of. They're not kids looking for some banter. They've graduated into bored teenagers robbing and destroying things and burning the evidence. They'll graduate to other things cause no one will stand up to them, catch them. They've no morals cause no one shows moral courage around them. Destruction is around them. Accountability isn't. They'll move from lighting bonfires and robbing kit bags to burning down buildings and looting lives, cause they're bored, cause no one's brave enough to challenge them. And if they are stopped they'll buck against what stops them, they'll react by rioting and doing what they know how to do – getting away with it – cause everyone else does. They'll take what they can. They'll run wild if they can. And I'll see it coming because I'm just like them. Everyone's like them; just some are held back by the fear of being found out. The Droogs are clear of barriers because they either don't believe they'll be found out, don't care, or don't know what they do is wrong. Their violent freedom scares me, fascinates me.

I speed up and take the steep slope back to the school and when I'm on the other side, glance back into the darkness.

I've got an insight into what they'll be doing in the future. I'll see their violence coming and make sure I'm out of town when it arrives.

★

A&R from major labels are probably schooled on how not to react when they hear something impressive. Barry doesn't react when we finish. He's good.

No sound. No guitar feeding back, no heavy white noise, no screeching. Mono's amp isn't on. Mono's guitar isn't plugged in, cause Mono's not here. And without his guitar, the room, once the song ends, is kinda quiet, weirdly so. Everyone looks to me for some reason. The drummer, hand on the cymbal, looks at me, Steve, bass in his hands, stares at me, and Derek, leaning into the microphone stand like he'd collapse if it wasn't there, looks at me sheepishly. I dunno. They're all looking at me as if their eyes have a question and I should have the answer. Even Barry's looking at me, as if to say, 'Where did they come from?' They being the beats. My hip hop beats and samples. The ones I got just before Christmas.

'Well, there ye go Barry. That's the Terrors branching out. Not quite what you were expecting, but like we said, something different, yeah?'

Barry frowns, like he's stuck for words, nods his head, an impressed smile, and he shifts, finally, after literally being rooted to the spot against the wall for the duration of our new song.

'No, no,' he says, rubbing his chin, 'not at all Bob. B-but the beats man, the beats.' And he looks to the ground and then rubs the back of his head, 'I mean, like, lads, the beats, the sound.' He holds out his hand to me, his palms upturned, 'The keyboards – wow,' then Steve, 'and the bass,' then the drummer 'the backing drums – the live sound over the beats,' and then takes his stare from the floor up to Derek. Barry's eyes are wide, he points at Derek, does a gun with his fingers and says, 'The melody man.'

He blows out a breath, a kind of 'phew' and smiles, circles the room with the smile. 'Lads,' he continues, like he can't stop talking or something, 'that's it man, that's it. One song guys – one song. You've got it. Granted – the early demos are what, two, three good songs – one single there for sure – and now this. Wow, this, this tempo, the new sound – I mean, I'm blown away. I can bring this to my bosses guys.' He nods as if he can't believe what he's saying and begins to rub his chin again, thinking hard. 'I mean,' he continues, almost talking to himself now, 'I've never given all of my bosses a listen at once. Like we all do demos, yeah, but this. They won't be expecting this. This is my breakthrough,' he stops himself, and looks up, like he forgot we were in the room, 'sorry, *your* breakthrough.'

He goes on for a while longer. I can tell the lads are uncomfortable too with him losing his cool like this. So much for composure. Only a few months ago he couldn't get out of here quick enough. To get him down here took some doing. And now to see him like this, delighted with what we have, is kind of jarring. Weird. Can't help but feel a little wary of him. He's been in the job for four years. Four years as head Irish A&R, a fully paid member of staff for the label in London, and he's still to get a band signed. Must weigh heavily.

After some more waffle, saying he'll arrange a recording session for our new song, or a showcase in London, he leaves.

The moment the door closes and he's gone the lads all break out the smiles and do secret, whispered 'yesses' and look to me, delighted. Steve high-fives me like we're kids, and goes, 'Nice one Rob. Deadly buzz. Got any more?'

'Not yet. Gimme time.'

'Quality.'

And we're all buzzing.

Derek and the drummer are talking about a new session, and Steve's saying to me, 'Imagine a showcase with the head of A&R in London, Rob. Imagine.'

And I say, 'I know, I know,' just to say something cause I can't take it all in, this turnaround, this sudden change in fortunes.

'Mono's gonna be delighted,' Steve says, 'you were right Rob. You were right, he'll defo go along with everything now he knows what it's gonna do for us.'

I don't hear the door open, but from the corner of my eye see it move. At first I think it's Barry back to slobber all over us. It's not. It's Mono. The room dips into a sudden silence. We're caught rotten. We would've had to say it to him at some stage anyway. He stands in the doorway, concerned look on his face, trying to compute what he sees. It must click cause you can see all the options of how to respond go through his head. You can read it in his eye like a slot machine with all the things flying past the viewer. Ding-ding-ding. I place my bet on violence. Confrontation.

'What's all this? I just saw Barry go out.'

'You talk to him?' I ask.

'No, he was too far up the road.'

He steps into the room. No sign of the mood yet.

'Well,' he says, 'yis forget to tell me or something?'

The rest of them are finding chewing gum stains on the carpet suddenly interesting.

'We just thought—' I say, but Mono cuts me short with a, 'Shut it you.'

I'm stuck behind the keyboards. Enclosed. He's lucky. Can't act. Won't act. Have to keep the lads on side. It's coming though. One of these days I won't be stuck here behind my keys and I won't have to answer to the lads.

'Lads,' he says, moving into the room, 'what's all this?'

Steve finally looks up, 'Relax, Mono, we just thought it'd sound better – clearer with no guitar for today. Barry had an opening to see us and we knew you weren't into it. You said yourself it's cool for all of us to try new things in rehearsals. We just thought . . .'

'No guitar?' Mono shouts, rubbing his face, 'no guitar for like, when Barry came in?'

'Rob got some new sounds,' Steve says, trying to explain, 'new beats on the computer. Hip hop kinda things. They're deadly. We sent Derek a rough recording an Derek got a deadly melody, real catchy chorus, real catchy.'

Mono just stands there. Devastated.

'And it's just, what,' Steve looks at me, 'a three chord trick?'

'Four,' I say.

'Four,' Steve says, 'sorry. And we got it together last week.'

'When?'

'Before you came down.'

'And yis never told me?'

I step up, 'We know how much you're against the whole hip hop beats thing – we didn't want to—'

He cuts me off, his face all pained, 'Aahh, give it a rest Bob.'

'But we had to get Barry down,' Steve continues, 'it's quality. Quality. And Barry was blown away Mono. He was blown away.'

Mono doesn't know what to say.

'And,' Steve goes on, 'we've got a new session or showcase outta it.'

The rumble of a band next door undercuts the silence.

'Really?' he says, finally.

'Yeah,' Derek says.

'Barry's gonna give us more recording time?' Mono licks his lips, stops dead, looks around the room. 'More time to record? Okay then,' he goes and unhooks his bag from his shoulder all in a hurry, 'I was only comin in here to get my acoustic cause I wanted to record a new song and give it to yis – but I might as well play it now. If ye like it we can play it, yeah? Maybe record it with the other song or add it to the set for the showcase. Yeah? New ideas? Up for it?'

Everyone looks at me. Me.

'I mean,' Mono continues, not wanting to lose the room, 'if we're giving the hip hop thing a go, we can give my stuff a go, yeah?'

I just shrug a, 'Yeah, why not?'

I play along because they do. But I doubt they're really taking this nonsense seriously. They're humouring him, have to be.

★

Thursday in Balbriggan is court day. Me and Lauren see the heads shaping away outside the courthouse on our way to lunch. All sorts of them, tracksuits tucked inside the white socks, hoods up, big dyed blonde hair shaped around the fringe – the town's baddies. We move by them going to the new Bagel Bar.

A lunchtime con job: I hate bagels.

'Mmhh lovely,' I say, wiping the mayonnaise from the side of my mouth, 'this is lovely.'

A text beeps in my pocket: *Did u take money out 2 pay rent?* Jen.

'Who's that?' Lauren says, her hand over her mouth so I can't see the food while she talks. 'Your manager checking in?'

'You're not far wrong,' I say and take a slurp of tea. I put the phone back in my pocket on silent.

Lauren looks at me like she's working something out.

'Ye know,' she finally says, 'I always knew you weren't a teacher, like really, you know, a lifer.'

'Thanks for the vote of confidence.'

She flaps at me, 'It's a compliment. When I saw you last year I asked one of the girls who you were. I thought . . .' she smiles, eyebrows raised, kinda shy.

'Go on.'

'I thought you were, god, I don't know, a visitor, ye know, giving a talk or something. You . . .' she studies my face again, 'you had this, this distance. I'm not expressing it right.'

I don't know what to say so I just nod to encourage her.

'I just knew,' she goes on, 'that you'd do something different – and I was right.'

I hold up my hands in protest.

'We're not signed yet – we're not there yet, nowhere near it yet.'

'But, ye know – from what that A&R guy said about that new song, you've hit the jackpot.'

I fall back in my chair, rub my face.

'You're sitting on the winning lottery ticket – you could at least look excited. No more smelly teenagers, moaning teachers, arrogant principals, stuck-up parents.'

'I know, I know.'

'Well then,' she whispers, 'cheer up.'

I turn my cup, pick at a sugar pouch and crush it, fold it.

'Rob?'

'It's not as simple as that,' I say.

'What?'

'The lottery ticket – the winning numbers. It was a once-off.'

The bagel's held before her face, mid-bite.

'It was a fluke. A once-off fluke.'

'I don't get you.'

I tut, pause, 'It's not mine,' I say quickly, like I'm pulling off a plaster.

'What isn't? You're not making sense.'

My phone vibrates. The silence. Plates and forks sing together. The coffee machine steams. Condensation creates slalom tracks down the window. Bagels crack as teeth sink in and take unfulfilled bites.

'The song – remember. The hip hop beats and the sample. The structure. The whole thing. It's not mine. I-I, I dunno, I copied it, cut and pasted it, robbed it, took it. Whatever. It's not mine.'

The hoodies from the courthouse swagger by the window. She studies me, her bagel half eaten on the plate. Her chin's resting on her knuckles, like she's posing, framing her face. Her eyes remind me of an ocean you'd see on travel ads. So clear and green and exotic. Beautiful.

'So you've taken something that isn't yours and made it into a Terrors song?'

'Yep. And I don't think I'll be able to do it again.' My leg trembles under the table.

She shakes her head, 'Do you know anything about art? The lengths people go for their art, Rob? It's people like you – the boundary pushers – who move art forward. If this Barry – the A&R guy – was as blown away as you said he was, whatever you've done, whatever you've copied has worked for *you* – the Terrors. What artists, writers, musicians have you read about that played it straight?

158

Huh? What artists do you know closed their eyes to all influences, put the blinkers on,' she puts her hands to her temples to show me, 'to make pure art?'

I shrug.

'None. Cause they don't exist – and if these guys do exist no one hears about them cause they're *bor-ing*.'

She stops and a guilty smile creeps up the side of her face. She raises an eyebrow, puts out her hand and touches mine, 'So what *did* you do? How did you create this masterpiece?'

I pull my hand away.

'Doesn't matter,' I mumble.

Her mouth opens behind a smile and morphs into a shocked O.

'Secretive, and sultry. How interesting.'

'It's not about the taking. I can deal with that. That's grand. It's the consistency. I don't think I can – I can't see how I can do it again – keep the A&R lad and the band happy, believing in me.'

She goes all serious, places her hands wide on the table.

'What would you do for your art?'

'I dunno.'

'What is art? What makes good art?'

'I dunno.'

She shakes her head. 'Art is a voice. You're in a position to have a voice. This music will be heard, whereas if you don't do this music, it won't have a voice. It won't be heard.'

She starts pouring more tea and goes, 'Shakespeare. *Romeo and Juliet*. You're an English teacher. You tell me – he wrote it, right?'

'Yeah,' I say, 'well, yeah and no.'

She points at me satisfied, 'Exactly. He took the story from someone else and made it his. He did it with loads of plays. Someone had the story, he just published it, performed it, whatever. It happens all the time in the art world too. Plagiarism, forgery. They're big business. You just put something out there that wouldn't be out there otherwise. Do we care we never heard about the *Romeo and Juliet* not written by Shakespeare?'

'No.'

'Exactly. So why should you? Whatever formula you used for your first song – use it again.' She holds my hand, 'And I want a percentage of the profits and a thank you in the sleeve notes.'

We cheers our teacups and I pretend to be relaxed and at ease but my leg's still trembling under the table.

Afterwards we stroll back to the school and I unlock the heavy chain at the wooden hoarding and hold the door open for her and say, 'After you,' and enjoy watching as she skips by and turns on her heels.

'I was thinking of doing that first aid course next month,' she says, waiting for me to lock up before we move off.

'Were you, yeah?' I say, pretending to be interested. 'I heard about that alright – but it's not on til seven in the evenings or something.'

She nods and we walk. Brief scent of perfume. Kids' eyes smiling out windows.

'Joe the caretaker said he'd lock me in after six while he goes home for his dinner.'

'Lock you in?'

She glances at me, eyebrows lifted, 'I'd be all on my own from six til seven, imagine, waiting for my first aid.'

'No one else from the staff doin it, no?'

'Not at the moment,' she says keeping those eyebrows arched, suggesting something. I tell her I'll think about it. Play it cool.

We stop at the entrance to the school building. She puckers up and roots in her bag for something.

'It'd be nice to have some company,' she whispers and takes out some lip balm and starts sliding it slowly across her bottom lip and then her top lip, hint of tongue breaking through, 'especially in the dark evenings.'

'But the shutters'll be down.'

'You never know what lurks outside.'

The bell goes. Those three single notes, ending the fun, starting the misery.

'I'll think about it,' I say and we're moving together through the door as kids swarm. Just before I go into my room she goes, 'Don't forget what we talked about,' and we smile and I close my door and check my phone.

There's a voicemail from Jen. I listen to it before all the students arrive. She's moaning, saying she's been calling me for ages and I'd told her I'd be off between half eleven and twelve and I better have paid the rent on time cause it'll effect our credit rating. We've got to make sure our credit rating is clean for when we go for mortgage approval, she says. Don't forget Rob, she whines and hangs up.

First aid is something I've given a lot of thought to. I could do with learning how to act in precarious situations.

*

'If it's all about the money, Jen, I don't see why you wouldn't consider it.'

She slams her hands down on the couch and moans through a closed mouth.

'Cause I've told you. It's not right. It's no way to start off a new life.'

For the sake of the argument, to win the argument, I've upped the ante and told her I was talking to an old school friend who works in an estate agents in Balbriggan. He was asking me what I was up to and I didn't want to give him the satisfaction of looking down his nose at me so I'd said I was house hunting.

'It's not right. It's not right, that's the end of it Rob.'

'Oh, but you'll keep tabs on every penny, every single penny I spend on the band, and goin out and all that lark, and it makes up what? A couple of grand a year and you won't consider saving twenty, thirty, forty thousand quid on a house this way?'

'It's wrong. It's karma. You can't start your life – live off some other person's misfortune. I couldn't live like that.'

'Well I could.'

'Well then we differ.'

'We do.'

The muted television strobes over us, adding to the manic feel in the room.

'If they can't abide by the rules, do it for themselves – they deserve to give up the house an for us – for a lot cheaper – to take advantage.'

Her bottom teeth come out and she raises her voice, 'You don't get it. They don't *give up* the house. It's *taken* from them. It-is-repossessed. It-is-robbed-from-them. And if we move in we benefit from it.'

'It's not *robbed*. How can it be robbed if they don't own the house in the first place?'

She stands up, goes all stiff, her fingers spread out and tense by her hips, 'I'm not listening to you. If I find out this estate agent lad is tipping you off to repossessions and we go and view it, I'll never speak to you again.'

'It's a way of getting ahead.'

'I'll never speak to you again.'

'Don't expect me to look for more houses so. I try and help and you shoot me down.'

'Fine. I'll do it all. I was anyway,' she says and she turns and storms out, slamming the door as she goes. I smile, bring the volume on the television back up and stretch my legs out on the couch.

★

As ever, the train's empty heading back into town in the afternoon. It's the same as the mornings. I'm always heading in the opposite direction to the flock. I sit in a four-seater, put my bag to the side and put my head in my hands. I try to leave the anxiety behind in the school, but I can't. I bite my nails and pull at my hair. The train chugs into gear and eases off and we're moving away from the platform, onto the viaduct with the harbour below on the left, the town out the window to my right. Another no-show from John, another opportunity lost. I'm running out of time. The less you have of something, the more valuable it becomes.

I put the headphones on, play a Terrors tune to try and concentrate on something, take my mind off him. The sun begins to flash through the viaduct bars like in a music video. The song starts up and I'm watching one of these real cool, arty, smooth 8mm long distance shots of the gritty urban setting of the band; the streets telling a story, the landscape explaining the contours of the music. I get lost in the journey until the song ends, the hi-hats die out. In the silence between tracks I hear the heavy door between carriages slam and before another song begins a sense of someone standing over me pulls my eyes away from the sea.

John stands there, although for a second I don't recognise him with his baseball cap, the big puffy jacket, the big chain outside his jumper, his headphones and the lumps on his face. He looks older. Worn down. You'd pass him off as a twenty-year-old at least.

He says, 'Hiya sir,' real casual and nods to the seat in front of me, 'can I sih down?'

I move into a tighter ball and take off my headphones, go, 'Course, yeah, course.'

He shifts in and bumps his leg off my foot and whispers, 'Sorry.'

'Where've ye been?' I say.

His bruises are still visible.

'Nowhere sir. J-just wasn't well an my mama said like, if I wasn't well I-I should stay at home.'

'What ye listenin to?' I say quickly, to get us away from the reason he wasn't really in school: losing his brother's runners, feeling his brother's wrath. He looks embarrassed for a second and pulls the lead from the headphones out of his pocket to show a jack – with no device on the end.

'Nothin – my-my brother won't let me, he like, he won't let me near anything cause like . . .'

'It's okay,' I say.

'B-but ih-it's grand sir, cause like, since you took my boombox an my mp3 goh broken I-I just think of music an stuff in my head, like, all the time. Ih-it's cool.'

'But why bother with the headphones?'

'Why not? An-an it's quieter like, with them, yeah?' he giggles to himself. 'The music I hear in my head is better than the rest, and they look cool.'

We smile together.

From running out of time and opportunities, I have a surprise forty-minute opening. I let my shoulders go, relax. I ask him what he's doing on the train and he tells me his brother forgot to tell his ma he was rehearsing for the school choir.

'So she went without me.'

My face must read like a question cause he continues, 'To gospel practice.'

He smiles and looks out the window. He tells me it's in Blanchardstown and he's doing well in school and Miss Holmes is using him for keyboards after I talked with her, and his mother's coming to watch him play in the National Concert Hall. He takes a deep breath when he's finished, content with himself, and he slumps back on the seat, spent, and looks at me closely. His thumbs wrestle on the table.

'B-but my mama say I might need more letters, from school like, sport and choir yeah, we-we might have a better chance and stuff.'

'For what?'

He goes to speak and stops, looks confused and then says, 'Eh – thingy. I dunno. Just – I gotta be good an try an be a success for my family, yeah?'

'Oh.'

He nods as if his own vague explanation has satisfied him and he looks at me all worried again.

'How long you been workin here?'

'Here?'

'The school.'

'This is my second year.'

'Two years? Mmmhh – I wanna do mechanical engineering after I leave.'

'Yeah?'

'Mmhh – I have ih all planned out, like, if I don't do beats an stuff. An I don't know if I like, if I will cause they is way too much hassle with them sir – I'm gonna do four years, bout four years, get a proper degree an if, if I can geh a good job here, I'll get it, if I can't I'll move to Australia slash America – some kinda big country . . . and live a life. What you think?'

I look at my watch. We've got plenty of time.

'Cool. Sounds good. But what about music?'

He looks out the window, ignores my question.

'How much does college cost?'

Maybe he just didn't hear it, or was preoccupied by his own question.

'I dunno John. Don't worry about it til you need to.'

'Yeah but like, I wanna start planning an stuff now, yeah? Like – be good in school – do good like you said I could – not just in music an stuff – but life. When-when you went to college how much did it cost?'

'Eh, five hundred euro a year to register, I think. Thereabouts. But I was lucky, I had a job.'

'Ah, my mama's gonna pay for me. Five hundred euros is okay.'

I think about asking if he's considered a foreign national. But that's pointless. It'll be ten grand a year if he is, or more. Think about telling him that fees are back, registration costs are up. But hold off. He needs something to work towards. We all do. I just say, 'That's great John. You should think of studying piano though – music or something. Use your talents. Especially the beats.'

He shakes his head, 'Nah, I'm more into drumming now.'

'You drum too?'

He starts to drum his fingers on the table as he speaks, 'Uh-huh. All styles. Congolese, Nigerian, Angolan. They are different . . . but they're like, for a black person, the easiest, eh like, lets say if you're Nigerian. If you're Nigerian the easiest beat you're gonna catch on first is Congolese – sorry, it's Nigerian beats. If you're Congolese the easiest drum you're gonna catch is Congolese.'

'What about Angolan?'

'Angolan is more like, it's more hip hop beats. Kendora, yeah?'

'Really?'

'Yeah . . . it's cause, mostly Angolan songs it's more like hip hop beats.'

'And is that why you can do all the beats on Reason on the computer?'

He shrugs, 'Yeah, maybe.'

'I'm interested though, John. How are you so good at the beats? Like, how do you make a song like you did before Christmas on the computer?'

'What song?'

'You know, the one you played for me on my Mac.'

'Oh, that one. Ih-it's really easy like.'

'How easy? Tell me.'

I concentrate hard, block out everything flying by the window, the noises in the carriage. His face goes dark, his brow creases, he stops drumming and his eyes blink, quick blinks, and you can tell he's in front of his computer.

'Right, okay, like first thing is you geh Reason Four, yeah, first thing is you get the tool window – find a mixer – I-I use mixer 14.2, click on tha an like, drag it over and drop ih.' His fingers do the actions on the table as if it's his mouse pad.

'Next things – eh, get Redrum drum computer and then you can like geh a beat. Get any like, drum patch. Hip hop kit number six, what my saying, hip hop kit four I use. Solo any, go through all them, get a sound – claps, kicks, snares, hats, yeah? Whatever. I-I-I always start with like a basic beat,' he does a deep boom with the heel of his palm on the table and a light smack with his fingers, 'like a kick drum an a snare. I do a kick, put ih down on like number one and eight and nine. Run ih – hear the bare beat, yeah, like take a clap, snare, put it down on say like, a five an a twelve or thirteen. Layer up the kick with some more kicks and change the velocity so it's better – after messing you get hi-hats,' he makes the noise of them with his mouth, and I'm trying to remember keywords but he's going too fast. 'Put a hi-hat pattern down – like – wherever you feel, shorten the hi-hat or put some sorta reverb – whatever reverb thingy and tha-that's the basic beat, yeah – b-but then you want like, me like, I get the bass sound on NN-XT. It's a sampler sir, and get the sound from patches. Get like the riff on your keyboard . . .'

I can do that.

'Get a loop on. Loop between one and four bars and create your notes over the beat . . .'

I can do that.

'Shorten the pattern like, quantize the notes – only seventy-five percent, cause like, you wanna give a real feel for ih – copy an paste the line, make sure you snap the grids on so it lines it up . . .'

Can't do that.

'You wanna get some cool samples, me, I go into another NN-XT and grab a sound and I sequence it, double click on ih so you have your information on. I sometimes quantize it – fifty percent, like, to keep it loose an if I wanna nother one I geh another rack window an layer stuff . . .'

Can't do that.

'Tha – that's ih.' He smiles, 'The basic track.'

'Cool,' I say, gutted, freaked, more confused than when he started. There's no way I can do it.

'So you must have done loads since Christmas?'

His smile slips away and he shakes his head.

'A few. B-but I have to give two away an stuff, for some stuff.'

'I thought you were gonna keep them for yourself John? That's what we agreed.'

His eyes expand

'I will sir, like, I am, but, like them crews, the Brigz Boyz an the other new crew, I-I was meant to give them one song, yeah?'

'Have you?'

'They already gave me something, an I hadta – but now they. They like, they won't stop askin me for more.'

'Hold out. They're going up in value. Imagine what you can get for them in a while.'

He squirms, bites his bottom lip.

'I dunno sir, like they, they, they're not happy – they're like *goin crazy*.'

'Don't underestimate yourself. Wait a while, get maximum value. How many more have you done now?'

He shrugs his shoulders, holds out the palms of his hands.

'None – an I told ye I would, but,' he looks out the window, sniffles, 'but, I have no computer now cause,' and his voice whispers the last line, 'my brother won't let me cause I lost his runners.'

I'm finished. The band's finished.

'No more?'

He doesn't answer, just leans his forehead against the window and stares out. No one else gets on our carriage. No noise. But it doesn't matter. We've nothing more to talk about. I've no more questions. I join him staring blankly out the window. He has nothing more to say either. He just leaves his head against the window watching the ditches turn to DART stations, turn to the city, and to our station.

I get up when we get to Tara Street. He does too. We walk together out of the station, him still in his funk, me thinking of things to say, racking my brains trying to find a way I can make something happen. We're about to split at the Butt Bridge when I take his hand and we shake. The traffic's mental around us, the people rushing through it to get to the train, bumping and brushing us as we stand there.

'So you've no other computers?'

'Wha?'

'For your beats.'

He shakes his head, 'My brother's was it . . . it was a present. Look, I gotta go.'

He tries to move his hand free from my grip. The traffic lights go green. He pulls away, looks at me, at my hand, 'I gotta go sir.'

'What if I got you a laptop?'

He looks at me like I just slapped him.

'Huh?'

'A computer. I can get you a Mac I suppose. To write more songs. I feel guilty you lost the runners at the match. A Mac. Just for a lend now. No one needs to know.'

The lights are zapping for him to cross. His jaw drops and morphs into a smile.

'You-you-you'd gimme a laptop?'

'For your music.'

He laughs. 'Ah man,' and his grip tightens and he starts to shake my hand again, rigorously, 'that-that's like, amazing sir.'

'What are friends for? But it'll be our secret. And no more giving your beats away – okay?'

'Yeah cool,' he says, looks at the green man turn orange, pulls away from me and goes, 'greah, yeah. I gotta go sir – thanks so much sir – that's great. Thanks so much.'

And he jogs across the road and over the bridge, his big frame lumbering through the crowd. I let the tension deflate, lean against a wall, compose myself and look into the Liffey, rest my eyes somewhere easy and try and work out what I've just got into. Steve has a computer. We can play the beats off that for now. I let my bag slip off my shoulder and I crouch down, run my hands through my hair, think, think of what I'm doing and how it'll work. Two more tracks – one more track and I could take it back and no one would be any the wiser. One month. A month loan. Three weeks. He can work fast. I won't give him a choice. I haven't got a choice.

February.

So Oasis and Blur open up another world of music. Cream and Lynyrd Skynrd, Hendrix and the Beatles and the Stones are the start. Ocean Colour Scene and Paul Weller – post Style Council – follow, and of course Weller leads to Fred Perry, Ben Sherman and Clarkes. This takes me to the Jam. The Faces, the Who, the Small Faces. The style and the scene. Organ and piano and keyboards are in the thick of the songs, almost centre stage, or at least sharing the stage with guitar. Seventeen, eighteen. Another major junction. The Small Faces bring me to Tamla Motown and the Northern Soul scene and all of a sudden we're playing Mod covers and going to clubs, hearing DJs pick out tracks, little small 45s that no one's ever heard because that's the scene: play music no one has unearthed, so they can hear it for the first time and dance. I'm dancing but unsure if I'm dancing like Jimmy form *Quadrophenia* cause that's how he dances, or dancing like Jimmy cause that's how 'Green Onions' makes you dance.

Mono argues we should be playing Thin Lizzy and Led Zeppelin covers instead of the Who and the Faces. When we get a gig – a headline slot – at a scooter rally in the Bray Head Hotel it's settled: we're going down the mod route.

Bout twenty of us, Jen and all the other girlfriends and mates, book rooms in the hotel. The rest of the rooms are packed with English heads on their Vespas and Lambreattas. Old school mods and Northern Soul enthusiasts.

There's loads of quality DJs, their top buttons closed, dancing with their necks, spinning deadly tunes on Friday night. We're the only live act for the whole weekend and we're playing Saturday night and there's a mad buzz about us cause we're so young and the promoter has talked us up to anyone that'll listen.

The PA is useless but we still blow the place apart. The hall's packed with ultra-cool mods, their scooters parked in front of the bay window to the left of the dance floor – grooving and gurning to our tunes: 'Tin Soldier', 'Sunflower', 'The Circle', 'Going Underground', 'The Seeker', 'My Generation', 'Louie Louie', 'You Really Got Me'. We come off stage and our mates swamp us as the crackle from an old 45 spikes and the turntables start up again and the whole place heaves.

It's our first taste of an all-nighter club and everyone's taken in by the euphoria of the chaos and the camaraderie. Old heads, their severe fringes and whispy locks, come over to me and Derek and Steve and shake our hands and pat our shoulders and say in their English accents, 'Topper our-kid,' and 'Great set lad, great set.' I'm standing with Mono at about four in the morning discussing our performance when a DJ comes over, sweating, and grabs both our hands and says, 'Nice keyboards, son, nice keyboards – well done. Well done,' and he walks off without a mention of the guitars.

'He's right,' Mono shouts in my ear while dancers do high kicks and flips all around us, 'the keyboards sounded deadly tonight. Really made a difference.'

We've been playing together for two years and it's the first time he's ever commented on the keyboards. I just go, 'Cheers Mono,' but I dunno, whether it's the drink and the high of the whole weekend, the music or the dancers, I feel like crying. For the first time in my life I feel like I belong, like I'm part of a gang – the band – and I know I won't be leaving their side anytime soon.

★

I get back to my room after a brief meeting with the guidance councillor. Asked me to, 'have a chat.' Seems I'm the go-to guy about John. He's been strange lately, she said. Detached.

I sit at my desk and look to that partition. The illusion of a wall. An illusion of security. Easy to forget that the cracked wood, all shiny and polished, covered in all those pictures and posters, is a fraud wall. One push and it folds in on itself like a big accordion.

I hear someone rustling around next door, a chair moving, a computer snapping shut and I think of getting up from my desk and going in to see if it's Lauren and forgetting about this pressure. A voice speaks. A few dull sentences and then, 'Now when you're finished that,' I hear Lauren say, 'get started on *The History of Impressionism*. Okay?' Her voice is an Eno soundtrack I could float in forever. There's no response, and I hear a door open. 'Kembo, do you hear me?' she says.

There's a hint of a grunt.

'And Bruce – Impressionism. Okay? I'll be back in a minute.'

Another grunt. And the door closes. And I come back to earth.

They stay silent for a second. Kembo and Bruce. Bruce Sembola. Third year like John. Congolese though. I wait for the voices to be sure it's them.

'Y-you have to beg miss to let you do honours. I h-had to beg her to be put back into ih.'

John alright. His voice is hushed, but deep, clear behind the partition. He sounds like he's at the top of the room. The front row of Lauren's room. But that's at the opposite end to my room. Behind the divide.

'Why would I beg to do higher level – I got an A – why would I do ordinary level?'

Bruce. His voice has a deepness to it, like John's, but an octave higher. I can picture him a few seats away from John in his baggy school jumper, his thin frame, those thick glasses like Malcom X or Spike Lee. More Spike Lee cause of his teeth and skinny face.

'She put me in ordinary level. Are you mad?' John.

I can hear a fist pounding the table. They giggle.

I get up, quietly, and move to the back of the room and stand at the door between us while Bruce says, 'You don't deserve to be there John.' I think about opening the door and calling him out and dis-cussing the issues some of the staff have with him – or the issues he has with them. Do I wanna be that teacher? I don't, but I stay up that end of the room anyway.

'You just jealous boy,' John.

'Jealous of what? You? Ordinary? Man – you don't have nuthin. You don't have a crew. You're out by his own.' Bruce.

'I don't have a crew? I'm one man,' John, the whisper developing, the boom of his voice increasing, 'one – one man crew singer Bruce. Have you heard my song? Mr – Mr Lynch,' my ears prick up and I sit on a table beside the door, 'he – he thinks it's greah. I don't need a crew. My beats ain't for sale no more.'

I just sit there, slump, and rub my face.

A tut. A laugh. Bruce: 'Mr Lynch, chap, he's a racist freak. I wouldn't listen to nothing he says cause your beats ain't nothing now.'

'Well, he-he, he's cool, he's okay. I know him.'

'Chap, no you don't. He's like the rest of all them haters. Always on our backs cause we're kids an we're black. You watch out boy, he'll disgrace you, you watch.'

'He's noh. He says my music's greah, he listens to ih and he says it's greah.'

'Yeah, whatever, but you still out by his own John. Big style. No crews. No nothing. Me an my crew, we're dancers – we have rehearsals – we have Funsho an Hassan an Toba. Man we are the *Three Star Boyz* crew and you out by his own crew now.' Bruce giggles and then says under his breath, 'Mr Lynch,' and I think, defend yourself John. Defend yourself.

I'm intrigued though. It's just like me and Mono when we were in school. The push and pull. The knocking of another ego to build up your own.

'You don't know nothing John. You don't know nothing.'

'Yeah I do,' John says and there's an edge to his voice, 'yeah I do. I'm the best at writin beats – all the lads, Jordan and Tunde and Mr Lynch, he-he says I am. I'm the best at writin beats man.'

'You wish.'

'I'm the only one tha – tha . . .'

Bruce starts to interrupt him, 'No you don't.'

Anger rises in John's voice, 'Right,' he shouts, 'I'm the only one. I'm the only one tha . . . tha makes original beats.'

'No you don't, no you don't no more. Ask Hassan.'

John does that backward kiss thing.

'All of you steal your beats from other people.'

'I rap, an we don't steal beats.'

'This is the only – wha beat have you made tha we heard? What beat have you made?' John must start hammering with his fist on the table cause there's a pounding as he says, 'Bring-me-a-beat—'

'Guy,' Bruce interrupts.

'Don't – don't *guy* me. You-do-not-make-beats Bruce. Bring me—'

'Listen,' Bruce pleads.

'Don't – don't *listen* me.'

Even though they're arguing their voices try not to override each other in case they can be heard.

'Listen,' Bruce strains, 'go check it out.'

'Don't – don't – don't, no, no . . .'

'Ask Hassan, ask Hassan . . .'

'Bruce, Bruce, Bruce . . . there's a reason, your beats, you, you get like beats that are ready made.'

'No it's not.'

'Beats that are, are together already – y-you do not play yourself – you don not play yourself Bruce. I play myself. I-produce-the-beats. I use my own keyboard,' John says, his voice becoming aggressive, 'when I *play* it,' he draws out the word play – emphasises it, 'I do no copy it – I don't get ih from software. I *play* it.'

'But John, people can make the beat on software now. Easy.'

'They can, b-but that's like cheating. That's not righ. That's cheating Bruce. I-I don't cheat Bruce. An – an dat's the difference.'

'But everyone's cheating then John. Everyone in this whole world cheats. Look, look at the teachers. They do nothing, they cheat us. Everyone's a cheater. You're on his own.'

'No they're not.' A drumming, slow and deliberate starts on the table again, 'No-they're-not,' and he whispers, almost to himself, 'Mr Lynch – he ain't no cheater.'

My eyes move from my hands, all red and sweaty from being twisted and turned, and look to the posters and media studies projects hanging loosely from the partition wall. Headlines about politicians, banks, promises and accounts, half-truths and non-truths, forgotten truths.

I can hear them next door. I can hear the hushed insistence of musical opinions, I can hear the voices, the argument, the one-upmanship – and I smile. I laugh through my nose cause I can hear them, but I can see us. Me and Mono. Down the back of class, our hot flushes and the awkward glances, stances, the passion in your belief that one thing is not the other, that what we say then, in that moment, in that argument, how thoroughly we argue, knowledgeably we insist, show our depth of listening in music – our music – the Small Faces are better than the Who, the Stones better than the Beatles, it'll make us what we want to be in other people's eyes: respected, acknowledged, cool.

Music makes us. The albums we choose, the videos we watch, the lyrics we love as teenagers, become us. Just as the Nike swoosh or the Adidas three stripes define who you are as a fifteen-year-old, the songs you believe in become you. The beginning of you.

'You are not the best at beats,' Bruce whispers after their pause.

'Yeah I am.'

'No you're not. It's Oscar.'

'Wh-who's Oscar?'

'He's a black guy – lives outside the town – comes here, to Balbriggan, just for a sleepover. He – all the crews use him.'

'So then, as in here. This town. Balbriggan town. I am the best.'

A tut, 'He's class John – you can't compare to him . . .'

'I can compare to him . . .'

Bruce cuts him off, 'Cause he's the only one, like, started the crew. He started teachin me. He's really good like, he makes like . . . Tallaghtboys and Lucanboys helped them out.'

'Well, I don't know them, sorry.'

'He's in college – that's why you can't see him here – but he's really good. Some boys playin his beats in the city. He's big. Real big'

A lull. I hold my breath, just in case they can hear. What am I doing? Listening to two fifteen-year-olds argue about music. Desperation? Possibly. Inspiration? Hopefully. Am I too old for this game? Maybe. Next door was me and Mono ten years ago. And this is me now. Hiding, peeping, listening in on kids for insights. I was John once. I had an identity through music. I knew what was what. I had direction. Ambition. Ideas. Ideas greater than this, surely.

'You see John, you gotta know, like Oscar, he knows. People dunno difference between rap and hip hop. Oscar does – he-he can show you. He can *teach* you.'

'Teach *me*?' there's a tut and a laugh. 'I know there's a difference. You can rap in a hip hop song, you see—'

'I know, see the lyrics that they use, hip hop they have—'

'The basic thing Bruce . . .'

But Bruce won't shut up, so John just keeps on going, talking over him about beats and random effects and then he makes these weird noises with his voice 'paawwm, paawwm, paawwm.' He doesn't stop there but continues, 'Y'know like Bruce, usually rap has like, only three chords in ih, like, like you would like, play only three chords in the whole song an, an just rap n lyrics. Hip hop can have up to six chords, four, four chords an five chords an you can sing in ih as well an you can rap in ih. But rap – you cannot sing in rap cause the beat on ih won't go with singin.'

John understands music in ways I never did as a fifteen-year-old.

'But,' Bruce adds, 'if you're into dancing like me an my crew, you know the beats – but, oh, I forgot, you don't dance, so it's okay.'

'I don't wha?'

'Only dancers know.'

'Tryin say I don't dance?'

'That's the thing I said.'

'Bruce when I bust moves right, the heavens come, the heavens themselves comes on fire.'

Bruce laughs, 'When you, when you enter the dance floor everybody has to clear cause you jerkin and bumpin off them.'

More giggles and laughter.

'Of course,' John announces, proudly, 'make space for the king.'

They laugh together and I wanna join them, just be there, buzzin off them, shootin the breeze. Having fun talking about music. The band don't do that anymore.

They giggle and you can hear them breathe and tap on their tables.

'If you, if y-you have a sense of music you can make beats easily,' John says.

Is he talking to me? Is he taunting me? Is he more talented, inventive, gifted than me?

'It doesn't have to be hip hop or rap,' he goes on, 'I can do hip hop mixed with rap, and jazz mixed with classical mixed with electro mixed with gospel mixed with soul.'

'No you can't man. No one can do all them things. Man, they is too many things to mix in music.'

'I can. Me, I can mix all them things. Music is music Bruce.'

'No it's not John, no it's not. Rap is rap an hip hop is hip hop. You cannot be out by his own an say you can mix all them things.'

'But why not? Me, I got my iPod an I hit shuffle and it makes no difference what comes up cause all my favourite people get mixed up an I love tha. An then I, like I just go to my computer an make songs.'

'Yeah – but you need a computer man. I heard bout your brother – your brother's computer.' A giggle.

'No you didn't, no you didn't cause I have a Mac now.'

I stand up, prepared, ready to bust in the door.

'You don't have a Mac.'

'Yeah I do, yeah I do. I don't just like write beats on ih, I can also write songs.'

'You have no Mac John.'

'Yeah I do, I like, do composing, singin on ih, an I'm tryin, I'm tryin out rappin – but except I cannot freestyle.'

He's kept our secret. I sit back on the table, breathe easy and continue to stare at the partition between us. All those pictures of men in power, suits and ties. The veneer of civility. Morality. Honour. Dignity.

'Tunde says you can freestyle.'

'Really?' John says, surprised, probably cause Bruce is giving him a compliment.

'Yeah you can John. You have a brilliant, like writing book you never uses. All the guys say tha. I'm only dissin bout the beats. But guy – you gotta give crews your beats, otherwise like, no one will care no more for them.'

'Nah, me like, most of you dedicate your brains into all this, all this rappin, hip hop an all – but me, I-I got a plan – I'm, you don't know how to get value for your beats.'

I stand again. Go to the door. Take the handle. Hold it. Think about what I'm doing. Think. Think. Stop thinking. Just do it. No one will get hurt. No one will know. And if no one knows – well, if no one knows, who's to say anything has happened other than what they are given? What I give them.

'I don't care too much about those kinda stuff,' John goes on, whispering now, 'I will write, like, my own personal songs, like, j-just for fun but, mainly like I wanna spend this day, my days, writing music. Most of you Bruce, you do this and post it on YouTube cause you expect to get big. Because that's how Soulja Boy made it.'

'I don't wanna be like . . .'

'I'm not tryin to win any . . .'

' . . . famous, but,' Bruce continues.

'I'm just,' John says over him, 'if I swear, if I like, write a song and a very famous artist see ih, an tries to gimme a contract I w-will literally turn it down cause I'm not lookin for that kinda fame life, but, but if ih means I can make my family happy an stuff, geh dem to stay here in Ireland, then I will. I will.'

Bruce tuts.

'They may look happy and okay with ih,' John continues, 'fame like, they may look happy an okay with ih, but truly, nothing good comes from music, there is always consequences, yeah, behind every single good thing. A producer Bruce, that's different. An some money to make my mama happy. Do da righ thing, yeah. Make something worth something so I can stay here an be the best in Balbriggan ah the beats.'

I just stare at the door. Stare. Blankly. New wood, tainted varnish, fading newspapers.

'Man,' Bruce says, 'if I was like, famous an I had Miss *Lauren* Fields, John, there'd be no bad consequences. Just happy, happy endings, uh-huh.'

'Oh yeah,' John says through a laugh. Bruce giggles and from behind me, loud, jolting, shocking, a voice says, 'It doesn't sound like you're doing your work, boys,' and the laughing behind the partition stops like it was on a CD and I look around and see Lauren standing there, her eyebrows arched, head tilted to me, like I'm in trouble too.

Her arms are folded and she walks towards me from the side of my desk. I wonder how long she's been there. I laugh it off.

'Kids,' I say and let her by. She opens the door between our rooms, and looks in to the lads, 'I hope the work's done, boys,' and there's a mumbled 'Yeah miss,' and 'N-not yet miss,' and she smiles to me and I feel like I should say something. But there's nothing to say. Totally dried up, until, 'I'm on the course.'

She steps back into the room.

'The first aid?' she whispers, and behind her I can hear them hush.

'Starts last Thursday of the month, yeah?'

She thinks and nods, then smiles.

'Just the two of us.'

'Just the two of us,' I echo like a dope, and nod to the room, 'they behaved for you anyway. Just makin sure ye know, cause I couldn't hear a word they were saying – just mumbles.'

'Okay,' she says, a wary face.

'Mumbles – so I was just making sure they didn't mess around or throw stuff cause you can't really hear what people say next door.'

'Yeah you can. You know that better than I do Rob.'

'Yeah?'

'Yeah.'

'Well, I couldn't hear them anyway.'

'Strange that.'

'Yeah strange,' I say and I retreat to my desk.

Just as I sit she goes, 'You staying around for long?' and I look at my phone and say, 'Not really – rehearsals,' and I think she looks disappointed. I know I am.

'Another time,' she whispers and frowns and closes the door. I can still hear her through the partition though. 'Okay boys,' she says, 'let me see your work. If it's done you can go – Bruce I'm sure you and your *Three Star Boyz* crew are waiting for you for dance rehearsals,' and Bruce goes, 'Wha? How you know about them miss?'

I shake my head and hold it in my hands and Lauren goes, her voice louder now, as if she's facing me, 'Teachers know everything Bruce. We hear everything.'

★

Anyway, me and Jen are stuck there, looking through bulletproof glass at this dope chatting away to her friend, a lodgement slip in her fingers, her back against the door keeping it open. That little red button flashes WAIT and me and Jen obey, waiting for her to close the door so we can get out of this security lock mechanism thing. I know they use it for criminals, potential bank robbers, but this is ridiculous. We don't even look like criminals. We're not wearing suits.

Jen knocks on the glass and mouths, 'C'mon,' to the lady. Although it's claustrophobic, I've no problem watching, obeying that flashing sign. A green yoke lights up and Jen kind of hits it, palms it, tuts and pushes through. And we're in. There. Here. At our appointment.

A suit takes a firm grip of my hand and shakes it. His other hand holds his tie as he leans over the desk, reaching out to us. Getting a feel for the suckers he's gonna drain for the next thirty years.

'So,' he says, lifting up all our forms, glancing again at Jen's precise BLOCK LETTERS and my casual scribble.

'I believe you've spoken to Philip over the phone, so you know this will just be . . .' A joke I reckon. I've seen the news. But I play along. For Jen's sake. Keep her happy. Nothing will come of it. Surely.

'Yes, yes,' Jen says, nodding her head, all efficient, like she does when she turns into her manager mode.

'So, you've been saving for the past . . .' he flicks over a page, 'two years?'

'Well, longer – we've been living together, paying rent for the past two years. You should have a record of our landlord's rent book there.'

More page flicks and 'mmhhs' and I'm surprised we're not in an office instead of just behind a little divider. I can see the Bureau de Change, the cashier's desk, the bored, inconvenienced look on her face as she counts out the money.

'And you're in?'

'The private sector,' Jen says, 'you should have it there – the average industrial wage, as they say,' and he shares a giggle with her.

'And you . . . ah yes, public sector.' And he looks for the figure in the forms.

'Not quite the average industrial wage,' I say, just cause I can't help it. He looks at me, as if he doesn't know what way to take me, so I continue, 'Now that we're taking a whack for you lot.' His chin goes into his neck, bulging at the collar, and he smiles a fake smile to Jen; looking for help from the private sector worker.

'But sure we're all public sector now, aren't we?' I nod to him and tap his computer, 'What with all our taxes an all floating around in there.' I don't know. It just comes out. His laugh is a weak one, and he does this thing with his mouth, all teeth, lips parted, like a smile – but not. A face. Some sort of face with teeth. An apology? Not likely.

'Well, regardless, everything looks good,' he says. Good. Surely not. I've no idea how it can be good. There's red tape, mountains of it. Loads of it. We couldn't have cut through it all. Jen couldn't have. How could she have? I thought this would just tide Jen over for a while. A discreet refusal. Maybe another time. Good?

They waffle on without me. Despite me. I'm sweating. Feel sick. I look to that glass door, the glass holding room, and see it opening, two lads bursting in, balaclavas on, shooting the ceiling – wham – and shouting, 'Everybody get down!'

He says some stuff about the European Central Bank and interest rates and fixed rates and variables and I know that'll never happen. Gunmen will never come in and put a hole anywhere. This is an Irish bank. Nothing ever happens here. Ever.

'Six months,' a voice says.

'Rob,' Jen whispers, pinching my knee. My eyes move from the floor, 'Rob, is that okay with you?'

'Mmmhh?' I mumble and he purses his lips, like he's appraising me.

'Six months,' he says, 'and we'll reassess the application.'

Six months. Unbelievable. Incredible what a few signatures and a payslip and a fake letter from the principal can do. Jen said they just wanted to meet. This can't be happening.

'Will the mortgage approval still stand?' Jen says. I'm firmly back in the room. In that seat. Still stand?

'It more than likely will – but the terms may change.'

Thank God.

'With regard to?' Jen asks.

'For one, your deposit,' he says, and he presses his lips together and brings his hands up in front of his face as if he's praying and spreads his fingers wide like a net. 'At the moment – as you know – we're offering ninety-two percent, but more than likely it will change to ninety percent.'

We, Jen, couldn't possibly front up another two percent. But just in case I say, 'That makes sense.' And they both look at me as if they forgot I was there. 'The more we give you, the less you wanna give us.'

He chuckles confidently, dismissively, and goes, 'Oh, that's not an issue,' pauses, takes a breath, looks to Jen and smiles. 'On that note . . .' and laughs with her as he steps out from behind his desk and goes away to get some more forms.

Jen turns to me, wide-eyed, shaking her head, talking through her teeth, 'I cannot believe you. If you didn't want to come you should have just said.' A real tense silence clings to us. People go about their business talking and queuing. She takes her bag and starts to go on about me sabotaging her happiness and how embarrassed she is and how I can wait for yer man to come back with the information booklet and she storms away and goes for the door and slips in before it closes over. I'm after her but I have to wait til the other door closes on the far side before I can leave.

I catch up with Jen on Georges Street. I wanna stop her and shake her. But I don't know what to say.

'I'm not sabotaging anything. I do want this Jen . . . just, just not now.'

She looks up to me and shakes her head and smiles a kinda rueful smile.

'I mean, not now that we're this close – this close to getting signed. I mean with this London thing – it could be . . .'

'It could be, it could be, it could be. It could've been great two years ago. You were close two years ago – and you'll be close in another two years, Rob. It was over last year. You said it. You said it yourself. It was over. It's over.'

'It's not,' I say, shaking my head, quietly defiant.

'It is.'

She grabs my hand but it's my turn to pull away.

'Rob,' she calls, kinda jogging to keep up with me, 'Rob.' I don't stop. The buses. The hardware store across the road. Wild Child's gone from beside it.

'Rob – listen to me. It's over. Why don't you understand?' She sucks in a breath. Hot air from the launderette beside the bus stop, Chinese store, out of use discount store. Hasn't been open for years. Waste of space. Prime retail. Prime spot. Great bar? But the Long Hall is across the way. Keep walking. Mad red and white awning. Wood. Clean colours.

'I don't understand.'

Dunnes Stores' head office. Their homeware store closed down a while ago. Number 16 bus. Taxi. Traffic lights. Wait.

'Talk to me Rob.'

Green man. Go. Capitol. Never have, never will. Pint there. 747 Travel. Smooth curve off up to that Argentinean place. The hotel. Back of Christchurch.

'Rob,' she shouts, kinda screams and a Hindu or Pakistani woman jerks away from us, frightened or shocked. Bald Barista. Winding Stair Cafe. Winding. Widening stair. Widening gyre.

'I'm desperate!' I shout.

I stop walking and turn and face her. Her smeared eyes. Panda face. Heavy breathing. Short, small intakes.

'I'm desperate okay,' I say, lower now with this quiver in my voice, 'you happy – I'm desperate to get outta here, away from there.' I point vaguely at my school all those miles away. 'I've done what you asked, I've got my job, we're living together, I'm saving. But. But, just gimme one last piece of hope.' I take her hands and go, 'Have you ever Jen – I mean, ever, just wanted something so bad, wanted to succeed so much, not to fail so much, just, just win for once – do something, make all the years of everything worth it, worthwhile Jen, that you'd do anything?'

She goes, 'But you are—' and I cut her off and go, 'I need the band to be worthwhile Jen. I need the last ten years to be worth something.'

'But what about the house,' she goes, 'our house, us. Am I not worthwhile?'

'You are,' I say, insist, insist by taking her shoulders, staring, trying to find that connection, just trying to put everything I wanna say through my eyes because the words are dying in my mouth. Failing.

'We can still have all this – do this; the mortgage and all the rest – but now Jen – please, just cool the jets.'

'But it's two percent if we—'

'Well then it'll be two percent more, but at least I'll know I've given the band a hundred percent. Just one more push Jen. Please. Please let me make Camden work. We can do the house thing down the line. Just not now.'

'But it's started,' she whines, 'and houses will never be cheaper. This is the bottom end.'

'Well then let it run out, let the prices go up. We'll be payin long enough.'

'You said Rob, you said you'd go along with it,' she says and I go, 'I didn't realise we could really get signed now.'

I breathe deep and look around and see the glances we're getting and start to walk again.

She follows me and says, 'And so, if you're signed our life ends?'

'No, no,' I insist again, 'just where it's going changes, changes from what it is now.'

'But I like what it is now. Where it's going.'

'It can still go there,' I say, 'but not now, just all this is bad timing.'

We walk on in silence. It's not until we get to Camden Deluxe that Jen whispers, 'Okay Rob, this London thing – and after that, I dunno. We've six months on this approval. I don't want to lose it . . .'

She trails off and I get what she's saying. After ten years I get what she's saying. I'm glad she didn't finish the sentence. Relieved really.

'Okay,' I say and we move under the flashing neon, the fake glamour of Camden, a weird buzz between us. We're at peace though, holding hands and at rest with one another, settled, like a stranded boat waiting for the tide to ebb back in before the leak becomes apparent again.

We will sit together in the apartment and watch something tonight. We will eat dinner and find passersby out the window to talk about. We will say whatever comes quickest, easiest. We will go to bed and we will make love, just to show each other that everything's as it always is. Always was. We will turn our naked backs on each other in the orange streetlight darkness, the net curtains casting shadows over us and we will stare at separate walls. We will think separate thoughts, silently, unblinkingly, unfortunately, inescapably, and we will come to the same conclusion before sleeping and hopefully find in our dreams a way of being happy that we can't find, or won't find, in our collective lives. And then we will smile.

*

There's a heaviness in the air. It's not the muck or the sweaty jerseys and socks. The kids are sitting there, quiet, when normally they're wired after training, all loud and giddy. But the final looms. Their big day. Most of the school's going. Principal and all the teachers. Flags and banners. Lauren and the rest of the art department have got in on things with a: 'St Michael's College – our eleven heros.' I haven't the heart to point it out to her.

I give the whole 'make us proud' speech and ask John to wait outside for me while I lock up. He just nods, no real response. Doesn't even say anything going out, just keeps his head down, serious face, lost in his thoughts.

The school's silent. He's not outside. Chicken fillet roll wrappers and Tayto bags skip across the pitch like they're being pulled on a string and I follow their progress until they bounce away off the grass and onto the road at the gate. Then I see him, legs spread, body snapped to attention like a baseball player, his plastic kit-bag the bat. The Droogs are there, circling him, making to throw digs, pushing in, pulling out in unison. I look around, see who can see me. It's bright. I'm out in the open, a responsible adult witnessing a fight. Anyone could be watching, judging, so I start to jog. As I jog one of the Droogs, Colm, makes a dive for John's plastic Spar bag yoke. John moves aside like a bull-fighter and smashes Colm, busting his nose as he goes, knocking him to the ground.

The other two jump back at the shock of the connection. John jumps on top of Colm and starts pounding him. Taidgh jumps on John's back and Andrew goes for the plastic bag. Singularly weak. Collectively brave. I arrive on the scene and first pull Taidgh off John, then somehow manage to shoulder John off Colm. John falls to the side, retaining a grip on the bag Andrew's trying to snatch. It rips and his gear gets flung across the grass.

Colm's moaning. Holding his nose. Taidgh's face is all red and Andrew's is pale. John's on his feet and they're all just sucking in air, composing themselves, staring at each other. I get between them and try to calm things down, get to the bottom of it all. They were friends once. John says they were trying to rob him, and the others, Andrew in particular, says something about football gloves being his. John fixes his school jumper and says, 'You-you gave them me.'

'I didn't give them to ye,' Andrew goes, 'you were meant to pay us back . . .'

'I did,' John shouts, desperation in his voice.

'It's not enough,' Taidgh roars, his tongue between his teeth, his eyes massive, 'we want more.'

I look at John and he presses his lips together and shakes his head. Colm spits, blows snot and clotted blood from each nostril and goes, 'Doesn't matter now cause yer dead.'

'I thought you lads were friends. What's goin on?' I say.

'We were never friends,' Andrew butts in.

'Tell me what's goin on or I'm gonna have to tell the principal.'

'Tell him,' Colm spits, 'tell him and I'll tell him what your favourite nigger just did to my nose – one more fight – I heard – an he's gone . . .'

Andrew slaps Colm's back and Taidgh whoops and they move away out the gates.

I turn to John as soon as they're out of sight. He's down on his hunkers collecting his boots and gloves and schoolbooks. I ask him where his school bag is and he does the backwards kiss and shakes his head.

'Oh,' I say, kind of whispering to myself. I remember the rain, the penalties, the anger, the missing school bag, the melted runners and see the ripped remains of his new plastic Spar bag floating away across the pitch. He straightens up and looks down on me, his face all serious.

'Y-you shoulda like – just left ih sir. Like me, I – I can do my own fights,' and he turns and heads back towards the school. I shout after him, ask him where he's going.

'The ditch,' he says, his head high, talking to the field, answering to no one. 'I ain't goin out the gate sir,' he goes on, 'cause dey, dey, dey'll be waitin for me, an – an I have a place.'

I catch up. Skip between his strides. He doesn't even acknowledge me, eyes on the ditch and the ghost estate behind it.

'What place?' I say

'Just a place.'

'What was that all about back there?'

'Nothin.'

'Nothin?'

'Yeah nothing. Leave me alone.'

'Where are you going John?'

He stops and turns to me.

'W-why you care sir? Why you like – always askin me questions? I – I have enough questions from everyone.'

'Who's askin ye questions? Are they at you?'

He blows out a breath and looks at the clouds, 'Man – y-you just ask me more questions. Everyone – everyday, they like, askin me questions. I goh a place okay – tha I will like, hide out til I know they're gone.'

'Where?'

His eyes betray his silence and they return quickly from the empty houses over and through the ditch. His head shakes.

Although I kinda need to, I don't probe any further. He moves off. I follow again and go, 'Who's askin ye questions John?'

'Everyone,' he says, 'these guys an my mama's thingy – the,' he stops and closes his eyes and struggles with the word.

'Friends?' I say.

'No-no. My mama's judge guy.'

'Solicitor?'

'Yeah him and . . .' the sentence trails off and he's moving again, the books, the boots, the gloves, the socks cradled in his arms.

That thought won't leave my head. I've got a question that needs answering. But I'm too aware of the weird buzz he's on. He must sense me, hear me behind him, swishing through the long grass, cause he stops and turns, just at the dip into the ditch and shouts, real rough, big boom, 'Leave me alone. W-why you follow me sir? I didn't do nothing – leave me alone.' I bite my tongue and think how ridiculous, out of place what I'm gonna say will sound – but he's gone before I can say it, down the ditch and propelling himself back up the other side.

He stops on the far side. Doesn't move. Just stays there with his back to me, his shoulders easing, rising, easing. I need to say something. Something reassuring. Something a teacher would say – a friend might say – but that one thing just lodges itself in my brain. It won't move. To say it though would be to give the game away. He's not stupid. So while I'm there deciding what to say he goes, 'I – I'm sorry sir.' He turns around slowly, his bottom lip stretching, his shoulders still rising and falling, and we face each other over this mucky divide.

'I – I,' he goes on, 'you are like, I dunno. Ih – it's hard cause everyone, my mama, my brother, my sister, my uncle, the judge thingy, the people from the thingy, they're all like, askin questions, stuff like, all the time sir, an me sir, all I wanna do is like, play, play my music and sing my, my gospel and do – do – do my beats on y-your Mac an play football an I ain't goh no time. So I'm like, thingy, sorry sir. You, you, you don't be askin, like all the others, the questions an all – you don't be, you're not like them.'

I nod, rub my chin, take a deep gulp, hold it back.

'So, you're making use of the Mac John, yeah? That's something, isn't it?'

He nods, but I can tell he's not listening. He's looking around me, past me, before finally, his eyes rest on me.

'I knew you were like, me, I thought last year you-you were just like all them others. B-but like, ah-after the fight in September, I knew you were different.'

'Yeah?' I go, hearing the crows in the trees for the first time.

'Yeah, like me, I-I used to be a pussy w-when I was back in, when I was back in primary school in Angola everyone used to walk all over me, yeah?'

I listen, forget about everything and just let him talk.

'I-I wouldn't say anything. They would come an slag me or bully me. I wouldn't say anything. I'm really surprised why, like, why I'm like, independent like here in Ireland. I'm not afraid. I dunno – maybe the school's too soft. I dunno. But I just started like standin up for myself. In Angola when I was in primary school, like people were actually annoying me an I wanted to stand up for myself but I actually just couldn't, cause I was like small an tiny. They'd beat me up and a female girl beat me up once.' He starts to laugh at the memory.

'Sh-she beat the crap outta me an I went home crying an I wouldn't tell my mama cause I was scared to be a snitch. Everyone though – here – is a snitch. They all tell tales, they do things noh like – to your face and stuff – they go off an do like, things behind your back – but you – you sir – in tha fight like you didn't snitch, an you weren't afraid and like in Angola like, if you misbehave or something they make you go to the corner, kneel down, hands up in the air. Everyone lookin at you. It's so embarrassin. You're there with your hands up in the air like a little weirdo – b-but sometimes other teachers – the good ones – no messin sir, would hit you, and me, I prefer that cause the stuff is over and you don't get all embarrassed and you're not like a weirdo out on his own in the corner of the class. Tha-that's why you sir – I like you.' He smiles. 'You don't make me be like a weirdo or be a snitch. Eh-everyone – all the other teachers are like – afraid of me so they snitch to you or the principal. But you sir – you aren't a snitch or a racist. You're not like them.'

'Maybe I am and you just don't know it.'

He laughs.

'Well, that's what Bruce thinks anyway, John.'

He stops laughing. He looks shocked.

'How you know tha sir?'

'I know everything.'

He laughs again.

'No way sir – you ain't a racist. Y-you gave me your computer an I like, I got like two – nearly three new songs on it an all now.'

He adjusts his books and the boots in his arms, all proud, 'You'd love them sir – ah-after the mid-term they'll be finished an I'll bring them in to you to hear first, cause everyone wants them then. You're right. You'll listen to them, won't you sir?'

'No,' I say and we both laugh.

His lips dip as if he's settled something.

'Okay sir,' he says, 'talk to ye,' and he turns and I call after him and say, 'John,' and he turns back to me, his head raised, waiting.

'Don't worry bout those lads – I'll give them a dig the next time they annoy you.'

'No you won't,' he smiles.

'I will.'

'You won't, cause you'll only hit them if they try and get past you like I did – and you sir, you won't stand in their way, so you'll never havta hit them.'

A flock of birds rustle the trees and flutter off. He's turned again, the smile gone and I shout after him, 'Stay safe,' but I just see his head nod, like he's heard me and I watch him pick his way through the debris, manoeuvre around his new obstacles, disappear behind the big cement tubes. I bite my lip and try and shake off this feeling that's crept up. A weird downer surrounds me, like I've done something wrong or let someone down. I can't put my finger on it, trace its origins. But it's there, beginning to nag.

★

We're in the studio recording the two new tracks for Barry and the label in the UK. The song I got together, the one with the hip hop beats and sample, is finished. Done. Dusted. Sounds whopper. We all recorded our parts separately in the morning and the producer layered them all back up afterwards and it came out unbelievable.

Cause we're running short on time the producer has us all in the live room, set up and ready to play Mono's folk thing together. There's curtains and carpet on the walls and the foam stuff, like a black egg carton, is on the ceiling. The sound is mad and compressed.

'If yis all play together it'll make the song sound more organic,' the producer said.

'Why didn't we do that with the other song?' I asked.

'It didn't call for it,' is all he said.

So we're set up, Mono with his acoustic, the drummer with his brushes instead of sticks, Steve sitting on a high stool and Derek with his headphones.

'What sound you gonna use?' the producer says to me.

I shrug.

'He's not playing on this song,' Mono says, 'we're leaving the keyboards out.'

'You're not leaving the keyboards out – I never put any in in the first place,' I say.

'Cool – okay,' the producer goes, 'eh, well, then, you might as well go and get us all some booze.'

Everyone smiles.

'Bout time someone gave him his true role,' Mono jokes.

Steve joins in with, 'You've found yer callin Rob – you're our skivvy.'

More laughs and the producer settles us and says, 'Honestly though, can ye go to the shop and get me a few beers?'

Just as I'm leaving I hear Mono mention Jen.

'What's that?' I say.

'I'm just sayin ye probably have to ring Jen anyway, tell her you're gonna be out late.'

More laughter and head shakes and I turn and go, 'Leave it out lads,' and they snigger together like they used to do when we were teenagers.

They're in the middle of a take when I get back from the off-licence. I go into the producer at the desk and look through the big pane of glass at the lads playing away in the live room. They look weird – but happy – as a four piece.

'Sounds great,' the producer goes.

'Yeah, but not as good as the other hip hop track, no?'

'Eh, dunno lad,' he says, 'they're both very different songs.'

'But the other one's better, surely.'

'Does it make a difference?'

I look to the four content faces.

'Yeah, it does actually. A big difference.'

'You're on the same team though lad, you should want all your songs to be as good as the other.'

'I do. Just once mine's better.'

'Depends,' he says, concentrating on his faders and knobs.

'On what?'

'On who's listening.'

The song ends and the producer talks into his mic at the desk and goes, 'Sounds great lads, really great. Gonna get you to go through it again. Once more from the top.'

Derek leans into his mic and goes, 'Is Rob there?' and I hope he's gonna say I should come in and layer things up with some organ or something.

'Yeah,' the producer says.

'Tell him to get in here quick,' Derek says, 'we're all parched,' and he looks around and they all burst into hysterics.

Looking through the glass I see how things may go. I grin and bear it for now, lift the bag of booze and bring it into them, worrying as I go, already, about the quality of John's next two hip hop songs and how important they've become.

★

I've my big ear-muffler headphones on. I want to listen to our new recordings, rough mixes, every opportunity I can get. If Lauren sees me with them on she'll want a listen. Haven't had a chance to talk to her about the recordings yet. Haven't had a chance to talk to her about much of anything really. Have just seen her in passing. She hasn't had time to stop. She seems aloof.

My heart jumps, flutters, all those clichéd things, when I see her through the glass. I nod and smile when she comes in and I pull out a seat and take my headphones off and hear bagels crunching around us. She mouths, 'Hi,' and smiles and nods to the headphones and goes, 'What ye listening to?'

I shrug and say, 'The new recordings we've done.'

'Great,' she says and unravels her scarf and sits.

'Sorry I'm late,' she continues, 'had to give some extra work to one of the leaving certs. Not that it makes any difference.'

'Yeah?'

She takes a hold of the menu and blows her fringe away from her eyes and says, 'Yeah, he hasn't noticed.'

I frown as if to say 'Why not?' But I'm sorry we've gone off topic. She seems cool with me.

'He's too busy with other things – like being seen to be a good principal as opposed to being a good principal.'

'I didn't know you had a problem with him,' I say.

'Well, if I didn't before, I do now,' she goes, 'word has it I could be let go.'

'No?' The word is said more in shock than as a question. No. Surely not. No.

A waitress comes over and disturbs us. We both order tea. I ask her if she's eating. She waves me away.

'Yeah,' she repeats when the waitress leaves, 'I hear we're down on numbers for next year. The Community College are fightin back. Imagine.'

'But you, you can't be. You're Art. Everyone loves art class ... don't they?'

She pulls her fringe away from her forehead. I look at her, the lip gloss, the perfect hair, smell her smell and think is this what I want? Or is it just something I think I want?

'You kidding me? It's all about the "knowledge economy" now. Maths and science are going to save our souls and dig us out of our hole, not art. Art is for the affluent, don't you know. No students, no third choice art teacher.'

'But what about me? We started the same time – I mustn't be safe either.'

She smiles a sad smile.

'Don't be silly,' she says and she takes the little teapot from the waitress and I take the cups. 'You're the cream of the crop at the moment with the football final – against the CC, of all schools. And Kembo. You're the talk of the staffroom with how you've calmed him.'

I shake off her praise.

'But who'll I talk to?'

We smile together like it's a joke. But I'm serious.

'Really though, do you know for sure? Who told you?'

'He did. Warned me I might need to start sending out CVs. Told me all about the numbers. Didn't know it was so bad.'

'And are ye gonna start looking?'

'Thought about England,' she says.

I try not to seem too disappointed, freaked really.

'Really?'

'Yep.'

She pours her tea, the liquid spills from the spout onto the table and she soaks it up with napkins and makes to speak but doesn't. It seems like she wants to say something. A new silence is lodged between us. I wait.

'You could . . .' she says, but stops.

'Go on.'

'You could come with me,' she whispers, her lip caught briefly under her teeth, still dabbing the napkins, 'all the good bands I know made it big in London. Why can't the Terrors?'

We share a laugh. A small, strange laugh. I can't work out whether she's serious or not.

'Why not,' I say.

'Exactly, why not,' she repeats, lifting her eyes from the table.

Forks on plates, coffee machine steaming, voices whispering.

'You could you know.'

I open my eyes bigger, a lazy response. A scared one.

'You could,' she repeats, 'you're young. We're young – no ties, no pressure – you could drop everything and go. Just go. Get the Terrors to go. There's nothing here for us. London is where it's at.' We share another laugh as if the laughter will take the strain of the seriousness of her words away. Ease the pressure of opportunity.

Her words stun me, like, I dunno, someone coming up and whacking you in the stomach. A sucker punch. My head is clear. Was clear. Is always clear. But this. This is new. Unseen. It's not the head I can think through anymore, it's the heart. And the heart is muddled. It's a weird sensation. A sick feeling comes into my gut, like all the lies I've told myself, all the truths I've dodged, ignored over the years in that blind pursuit of the dream with the Terrors, have finally reached breaking point and it's blurring my vision. Just go. I could just go. Leave ten years with Jen behind. Ten years – on and off, in fairness – with the Terrors behind. Just go. But I've invested myself in these things. It's not just time I've given, it's myself. I am them. The Terrors are me. Jen is me. I am Rob, I am here, the person I am because of them. There's the clarity. That's the head.

'It's a thought,' I say.

'Doesn't have to be.'

'No it doesn't. But there's four others in the band. Getting them to London next week is a big enough job as it is.'

She looks at me with wide eyes, shocked, and goes, 'Oh, I forgot all about that Rob. How you set?'

I'm about to say, 'not great,' and dive into what went on while we were recording over the midterm but another teacher comes in, sees us and comes over.

'Hi you guys,' she whispers and Lauren looks at me and there's this awkward silence. Lauren pulls out a chair and goes, 'Sitting down?'

When the other one disappears to the toilet Lauren nudges me and says, 'Are we still doing our mouth to mouth?'

I must look confused cause she laughs a little and goes, 'Our first aid course. You're still going aren't you?'

'Course,' I say, copping.

She smiles and nods to herself, pleased almost. 'We shouldn't be disturbed then.'

We're back. It's back on. She didn't catch me. I smile and feel she's interested again.

★

There's an awful racket coming from the kids behind me in the stand. Some of them are shouting, 'Bal-brig-gan, Bal-brig-gan,' forgetting that both schools are from the town. Dopes. Since both finalists are from Balbriggan we're playing on the main pitch in the Glebe. One stand, two dugouts and a lot of advertising boards. The fans are huddled in the one stand and their chants are bouncing round the pitch. The players can hear the stupid roars and shouts too.

So the chanting is going on, and on, and on, Bal-brig-gan, Bal-brig-gan, and the principal, Peter Shields, is on the edge of the pitch, his slacks tucked into his socks, his tie loosened, his windcheater open, shouting orders to my kids – my kids. I've traipsed all over North Leinster – got lashed on and abused by patronising coaches – and he turns up to the final, never even asked me how we were getting on during the year, and he's barking orders like they're his team. He's a red-necked bogger. A Gaelic man. Hasn't a breeze, not a breeze and the lads are looking at him, big furrowed brows, frustrated faces and then looking at me as if to say 'wha?' I'm just shouting a few things –

but I'm so annoyed by yer man, our principal, the dope shouting, 'Get it up the field there boys!' and, 'C'mon, put your back into it boys!' I couldn't be bothered. He doesn't even know their names. And to top it off Lauren's there, in the stands, looking down on me.

At least we're not losing. But we are under a bit of pressure. There's twenty-odd minutes gone. It's tight. John's made a few good saves. And one major mistake. Nearly let an easy shot drop over the line. Don't know if his ma or brother are here to see him. I know his sister isn't even though the rest of the school are. The press are here too.

'N-newspapers sir, that's the main thing, pictures is greah for me sir,' he said. Coverage is success. I can't work it out.

Bout twelve minutes, maybe ten, before halftime, I take a quick look around at the dugout and see the subs all huddled together, quivering, so I let a yell, 'Get out there an warm up!' and this lad, Neil's da, catches my eye. He's leaning against one of the big flood-light poles, hands in his tracksuit top, like he knows what he's doing or something, and he nods to me and kind of smiles. A smile of recog-nition I think. I just raise an eyebrow and nod back to him, to acknowledge him, and he takes this as a sign to come over to the touchline.

We're standing side by side, him all relaxed in his tracksuit, his hands still in his top, me all on edge, and he takes out his hand and goes, 'Alright our-lad.' We shake hands, he grips me a bit too hard and sniffs and nods out to the pitch. I turn back to the match.

'I'm Damien Ryan,' he says, 'your sub goalie's da.' And we're standing beside each other, but not facing each other, so it's like we're looking out at an audience and we're on stage.

'Yeah?' I say, casual, cause I know full well who he is. He's come to all of our games and watched us from afar. Typical, at a final he decides to come over. He just stands there for a while longer, sniffling, spitting, watching the game and I'm thinking, does this lad want to feel important or something, or does he want to help or be seen to be involved? Or is it about Neil being on the bench? And then it comes.

'I've a spare kit goin from the local GAA team.'

'Yeah?' I say and roar at little Rico, trying a few step-overs in our box.

'Yeah. I thought you lads could use it. The one ye have there's a bit wrecked.'

'That'd be great,' I say, not looking at him, keeping me eyes on the game.

'Of course, I'd only be offering it if my Neil got some use out've it, ye know.'

'Shame,' I say, eyes forward, 'I'm sure the Gaelic team could do with it instead.'

'The Gaelic team aren't in a final,' he says.

There it is.

I roar at Abdel, our centre-back.

'What ye think?' he says.

'Great, I'd love a new kit. But your lad won't get any use out of it today.'

'Ye sure?'

'Yeah.'

'Yeah?'

Yer man pats my back and says, 'Okay so, I'm just going over to say hello to Peter.' The principal. I stand there and watch him stroll away. I see him pat our principal's back and shake his hand. They glance over to me and laugh then go all serious and shake their heads and keep patting each other and conspiring. The principal's face goes dark and his eyebrows dig deep.

I'm dealing with an injury on the sideline when the half ends. By the time I get to the players the principal has them circling him, and he's there, finger pointing, shouting, roaring, nearly spitting in their faces, giving them a real going over. I squeeze by John and get into the centre of things, beside the principal. He's saying, 'I'm making one change,' when I butt in and say, 'Sit down lads, sit down,' and their eyes go from the terror to me and I just get in there, don't let him speak, just say anything that comes to mind.

I can feel the principal looking down on me as I talk. I carry on for a few seconds before turning and lifting my chin as if to say, 'what?' He nods for me to go close so the kids don't hear.

'I'm making a change,' he hisses, 'putting the sub goalie, Neil, on.'

'No way,' I say, quick as anything.

'Your goalie isn't doing well. And I've decided, Neil deserves a chance.'

'No way. He's our captain, he's got us here. He's staying. That lad Neil doesn't even play. He's a Gaelic player.'

'That's irrelevant. Now, put him on Robert.'

His bottom teeth drag at his lip, spit coating his lips. The kids begin to squirm.

'The only reason he's here is cause he plays Gaelic. He's only a backup.'

'This isn't a request Robert. If you don't, I will.'

The whistle goes and they make to run off, but I stop them with, 'Ref – change.' The principal pats my back and walks away and all the young faces look at me with horror. I call Neil over and tell him to take off his jumper. His da watches me from afar and nods to the principal as he folds his arms and settles beside him.

'Okay Neil,' I say, 'you're going on.'

He pumps his fists and then I call to JJ, our left back.

'JJ, you're off.'

Jaws drop. Neil's jumper stays on his shoulder.

'You wanna go on or not?'

'But, but I'm a goalie, sir.'

'You were. You're a left back now.'

All the players are out on the pitch and the ref whistles before the principal notices.

Nothing happens in the second half until about five minutes from the end. We score a scrappy goal. But a goal. There's a mix up in the box from a corner and who else, but Rico pokes the thing in. I turn to the principal and smile. He doesn't respond, still smarting. And then right at the death, Neil, who'd been a passenger til this point, goes and hacks a lad in the box. The ref storms over to him and whips out a yellow card, holding it between his forefinger and thumb like it disgusts him, and points, all theatrical, his chin lifted up, to the peno spot. Their coach is nearly in the centre circle, going ape, rubbing his bald head, hand cupped, roaring at his kids about who should take the peno and there's chaos behind me in the stands – boos and screams and, 'Come on Community College!' and, 'Saint-Michael's, Saint-Michael's!'

The noise ebbs away. The ball's on the spot and you can hear the ref tell everyone to stay outside the box and the principal slides up beside me and kind of whispers, 'The NN.'

'Which one?' I go.

'Your goalie.'

'Pereira.'

'He'd better be worth it.'

'He is. He's great,' I say and hope, genuinely hope, he can shine, claim some glory for himself. Be a hero.

He saves it. The stand explodes. They get a corner from the save.

We settle down celebrating and John ploughs through the crowd of players and claims the high ball. We clear and the whistle goes. The principal shakes my hand, tight lipped and goes, 'Thank god for that. Well done Robert,' and steams onto the pitch and starts lifting up players as if they're the trophy themselves. A crowd runs onto the pitch too. John's hoisted up by the lads, and they bounce him round and cheer and he's delighted, big smile and luminous gloves waving to the stand.

Your man, the da, walks by and I call after him to drop the jerseys into the school whenever he gets a chance. He forces a smile and slips away.

John emerges from the celebrations and comes over to me and says, all breathless and excited, 'Are any, any newspapers here sir?' I pat him and tell him not to worry, they're all here, he's the captain so he'll be in all the papers, all the pictures. 'You're a hero John,' I finish and he goes, 'thanks sir – thanks sir,' and I say, 'No bother John. You deserve it,' but leave it at that. There'll be other times to talk about other things.

He shuffles back onto the pitch to collect the cup and I see him peering into the stand, searching for something, or somebody. I look to where he's looking, but there are no black faces there. Lauren waves to me and I wave back. It feels good to be on a winning side, regardless of how I've got there.

★

The microwave pings. Jen gets up from the couch and goes into the kitchen. She returns with our plates. The lasagne is steaming. She places the plates on the coffee table at our knees. Jen's face is lit on the side away from me by the television. It's the only light in the room.

'Thanks,' I whisper. She mumbles something and nods, but keeps her eyes forward.

I lean down and take a bite from the lasagne. It's rubbery. Too dry. It was fresh on Monday; today's Wednesday. Doesn't taste like it did. Doesn't taste the same. Wonder if Jen notices how time can have that effect on things.

'The lasagne's lasted hasn't it?' I say.

Jen turns to me, distracted by what the reporter's saying.

'What?'

'The lasagne,' I repeat, 'it's lasted well.'

'Mmmh,' she mumbles, 'it'll do.'

And I think, actually, I'm beginning to feel maybe it won't.

We eat in silence, just the reporter's voice, the country twang informing us of words and phrases we thought we'd never come to care about.

'My team won the cup today,' I offer, just to put something into the void.

'What team?' she says, still facing the TV, not even moving her head to receive her food.

'The school team I manage. Under Sixteens.'

'Did the principal say anything? Was he there?'

'Yeah, he was. Said well done.'

'Good.'

She turns to me.

'That won't do you any harm at all. Has the school won any other trophies this year?'

'No.'

'Good.'

She turns back to the TV. I shift on my seat. Touch her arm and smile.

'Do you remember, Jen, when you took a day off school to come an see me play in the final when I was in fifth year?'

She raises her chin and looks into a space above the TV and mumbles something.

'Remember, me and Derek were on the school team. It was up in Drogheda. And you went on the bounce so you could come up and watch me.'

'Oh yeah,' she says and a smile breaks out and she shakes her head, 'that was a great day.'

'It was wasn't it. It's mad how great days stick in your memory when you get older.'

She nods, still smiling and goes, 'Yeah, me and Michelle and Aine Smith went. We got the train up. Aine was going out with Paul then. Remember Paul. He went to the school you guys were playing against and god, she was going on and on about some trials he had and how great he was and how he was gonna become a professional player and they were going to move to England together. He didn't even get on. He was a sub. And you weren't even that good and you got on.' She giggles. They way she says *you* annoys me. 'She was mortified. Aine was mortified. They never made it to England. God, they never made it out of the town. And all of her talk. Didn't you guys win?'

'You know we won. I scored the winner.'

She looks at me, eyebrows down, 'Did you?' and smiles to herself as if she's satisfied with something new.

'Do you not remember me pointing up to the stand and waving to you after the goal?'

She shakes her head and turns back to the TV.

'No, sure me and Michelle were busy with Aine. She was mortified about Paul. She never lived it down.'

'Oh,' I say, quietly, and turn back to my dinner.

We finish the lasagne. Nothing happens. Jen just keeps her eyes on the TV.

'You know I'm off on Friday morning,' I say.

She responds with a, 'Mmhh.'

I look at her side profile, see the lines on her face. There are parts of her face where her makeup has faded. There's a glow of fur on her top lip. It appears and disappears when the light from the screen catches it. She doesn't notice me noticing her. And I think, if love is blind, how come I'm beginning to see these things? And when I see these things, how come they seem like imperfections? And if I think of them as imperfections, how come I've never seen them before? Maybe I was blind, blind to everything about her. Her imperfections, her ways. Things are beginning to clear up. There's the head. That's the clarity.

'When are you back?' she says.

'Sunday sometime.'

'Okay – I might not be here. Some of the girls are calling over. We might go out. But if we're here Rob, try not to have one of your heads on.'

'What you mean?' I say.

'You know what I mean,' she whispers, still looking at the TV, 'no sleep, big pale face, bloodshot eyes. Please. We're a bit past that aren't we?'

I shrug.

'It's London. I'm on holidays.'

'Well – I might have houses organised for Monday or Tuesday too. I don't want to be dragging your comedown face around with me.'

'Monday or Tuesday?'

'Yes. Monday or Tuesday.'

'But what if Camden goes well?'

'We'll cross that bridge if we come to it.'

I just look at her, but her head's still turned away towards the screen. And there, at that moment, as if my eyes were like, I dunno, binoculars, and they were a tiny bit out of focus, and suddenly a word, a nudge, something puts them in focus and her side profile becomes razor sharp, like High Definition after watching a snowy screen. Everything is clear. Everything. Dust on the mantelpiece, the fluff on the floor, a mark on the TV screen, scratches on the walls, stains on the carpet, burns on the couch, hot-rocks on the rug, the lines on her face. Everything.

'I'm doing a first aid course. It starts tomorrow,' I say.

She doesn't turn.

'That's good. Does your principal know?'

'No – but I don't see what difference him knowing makes.'

'Tell him. It adds to your CV.'

I don't answer.

'I'll take the late train home. It's not on til seven.'

'Okay,' she says.

'Another person from work is doing it, so it won't be too bad.'

'That's good.' Eyes forward. Always eyes forward.

'Yeah,' I say and continue to sit there and look at her like I've never seen her outline before. She doesn't notice. She's too wrapped up in other things to notice me.

★

'Oh.'

It's all Lauren says as she pulls away from me. The word kind of escapes the moment our lips part. She wriggles her hand free and the only sound, only sound, is my belt buckle tinkling. There is nothing to say. No words to cover up the embarrassment, no joke to cut through the atmosphere. What was only moments ago such a passionate embrace, has deflated. Gone flat.

'Oh.'

It's not even a word. But she's translated, in that sound, so much confusion, disappointment, surprise, I can almost sense the line of ex-boyfriends, conquests, peering over her shoulder, eyebrows raised, hands over their mouths, giggling – sniggering.

I get this feeling, a flash from one of my first visits to the Temple Theatre when I was around eighteen. Me and Mono and Derek and Steve are moving through the crowd to get closer to the speakers, big mad ten-foot monoliths, creaking out some filthy, absolutely filthy hard-house, and the place is soaked, soaked in sweat, beads of the stuff spraying everywhere cause people are literally head-banging, raising their faces to the stage, eyes closed, feeling the heat of the lights, letting the DJs – Tidy Boys I think – do their thing and just losing themselves. All kinds of heads. But everyone, regardless of their Reebok classics, their gammy Levi 501s, their striped Henri Llyod round-neck jumpers and gold chains, has one thing in common with me, us, the lads, everyone – they're off their rockers. The music, the track they're playing is being cranked up, like, really, really, really cranked up. And you know it's late, maybe too late, cause they should've got off the stage ages ago, but you're pushing, everyone's pushing, mad for one more tune, one more tune, and the DJs start the build-up with the snare going 4/4, then 8/4. The bottom end drops out, the strobe goes with the snare, just black and white, black, white, the build-up and the snare kicks on to 16/4, like a marching band or something, the drum roll gets more intense, snap, snap, snapping away, up to 32/4, cranking up to 64/4 and the snare is getting so fast, the treble so thin, the strobe just one white blinding light, the crowd so loud, the build-up so high, the buzz so incredible you're gonna explode and everything drops out, for one second, before boom – the massive bottom end bounces in, pounds the speakers, shakes the floor. Only it doesn't.

In the anticipation to go off on one with the rock steady, bass-drum, snare, bass-drum, snare, you don't cop for a second that nothing's happened, the euphoria has peaked, the build-up was it, the anticipation was without foundation, the rug has been pulled from under you. The track's over, the night's over. What was the greatest build-up ever will never see the expectations met. The juice is gone. The buzz has plummeted. You're unfulfilled and left dealing with it in the horrible white light.

That's it. That's how I feel. It's never happened before. Swear.

Lauren's kinda embarrassed and she gets up on her knees and creases my coat under us. She goes, 'I thought you liked me.' I prop myself up on my elbow. Say nothing. We don't laugh. There's a time for jokes. This isn't it. She pushes off the floor and gets up and brushes herself smooth. She stands over me in our little valley of chairs and tables. I'm speechless, sprawled out on the coat. She raises her eyebrows, flushed face, goes to say something, stops, says, 'em,' stops, nods to the door, stops, holds her hands together, unclasps them, fixes her hair, holds her hands together again and goes, 'I eh, I thought you fancied me Rob.' And just for a flash, I see hurt in her eyes. Like I've wronged her.

'I do,' I respond, dry throat, feeble words. The words make her wince and she goes all quiet as if we're in a library or something, 'I'll give you a minute to get yourself together. I've gotta go to the loo anyway. It's nearly seven.'

'It's not, it's only quarter to.'

She smiles, 'Well, the caretaker'll be back soon. I better get ready. I'll be back in five, okay?'

The okay is barely audible, like she's talking to a baby or something. She goes. I'm alone on my classroom floor.

To think, about two hours ago the world was at my feet. I went for a walk around the town. Couldn't sit still in the school. Waiting. Excitement. The build-up. There was a mist coming, shrouding the school in this fresh cloud. I was biding my time til the school emptied and only Lauren would be left. So anyway, I walked downtown. Got cash out. Last day of the month. Thursday 28th. This time tomorrow I was thinking. I'd be in London after the flight at ten. I'd be soundchecking at four. Out for dinner at six. Back at the venue at eight. On stage at ten. The gig of our lives. Maybe that added to the nerves. The tension. Something did. Something wasn't right. Isn't right.

Joe the caretaker met me at the door to the school and said, 'Don't forget to lock up, yeah,' and I held up the key, looked at all the shutters rolled down over the windows and smiled. But as he got in his car Lauren came out to the door and said, 'There you are,' and I smelled that smell, saw the lips, saw the eyes. I instantly felt this buzz in the air. The anticipation. So I just waved at Joe, closed over the door and followed Lauren's scent into my room.

How do you go from that stage where you're just talking, like all casual, playing that game, that distancing thing where you know it's on – but you just don't know how to show you know? We were sitting on tables across from each other. Facing each other. There was this sick feeling growing. The gig in London, yeah, but knowing the school was empty, and just the two of us were free to do as we pleased was all too apparent. All the bravado, all the innuendo, the raised eyebrows, the talk, the smiles and the laughing at jokes that were lame, the hair tossing, had to come to something. I had to act. How did I act? I laugh. How did I act? How did I act ten years ago? That was the last time a leap of faith had to be made. Leap. It was a leap. The space between tables is the distance travelled to change your life. What did I say? Did I actually say, 'you're beautiful'? I couldn't have. I did. Did I get up, ease off the table, shaking cause this thing has been coming, building since September? No, last year. And I've seen that moment. Imagined it. Visualised it. Almost felt it. So, I leaned out. I did, I did. I leaned one hand out, my right one. God. I actually moved my right hand up to her face, and I touched it, actually stroked her cheek, brushed by it, the warmth, and slid that hand over her ear, felt her hair. The hair was silk. The hair was velvet as it slipped through those fingers and she moved it away from her face too, and we touched hands in silence, and I leaned down to her. Her eyes melted into mine and she didn't move. The signs were right. Real. Clear. I wasn't misreading them. And in that moment, that second, the heart-beat before our lips met, all the possibilities, the consequences, the repercussions flashed and faded, and became that kiss. Those lips. Not Jen's lips. Ten years. All the glances, the thoughts, the doubts and jealousy. I'd done it. If nothing else happened I had done it. If nothing else happened. It did though, didn't it?

Things got more intense. I took my coat off and lay it on the floor, in the gap between the tables. We giggled. Laid her down. Side by side. I kinda manoeuvred on top. No, not on top, at an angle. Everything was in working order. Was it? Working? Can't remember. Was mad into it. And we stopped to giggle again. The build-up. Cranking up. And I'm thinking, *this is amazing*. We're in school. School. The floor. The chewing gum. The snare. 8/4. The seats, the tables, the posters, the whiteboard, the lockers. 16/4. The staffroom, the office, the toilets, the students, the teachers, the parents, the meetings, the tests, the copies, the books. 32/4. The library, the gym, the footballs, the jerseys, the pitch, the students, that student, the beats, the Terrors, my Mac, my computer. 64/4. The dig, the detention, the team, the beats, the demo, the showcase, the beats, the Mac, the trophy . . .

'Oh.' Is what she says. All she said? 'Oh.' Oh, oh. What's oh? Disappointment? Ridicule? Shame? Anger?

I'm back in the empty room, dealing with what went wrong when the door opens. I presume it's Lauren back from the toilet and I'm buckling up, on my knees, ready to explain myself, the stress, try again, go again. But a dark face. John? Enters.

'S-sir.'

Not now. No way.

'Get out,' I say, the buckle tinkling, struggling to my feet, 'get out.'

'B-but sir, sir,' he says, panic, sweat on his face.

'Get out John!' I roar.

'S-sir.'

My belt buckle. My hands. My coat like a bed.

'Out John!'

Moving towards him.

'S-sir plea—'

'Get the fuck OUT!'

A shout. A roar. Finally the belt clicks in and he looks at me, shocked, disgusted. That face I saw after I clocked him in September, only there's something added; an extra turn in the eyebrows, an extra layer of complexity, hurt or confusion or something. Everything is there in that look. He's realised his mistake. He's seen me for what I am. He's seen through it all. Just him. Only him. His eyes show it. Disappointment. And he turns and runs, a school bag, new thing, heavy looking, bouncing from his shoulders as he goes.

I watch him leave through the main school door. He swings it back and a brief square of white plastic, a laptop? flashes in his hand. I shout 'John!' but the door closes over as I do and it whips back with a clatter. He's gone.

I scan my room. See the gap between the bottom of the blinds and the foot of the window. If he crouched down to look in he could've seen everything. Everything. I look at the coat on the floor. Grab it. Turn off the lights, scan the corridors for a sign of Lauren, see she's not there, and walk, fast, out the front door after him. It's cold outside. It's getting dark too. Nearly dark. The fog is thick. That February bite is in the air. The mist is freezing. The sun's gone. So is John. But I know where to go.

The long grass slides against my jeans. I button up my coat and smell Lauren from it. Even though it's getting dark, I can see the ditch, vague and blurred in the distance. Car lights take a turn into the school and shoot down the road behind me. Joe's back. An orange streetlamp lights the far side of the slope into the ghost estate. There isn't a sound. Not even the seagulls are circling. The mist has gassed the town. Total silence. Just my breathing follows me as I run down the mucky slope and back up the other side. My breath fogs my view. Voices, broken things, come through the mist. I cock my head to hear them through the darkness. More than one. I know he'll be in here somewhere.

All this rubble, broken bricks and stuff, all unsteady, unused grids of metal wiring, clatter under me while I'm walking away from the ditch. The houses in the distance are like black cut-outs against the orange glow from other estates. Just an outline, no detail, and on I go. The big cement tubes, stacked on top of each other, block my view of the houses the closer I get. I make to walk around them. An orange sliver of light, sneaking in from somewhere far away, lights the front of the houses; the cracked windows, the broken drains, the scaffolding. I can see the scaffolds through one of the cement tubes. More voices. I stop. Bit freaked out. The cement is rough, cold to touch. I ease to the side of the tubes, keep my left hand on one. Hiding. I dunno. Again the voices. They're bouncing round the estate. Echoing. Shouts, random roars. No words. Echoing but blocked, muted by something, and I think about shouting, 'John, John.' But I don't. Can't.

A flash in the scaffold, the clear plastic sheeting on a top window beside it, something catches my eye. I'm not walking now. I'm still, kinda crouched beside these massive tubes. Being cautious.

'Leave m-me alone,' comes through the clouds. The plastic sheeting whips, snaps at the top window – no glass – from the house with the scaffold. Muted laughter follows the plea. A horrible sound. I stay rooted.

'G-get away!' comes through the silence, and finally, at the top window, bout a hundred feet away, I dunno, bout half a football pitch away, John appears. He scrambles through the top window and eases himself onto the scaffold. The laughter turns to angry shouts, fills the whole estate, bounces through all the tubes like it's being compressed, played through a set of headphones or something. John stands on the scaffold and you can hear the noise of scraping metal, steel and wood clattering. Three figures appear, just their upper bodies, at the window. John must see them cause he starts to hoist himself, all awkward, down, legs first, resting his stomach on the edge of the scaffold, easing, starting to ease down the twenty-odd foot drop to the ground and the unknown below.

They don't say anything, the three shapes. Just jeer and I can see one of them, the thin one, smaller one, climb out on the ledge of the window, straddle it, and begin to shake the scaffold. Rattle it.

'Stop ih – stop ih!' John shouts.

I should be there. I should be running through the rubble, saving the day, my cape flowing behind me. But I'm not running. I'm me. I'm the observer. The teacher. Those that can, do. Those that can't, teach. I'm not in the open now. Can hide, will hide.

The other two start to shake the scaffold. Just rattling it, for like, a few seconds. John's still on his stomach, his chest still on the wood, his legs dangling free and the, 'Stop ih – stop ih!' becoming more desperate and it all happens so quick, too quick, the rattle getting more intense, just for a second, two seconds, and he goes, 'Okay, I'll g—' and he lets go, drops or whatever – loses his grip and flips, falls, just a big blur and there's a thump. A small crack or something hidden under it. The scaffold rocks to a standstill. The rattling's stopped. The figures disappear from the window and seconds later they're at the front door. There's murmurs. No laughter. No shouting. Nothing. They must stand over him for a second and then they're gone into the darkness, lost in the mist. And in that moment I'm all too aware of my heart beating, my breath floating, the cold touch of the tube, my presence on the estate.

My hands begin to shake. I try to move. Don't move. I swallow the mist. Gulp the air. The little bits of rubble are snapping, cracking, rolling under me as I'm moving and at first I'm relieved cause where he lies is black. Dark. In the shadows. I think maybe he's gone. But I'm getting closer, walking closer, over the muck, through a puddle, the long grass, closer, and my eyes are focusing, the mist disappearing, the shadows separating, fleeing from the scene and he's becoming clearer. His outline amongst the shadows, unlike all the jagged and rough verticals and horizontals, is becoming more pronounced; the dark slopes and bulges, soft lines of a body. John.

I dunno. I'm over him. Just standing over him, and I'm holding my breath. He's sprawled out on his back. His arms are spread wide, his legs at mad angles, but his head is arched back, as if there's something big stuck under his body. His bag?

Like a camera or something, I pan up to his face. Haven't taken it in yet. Don't know why. Maybe I know. How could I know? But Jesus his eyes. Those eyes are bright in the darkness; the weak second-hand light, the eyes reflect it. But there's none there. In him, the eyes. Nothing. No light. Those eyes. The mouth like it was about to call out, wedged open, no fog, nothing smoking up. Something behind his ear catches the light, finds the light, seeps out from behind the head into the darkness and trickles over the rough broken lines under him onto the wasteland.

March.

Some geezer goes, 'Sorry mate, no one said nothing bout no keyboard stands,' and shrugs and pulls on some more gaffa tape and goes on fixing leads to the stage. Keyboard stands were definitely included in the tech-spec. My synth, my little mini-Korg, my mixing desk, my sampler are all there and nothing, not one piece of apparatus to put them on. So I get two hard cases, an amp and a table, a round rickety thing, and pile them together and use them as stands. I'm playing bum notes in the sound-check cause the keyboards are rocking. I'm not shaking. Everything's a mess.

The place, surprisingly, fills up. We stand at the bar and scope out the punters. We nudge each other and nod to lads we think might be the head of A&R. I have a few pints while the support bands play. Steve notices and goes, 'What ye doin Rob?' and I go, 'Nothing, just enjoyin a few pints – it's London.'

'Yeah, but you never drink before a gig,' he says.

'Well I am now.'

'But that's ridiculous – you'll be all over the shop.'

'I won't,' I say, 'relax. Just takin the edge off. I'll be grand.'

He shakes his head and takes a deep breath, as if he's not convinced.

The first few songs are a bit of a blur and I turn, instinctively, to press play on the computer for the new track. It's not there though. The computer. Why the Mac's not there flashes. But I don't follow the thought to its conclusio— I blink, shake my head, look to Steve. His face's lit by the laptop screen and I see him begin my beats on his computer. The whopper beat. The sound of the synthetic kick drum is massive. Huge. Shakes the floor. The crowd roar, mad shouts, and I start up one of my real sharp arpps. The place is kicking. I concentrate. Concentrate hard on the keys, just my keys, the white keys, the white keys, the arpp, chord change up to F sharp, down again to the white keys. Concentrate. I focus like I've never focused before on what I'm doing – only what I'm doing. Don't think about anything but what I'm doing. Why am I concentrating so hard on what I'm doing? What am I blocking out? What I'm doing. Who am I and what can one person do? What should one person have done? I'm finding it hard to focus. Left my phone under my pillow that morning so I've no connection with the goings on in Ireland. Dublin. Balbriggan.

The gig's over and I'm off struggling to get served at the bar when someone taps my shoulder. I turn around and almost fall, stagger back into some punters. This tall, big square-shouldered black lad, real trendy glasses, mad headphones round his neck, tight afro, is standing there. I see him there, cause I'm there, obviously – but my mind's gone, like it shoots instantly, over and away to another place. The lad holds out his hand and goes, 'Awite mate. Top set.' I take his hand, see the flash of his palm, shake it, feel the roughness. 'Tellya what mate, your last two tracks, wicked tunes, yeah,' he says, all friendly, familiar almost. 'That last track mate – the beats – they were phat,' he stops and dips his lips, 'they were wicked man – you guys killed it.'

The words, talk of the beats, I dunno, everything, I bottle it, just say, 'Killed wha?'

'The tunes, man,' he says, confused, 'the tunes, man.'

The penny drops, I breathe and say, 'Cheers, nice one, cheers,' and turn my back on him, face into the bar, catch the barman's eye and shout, 'Triple vodka and Red Bull please – in a pint glass,' and he pours me these tiny measures and when I turn around your man's still there. It's like the only black lad in the room has come to haunt me. I smile my best smile but make to brush past. He doesn't move. He goes to shake my hand again, notices I've the drink, stops and goes, kinda shouts in my ear, 'Sorry mate – shudda introduced myself. I'm Kele.'

It sinks in.

'Barry's mate?'

He smiles a mad satisfied smile, raises his eyebrows, eyes like a cat behind the thick frames, 'Kele Cole, head of A&R at—'

I don't, can't put my drink down quick enough. I hold it between my arm and ribs. Shake his hand again, 'Rob, Rob. Nice to meet you. Sorry, I wasn't expecting . . .'

I stop. He smiles, dips his head, like he's heard it before.

'No,' I protest, 'wasn't expecting to meet you here, now, after the gig an all.'

Everyone cops who he is when I arrive with him and they jump off the stage and circle round and offer their hands. They fawn over him and laugh at the stuff he says. I step back from it all and watch him in action, listen closely to what he's saying, listen to the London accent, listen beyond his London accent, watch the way his body moves. Try to read him – see if he's the same as Barry. Anything like Barry. But it's not Barry I see in him. It's someone else. Someone else's image flickers. Much younger. He's looser, freer with his limbs, slumped, shuffled, slouched. His head sinks down his shoulders like the other kid. The student. My student. I neck the rest of the vodka. Turn for the bar.

When I return I feel a bit happier. Bit more distanced. The music's loud, the place is hopping, and our new friend keeps sipping away at his sparkling water and throwing his head back and laughing at whatever jokes are being told. They continue laughing when I join them and Steve says, 'There's the man himself now.'

They open up to let me back in. Your man Kele goes, big pretend shocked face on him, 'This can't be him – this guy's white.' They all burst into hysterics. He keeps on going in his stiff London drawl – oh so cool – 'Surely the guy who wrote those beats was black,' and he knocks on my head and goes, 'Hullo mate – is there a black man in there?' Just cause he's black he thinks he can take liberties. I brush his hand off, fairly aggressively, the Red Bull spraying over his skinny chinos as I do. He jumps back and goes, 'Wow – easy there mate. Just havin a laugh, yeah?' So I go, 'Well it's not funny man. I wrote the beats. I'm writin more beats. It's just rhythm. Computer programs. Why ye makin such a big deal bout it? White – black, anyone can make them. I did. Okay? They're mine.'

Five sets of stunned eyes look at me like I've just puked on them. I take a breath, wipe my lip, bit of spit hanging onto it, and realise, maybe I did – in a way.

Yer man Kele holds up his arms like I'm gonna shoot him an goes, 'Whoa there mate. If you guys have issues, ye know.'

All four of them, the lads, fall on him with, 'No, no, Kele' and, 'Not at all, not at all.' Mono looks at me like I disgust him. Steve takes time out from going, 'Yeah, yeah, how interesting,' to give me the daggers too.

But I can't stand it. Yer man, I dunno, take away the glasses, the London accent, the buttoned-up shirt, the too-trendy suit jacket, the ego, the slacks; take his stiffness away, and it'd be him. The student. Him. I can't help but notice it. Him. I knock back more of the vodka and Red Bull and leave them. Get more. Take a few shots. Go back to them. Him. Still looks like him. Knock back the pint of vodka and Red Bull, go to the bar, return, and still it's him. He shakes my hand and says real slow, like I'm simple or something, 'I-look-forward-to-hearing-more-of-those-beats-mate,' and I sneer, 'Whatever – if you ever hear dem, causeIdunnoifyouwill,' and he looks confused and turns to Mono and embraces him like they're brothers. The room sways. Think he takes Mono's number cause the bright lights of phone screens are wobbling in front of me and he's gone and the lads are surrounding me, shouting, 'What ye think yer doin Rob?' and, 'Get a grip man – spillin drink all over him,' and, 'What the hell – goin on about the beats and black men – what're ye like?' and I shout 'IdontcarewhatyouladsthinkIjustwannaget . . . locked.'

Mono moves forward and starts mouthing at me, 'You're killin us Bob, you're ruinin the buzz,' so I lunge for him cause there's nothing else for it. Lunge, just throw myself at him, cause his face starts to look like the student's, and at this point, it's annoying me. We fall back against the base of the stage and glasses drop off the edge of it and smash everywhere – sounds worse than it is – and we're wrestling on the ground, sapped, hands on my shoulders, on my legs, names, Rob, Rob, Rob, shouts and music, some Libertines whacking away and all of a sudden the little grips on my shoulders and legs are gone and these mad rough, real rigid gruff things reef me, lift me up and I'm in the air, big lads in their black suits and dickie bows are mouthin off and I'm roaring 'getoffme – getoffme.' But they're not listening and my head is shaking like mad, struggling, lights veering everywhere, my body stretching out and I'mkicking-andkickingbutthey'repushingmethroughthecrowdandthroughthebar

andbeforeIknowitthey'velaunchedmeoutonthecoldcoldstonesand-
I'mfreezingandIlookuptothemtoshoutsomethingandoneofthebou-
ncerssays'shutitpaddy'andIcantbelieveitcausehe'sblacktooanditishim-
itishim.Thatstudent. It'sJohn.

★

Jen's in bed when I get home. She mumbles something about being so late. I don't tell her about the delayed flight. Just shush her and spoon her. She's cold. I don't tell her about the horrible atmosphere over the weekend. The silences. The accusations. 'Why were you so late back Thursday too?' she whispers, half asleep, half awake. I pretend I don't hear her. Don't want to tell her the truth. Don't wanna tell her about staring at John flat on the ground and just turning and running out the gate, not looking back, sprinting away from the responsibility, the repercussions, everything. Ensuring I made the flight the next morning. Don't wanna tell her about getting on a train, getting off the train at Skerries, getting back on a train to Balbriggan and calling 999 from a phone box, bottling it, hanging up and leaning my head against the ruined plastic before calling again. Don't tell her I put on a voice and pretended I'd heard screams from the ghost estate. Don't tell her I made this call more than an hour after I saw it happen. Don't tell her I got back on a train to town and got locked, I mean, absolutely destroyed drunk in Anseo before staggering home and puking. Don't tell her I puked on Thursday night, Friday morning. Don't tell her I nearly missed the flight because I was sick, all over the shop. Don't tell her about the gig and getting wasted there too. Don't tell her anything, because anything I say will only remind me of what I didn't do Thursday evening. I didn't stay and help him. Don't wanna tell anyone that. Don't need to remind myself of it either.

★

Monday-after-a-weekend-session tired is different from any other tired. Add to that the build-up of tension thinking about what will meet me when I get to the school and I'm a wreck. But the school is eerily empty. The vice-principal's waiting at the staffroom door and orders me to the principal's office. I think I can hear whispers behind her. I don't have time to react, just say, 'okay,' and turn.

I'm watching the carpet, trying to compose myself when Lauren literally barges into me on her way out of the office. We're both stunned and there's so much I need to say it all gets clogged up and she attempts a smile and nods in to the principal.

'Is that you, Robert?' I hear him call and Lauren lifts her eyebrows, blood-shot eyes, and scarpers.

He's behind his desk, his tie unravelled, his top three buttons undone, elbows on the desk, hands holding his chin, his face in deep contemplation. A slight movement of the head tells me to sit. A clock ticks somewhere on the wall and all of the head-office charters and folders on policy are opened before him. The CCTV screen, black and white and fuzzy, is staggering on pause behind him. He breathes in, a deep, theatrical breath, and closes his eyes again.

'Robert,' he says, his eyes still closed, 'we find ourselves in an awkward position now, don't we?'

I shrug. I'm not going to hang myself that easily. His eyes open.

'We're in a mess, aren't we?'

'In what regard?' I say, feeling like I should say 'sir' at the end of my sentence.

His lips dip. I take the opportunity to try and swallow. Get my defence sorted.

'Every regard. Every regard, Robert. The cameras only tell us so much. But you and Lauren were here on Thursday evening, am I right?'

'You know you are. I just saw Lauren leave. But I left early. On Thursday. I was gone by half, maybe quarter to.'

'I know. But the cameras are the problem. Did you see him, Robert? Did you?'

I blow out a sharp breath, 'Who? I don't get you.'

He rubs his chin, contemplates his next move. 'This is exactly what we didn't need. He was to be deported. I had written letters of recommendation – lip service – for him and the sister months ago. To be seen to be doing something. But we knew it was coming. Did you know that?'

I shake my head and remember the letter I wrote.

'Yes – his brother was at home when they came on Thursday. They got him. But the others were out. They heard. They ran.'

He sighs.

'If only they'd been . . .'

He stops.

'Now, like I've said to the rest of the staff, Robert, this is a defining moment for the school. Our numbers are down. The Community College is striking back. We've somehow, somewhere in the last two years got a reputation for . . .'

He stops, winces, lurches forward, 'The captain, Robert? Did the boy have to be the captain?'

I'm speechless. Don't know how I should react.

'John? He was a leader, sir.'

He winces again, 'But surely there were other, leaders . . . surely. Leaders from the town. Sheridan? Richardson? Locals?'

'No,' I say, 'no, actually there wasn't.'

He tuts, 'Nevertheless Robert, he was, he passed through this school on Thursday as an illegal immigrant. We have it on tape. He was spotted on his way in. Illegally. Now it looks, we look . . . I cannot be seen to have been welcoming him, or now that he is gone, mourning for him. There are many, many in the town who would cause uproar if we're seen to encourage his renegade behaviour – his sister's behaviour – and the mother's.'

I just nod.

'Now, head office will provide a general statement on the matter – but for now, and I believe the funeral is on Wednesday or Thursday, for this, I would like you to be the school's representative.'

'Funeral?' I say, shift on my seat, my stomach lurches, 'sir, I – I'm in no position to . . .'

'Robert,' he says, a hand up to stop me, 'you're the man who made him captain, the man who got him that picture with the cup that's going to be in every blasted newspaper around the country. You're the man the staff say was closest to him. It's fitting – it makes perfect sense – you should be our envoy.'

'But sir—'

'Robert, this will be of huge personal benefit. A favour for me. I simply cannot be seen to go to the service – especially, especially if as I've heard, his mother, and sister, will be attending.'

I slump back on the seat. Now that I've heard it, it becomes real. All the badness, the weekend, everything's leaking out of me.

'This is too much sir,' I say, 'this is too much. I can't be dealing with this – honestly. I can't be dealing with this. He's dead?' My shirt feels damp. I move my arms and feel the drips slide from my armpit.

He closes his eyes and goes, 'I know, I know. But this was no accident.'

He waits for my response. I nearly say something.

'It was always going to happen, an episode like this. Granted they say he was trying to hide, messing, but it was always going to happen with one of these students. The cameras are the problem.' He looks behind him to the jumping snow screen and shakes his head like it disappoints him.

'Did you see all the press at the top gate? They want answers. Why was he coming into the school when he was to be deported? They want the video.'

The game's up. I'm caught. It's over.

He stops, opens his eyes like he's remembered something and goes, 'But Robert, this is the last of it now.' He looks to the door and whispers, 'Next year, as of next year, things like this won't be an issue.'

I must look confused cause he goes on, 'Our admissions policy is changing.'

A slight transformation occurs on his face. The weariness shifts and I think a hint of a smile creeps up one cheek, 'As of next year we're not going to accept any students who have an exemption from Irish.'

'Irish?'

He nods a satisfied nod, 'Irish. If they can't take it as a second level subject they can't come here. They can go to the Community College.'

'But, can you do that?'

'You can if you've got balls, Robert.'

I'm confused now.

'I thought our numbers are down?'

'They are,' he says, 'but long term, this will have an impact for the better, long term. That's why it's important you – you go to the service. Not me. You. You're just the soccer coach. Soccer accepts everyone.'

He stands up and puts his hand out for me to shake. I'm so tired, dumbfounded, shocked, distant, confused, nervous, I dunno, anything and everything, I get up and put my hand out too, unsure of what he's playing at, what he knows.

'This won't be forgotten Robert – believe me,' he says, patting my hand, 'this won't be forgotten.'

I get up to leave, escape, when he says, 'We're alright though.' I can see the corridor. 'All we have is him climbing over the boarding at the back entrance. The other cameras are broken. Vandalised. It could have been worse.'

I'm away into the dark corridors. Don't bother with my room. Just go straight for the door and the train home. Just get out of there. Headphones on, head down, away from him, out of there.

★

The radio fills the void. The emptiness. Silence is the problem. Space to think. Don't want it. Don't need it.

It's barely bright out. The days are getting longer – but this one's getting darker. The light from outside is weak and only the headlines on the inside pages are readable. One day of front page news and he's pushed aside. '*The good guys run for their lives in our Wild West System.*' And under my pen, my fingers, the good guy stares back. The good guy everyone in the country has an opinion on. An opinion about. An image to frown over. Big smile, blue jersey, shinning trophy.

The door closes before I notice Jen standing in the hall. She smiles and breezes in. She drops her bag on the newspapers and pulls out a chair and sits down and I can tell she's in good form. I move her bag off the papers, real gentle, and leave it on the ground. She looks at the bag and then looks at the table, covered with the papers. She frowns and shakes her head and goes, 'Why you buying all the papers again Rob?' She looks closer at them, spots the pages I've opened them on. The pictures. The headlines. Her neck arches round to try and read some sentence. I hear a tut.

'Rob, what's with all the papers?'

'Nothin. Just reading them.'

'You never buy papers – and then yesterday and today. I mean . . .'

She stops, turns one round so she can read it, 'I know it's sad he's dead and you taught him, but how many papers do you have to read?'

'I dunno.'

I begin to feel foolish; only because I see things from her point of view for a second.

'It's just, I dunno, I don't wanna miss anything – ye know? In case like – I dunno – something new turns up.' She puffs out her cheeks and looks over the tabloid in front of her. Music starts up on the radio and the DJ, this dope, keeps talking over it.

'You won't miss anything,' Jen goes. 'Rob – hello – you won't miss anything. They'd tell you in school. What's there to miss anyway? He's dead. It was a freak fall. And his family are still on the run. It's sad. But there's nothing to miss.'

'There is,' I say.

'Is there?'

'It's a big deal Jen. There's all sorts of problems there now cause of it.'

'Problems that don't concern you. Jesus – look – this is getting a bit much.'

She starts to shuffle through the papers, 'One, two, three, four, five, six, seven – seven newspapers. How many pictures do you want of him? I know it's sad – but he was only a student after all.'

'He wasn't *just* a student.'

She frowns, grimaces almost.

'I don't get you.'

It'd nearly be easier to just tell her the truth. The truth?

'He wasn't just a student.'

'So he was a friend? You had him over on weekends for a few beers?'

'No, it's not . . .'

'Did you hang out?'

'No Jen, not . . .'

'Did you have a special bond? Did he look up to you?'

'Don't be silly Jen. It's just, he's dead Jen. It's a big deal.'

'I know it is. But I doubt every teacher that knew him is buying every paper to read every word being written about him, are they?'

'No.'

'Well then.' She takes my hand, 'You're taking things too far. Sure, he was to be deported. You wouldn't have seen him again anyway.'

'But—'

'But what Rob? You're going to be teaching for thirty years – at least. And God, it's depressing – but there will be kids that pass away. You can't get like this for all of them. I know it's raw – but this, all this is unhealthy.'

'You don't get it. It's different.'

'How?' she says, kinda pleads.

'It just is.'

I see the face and the trophy. A local band are playing on the radio. They're brutal.

We listen to a verse and Jen starts to bring all the papers in line, tap them on the table, get them together before going, real casual, small grin, 'Well Rob,' tap-tap, her eyes peeking over the flopping broadsheets,

'I've something to take your mind off it. I've got an appointment for us on Thursday. Two o'clock.'

She's tentative, waiting for my reaction.

'Thursday?'

'Yeah. Marino. Three bedroom. You'll love it.'

I rub my nose, look out the window, up and to the left, to the silhouette of the steel railings, the locked gate. People passing outside.

'I can't make it.'

'But you said the school had a half day.'

'They do.'

'Rob?'

'They do. It's just that I'm busy.'

A couple breeze by, holding hands, a frozen pizza under his arm. Jen's voice rises and she goes, 'Rob – look at me. You – you said the school has a half day.'

'They do.'

She's staring. Really staring. Not blinking. Focused.

'Well . . .'

'I'm, I've to go to the service.'

'What service?' She puts her hands up as soon as she says it, shakes her head and smiles. I say nothing.

'The service?' she whispers. 'And can no one else, no one else in the whole school go to this service?'

'No. It's just me. They asked me. It's a good thing Jen. The principal asked me. You're always goin on about—'

'The principal asked you to go into an African funeral – a dead boy – on the run from the government, his brother on a plane already, probably back in Africa now, his ma and sister on the run, in hiding, the town about to explode and it's a good thing that the principal opts out and you, *you* have to go. You're honestly telling me it's a good thing you've been asked? Think.' She taps her temple and laughs, kinda scoffs, 'Rob, c'mon. There's a line. You're crossing it. I've a house – we're booked in. You said—'

'I know what I said.'

A beat bounces out of the radio and this real dirty synth breaks in. I recognise it. I know it, kinda feel I should know it, like your own voice being played back but not spotting it for a second.

'Thursday,' she says, 'Thursday is the first with this lot. I've already cancelled yesterday cause . . .'

It's us. Our new track. Live – going out on the radio. The beat, the synths, the sample.

'Sshh sshh!' I spit, real loud, my hands out, palm across the table, nearly touching her nose, 'It's us, it's us,' and I get up from my seat and make to go over to the radio above the TV. She grabs at me and goes, 'I don't believe this.' I shrug her hand off and move.

She's shouting something from her seat. An orange street light colours the side of her face. I turn back to the radio. There's loads of dust gathered on top of it. Derek's voice sounds mad. The whole thing sounds mad. The new recording. The new beats. Live on the radio.

'ROB!' she screams, roars. I mean she roars it. Really belts it out, big furious face on her. The first chorus kicks in – just two minutes twenty left.

She kicks the chair out from under her. I look at her, keep my ear to the radio. She's screaming, 'Two o'clock Thursday. Do you hear me?' and she pulls the papers together, terrible racket, tries to scrunch them up into a ball but they're too thick all together and she flings them, flings them across the room at me. They make it half way. Some scatter, sheets flipping up, like they catch a wave or something and float, sweep to a rest. Others hang, sprawled on the back of the couch and under chairs and even under the coffee table.

Second chorus. Bout one minute thirty left.

The hall door slams. The song plays on, middle eight, third chorus, outtro and yer man goes, 'That's the latest track from up-and-coming electro-folk-rock outfit the Terrors. Getting a lot of attention right now these guys,' and the front door booms and Jen's legs storm past the railing out the window above. All I can think is that he called us 'up-and-coming'. Up-and-coming. What's it gotta take to be the band that are at the top and have arrived? And then the word 'folk' registers. Folk.

I sit on the couch and pull up the papers and flatten them out on the coffee table. The trophy. That smile. The shake of the scaffold. The lonely rattle.

Words. The headline again. Page seven, 'N'kembo thought he was safe here.' Some reporter – probably never set foot in the town – probably never heard of the school, the problems, writes from her ivory tower back in broadsheet base camp: '*Balbriggan has been held up as a model of ethnic diversity, but there are concerns that underneath an already thin veneer, lies racial unrest, made worse by non-existent community facilities, poor cross-community communication and entrenched stereotypes. All have been highlighted by last week's tragic death of N'kembo Pereira.*'

I read on, get half way, give up and close it over. Nothing. Open another and read again. 'There can be no retaliation,' the headline says and another talking-head goes, '*as tragic hero N'kembo Pereira is laid to rest this week, emotions will run high with a distinct sense of anger among the ethnic community at his needless death,*' and I read down to how the writer's opinion is that had the death been a murder – racially motivated – then the sense of anger would be justified. Racially motivated. Murder. These words send a shiver through me. I freeze up, nudge the paper away, the word away, think of what I saw, look into my version of events and try to equate that word with them. Can't match them up. Something won't let me. Something holds me back.

Everyone who matters has an opinion. A voice. A way of viewing the cause, the action, the results, the reaction. Everyone has a way of dealing with it; everyone apart from the person who viewed the events as they unfolded.

I read and re-read, look at the pictures of him, the words they say about him, try and find a suitable opinion somewhere around or in between all the opinions. Try to find some sense, some words of advice, a calm voice, a new voice, a voice that knows what I can do, should do. A voice that rings true. Cause my own's gone missing.

★

The looks white faces give us are almost as threatening, distrusting as the looks from the black faces. Women in dressing gowns and men in muscle tops are out on their little one-foot metal balconies, smoking over the edge, judging us as we walk into the estate. The once white buildings, square blocks shoved onto a path, are starting to crumble. The houses, buildings, curve like they're part of a maze or something. But there's no centre – just a round and round mess of discoloured, fading whites and stained windows. The school's a five minute walk back into town, my ma and da's a fifteen minute walk away, but this is another world. One I don't know.

A big crowd of black people, Africans, adults and kids, are shuffling around at the entrance to the townhouse complex. Some kids, in their skinny jeans, buttoned-up shirts and pretend glasses, kinda hiss, tut and do the backwards kiss thing in our direction. The adults, some in suits, dark black cheap things or dazzling white things and women in mad yokes, big head pieces and colourful togas or something, watch us silently.

Just as we get to the house, step off the road onto the path, into the doorstep, a small black lad, probably thirty or so, blocks our way. There's loads of freckles, dark patches, spots under his eyes, on his cheeks. Lauren's hand searches for mine. She squeezes my wrist. It's the first time we've touched since that night. We've spoken since then in the school, but only briefly. The day after I met with the principal. She tried to make me feel better about my mishap. But I was too embarrassed to talk openly. She never asked if I saw John. Presumed I missed him when I ran. She never questioned me. Just offered her condolences. 'He was your student,' she'd said, 'everyone knows that.' When I told her about the principal's suggestion I go to the funeral she offered to go with me. I was relieved to have someone by my side.

'Who-r-you?' the lad says, all burly and rough, and before we can reply he goes, 'No police – no emmagrasheon, nobody. Dis is a funeral. Leave us.'

Lauren whispers to him that we're teachers and we've been invited by Pastor Taiwo. He raises his chin, lips puckered, and flicks his head to the door.

The hall is dark. There's loads of people, loads, inside lined along the hall walls. Both sides. Some acknowledge us, others keep their heads down. There's some mad kinda gospel music, thin and distant, coming from a stereo somewhere, floating around the place. Food smells waft from the kitchen. Forks and knives spark off plates. Lauren lets go of me cause it's too cramped to walk together. I dip my head, cross my hands and look sad, quiet, harmless, all the things you want to portray. I keep on walking these little half steps, slowly brushing by the mourners, cause I don't know what else to do. Meet the mother? Hand over the carefully worded letter of condolence on school headed paper, nod and be polite, and leave. That's all I'm in the house for.

I stop, immediately, as soon as I see the bottom of the coffin; the silk white cloth like a blanket, bunched and bright. Didn't expect it. All eyes see me, watch my next move, watch me secretly panic, stall at the door. I don't follow the wood up to the head. Just the bottom. The mounds were his toes point up. There's loads of candles and the blinds are drawn. It's dark. Stuffy. A real strong smell of food mixes with the candles. I search out the sobs and the words, and sitting on a chair, hands squeezing a tissue, face all wet and mouth just a blur, is John's mother. Only met her once. But remember her face. Last year. And beside her, almost mirroring the shoulder shake, the hunch, is Isabel, his sister. The room is cleared in the middle, but completely surrounded with an African guard of honour thing. Arms folded, jaws tight, they watch me silently. I fidget in my back pocket for the card and the letter, and just as I make to go across to the mother the gospel song from the stereo comes to an end. Sniffles and blurred words, our feet on the wood. Still no music. Plates rattle out of sight. Stop. Nothing.

I reach her. She looks up at me, her mouth, bottom lip dragging down on her chin.

'Mrs Pereira,' I say, low, cause there's no music, and everyone, everyone is listening. The sniffling's even stopped.

'My name is Robert. We met before. I was John's teacher. I'm very, very sorry for your loss.'

She doesn't respond, so I go on, tell her I was his football coach. She smiles and shifts her tissue to her left hand and offers me her right hand. It's wet and huge, rough like John's.

'Kembo,' she whispers, 'he love fut-ball,' and she motions to a space behind one of the onlookers. I follow her nod but don't see any-thing. She speaks in Portuguese or something and the figure moves and I see they've set up a table beside the coffin, two candles framing that picture of John with the trophy. The silver cup, that shining smile. His medal's beside it, nestling on top of the white cotton in its little black plastic container.

'He was a great player,' I whisper.

She stands, eases up and takes my elbow, kinda links me. Her chin points to the coffin and she shuffles over – me hooked onto her – to the foot of it.

The long, half hidden body confronts me. I can't but look up to his face. The white silk is tight around his ears. His hands are at rest; no more drumming on my table, no more handshakes. His mother starts to tremble beside me, her arm still connected to mine, and she starts to say, real loud, shockingly loud for the room, 'Why he havta go? He love fut-ball. He only a boy,' and she's sobbing, shaking, 'only a boy.' I'm stuck beside her, staring at his face; it's far away, closed off from us, like he's got headphones on and he's lost in a song. I hear the scaffold rattle, hear his last words, hear the nothingness between the fall and the landing, hear the thump and the crack, hear the mother begin to wail, wail, her arm coming loose and she's wailing and speak-ing, kinda shouting in some other language, and the candles are flick-ering, throwing shapes over the tip of his noise, his upturned chin, his closed mouth.

Someone's comforting her now, and for a flash I think, but know whatever I say would be useless, too late, too cold, too callous, too much. Too dangerous. I imagine the faces, the reaction in the house, outside the house, the town. Lauren. All my knowledge, my thoughts, my information, bottled up. The time wasted between train journeys. But he was gone already. The candle flickers. Sends shadows across his face, shifts shadows around his mouth. He was gone already. You were gone already.

H-how do you know, like, I was gone?

Still she wails.

Did you, you check my pulse an stuff?

No.

Did, did you crouch down and put your ear to my thingy, my heart?

No.

Ear to my mouth?

No.

W-well then – how, how did you know?

There was no smoke   breath. Nothing floated up from your mouth. It was gone. You were gone.

Ah-ah-and you, you turned away, walked away, your back on me without even like, calling for like, an ambulance?

I considered it.

Considered ih?

Yeah – but, I was confused.

Confused?

Shocked.

Sh-shocked?

Afraid.

Ah-afraid?

Yeah – afraid. Afraid of everything. The three of them, his father, missing the plane, missing the gig. Being discovered . . .

Discovered?

Discovered – found out. Found out for being what I am. What I really am.

W-wha are you?

The wailing's loud. The foreign words, woes, lamenting, all of it's a blur, and his face, that calm face just resting there – the mouth closed, is too much. I mumble something about the toilet, squeeze past the two massive lads, and just out the door at the stairs, spot the source of the music; his boombox hidden under a chair in the corner.

It's dark upstairs. Empty. The landing has two small cracks of light seeping into it. I push one door open – see the tiled floor of a bathroom, turn away from it and push the other door. Stapled soles from old worn school shoes are inside the door. I stretch out my left hand, ease the door open. The sun drenches the room through the nets. I squint. There's two single beds, a desk, posters of some rap star or something, a map of the world and a flag, top half red, bottom half black, with a yellow emblem that looks like it's Russian. I step onto a stained carpet, see the schoolbooks stacked randomly on a bedside locker, see his luminous green football gloves lying limp across the pillow, see big headphones beside the books, a small digital keyboard standing on its side against the wall, see a laptop cover – sleeve thing on the desk – and the school's grey goalkeeper jersey pinned to the wall over it. Step over to the desk, pull out the drawer where the cover is, and take it up. The initials RL, fading, are on the bottom corner, written in my hand a year or so ago with a whiteboard marker. The sleeve is there, but the laptop isn't. I look under the desk, go over to the schoolbooks, sift through them, look behind the keyboard, am moving the keyboard when a voice from behind me goes, 'There you are.'

I turn immediately and see Lauren blowing out a breath of relief. 'I thought you'd done a runner. Taking one last look?' and she presses her lips together, like I'm so good. But I'm so bad. I leave the room quickly and say, 'Yeah. Let's go.' She whispers to me as we go down the landing about a rally being held in honour of John and in support of his mother and sister.

'What's the point?' I say as we take the first step. Lauren leans in close and whispers, 'Don't be so defeatist. I was thinking some of us should go. It's the least we can do.'

A low wailing starts up from the front room before I can respond. A small black man, grey woolly hair, strides in from the kitchen. He's wearing a pink silk cape and dress type thing. When he swooshes into the room the wailing becomes even stronger and me and Jen look at each other and decide it's time to go. I'll leave them to their funeral, leave them to their rally too.

★

Barry takes out his little black book and places it on the table beside his plate of sushi. He goes to open the book, stops – says, 'I almost forgot guys,' and takes his saki, holds it above the candle in the middle of the table and goes, 'here's to a great gig in London – well done guys.'

After taking a few mouthfuls of his sushi – big expert with the chopsticks an all – Barry finally opens the book. Everyone else, Mono, Steve, Derek and the drummer, are all dipping their sushi into the soy sauce with their chopsticks like they do it every day. I just lob the odd bit in with my fingers. One, can't use chopsticks, two, I hate fish. Despise raw fish. And three, I don't feel like eating. Can't eat. Haven't been eating. The drummer just keeps munching like he's never eaten before and wolfs down more of the stuff. Free food.

'Okay,' Barry says, finally, signalling it's business time by knocking the book on the table. He wipes his hands in one of the silk napkins and dabs at his mouth. The drummer just keeps on munching. Everyone else drops what they're doing and stares.

'Now,' he runs a finger down his notes, 'the gig went well. Very well.'

Everyone exchanges glances.

'Kele really likes some of the songs. Has issues with the set structure – some of the sound – one or two songs and stuff. But, yeah, overall, he liked you guys.'

Suppressed smiles.

'He likes the new stuff, the two recorded tracks, he thinks they're great. That's the future there, and those two new demo songs you gave me – I'm gonna send them on to him too. So we're looking good.'

He holds up his saki and we all do the whole cheers thing again.

'I'm telling ye, it's lookin good lads.'

'Two new demos?' I say after there's a lull. Barry looks confused.

'The folk ones,' he says, ridicule in his voice, almost impatient, 'that you guys sent—' I stop him mid-sentence.

'Who?' I say. The Tetris blocks. Into place. Fall. Barry turns to Mono. Mono looks to his plate, moves some sushi with his chopsticks. The voice of some karaoke queen starts up behind us. Clatter of plates. Steam and chefs. Barry raises his eyebrows, goes, 'Oh-kay guys,' and closes his black book.

'Well, as I said, I'm sending Kele the two new demos – he has the old ones. Oh, and,' a smile, 'I forgot to tell you, he's coming over in May to see you guys so, eh, it's show time again.'

Everyone stays quiet. No one raises their heads.

'It's all good guys, yeah?'

No response.

'Guys, who died? I just said the boss was comin over to see you play again. Nothing?'

Mono puts out his hand and goes, 'Nice one Barry – cheers. Appreciate it. We'll be in touch,' and Barry goes, 'Don't worry about the bill – I'll sort it,' and he flashes a gold card and leaves.

I wait til he's out the door.

'Two new tracks?' I say, daring someone's eyes to meet mine. 'When did ye sort them?

Mono looks up, his jaw clenched, and shrugs. Shrugs like it's grand – everything's cool.

'Me and Steve had a few days off after London. We went in and just put down two new tracks. Sounded good so we passed them on. Like ye do.'

'But you said,' I look around the table, 'yous said we should cool it for a week.'

'No, no Bob,' Mono says, looking to the lads for support, 'we said *you* should take it easy – after the mess *you* were in.'

'I wasn't that bad. I wasn't that bad. Was I Steve?'

Steve messes with his sushi and says, real low, almost too low to hear under the karaoke, 'You were in a pretty bad way.'

'But yis don't understand lads, seriously, yis don't understand,' I say.

'Get a grip of yourself,' Mono responds. He's mocking me and the sacrifices I've made, the things I've done.

I just lose it, pull the tablecloth, lift it and flip the sushi nonsense everywhere. There's gasps from all over the place. The karaoke singer stops and there's some Chinese or Japanese being shouted in the kitchen. I don't move. I stand there staring at them. Not walking away. Staying there. Let them see me. Look at me. I look at each face. Steve is kinda frowning, grimacing, like what I'm doing is actually hurting him. The drummer's just shaking his head, mouth full of sushi, eyes on the bare table. Derek's sat back on his chair, brushing his trousers off. And Mono. Mono's looking me straight in the eye, a calm smile on his face.

Two bouncers or waiters or chefs, I dunno who they are, appear from behind a cloud of steam in the kitchen like cops in some bad movie and this scene suddenly feels like I've played it out before.

I brace myself for the struggle.

★

Okay, the placards, with their big printed words – bold and typed – not scribbled and coloured in with markers like I thought they'd be, are way too professional to be made by kids. A rally organised by friends, attended by friends is what Lauren said.

The demonstrators are in a tight little group in the pedestrian area of the square, sandwiched between the library and the courthouse, looking out onto the town's main road. There's about thirty, maybe forty people. All kids. Only one adult. Think she's a councillor. Seen her face on all those posters on telegraph poles for town meetings. So it's all kids. Mostly black kids with the real professional placards saying 'LET THEM STAY'. No parents. Probably afraid to put their heads above the parapet. I can guess why.

An official-looking red haired young one comes towards the group and I take this as my cue to melt away – join Lauren and two other teachers who've just got out of a car and stood a few feet away from everyone. The red haired young one has one of those hand-held speaker-mic things, the cone and an electric cord connected to the walkie-talkie part, and a clipboard. She gives the mic to the councillor and there's a screech as she gets the thing comfortable and raises the walkie-talkie part to her mouth and coughs, clears her throat and shouts, 'What do we want?' The group of kids raise their placards, like they've rehearsed – cause it doesn't feel spontaneous – and shout, 'Justice for Kembo!' and she goes, 'When do we want it?'

'Now!'

Lauren waves, a big smile, and goes, 'You made it – thanks.' The other teachers, women in their thirties, look at me like they know what I'm up to.

'This all of us?' I go.

They nod.

'Shame more couldn't be bothered,' I say and Lauren rubs my arm and goes, 'I know, I know.'

This 'Justice for Kembo,' racket goes on for a while. The councillor's like a conductor in front of her orchestra, prompting and controlling them in their boring chant. After a while they expand into, 'Justice for Kembo – Let them stay!' and it starts to repeat, over and over, a simple beat, the rhythm dictated by the consonants; 1-2-3-4 – 123. Slow for the first bit, fast for the last.

The councillor raises her hands to calm them and the rabble-rousing dies out. I can't see anything beyond the kids, but behind me, there's a few pubs and the bank, and people are gathering. Heads have come out of the pub, smoking, pints in hand, and they're smiling – like this is gas. But their smiles are weird things. I dunno.

Anyway, she pauses, the councillor, keeps the microphone thing to her lips – waiting for the right moment and finally goes, 'One brother is dead. One brother is deported. A mother and daughter are in hiding. This is Ireland's answer to the immigration problem. This is *our* government's handling of the immigration problem.' I don't know why she bothers with a mic cause she's roaring into the thing, loads of screeching and stuff. I look over my shoulder and see some of the pint drinkers come across the road.

A car horn barmps and someone shouts with approval and the councillor ignores it all and spits, wide-eyed and crazy, about a family on the run. The pint drinkers arrive on the scene. Passersby saunter to a stop and raise their heads to listen, a smile of entertainment lifting their lips. The councillor screeches through the noise about criminals who've robbed hundreds and billions and are being bailed out and supported while the state goes after the little man, chases him to his death and then hunts down his family. 'It's barbaric!' she screams, shouts to the street as if they've made the decision. 'Barbaric!'

The councillor runs outta steam and the crowd goes quiet. I'm looking around, seeing who they're aiming all this noise at cause – bar me, and the few teachers, the councillor and the drunks, the passing cars and the fat photographer from the local paper – I don't see who else is listening. John's gone. It's old news. Only one mention of his name in all the papers in the last five days. The rest of the family are, if they're lucky, a small column in the national news section. No one cares anymore. Which isn't necessarily such a bad thing, really.

I'm lost peering round my old town square when from nowhere the councillor's beside me, her metallic voice having stopped the chanting, and she's talking to me, right in my face, but she's speaking into the mic thing, so the entire square can hear too.

'Here's the teacher,' she says, 'the only teacher, the only person to highlight his plight and show him some compassion.'

The whole town is staring.

'He's here to say a few words,' and she shoves the walkie-talkie part to my mouth and as I go, 'No – no way, sorry, no,' I can bloody hear the metallic version of my words come out of the speaker cone thing. Her thumb is on the voice button. The bitch. The crowd start up, 'Speech, speech, speech,' and I'm goin, 'No, really,' and I can still hear my own voice and it sounds so weak on the yoke and her hand is wedged, can't move it, real strong on the button. The walkie-talkie bit is touching my lips, her spit still warm on it, and it's so quiet now, so quiet, you can hear my breath as I struggle. The silence is massive.

Horrible. A teacher's hand – could be Lauren's – nudges me forward.

'What's done is done,' I say, my voice all croaky and trembling. The megaphone screeches and the councillor shifts me round, moves me to the side, back a few steps. She backs me into the group so I'm in the thick of the placards, looking out onto the main road, the drinkers, the teachers, the passersby, a hooded figure in the distance.

'Okay,' she whispers, 'you're good. Go ahead.'

I cough to try and clear my throat and it makes the thing screech and I say sorry to her but it comes out everywhere, echoes around, like I'm apologising to the town. It feels mad to be heard. I've nowhere to put my hands so I take the walkie-talkie bit and go, 'What's done is done. Our friend, our student is dead. There won't be justice for him.'

I've run into a cul-de-sac.

'But, em – for him, we can work, and today we can demonstrate for his family to live the life he would've wanted them to live. Eh, that life would've been in Ireland.' There's a huge cheer behind. It moves through me. Lauren presses her lips together and nods, almost prompting me.

Feedback, throat clearing, nose sniffle.

All of a sudden I'm part of the group instead of just an observer. A bit of a rush goes zipping through me and I take a hold of the megaphone thing with my other hand, feel the weight, and get comfortable with it.

'We can't dwell on the past – but we can dwell on now. Isabel's part of this community. Just because the law says she hasta leave doesn't make it right. It doesn't make it just.'

Another cheer and a car horn barmps.

'Think of the money that's been spent on educating Isabel . . . four and a half years, and at the last hurdle, when the government could see a return on their investment, they ship her off.'

A group of young lads approach from around the corner of the bank. The red haired young one has a phone held out in front of her like a cameraman.

'Just because you're told something doesn't mean you don't question it. You kids are right to question her deportation, you're right to challenge it . . .'

'What about precedents?' someone shouts. Beside the teachers there's a man in a suit, suitcase and umbrella in hand, chin raised, mouth open from disturbing me, 'The law is the law, son. Nobody should be above it.'

There's boos from the kids behind me.

'If they were asked to leave,' the suit continues, 'it's cause their claim was bogus.'

More boos and shouts.

'They just want a better life,' I respond through the thing.

'There's a coupla million Africans our, who'd like a better life. We let them all in?'

Laughter from the pint drinkers and the kids that've just arrived. Hoodies and tracksuit bottoms tucked into socks.

I'm knocked outta my stride and go, 'I'm not, I'm not sayin that . . . it's just, John is dead. He ran to the school for help – we didn't . . .' and behind the growing crowd I recognise the hooded figure. Andrew, half his face hidden by a shadow, is smirking. The Droog. Haven't seen any of them since . . . since I last saw them. He's across the road, leaning against the bank, listening to me. Observing.

The megaphone screeches. Someone lobs a can of coke towards us but it goes too far. Another can flies through the air, the coke trailing out like the tail of a comet. It smashes off a placard, sprays everywhere. The councillor snatches the megaphone and starts shouting,

'Please, wait, please, this is a peaceful—'

A small group of the protesting kids break away, sprint after the can throwers. They haven't got far to run cause the can throwers don't move. Shape up for a row. A pint glass smashes, there's placards on the ground, going through the air and Andrew, the Droog, is still, like a statue, at the bank, just looking over, watching me. Detached from it all. The councillor's voice is shouting, 'Please – please, peaceful rally, this is a peaceful rally,' and sirens are coming and there's cars stopping, tyres screeching and Lauren and the other two are getting into a car, her hand beckoning me but I'm standing there, transfixed by Andrew, the sirens getting closer, faces and fists meeting, slapping, wet thuds, placards snapping, and like before, I can't move.

★

The keyboards are loud and clear. Everything's going smoothly. All of a sudden the Stone Roses thumb a lift, introduced by a friend, to show me how Oasis ripped them off. It's non-stop, all this ripping off. What a discovery though, the Stone Roses. I veer off to the Happy Mondays, Joy Division, New Order. 'Blue Monday'.

My early twenties are a maze of turns and new signposts, all-nighters and earth-shattering conversations off my head discovering the intricacies and genius behind the music I love. I'm sitting on a couch, sweating and gurning til the sun bursts our bubble and infiltrates the room we've melted into. Chemical Brothers, the re-emergence of Prodigy, Primal Scream's *XTRMNTR* and *Evil Heat* and Daft Punk and Soulwax and *Satan's Circus*.

Me and Steve and Mono have our arms around each other's shoulders at a Soulwax gig, bopping up and down, cheering, going in sync with the rock-solid kick drum and Steve's saying, 'We gotta get more electro into our set,' and I'm going, 'I can get a synthesizer – do some mad sounds and arpeggiators and stuff,' and Steve's pogoing, nodding, 'Yeah, defo, big time – gotta be more dance man. Like them,' and Mono's adding, 'But they've no guitars – no guitar solos,' and I'm going, 'Guitar music's dead Mono – no one does solos. It's all about the keyboards,' and Steve's chewing on the inside of his mouth, real earnest face on him going, 'He's right Mono. Keyboards. We're so lucky we have Rob,' and Mono's stopped dancing and he's saying, 'I'm goin the bar.'

The potholes of my teenage years disappear into the distance and I'm on an autobahn. I'm cruising. I've found my crew. My niche. My mid-twenties and I'm where I wanna be with the perfect mix of guitar music – with all its fuzz and dirty bass – and dance music with its synths and arpeggiators and 4/4 beats. I find Death in Vegas, and my journey is over. There'll be other brief trips, but this is where I'll stay. Death in Vegas are what the Terrors modelled themselves on. That's what me and the lads want to achieve as our musical destination. That's what made us new and exciting. The mix of dance sounds and pure, raw power.

This lad Barry comes over to me and Mono after a gig on Steve's twenty-fifth birthday, introduces himself as A&R from a major label in the UK.

'Your sounds are amazing – the mix of the guitars and keyboards. You guys are ahead of the game,' he says.

'Nice one,' I say, delighted, buzzing.

'What I like about you guys is there's no egos onstage. The guitar makes room for the keyboards. You don't see that too often.'

'And vice-versa,' Mono says.

'What?' Barry goes.

'The keyboards make room for the guitar too.'

'Oh, yeah, yeah. That's what I was saying. No egos. You guys look and sound like a team.'

A team.

★

Again the key is in the door and Jen has it open, I've turned the television off and shuffled round on the couch to face her as she walks in. She's early. She said she'd be here at seven.

'You've changed your hair,' I say, like a dope, as soon as I see her.

She shrugs.

'I did that ten days ago.'

'Oh,' I say. So it's been over a week.

She doesn't move from beside the door. There's a bright square of light framing her in front of the hall. You can see dust and other stuff in the sun's beams floating discreetly between us.

'Are you sitting down?' I say.

She shrugs again. 'Is there any point? I mean, I'll probably just end up leaving anyway.'

'You won't.'

'I won't? And why won't I? Are you going to ask me to stay?'

'. . .'

'Are you?'

'Yeah,' I get up off the couch, 'I am.'

She smiles. It's not a smile I've seen before.

'Don't kid yourself. You didn't even miss me.'

'Yeah – I did. Of course I did.'

'Not one text from you – not even to ask about the house I'd booked for us to see and you expect me to believe you? Not one text.'

'I was busy . . .' I say it without thinking. Her mouth drops. 'No, not busy. I was giving you some time. Us time. But, I'd things going on too – like the band had a meeting and – just, it was busy. But not too busy for you.'

Her head shakes, she eases her bag down and folds her arms.

'And you're available now I suppose?'

'Yeah, course Jen. Course.'

This is new territory, a dirt track I've never travelled before. Things are so intense, the feelings so heightened, it's like nothing we've come across. The silence is loaded. A heavy, crackling silence. How can the silences be loaded with a person I've known for ten years? Ten years. Cars roll by above us on the road, someone laughs somewhere, the fridge clicks and starts to rattle. She breathes deep. I lean back on the arm of the couch. Fold my arms too. Nothing seems appropriate to say. We've spent so many years together, talked about so much, talked out so many things, this silence, lack of words, is weird, jarring, disturbing.

'How are you?' I finally say, sounding like a stranger. So precise. Proper. She looks up to the cars passing, a smile on her face again. She doesn't answer.

The nothingness returns.

The slow hum of the fridge. The clock on the mantelpiece used to tick too but the battery went a few months back.

'Do you remember when I went away with the girls to Tenerife?'

I nod. Glad she's talking. She breathes deep again. 'You called me every day Rob. Every day. Every night. Do you remember that? And your ma went mad cause of the phone bill.' She laughs to herself.

'Yeah,' I whisper.

'And you texted. Just stupid texts like "miss you J-Bunny" and "love you". And the girls, Rob – god. They made fun of you, god they made fun of me, but I knew they were freaked. They had fellas too. All of them. Not one text between them. But I loved it. I didn't tell you cause I knew you'd stop. But you didn't. You kept on calling, and texting. Every day and every night.'

'I just wanted to see what you were up to.'

'And you didn't last week? Do you have any idea when the last time you texted me to tell me you loved me was?'

'I dunno Jen. I do all the time.'

'No you don't. No you don't. You text me on New Years – you didn't say you loved me. You didn't text me when you were in London . . .'

'I'd things on my mind.'

'You didn't text me. One text to say you love me, you miss me.'

'I was, I had, it was mad Jen.'

'You don't love me.'

There it is. So simple. But devastating. Of all the words we've spoken, this combination has never come up.

'What? I. I—'

'You don't love me Rob. And I'm glad, cause you know what – realising this has made me see I don't love you.'

'But, I do, I do.'

She turns to me, mascara smeared all over her eyes, smiling, calm, 'You're a coward. A coward. That's all you are. You don't love me. You don't care about me. You're just settling for me – and you – god, you really had me fooled. You don't want a house with me, you don't want any of this.'

'I do, I do,' I say, whispering, cause shouting won't work, kinda pleading.

'You don't Rob, and you know what's pathetic – it's me, it's me that has to say it, cause you can't. You're too afraid to say it, too afraid what a bit of conflict will do to upset your stupid band and your boring life – your happy, boring life.'

'What?' I say.

'This, everything. You're afraid. You've been afraid to do anything out of the ordinary in case you miss out on something since I've known you. You're so boring – and predictable – and a coward. I'm done. I can't believe I've spent ten years of my life with you.'

'But Jen,' I say, 'it doesn't have to end like this.'

'What other way then? You'll just keep making sure everything else is achieved before you think of me. You've settled for me. And, god, what a fool, I was settling for you.'

I don't know what to say.

Nothing comes.

Nothing.

She turns to me.

'Well,' she says, 'aren't you going to say anything?'

Nothing.

'You've nothing to say?'

A real high-pitched noise enters my head. You can hear the traffic lights zapping away on Wexford Street when the cars stop passing. How easy would it be to say something reassuring. You can hear the bottom of trucks scrape off the speed ramps on Pleasant Street. So easy. But, at this stage, she wouldn't believe it. I wouldn't believe it. In the long run, and this has been a long run, it wouldn't be worth it.

'I've nothing to say.'

There's a definite jolt, a shift in her posture, her cheeks drop, the wind's taken out of her for a second. You can hear an ambulance siren wailing away somewhere distant.

My words, weak as they are, make her kinda crumble, collapse or something. She starts to shake her head, take double, triple breaths, suck it up, but her eyes water over and the impact of her words and my response explode inside her and she moves, grabs her bag and just at the hall turns, the sun now gone, the hall completely dark and goes, 'What a waste of time – what a complete waste of time.'

I don't respond. It is what it is. She's brought it on. I've accepted it. A long time ago if I'm honest.

'Would you have got a house with me?'

'I dunno.'

'You *duh-no*. We might have signed away our lives and you wouldn't have known. Jesus. Why, why were you with me?'

She just wants to prolong the pain, get all the answers she can while she's here. But I don't have any answers. Just an acceptance. An acceptance that what's come to pass was gonna come to pass.

'I dunno – I, I dunno Jen. You're my best friend. We're best friends.'

'Best friends? We weren't best friends ten years ago, and we haven't been best friends in a long time. Your friend?' She laughs, makes to go, turns away, turns back and says, mad serious face on her, 'I feel sorry for you. You don't have any friends, Rob, if you thought what we had was a friendship. We haven't been friends in months. How could anyone be your friend? You're a fraud.' And she turns and she's gone.

I sit on the edge of the couch watching the last of the sun creep through the railings above the window, cast their shadows across the floorboards. Those small flecks of dust float by, silently. Even the fridge doesn't hum – and the cars don't roll. I wait for my eyes to fill up, even a small bit of something to escape – but nothing, nothing comes. I don't feel like crying. Don't wanna cry. Don't need to cry. Shouldn't cry. I just sit there, let her words dissolve into me, go through my brain, into my pores, seep into my blood. I suck it up. Take it on the chin. All those clichés. It's over, after all these years, it's over. I am alone. I've been alone for a while now. And I've dealt with it.

April.

For days I'm sprawled out on the couch, hoping one of the DJs will play our tune again on the radio. Although the TV's on mute and I've got the remote in my hand and the radio's banging, it's the phone on the coffee table that I'm really interested in. It's been lying there, fully charged, for days. No text beep and vibration. No ringtone. Nothing. Anything. Not even a text from Steve. Even after I texted him and asked for a lend of his computer so I could try and get some beats going myself on the thing. I expected something from someone since we're meant to be playing for the A&R lad Kele in May. It's not an issue really though. I'm not that stressed yet. It's the same set as the London gig. It's the same set as the last few gigs. We just need to stay tight. And then there's Lauren. I've texted her – but she hasn't got back either. Haven't seen her in over a week. Easter holidays.

We're out of here in May. I'm out in May. I've texted Jen this – to let her know she'll need to come round and get her stuff and move it to wherever it is she's staying. Don't know where I'll go. Haven't thought about it yet. Will deal with it when I have to.

There's nothing in the papers; well, just a tiny column about the family still in hiding with a line or two about his death and the tragedy and all the usual. Things have gone quiet on that front. The election has taken over the space. Every man for himself I suppose, including the Droogs. Haven't seen them around school. Andrew hasn't been in class. Not a big deal. He has a habit of going missing for weeks on end. It makes sense they keep a low profile. Haven't thought about them. Try not to think about them. They're the issue. The crime. The problem. So I ignore it. I ignore them. Hope they continue to be invisible.

I'm nearly asleep, just dropping off on the couch, when my phone rings. At last. It jolts me, shocks me. A number comes up I don't know. Not in my phone book. Dublin number. Lauren. Clear my throat and answer, say hello like I'm just outta bed. It's been a while.

A voice asks if it's, 'Mr Lynch?'

'Yeah. Yeah, that's me.'

I'm disappointed.

He tells me his name – forget it instantly – and then tells me he's a representative from the constituency office of Balbriggan's local TD up for re-election. Forget his name too. He tells me the local TD would like to talk with John Pereira's mother and sister. 'See what he can do for them,' he says.

I don't know why he's called me, I say, and ask him how he got my number. He mumbles something about a friend in the town. I say it's great news someone is taking an interest and all, but I have no contact details and I'm not involved with the family in any way.

He's a bit confused now, saying he got my number from someone who was at the demonstration and he heard I spoke very passionately, forcefully he adds, on behalf of the family. I explain it wasn't set up like that, that I just happened to be there. The local councillor was running the show, I tell him. He tells me the TD would rather not deal with the councillor due to a conflict of interests and serious differences of opinion and so forth, and that the TD would very much appreciate it if I could take his number. I get a pen – write it on the fringes of one of yesterday's broadsheets – and tell him I'll pass it on to Mrs Pereira and her daughter, if it's possible. It would be very much appreciated, he says. I finish the call and sit up, rub my face and wish I hadn't answered.

But I did, so I put my runners on, grab a bit of change from the mantelpiece, get my keys and go out into the world, take the steps up onto the path, walk out from under the green shadows of the trees and go onto Wexford Street and towards Left-Click, the internet café, to get the number for that councillor's party office.

Outside the internet café is as good a place as any to ring the office. It's noisy from all the cars and all but I just wanna get done what I have to do. So I get a mobile number for John's ma, and forward it on to the TD. That's it. Easy. Once I've done that, in the space of what, five minutes really, I go to Roma for a burger and chips, and make my way back to the apartment to wait for a text from the lads, Lauren, or Jen and listen to the radio. Because I've nothing better to do. Nothing else to do. But for some reason, I dunno, burger and chips in hand, I just stop under the Camden Deluxe sign and stare into space and begin to think about what I'm doing – who I'm taking calls from and who I'm calling. The reasons behind everything. But they're not there, the reasons. They've morphed into this weird dream constructed from the stories pedalled about John's death in the press. The truth is an elusive strobe light that hasn't flickered in a while. All I'm left with is the imprint of the flash after its gone. A blur burned into my mind's eye.

If it happened again, I dunno, would I do it again? I did what I did but that doesn't trouble me. Weirdly, it's the other version of events, the one that's been made up in the papers, the events I've started to believe, that trouble me. The accepted story. I have this uneasy buzz about it, like, although it's the story everyone knows and accepts, there's something missing from it.

★

The principal stops me outside my room before I go in. I'm not in the mood but pretend to be interested since I reckon it's about John Pereira's family or something. He doesn't mention them but instead launches into this spiel about some first year parents ringing up about my lack of effort in class and not giving any homework and just reading from the book. 'I went next door when the room was empty,' the principal whispers as the kids pass, 'and I had a listen to you in action, Robert. It's not good. You could put in some more effort, you know.'

I can't believe it.

'But what about all I did for you, the school, over the last few weeks? It's been stressful. My mind's elsewhere.'

He grimaces and goes, 'I know, I know, but we're losing teachers and I'd hate to think your lack of performance could put you in jeopardy too.'

'But after what I did for you . . .'

'What matters is what we do *in-the-classroom*, Robert, not outside it. There are rules. Standards. We've had calls you see, from other schools, asking to speak to you about what you did for that NN. Your teaching comes first. Not your Non-National work. Quite the opposite if I'm honest. You've become synonymous – *we've* become synonymous with this whole mess. I mean, have you seen that clip on the internet?'

'Clip?'

'Fine, I asked you to make an appearance at the mass, but I knew nothing about the protest. Your words caused a riot. I mean, we've become the referenced school for their issues and your name is the one thing that keeps on coming up, time and time again. I fear it's going to become a tick we cannot shake. And now we have the Town Council wanting in on the act.' He breathes in deeply, exhales carefully. 'I'm afraid it seems your performance is suffering as a result of this newfound celebrity.'

'Celebrity? I don't see how my—'

'Was the speech really necessary Robert?' and he looks at me as if he's tasted something sour and he shakes his head and purses his lips. He dwells on the question, letting the accusation rest.

The corridors are quiet, my class behind me hushed; I make to go in to them. He puts his hand out to stop me.

'They're back you know.'

'Who?' I say, fake surprise, not knowing whether to play dumb, happy or sad.

He ignores my response.

'The mother rang me. I was to pass on her regards to you. I'm your new secretary. She asked for you in particular.'

'Okay.'

'His sister's returning to school tomorrow.'

'That's good.'

'Is it? She wants to thank you in person. I told her not to bother. You're too busy teaching. I'm right, aren't I? I mean, you are too busy teaching, aren't you?'

'Of course,' I say.

'Good,' he says and looks at me as if he's not satisfied. As if something else is still to be said. 'Okay then, better not keep you any longer,' and he turns and marches for the corridor.

The class are quiet when I enter. Qwuam, a first year, sitting in the same seat as John, is stretching over his desk with his hand raised.

'Sir?' he says, eager.

I lift my head to let him speak.

'Is it true you're the reason John Pereira's family are staying? That you helped when, like, no one else would? That's class. It's the truth, int ih sir?'

'The truth?' I go, shaking my head.

'My papa says so. He says you're a hero sir.'

'A hero?' I repeat. 'Don't be ridiculous. There's no such thing as heroes.'

★

Don't spot Steve for a while. Have to do a lap of the pub, look past the suits and ties, the after work crew. He's in the shade, at the back at a table with another shape. They both turn, must sense me descending on them or something. Mono. They muster small smiles. Lazy things. Like I've disturbed them.

'Alright lads,' I go, taking my headphones off, wrapping them round my iPod, 'wanna drink?'

Mono waves me away as if it's too much to ask and Steve says, 'No, no, we're grand Rob.'

When I check, I see he's not just being polite. They are grand. They're both in the middle of pints. I check my phone for the time, see if I'm mistaken. I'm not. I'm actually early. It's only five to. I turn and head to the bar for a pint. At the bar I check my messages to see the time Steve said to meet. No – I'm right. He said seven. He's obviously come earlier.

They shift around when I return. Mono, for some reason, goes to the other side of the table; so the two of them are facing me. Like an interview.

'Shame about the drummer not bein able to rehearse today, wha?'
I say. 'Especially since we only have a few left til the gig.'

They nod unconvincing nods.

'It was sounding good yesterday though, wasn't it?' Me again.

Steve mumbles something.

The drink is cold but vinegary. Too much gas. A sour pint.

'Gonna be some gig. Imagine the buzz when it gets round the
forums that we're playin to the head of UK A&R. Madness.'

Eyebrows are their response.

'Try and get yer laptop for me tomorrow if ye can Steve. I'll have
those beats any day now.' I just can't stop myself. Haven't spoken to
anyone in ages. Not properly anyway. 'I doubt we'll have them for
when yer man Kele comes over, but sure, we'll sort something. But we
defo need to get in tomorrow again. It'd be a waste of the week, the
month even, if we don't rehearse.'

They don't respond. Just little sips of their pints, their lips pouting
and biting the inside of their mouths. The silent treatment. I fly
through all the stuff I said to them in rehearsals the night before.
Nothing. I was in good form – surprisingly. Kept my head down,
head together. Granted, I didn't play along to all those acoustic
protest song things – couldn't. Well, wasn't bothered getting the
chords, finding a sound. It's a phase. It'll pass.

Mono's chest rises, like he's going underwater and he nudges his
pint away. Steve does this thing with his eyebrows and licks his bottom lip.

'About rehearsing, Bob,' Mono says and fidgets on his seat.

'Yeah,' I go, like I don't notice the weird buzz, 'what about it?'

'Ye know,' Mono says, turning his pint, 'maybe it'd be a better idea
if ye, ye know, if ye . . .'

Steve takes up the slack, 'If ye stalled it for a while.'

'Stalled it?'

Steve struggles, 'Stalled it, like just eased off rehearsin for a while.'

'Eased off?'

'Like, just take it easy for a while,' Steve says, a quick sup from his pint, 'just relax an stuff – don't worry about rehearsals.'

'Yeah – concentrate on yer beats.' Mono.

Now I'm freaked. Feels like there's gas stuck in my stomach. Mono wants me to worry about the beats. I'm missing a trick.

'Not for long like,' Steve says, 'we're goin grand with the new tracks. Sure our set's changing and ye know – you're getting a bit left behind.'

'It's probably just the pressure, Bob,' Mono goes, nice all of a sudden. Alarm bells. 'I mean – these new beats you've promised – they're never gonna come, are they?'

'They will.'

'Maybe they will, but they probably won't. We're probably not the band for them though anyway,' Mono says. Steve nods along, looks at me through his fringe.

I miss a beat. This is me falling off my bike, slipping off my pedal as a ten-year-old and whacking my nuts off the handlebar. That kind of sick. Shock. I'm in shock. Don't stand a chance here. It's an ambush.

'I don't get what yis are sayin. Yis can do without the sounds?'

The two of them wince. Mono nods slowly, as if what I'm saying doesn't matter, as if he was expecting this, as if he's thought everything through.

'Not just the sounds Bob.'

'Well maybe we can do without *you*. Hah Steve? We can do without you Mono. The whole folk thing is a joke.'

He shrugs.

'We've been thinking about it Bob,' Mono interrupts. 'Yeah – that new track, the beats are good – but you've offered nothing in months. Nothing. And this folk thing, the new tunes, regardless of what you think, they're really working – and Barry and Kele love them. They're the way forward.'

'Steve?' I say and look to him, crane over the table. He presses his lips and shakes his head, eyes down.

'So what are yis really sayin lads?' There's a quiver in my voice. I Sky plus everything. All glasses stop clinking. All laughing, banter stops sounding. Doors stop opening. Smokers stop exhaling. Cash registers stop registering.

'Maybe you need a change.' Mono.

'Maybe we all need a change,' Steve whispers quickly, like a comforting afterthought.

A change.

'You're saying I need a change or you need a change?'

They nod. Look at their pints. Keep looking into their pints as they take a long gulp.

'Which one lads?'

'Both,' Mono says, determination in his voice.

I fall back in my seat and go, 'I don't believe this,' and see the small drops of condensation race down the outside of my glass. I run my finger through them gently. Make a line across it quietly.

'But the beats,' I say pathetically, softly, still shocked.

'It's always something,' Mono says, 'look – we've got three folk songs. They sound great. You're not happy playin them. It's havin an effect on rehearsals, the other lads. It's not worth it. Let's just leave it at that.'

'Leave it at that?' I say. 'How are we gonna leave it at that. What about all the old songs? I wrote them. I won't let yis play them.'

Mono looks at me sadly. 'Bob, we all wrote them. Derek wrote the lyrics, you wrote the keyboards, Steve did the bass, I did the guitars.'

'But I came up with chord sequences, bits and pieces, verses for some songs and choruses for others.'

Mono looks at me like I'm stupid or something.

'We'll leave out all yer keyboards Bob. Give us a shout when ye remember what bits of what songs you made up and we'll leave them out too.'

He kind of smiles. Smiles. A real patronising smile. Steve doesn't look up. This is the end. I can't believe I never saw it coming.

I jump up. Their seats screech back as they flinch. I sneer at them and turn. This is the end of our road. Through suits and jackets, loose ties and locked secretaries, I push and escape. This is me in that freeze moment in the car while you skid. This is the brace, the hand on the dashboard, the weightlessness as you lurch forward, swerve left, pull around and flip, spin high into the air and turn before smashing down on the roof and sliding off the road, past the barriers and into the embankment. Hidden. I look up as I leave the pub, see beyond the strangers, catch a glimpse of Mono and Steve, big serious heads on them over their pints. I see the road I'm no longer on, that spectacular motorway, the new surface part financed by the record company. It's out of reach and they, Mono and Steve, Derek and the drummer, won't even notice I'm missing. My music is no longer part of their journey. I'm a ruin on the embankment. This is me walking away, silent, seething, sick, devastated. Finished with them. Betrayed by them.

★

My classroom is twenty-four feet by twenty-eight feet. Not twelve inches feet. My actual feet. I measured it today. Walked it. One foot, the other foot, heel to toe, heel to toe. There are two windows to my right that face onto a corridor. But the blinds are always drawn and shadows, like something from Plato's cave, pass by outside and hint at a world beyond the room. I try to imagine what the world outside the room is like sometimes. What's going on in other classrooms. What secrets other people have. Course at this time, half four on a Thursday, no one shades the blinds. I'm alone in the room. Bar the cleaners and Joe the caretaker, I'm probably alone in the whole school. Thought Lauren would be here for the first aid. She's not. She's not in today. Wasn't in yesterday either.

I think I've got tinnitus. A parting gift. The silence brings it out. What I'd give to have someone break it, shuffle in and disturb me. Slump down there at the front desk, bag on their shoulder, swing back on the chair, blow out their cheeks and tap away with their rolled-up baton. A steady, random drum beat. Or a knock. A knock from next door would be something. Just a head coming through. A peek to see if I'm here so we can chat. Talk about something.

I'm seeing things differently today. Feeling things differently. This room, for the first time, feels like a prison. My room is a four-walled, green-carpeted, low-roofed prison. I've been given a life term.

I am twenty-eight today.

I've reached the milestone, the mythological rock and roll age of youth and hope. Hope that you can achieve something great. I'm older than Kurt Cobain, Jimi Hendrix, Jim Morrison, Brian Jones. I'm officially their senior. And what have I achieved? What will I achieve?

So I'm in my classroom, a twenty-eight-year-old prisoner. I'll be here til sixty the way the government are talking. This is my life. Twenty-four feet by twenty-eight feet. I'll become one of those know-it-all scarf-wearing tossers, blown up by my own self-importance and grand words and quotes. But behind it all, the quotes, the scoffing at fifteen-years-olds who can't see the subtleties in Shakespeare's sonnets or don't understand the cultural references in some obscure novel, I'll be bored. Bored. The same room. The same desk. The same walls. The same partition. The same books. The same retorts. The same jokes. The same anecdotes. I will become a parody of myself, an embarrassment to my twenty-seven-year-old self, my twenty-seven-year-old self a vaguely recollected embarrassment to my fifty-eight-year-old self. And at sixty I will have forgotten myself totally. I will forget what I thought I could achieve outside this room. The hopes I let run wild in defiance of this room. I am twenty-eight today and I am older than the heroes that were always older than me and because they were older than me, their myth, the dream they lived was available to me. Available if I was ambitious enough. Ruthless enough, lucky enough. None. Nothing. I will never now live a life like theirs.

I will never achieve everything I hoped I was on the cusp of achieving. I am twenty-eight and I am not the person I thought I would be when I was twenty-eight. I am a failure. Death by drowning. Death by asphyxiation. Death by heart failure. Death by shotgun. I will not die in this room, but it will kill me. If I stay here I will ebb away. I will fade into something that wasn't what the twenty-seven-year-old me fought for. Death by cowardice. Not even the twenty-six, twenty-five, twenty-four, twenty-three, twenty-two, twenty-one, twenty-year-old me fought for this. Life will not begin tomorrow. It ended yesterday, it's ending today. That's worse than death. To burn out or fade away? Ebb away. Without a struggle. Without an argument. What could be worse?

★

A vague wave, salute of sorts, puts yer man back in his seat when I come down the stairs and into the hall of the rehearsal rooms. He lifts a finger in hello and slumps in his seat and returns to his computer screen. He mustn't have heard.

I go down the hall, stumble over an amp, adjust to the underground darkness. It's totally still. No one's in yet. It's too early. Most bands don't get in til six or half six.

No one answers the knock on the door. It's covered in carpet so it's a dull thud. I give another whack to be certain, move my ear away and pull the door open. Darkness of the carpeted second door. I push it open and root around, feel for the switch. Find it. Flick it. The light strobes weakly and bursts on, horribly bright, down on all the gear, our gear, my gear, their gear. It's all still set up from a rehearsal they must've had yesterday, or the day before. My keyboards have been pushed to the side.

Gathering my gear up is easy. Sure I've done it don't know how many times. Soft cases, hard cases, wind up the leads – my leads, my investment – click the stands and fold them up. Take each piece out of the room bit by bit. Leave them just outside the door. I pull over the outside door from inside the room. Then I push over the inside door, put my hands on my hips and survey the room. The corner where I played looks weird. Unfamiliar. It's a gaping hole in the history of the band.

The room lurches. Everything turns liquid. I blink. It clears. But only for a second. I breathe deep. A quick double breath, triple breath sucks in the dead air. Again the room wobbles and I lick the salt off my lip, snort, pull up the snots, close my eyes. Breathe deep.

This is me off the road, in the upturned car. I bend down and pick up the acoustic guitar. This is me struggling out of the car up the embankment, hopping the barrier and walking into the middle of our road. Their road. My autobahn. I feel the slim beauty of the neck of the guitar. The polished smoothness, the golden strings. I let the neck fall through my hands. Feel the gloss as it slides down. Hold it like a tennis racket. No – an axe. This is me on their road with a bomb. A nuclear bomb. I lift the guitar by the neck, over my head and turn to Mono's amp, size it up. An old Marshall yoke. I pull back, as far as I can go and put everything into it, everything, everything I have into the forward swing and I slam the guitar into the body of it, into the fabric front of the amp. This is a detonation, the blinding flash, the pure white boom and the slow fade to colour.

My eyes are kinda closed, watching through slits cause the wood's splintering, the strings pinging, flipping and whipping, twanging with every connection. I dunno, five, six, seven goes and it's a ruin in my hands. The neck, apart from the top E string, is disconnected from the body – what's left of the body – and is clinging like a sliver of nerve onto the bone.

This is the road wobbling, the dust rising before the tarmac cracks and the debris flies everywhere, gets sucked up by the tidal wave of power. As soon as I'm finished with the acoustic, ruined over the floor, I drop the neck to the carpet and look around, panting, wired, my hands searching in the chaos for another instrument.

I get lost in the rage and once outside, back in the hall – calm – the lad in the office is only too happy to give me a hand and help bring my gear up to the taxi waiting outside.

'You want me to get the guitars inside too?' he says, putting his hair behind his ears.

'Nah, they're grand for now. The lads should be along for them later. No rush.'

I don't want him to see the incineration, be exposed to the fallout.

He nods and goes, 'Cool, man,' and I take the last keyboard case from outside the room and turn the camera of memory on as I walk through the hall and up the stairs and out into the sun. After today, I'll never be allowed in the rehearsal studios again. This is a new wasteland. A radioactive nowhere now.

★

I missed the four o'clock train and the next one isn't until five so I've set myself up in my classroom with a cup of tea and one of the school's old laptops. I'm scrawling through the internet, bored, when I come upon us. Them. The Terrors. A small article on a national paper's website under the headline 'Word on the street... Be Terrorfied.' I gag, but it's an article. I read through the thing and get the most horrible sensation as I go, like the words themselves, those black letters, collections of tiny, tiny pixels are crazy little ants crawling through my eyes, down my throat, past my heart and into my stomach and burning, burning my gut. The writer – some music journalist hack – goes on about the hype surrounding their next gig and the record labels rumoured to be attending and 'fighting it out' for the band's signature. Fighting? Ridiculous. He then goes on about their 'dynamic new sound'. And then, right at the end he says, '*eyebrows were raised at the online release of their double-A side demo they made for a major UK label, but the retro-sounding folk music of 'Tomorrow' and the old-skool meets nu-wave beat rush of 'Things Will Happen' have excited fans and bloggers alike to such an extent tickets for their show in May are selling out.*' I have to lift my jaw off the table. I am sick. Sick. Absolutely sick.

The sun must burst through the clouds outside cause my blinds come to life. I can see a sliver of blue – just a sliver – out the top of the window, through the corridor, over the lockers and into the courtyard beyond. A little knock on the door focuses my mind, brings me back and I cough, clear my throat and watch the thing ease open.

Of all the faces, of all eyes, of all people I expected to see, this isn't one of them.

Andrew.

The Droog.

I freeze.

He lifts his head as he comes in to say 'Alright,' and shuffles past the front row, his big Mackenzie jacket rustling, filling the vacuum. I clear my throat. Haven't seen him since . . . haven't seen him in school in about two months. No sign of him or his fellow Droog Colm around the corridors since February. Spotted Taidgh once or twice, still with the mad eyes, crazy stare, but a bit subdued, less agitated. Quieter. Doesn't come knocking on my door anymore, none have til now. I cough again, shift back on my seat, bring my hands from over the laptop to the side of the chair and go, 'Andrew – long time no see,' normal voice, good pitch, nice and cool, all confident cause that's how I should be. Would be if there was no tension in the air.

I let the silence come between us. He seems taller than I remember. Bigger. His jacket rustles and he sits in the front row without being asked to. He glances at the old laptop with a rueful smile and looks away as if I've wronged him or made him come in for detention or something. I wait for his move. Nothing.

'Where's the rest of your crew?' I say.

He frowns, too cool for school, literally, and shrugs his shoulders, dips his lips and sniffles.

'It's very rare I'd see you without them,' I go. He just shrugs again. His nonchalance worries me though. He seems too relaxed, too in control, especially for a student who hasn't been in school in months. He should see me as a teacher. Have some sort of respect.

Attack is the best form of defence so I go, 'Haven't seen you in a while. Sick?'

'Nah,' he says, scratches at his stud earring, lifts his head and exposes his upturned nose, buckteeth.

The distant sound of a hoover starts up somewhere down the corridors. It's a faint hum to underscore his sniffles. He snorts next, takes a big chunk of phlegm and spits it to his left, onto my carpet and turns to me, his eyes daring me, and goes, 'You getting some sort of award sir?' It's so unexpected, the spit, I'm stuck for words, a reaction. I bottle it and look at where he spat, look back to him, see the overbite, the stud earrings, spiked hair, rat eyes and don't recognise him. Don't know who I'm dealing with. I let it slide.

'Award, Andrew?' I say.

'Yeah – me da says you're getting an award like. Yer da was telling my da. For doin stuff for the blacks an all.'

'Sorry?'

'Kembo,' he says and scoffs, snorts again. This lad is only sixteen, seventeen at most. I try to compose myself, assert myself. Act as a teacher would in this situation.

I tell him the award's not just for me. The hoover, a low hum, the head being snapped back and forth on the carpet, rattling as it goes, gets louder. A distant distraction.

'That's not wha me da says,' sniffle, eyes on me, 'he says tha you're getting loadsa stuff for helping Kembo.' He smiles. 'You,' he sniggers, head back, 'Helpin Kembo.'

This is not the coward I knew, the lad who hid behind his two henchmen for fear of being singled out. I breathe deep, think about how I'm going to approach this, how I'm going to break down this façade. Cause it is a façade. Has to be.

'Is everything okay Andrew?' I say. 'Are you looking for someone, cause I don't have time.'

'No – it's just funny – you gettin a award for helping Kembo.'

I do my best confused face. There's so many things flying through my mind I don't know which face to make, who to be. Why is he here? Has he come across something? The cement tubes, the orange light in the dark, the rattle of the scaffold, the crisp snap of the plastic sheeting.

'Is it? Delighted for you Andrew.'

His short chin drops into his neck, he looks at me dead serious, his tongue coming up over his bottom lip. He holds the stare, says nothing. No words, like he's in a trance or something. I'm pushing my chair back and making to get up saying, 'Right, let's go Andrew, I've had en—' when he cuts me off.

'Took me a while to work out why ye didn't.'

I'm like a statue, in an awkward pose, half up, half down, stuck, struck by his words.

'Why I didn't what?' I say, like I'm bored.

'Help Kembo.'

Still in that stance I go, 'But I did Andrew. You mightn't have heard – I helped his family.'

'But ye didn't help *him*, did ye?'

I sit, put my hands to my chin, hold them steady.

'What are you here for Andrew? I'm busy.' The friendliness has gone from my tone.

The noise of the hoover turns into a high whine. She's getting closer.

'You didn't, did ye? And you're getting an *award*,' he says, whispering the word 'award' as if he can't believe it.

I make to get up again and escort him out when he stops me for the second time. 'He was runnin away from ye sir – peggin ih. But why was he like, why was he runnin from *you*? Fair enough he was runnin from us. But, you?'

I sit.

'Nonsense Andrew. It's time you left.'

'And even after his accident on the scaffold yoke, you didn't help him or stay or nothing sir. That's tight.'

I am stunned. I clear my throat, twice, shift on the seat, fold over my legs.

'Where did ye hear this Andrew? Running from me. I wasn't even there. I don't have a clue what yer talking about.'

He tuts.

'I saw ye sir – hidin behind those big tube things – I saw ye when we ran. I thought you were gonna call the cops or call the ambulance or something.'

I should flip the table, shock him, throw a dig, choke him, kill him, hide from him, run out the door, do something, but I just sit there, real casual, my hands back holding my chin, my stomach beginning to turn, and I go, 'I wasn't there Andrew. I don't know what you're talking about.'

He shakes his head and says, 'But like, no ambulance come for ages sir. The lads went home an all an I went home. But I went back out, an again I was back there there was still no cops or nothing sir. I was freaked so I even stayed round the corner an all waitin for the ambulance and ye still didn't ring nor nothing sir. I was freaked. All we wanted was me gloves back. But what did you want? Cause you did nothin. That's real tight that is.'

'But if you made him fall, why didn't *you* call them?'

He looks at me with a new disgust, like I've just said something obscene.

'I didn't do ih,' he goes, 'I didn't do it. He fell himself or the others knocked the yoke by accident, but he fell. We were just messin. He fell sir and *you* did nothing. Why didn't ye do nothing?'

'I wasn't there.'

'And then I was thinking, why wouldn't a teacher call the cops or nothing and then I though you mustn'ta wanted the cops to come.' He stops and dwells on the sentence, looks beyond me, his voice hushed and goes, 'That's *mad*.' He smiles, still impressed with the scale of his discovery and all it brings. 'You musta done somethin on him or he musta wrecked your head sir if you never even called the cops or the ambulance – you never called no one. An then no cops come for us for days and you didn't help him. I was freaked sir, freaked so I was, but I never said nothin to the lads or nothin cause I know they'd go mad if they knew I saw ye an never said. But then I thought you were a beast sir – a beast. Tight for letting him die but—'

'I didn't let him die.'

'But ye didn't help him.'

'I did help him.'

'No ye didn't sir,' he says, smiling and shaking his head as he goes, amused at my insistence. 'I was there sir, around there an you weren't there an ye didn't squeal sir cause yer hidin something,' he smirks. 'Yer hidin something.'

'Get out,' I say, real relaxed voice, my collar soaked, my jaw shaking, but my demeanour cool, like he's talking nonsense.

He doesn't budge.

'And then he has that laptop of yours an all sir.' He lets a breath of disbelief out, his eyes widen like he's shocked, 'An he has songs on ih

– like a folder with music on ih called *Songs for Mr Lynch*. No beats for us, but songs for you.' He shakes his head. I swallow. Take a deep breath.

The scrape back and snap forward of the hoover is metres from the door. You can hear the cleaner on her earpiece to someone in Europe, shouting over the hum.

'That's mad sir. Was he writin ye love songs?'

I make to get up; he flinches. Finally, the real Andrew. He springs back, knocks his seat over and eyes on me, wary of me, inches sideways to the door. I stay seated. I won't catch him.

'What were yis doin sir? Somethin mad that ye want hiding anyways – an me da says yer doin great now cause he's dead with the awards an all from the town. Ye must be rich from ih. That's tight sir.'

'Get out.'

'Why'd he have yer computer sir? He told us he had no computer an he has yours all along.'

The songs. *Songs for Mr Lynch*. Wonder if they're finished. Wonder how good they are. Wonder what Andrew can do, could do, would do.

'Could be anyone's computer.'

'He dropped it sir when he was runnin from ye. I got ih when we were runnin after him. He was leggin it away from ye. And ye always have ih with ye.' He motions to the old laptop.

The hoover knocks against the radiator outside making a scaffold rattle.

'I have ih now,' he says and opens the door, letting the high end of the hum rush in. The hoover is right outside, the pull back, the snap forward, the foreign conversation. I give in.

'I want the computer Andrew.'

He smiles, looking to the cleaner and back to me.

'I'll give ye yer computer sir – but it'll cost ye.'

I scoff at him, make it seem like what he's asking for is ridiculous.

'Get a grip. You pushed him – you and yer mates. And you want money from me?'

He clenches his teeth, real serious and goes, 'I didn't push him. He fell. You're the one didn't do nothin. I saw ye – if I tell the lads about ye they'll want more money – the three of us weren't there – three of us against one.' He holds out three fingers. 'Three versus one. You were there sir. He had your computer, you were chasin him – he was leggin it away from *you* sir. I'll tell the lads you were there, I'll tell . . .'

'The others don't know?'

'Course they don't. Think I'd be here on me own if they did?'

He laughs to himself, settles his jacket on his chest, his tongue back on his bottom lip, the sniffle. 'I want money,' he goes.

'For what?' I say, my voice rising over the hoover outside the room. 'The laptop or for you to stay quiet?'

The cleaner shouts down her phone.

'I thought you weren't there sir,' he says, big delighted smile on his face.

'For what Andrew?'

'Both of them,' he whispers, barely audible.

The cleaner pops her head round the door, past Andrew.

'Okay if I go?' she says with a nod to the room.

Andrew smiles at her. She smiles back. I smile at them both.

'I'll be back in a few days,' he says and leans against the door, a new seriousness in his eyes, and goes, 'this is a joke. If he'd just givin us what we wanted none of this—'

'What did yis want?'

His eyes go wide like he's baffled by his own answer, 'Nothing, just some stupid beats.'

He's gone and she's crouched over the hoover, the noise of the thing swirling around the room. I put my head in my hands, cover my face and close my eyes. I'm swamped by the noise as it grows louder and louder until I'm groaning into my palms, groaning, just letting this noise out cause my head is in bits, my whole body is shaking, sweating.

While she clinks and clatters the steel legs of the tables and chairs I exhale through my fingers and wish I hadn't done what I had done. I wish I had stayed in the school and let him run. I wish I hadn't gone back to the studio. I wish all of this was over.

She's down the back of the room, facing away from me, crouching forward and back when I give the hoover an almighty boot. Dust explodes everywhere in a thick dirty cloud. It cuts off. The whine whirls downs into a wheeze and she's turned to me with a 'kulva,' and I'm pretending I only knocked into it on my way to my press. The plastic on the side is all cracked and broken and the dust is settling and she's saying 'kulva' this and 'kulva' that and I'm burying my face in my press and she's all angry doing all these hand gestures and I turn to her and she points at the hoover and hurries out of the room, the thing clattering after her.

'I'm sorry,' I call, but she's not listening and I put my head in my hands and try and deal with what just happened. The mess I've made.

★

The sea is a pane of glass you could walk all the way to England over. Just keep on walking and you're in a new world. New life. Imagine that, nothing needed only steps, the power of your legs. When the tide's out like today, totally out, past the lighthouse at the corner of the harbour, the trawlers have to wait under the horizon, surrounded by seagulls, until the tide rises and they can come back in. They wait patiently now.

Lauren's beside me on the bench, and after looking out on the boats, she turns and asks, 'Well, what you think?'

I shrug and go, 'Sounds great, really great. Fair play to you.'

Don't know what else to say. The truth?

'Do ye think himself will be angry?' Himself is the boss. The principal.

'Probably. But to hell with him. He deserves it.'

She laughs nervously. I do a fake chuckle. Don't feel like laughing.

'Good enough for him,' I finish and she breathes through her nose, lost in her thoughts. Still the boats, three in all, wait patiently for the tide, like they're parked, dead still, on the flat sea. She turns back to the beach, the blue sky, the wet sand, checks her watch and sighs. Her hand is on her lap. Mine rests on the worn wood of the bench beside her leg. Don't dare try and touch her.

'I've only got my head around doing the interview and they want me to be there by May. I mean, it's all very sudden. I've never lived in another country before.'

'Less time to think about it. Believe me, if ye think about things like this it'll drive ye crazy.'

'Suppose,' she goes and we both continue to look out past the lighthouse.

I try and cheer her, tell her a job in England is better than no job in Ireland. But she's having none of it. She pats me on the leg and talks about being too old for going over on her own.

'Wait til yer twenty-eight,' I say and she looks at me and realises she forgot my birthday. She puts her arms out and hugs me. Her sweet smell covers me, but it's a nothing hug, a waste of an embrace. She asks if I went out with lads and I use this as the time to tell her I'm no longer in the band.

She takes my hand and tries to console me. But I shrug it away, pretend I saw it coming. 'If I'm honest,' I say, 'it wasn't working for a while. She didn't understand where I was coming from.'

'She?' Lauren goes. I tut and smack my forehead, pretend I'm losing it. She asks if Mono might have second thoughts and I think about all the voicemails, his mouth roaring in my letterbox, the demands I pay for his gear and then tell her no, there's no chance.

It occurs to me then, while I spy the unblemished smoothness of the face I touched, kissed only months ago, that I could go with her. But I don't say anything. I realise the thought should, as we speak, occur to her too. So I wait for her to realise it, say it. I'm in no position to say anything. I'm the one who blew it – or didn't blow it – in February. She has to realise it as well, and if she does, the amount of time it takes her to suggest a move will indicate how serious she either is about me, or how serious that offer is. I wait.

The seagulls swooping over the trawlers, disappearing behind the lighthouse and the harbour walls; the trawlers still and patient; the horizon again, the smooth, levelled-off escape route from the town. From Andrew. From the truth.

I'm frozen by fear. Fear of what? I dunno, failure. I haven't been able to reach across the divide and try for a kiss. A connection. I remember the kiss though. Wonder if she does. I remember after the kiss too. I remember the scaffold. The cold, cold concrete. Paralysis.

'I'll miss the place,' she says.

'Really?' I say, a little laugh coming out with the words. 'What's there to miss?'

Her voice goes on about our friendship and the 'girls' in work, but I'm answering my own question. Nothing. There's nothing to miss.

'Hello,' she calls, 'what's wrong? You're not here. You're so quiet. There's something on your mind. If you wanna talk about something, just say it.'

Okay, I wanna talk about life, us, the possibility of us. How comfortable I feel in your company, how anything is open for discussion when you're around. How we listen to each other, laugh with each other, have supported each other. We could talk about my failure to rise to the occasion – a once-off – and my determination – no, my absolute insistence that it will never happen again if you give me another chance. Just one more chance. And Andrew of course. The pathetic situation of being held to ransom by a teenager. I need advice.

'Rob?' she goes, 'what is it?'

I shrug and go, 'Nothing. What do you want to talk about?' and secretly deflate.

She sits back down and from nowhere says, 'You could always come to London, start a new band – "Robert and the Rebels"', and she laughs in such a way I don't know whether she's making fun of me or making light of the thought of me fronting a band.

'That'd be something – me fronting a band alright.'

She bites the inside of her cheek, 'And it wouldn't be something coming to London?'

I just chuckle and go, 'It's an idea alright, isn't it?' and this big wedge of awkwardness arrives between us.

'But sure,' she continues, as if the silence was never there, 'you can't leave now – not in your finest hour.'

I look at her like I don't know what she's going on about.

'That ceremony thing, you know, the Town Council thing that's on in the gym in a few weeks. Everyone knows it's to honour you.'

I laugh her off, 'Gettaway outta that.'

She stares at me like I'm mad.

'C'mon Rob – everyone knows the Town Council's pushing this thing. They're saying you got Isabel and her mother's deportation overturned. They need the publicity.'

I flap away her glare.

'That's ridiculous,' I go, 'I didn't do anything. That politician did. Sure they can't use the gym without the principal's say so and he's not into that kinda publicity for the school. He told me. This is the last thing he wants.'

'I know,' Lauren goes, 'everyone knows. But he hasn't much of a choice. That's why you're gonna be the one the Town Council honours – not him, or the politician. It's good for the school name to be honoured and the principal's not seen to be involved with the politics. He wins both ways.'

'But I wasn't involved either.'

'If you were at the rally, you were involved. If you spoke at it, you were definitely involved.'

I pretend I'm not having a bar of it, but secretly let the implications dawn. She starts up about what they're saying in the staffroom about my speech on the square and the protest and all the publicity for the school in the local papers with pictures of the principal and his rallying call quote of, 'That's what can happen when a community comes together.'

Lauren gets so animated the more she talks about the principal's 'No Irish – No admission' policy and his attitude to Isabel's return, London doesn't come up again. Her leaving drinks do though. But sure, we just talk about who'd be up for it and where would be good to go. I'm not in her thoughts anymore. I pretend to listen but slowly resign myself to the fact that the invite will never come. She's gone cool since February. Things have changed. Something's changed. I just can't put my finger on it. Just can't get to grips with her. Anything.

'You'll come won't you?' she says, squeezing my arm.

'Where?'

'Where do you think,' she says, 'my leaving drinks. You'll come won't you?'

'Course,' I say and see the trawlers move, 'course. Wouldn't miss it for the world.' and I'm about to mention Andrew when she starts up about London and if it's a good place to live, and if a town hero like me would visit her. I don't say anything. It'd only upset her to hear the truth.

★

I've got, what, six black sacks full of clothes, bulging and ripping at the sides from being nicked off the edges of things. Three cardboard boxes held together with sellotape are full with DVDs, books, frames, cracked CD cases, sticky CDs. Just things you pick up over the years. Bits and pieces. I am twenty-eight. Six black sacks, three cardboard boxes, a bag full of leads, three keyboard soft cases and a sampler. I am retreating from the *big shmoke* to my ma and da's with my tail between my legs.

The couch still stinks. But I don't care. The green velvet has turned all shiny in parts from wear anyway. Some stains, hot-rocks, mark it too. But sure they'll be throwing it out. We should still get our deposit back though. Four hundred and fifty quid each. It's not loads, but not to be sneezed at either. I could use it for any number of things. Could stay in town, rent a room from some strangers, become friends with them. Weirder things have happened. Or I could just use the deposit to pay Andrew. Wonder if his da knows anything. Doubt it. The Droog. The new crew.

Before he arrived in the room there was this anxiety, this need to steer clear of all reminders of what happened that night. But since he's come in there's been a turnaround. His arrival has brought on a sense of responsibility, in some weird way, as if everything's my fault. I'm deflated, yeah, but weirdly resigned to the fact that something is going to happen. Feel sick about it, like in my gut, deep down. Scared. Things never happen. I am where I am and there is nothing I can do only deal with it and see what rolls out. It's a simple equation. Andrew saw me. Andrew knows the truth. The truth can be hidden if I pay him money. My role – responsibility can be shirked. It's so easy. No one need know. That's the main thing. Money equals silence. Silence equals normality. The only kick in the nuts about the whole thing is the songs on the Mac. I'm gutted. Absolutely gutted about this. Delighted I'll get to hear them, but gutted I won't be able to ram them down Mono's throat. That's the thing that really kills me. The fact I can't use them. The fact all this was for nothing. But then I get to thinking that maybe their gig in front of your man Kele will be a disaster. Maybe they'll fall flat on their faces and Steve, Derek and the drummer will come running to me having realised I am the Terrors. At least an integral part. They can't do it without me. 'Lads,' I'll say, 'I'm sorry about the gear – but look – I've got three banging new tunes – new beats – we're back.' Everything will work out.

Four hundred and fifty euro for the deposit would be a lot of cash for a sixteen-year-old. Five hundred euro. Give him five hundred euro to be on the safe side. Get the computer back, transfer the songs onto a USB key, then delete them. No proof. I'd be in the clear regardless of what he says. My life can go on as normal. Normality. That's what I've been anxious about. I've been mad for some sense of normality. Certainty. This will bring everything back down to earth. Five hundred quid will sort it out. That'll be me in the clear. Free of all this nonsense. All this conscience lark, the secrets and the dodging, the reminders, the looking at empty seats and freezing up. Put an end to all the regret, running away from things, running away to London. Thoughts of Lauren will end. She's not interested. Why would she be? London is an excuse. Kembo is an excuse. An excuse for failure. I can start again.

Because people do, start again. The Terrors are. They're still playing that gig. Must've got a lend of gear. Someone must've helped them cause that's what people do I suppose. Help each other out.

John didn't help the Droogs out though. Kept the beats to himself. Bad advice. The lengths people will go for a product. The rising costs and desperation for things not easily got. Black sacks and cardboard boxes. That's all I have. They're lying waiting for me to shift them. I'm in no rush. I've got a week and a bit left. So they sit inside the hall door in the shadows. Sometimes they're lit up by the sun coming past the railings outside the window and through the table and chairs. The dust is thick when the sun's rays warm them. Six black sacks, three boxes and my keyboard soft cases: the artefacts of a life; just like the luminous gloves traded for beats I told him to withhold are the artefacts of his.

May.

The crowd are like this season's shop window for BT2 and Topshop. I am not cool enough to be at this gig. If the lads weren't in the band, they wouldn't be cool enough to be at this gig either. Me and Lauren don't belong in this crowd, amongst these people. We're probably too drunk for them as well. They look at us with snarls, kinda Elvis 'uh-huhs', like we're the un-cool run-over that's to be expected when mainstream blogs and forums pick up an underground event and inform the uninformed. Cause that's what we look like to them: the uninformed. But I know these magpies of cool will just as easily dive in, take what they can and become vultures when this weird thing called the 'zeitgeist' spits the Terrors out.

'The others,' Lauren hiccups, 'did they not, did they not follow us up?'

I shake my head, lean in, cause Steve is giving the bass a fair few whacks to get the feedback going and create some sort of buzz.

'No,' I shout, 'they're not into this. I said we'd be back down to them in an hour.'

'So we're on our own?'

I nod and tell her it's just for a while and she says that's cool with her and she joins in with the crowd in front of us going, 'Whoo!'

We throw back our drink and Lauren insists she get the next round. By the time she comes back they've finished the third song. She hands me the glass of vodka and Red Bull and goes, 'Well, what you think?'

'It's weird – they're still missing the keyboards.'

No music's playing cause they're tuning up. Normally I'd be doing some sounds to cover up the silence. But there's a hum from the crowd like they're getting warmed up, getting into it. I wince.

'What kinda keyboards?' she says, her eyes looking tired all of a sudden.

I miss the question.

'Rob, earth to Rob, what keyboards?'

'Eh, just different things, like organ for the last song.'

She looks at me with this face.

'Organ?'

'Yeah, at the start like, chords with loadsa fuzz on them.'

She's about to say something but the drummer pounds in with a beat, whacks away, and the sound is so good, the drums so clear it's surreal and amazing and wrong. I've never heard us from out front over a PA before. They all crash in together and again, there's nothing to replace where I'd do an arpp. They need me. I'm missing, they must feel it.

'Ye see, there, there's where I'd do an arpp.'

'A what?' she shouts back, a hint of impatience lingering on the 't'.

'An arpp. Arp-pegg-iat-or.'

She shakes her head, makes a face and shrugs and turns her chin up to the stage. The music sounds good, but not as good as it could. We're too far back. Too far back to hear it as it would be on the stage. In rehearsals.

'It's not right,' I say, 'c'mon, a bit closer.'

She protests that it's too tight, but I convince her and we move sideways, find a gap and manoeuvre a few people out of the way and get nearer the front. We come out from under the shadow of the balcony and I look up into the shapes to see if I can see Kele or Barry or the other A&R lads who are meant to be 'fighting it out'. Flashes from the stage, brief flickers of strobe, highlight the bodies arched over the balcony barrier. Barry's there. I look back to the stage, get blinded by the strobe, shake it off, take a slug of the drink and turn back to the balcony and beside Barry I see John – Kembo – in his school uniform, smiling, lit briefly and whispering, conspiring with him.

The song ends and the whole venue erupts into a mad roar and applause before the lights go out into a deep depressing black.

'You okay?' Lauren goes.

'Yeah, yeah,' I say, 'course, I'm cool.'

'You sure? You're acting weird,' she says. 'Maybe we shouldn't have come. The others will be lookin for us.'

'No, no – I just thought I saw someone – doesn't matter. C'mon we'll stay for another few songs – I'm not getting them.'

'Getting what?' she says, her nose knocking off my cheek.

'Getting *them*, I dunno, I thought, I thought I'd recognise them. Feel something.'

'I don't,' she hiccups, 'get ye.'

'I dunno. They're our songs, but it's not the Terrors. There's something different. I dunno. I'm drunk,' I say and we do a cheers and down the rest of our vodka.

Another wave of sound slams over us and again I take Lauren's hand and we struggle forward, things getting a lot tighter the closer to the front we get. We're only about four deep away from the stage. It's loud. Really loud. But not as loud as rehearsals or on stage, like when you're in the thick of things, in the middle of it. Part of it. The thing itself.

A few songs pass. The crowd dip into hushed impatience after the initial rush of the opening. Two folk songs fall flat, new ones I don't know, and at one point, when Lauren's gone to the bar again, I hear someone yawn behind me and in one of those tender moments when everything drops out and it's just Mono's soft acoustic strum and Derek's whispered lyric, someone laughs. I can't help but smile. A big, cheek-bulging smile. Lauren gets back and we stay where we are, four away from the front. I still feel unfulfilled, cold though. It's like the answers I hoped to get, the quiet satisfaction of seeing them realise, once and for all, that they're nothing without me, is refusing to show. Their faces are blank. I dunno. I dunno what I was expecting, hoping for really. But whatever it is, bar the satisfaction of seeing the two new folk songs bore the place, there's nothing at all to cheer me.

Lauren's in my ear again, her nose, her hand on my arm, telling me she's still apprehensive, 'Worried,' she says, about London. Another song finishes, and the dry ice is gushing out with its low hiss all over us, and she's going, 'I met a few of them in the staffroom when I went over and they said it's great craic and they go out every week and all – but it's probably to some pub, some boring pub for all this lager lark, you know?' and I'm nodding, sympathetically, whispering, 'I know, I know,' before she goes, 'but I don't want that. You know Rob? I want this.'

'What?' I say, the low murmur of the crowd covering us.

'This,' she goes, her eyes closed and she nestles into me, her forehead between my chin and shoulder, her arm linking my arm.

'This?' I'm saying, about to launch into a spectacular speech about us and my problem with Andrew when Kembo's beat explodes through the speakers, warps the whole vibe and I'm looking up to see

293

Steve's face lit by his laptop screen and then he's turning from it and settling his new bass on his shoulders. The sample kicks in, the repetitive little riff, and Lauren's head is gone from my shoulder, her arms in the air and I'm stumbling past some random punters, pushing them out of the way, and they're all grooving, really getting into it, everyone's moving, and I'm at the front, fuming, sick and freaked, Derek's feet about my shoulder height, and there's this mad blinding orange light coming up behind him, like a ball of flames or something, and it's so bright everyone on stage is just black blurs and the drummer's kicking in over the beat and Mono's slamming in on the electric guitar and Steve's shaking the whole place with his bass line and I'm within reach of the mic stand, so close I can grab it, pull the thing from under Derek and ruin the song, ruin everything. I'm looking around at the heads all dipping and bobbing to the tune, my tune, my one breakthrough they've stolen from me that could've changed my life. I turn to the crowd, look on them as if I'm on stage too; only no one's looking at me, they're all looking up, their faces raised to the silhouettes and the orange light, smiling, really getting into the beats, the song, the band. They don't care about me, the smiling, bobbing fools. They only have eyes for the band, and ears for that song. The song they robbed from me. They robbed that from me, I feel like shouting at them all, they robbed that from me. But I robbed it from John. They've done more with it than I did with John's original; Derek's lyrics and melody, floating over the beats and the sample are quality. I turn back to the stage. See them play on, see Mono see me and play on, put more effort, more vigour or something into his playing when he sees me. He stares through all the flashing and the noise, the smoke and the movement, stares at me like as soon as the song's over he's gonna hop off the stage and batter me. So I stay away from the stage. Keep clear of him. The song pounds on, the second chorus and Lauren's beside me roaring, 'Whoo – it's amazing!' caught up in the buzz and I'm gonna roar back, 'Yeah, though it's still missing something, doesn't sound the same,' but don't bother. I know what's missing. Me. I'm not there. She doesn't care. No one does. I'm not part of the song anymore, my ambition doesn't drive them anymore. Their four collected ambitions now do. Their ambition is the song, all of the songs, and regardless of what I've done, what I could do, their ambition has outgrown mine, destroyed mine and become this thing that's swallowed me up and spat me out into the crowd. I am a spectator along with everyone else at the realisation of something. I am no longer part of the dream. That's why it sounds different. They're no longer my band, no longer my future. I can see the beauty of what I'm going to miss out on and it's devastating.

Everyone starts to pogo all around me – even Lauren does it – and I'm just standing there like a statue while the whole place goes in waves, up and down, up and down. With every nudge from someone jumping, I feel the dream I had of making it big with the Terror's finally dissolve.

From nowhere a big shove takes me off-guard and I'm knocked forward. I take Lauren with me and manage to push off the stage with one quick heave and just as I rebound off the thing a leg from on high flashes – Mono – and I instinctively duck and in the chaos of the noise and the pogoing hear a scream. Lauren's standing still, her eyes wide, looking at her blood-covered hands and her nose is busted. Still the crowd swamp, mindless, and she must kinda faint cause she disappears just as I take her wet hand and some of the dopes from work appear and collect Lauren under the arms and pull her out of the mess. I look up to the balcony to see if anyone saw the incident but Barry and Kele – and I think I spot Andrew – are smiling down on the stage, smug, content, ignorant of the crowd, oblivious to me.

All the concerned faces have Lauren in the back of a taxi when I get out and two of the girls from work get in with her and go, 'We're taking her home. Don't worry, it looks a lot worse than it is.' I can hear her kind of moaning, crying into her red tissue and her head's shaking and I try to get to her in the back seat, say something, but one of the lads stops me and goes, 'You've done enough damage Rob.' The taxi takes off and I don't bother arguing with him saying, 'I didn't do it,' because it was, in so many ways, me that did it. It wasn't me that kicked her, but I caused it. It wasn't me who shook the scaffold, but I might as well have forced him up there.

I walk away from the teachers and my mind goes back to the venue, to the bar, to the front of the stage, to the balcony, to the ghost estate, to the football pitch, to the classroom, to the beats. Everything is beginning to settle as I walk, the brief silences between the taxis and the screams and the queues and the sirens providing revelations.

What wasn't mine to give away has been taken from me and used anyway. After all my effort and ambition all I've got left are blood-stained hands, and lies.

★

The Mac's on the table between us, no longer white, just all scraped and dirty. Andrew's sitting down right in front of me – like I'd hoped he would – with this big satisfied grin. Mumbles, bursts of laughter, whispered conversations and shadows breeze past the blinds on their way to the gym for that big ceremony thing to mark John's going, Isabel's return. The principal called in the other day to make sure I'd attend.

'Course, yeah,' I'd said. He'd nodded, his lips stretched over his bottom teeth, and said, 'Good, good. After all of this nonsense we might have a sit-down? Discuss your options for next year. If things are tight here regarding pupil numbers I might be able to arrange something for you somewhere else.' He'd patted my shoulder and before I could reply, moved off, hands in his pockets, no sweat patches on the blue shirt.

I wait. Wait til everything has settled and the shadows have stopped going by and the laughter, boisterous stuff, inappropriate for the tone of the afternoon, is gone down the corridor. I look over the room, the twenty-four feet by twenty-eight feet, the posters, the pictures, the tables; size up my cage, take a good look at it, Sky plus it and then rest my eyes on Andrew. His hand is spread out on the top of the Mac doing a Mexican wave of filthy fingers, a slow drum, across the thing. His smile is gone and there's a tense, tight look on his face.

'Where's the plug?' I say once the laughter has disappeared.

He shakes his head, 'There isn't a plug.'

'So how do I know it's mine?'

'Cause it's charged.'

'Well, then, how'd you charge it?'

His eyebrows rise, 'Cause I bought a plug for it when the battery went.' He opens the computer and it hums and the screen flicks on and a password is required to go any further.

'I couldn't get near the songs,' he says and sniffles, 'cause after the battery went this came up.'

'And I suppose you want them now.'

He pushes a breath out.

'Droogz Boyz are finished. Couldn't be bothered. I just want cash.'

What a waste.

I take out the five hundred euro, all in fifties, and place it on the table. His eyes flick to my hand, his lips twitching, betraying the calm air he's trying so hard to portray.

'How much?' he says, sniffles like he does this kind of thing every day.

'Five hundred euro,' I say, real slow, to let the words wash over him.

His head nods, his lips dip.

'Cool,' he says, 'but I want more.'

I don't flinch. Do a sniffle myself, lean forward like I'm a poker player gonna show my hand and motion for the computer.

'Let me see the songs first.'

'Gimme the five hundred.'

I push the wad of notes towards him and he pushes the opened Mac over to me; it sticks cause of the rubber holders underneath and he has to lift it a bit. We stay seated, him counting the money, me typing the password, double clicking on the folder, looking at three songs, named song 1, song 2, song 3, and taking out my USB key and inserting it into the side of the thing. He stops counting and starts watching.

'Wha ye doin?'

'I need this,' I say, all innocent.

The three songs transfer easily into my USB with a triple ping, ping, ping, dead notes, nothing like the three from the school bell. I drag the folder to the trash can and throw it into the icon and there's a loud crunch, like paper being binned and I clear the trash can and erase all proof.

'What's that noise?' he goes, arching his neck, trying to see around the screen.

'Nothing,' I say and close over the laptop, put the USB in my pocket.

Andrew leans forward, fixes his hood, cranes his neck, sniffles, the teeth, the stud earring, the greasy wedged high spikes, the thin little upturned rat nose, the smirk of success.

'I want more.'

'Do ye now. And why should I give ye more?' I say, a croak in my throat, trying to sound normal.

'Cause yer a bitch – like Kembo.'

He laughs at me. This sixteen-year-old mess laughs in my face and goes, 'Ye don't have much of a choice, our.'

I reef the laptop up with both hands and in one swift action, so fast he doesn't have time to protect himself, lurch across the table and – boom – smash the white plastic into the side of his head. He's knocked off guard, forced from the chair, his neck whipping to the side with the crack and snap of the laptop and he falls like a boxer in one of those films, out cold, feet together. He lands with a damp thump, his jacket rustling while his limp body settles in the gap between the chairs and the tables behind him in the second row.

I look at the laptop like it's just appeared in my hand. There's a big nasty crack through the whole thing and it's hanging loose, split through the logo. I drop it to the table and it cracks again. I walk around to him and stand looking down on his closed eyes, his open mouth, his chest rising ever so slightly and dipping just as easily. I root for the five hundred euro in his tracksuit bottoms, get it and turn away, my legs light, my breathing quick. Leave him be, out cold on the carpet.

All of the fifties in one bunch make a fairly thick wad of cash. I open the door to my room and feel the weight of them bunched and folded together. I feel the dimensions and consider what the cash could've bought me – got me. Think for a second about whether or not I was right to take it back. How easily it got me the songs, useless as they are. It would've got me a silence of sorts for a while too. But that would've just been a fraud silence. An unreliable silence. A cheap silence. It couldn't have gone anyway near buying me a proper piece of mind, a real lasting silence, the type of silence that means you can listen to music again without wondering if you'll be caught, a kind of silence that will let you walk down the street and see a black face and not worry it's him come back to remind you what you did, and didn't do. But what I didn't do was kill him. That's the sort of silence I need, a silence that lets me forget this year and look around and start again, start on something new without the worry of being rumbled over something old.

I step out of the room. The principal's voice wafts like dry ice or something past my door from the PA in the gym, 'We want the best for every student,' faint words, 'regardless of their ethnic background or history.'

Applause rises like a heavy rain shower on the window beside the lockers. 'Thank you – thank you,' and the rain eases and the principal's voice starts up again about 'inclusion', and I look into the room one last time, like a criminal might look back into his cell before he makes his escape. I close the door over softly knowing where I'm going now will mean I'll never come back.

*

It's like a dream, or an out of body experience when the whole gym turns to me. Seats screech off the tiles and necks crane to take me in. I wait at the back of the hall for the echo from the mayor's words to fade and his last line to finish with, 'And for that reason, we'd like to present Mr Robert Lynch with this token on behalf of the town to show our appreciation for all he has done for our community.'

There's at least two hundred faces hushed and expectant watching me compose myself and move toward the stage. Ahead, above the figures on stage, there's a big sign saying: 'St Michael's College – Everyone Together,' and a huge, massive picture of a smiling John projected onto a taut white drape. There's a podium with the school crest on the stage too. The principal's there, standing rigid beside the mayor, who's beside another medallion wearer, who's standing beside the re-elected TD I got Isabel's number for. I flatten my jumper down and take the slow steps toward the stage and away from Andrew out cold on my carpet. A baby begins to cry in the distance. Maybe fifty, sixty metres ahead up on the stage these big, lonely, hollow hand-claps begin. The mayor starts off the slow beat like I'm a long jumper coming down the track at the Olympics and the TD follows suit and all of a sudden it spreads from the stage back, like a wildfire or something, and I stop walking, my breath taken away and at the front row, nearest the stage, a black figure stands up, and then seats are shifted and screeching mixes with the clapping and slowly, from the front again, people begin to stand up, big solemn heads on them, and for some reason – I dunno – maybe it's because they have a huge picture of him on the back wall behind them – like an icon, or a hero – I think of a time a few months ago when he's tapping a rolled-up piece of A3 paper on a desk.

He's slumped on the seat, chinning his scarf and I'm saying something like, 'Please John – enough – I'm trying to concentrate,' and he's saying, 'But I'm like, like I'm really excited sir,' and I'm looking up from some stupid copy going, 'I-don't-care,' and he's shrugging, tapping away saying, 'But I've gotta concert tonight cause I actually got baptised on Friday an I like – we're – there's a celebration an stuff in Blanch.'

I must stop correcting, peer at him with some sort of interest cause he's going on, 'It's like, technically, the law is, well not our law, it's written, it's written in the bible when someone gets baptised, the first act, well because we come to church . . .'

My hands are out and I'm waving at him, 'Eh, hello – John – zip it – I'm busy,' but he's leaning back on his chair, arms behind his head and he's saying, shrugging at me, 'I'm, this is detention sir – you – you can't,' there's a hesitation, 'you can't stop me bein excited bout getting baptised. We come to the church yeah, an the pastor will lecture us on what's gonna happen and w-wha-what to expect and if we're sure bout what we're doin, yeah?' he nods to me, makes sure I'm paying attention and I'm yawning going, 'I'm busy John – but I'm listening, even if I'm not looking I'm listening, okay, now knock yourself out,' and he's smiling at his little success as he slumps back again and starts saying, 'The pastor w-will make sure we're sure about what we're doin, yeah? And if we're ready to let everything go of this world and carry on with god's stuff an after tha w-we go to the water, yeah?' I'm putting my red pen down and sighing and going, 'John – enough with the "yeahs". I'm listening – even if I'm not looking I'm listening cause I'm correcting – but I'm listening, okay?'

'Mmhh-mmhh,' he's mumbling and continuing, 'so, we like go to the water – em, we went to the beach in town – this beach on the out-skirts of town – an the pastor goes in the water an stands like waiting, stands in ih, prays for ih, like, prays for the water for what we're about to do, an then a person goes in there an – an gets baptised an an ev-everyone has different reaction.'

'Okay,' I'm saying, eyes on the copy, 'I get it – you went in the water – well done. You got wet and now you're very religious and havin a party with god in Blanchardstown, well done.'

'No sir,' he's saying, hurt in his voice, 'it's crazy, ih-ih-it's hard cause like, everyone has different reaction. Like once when we were getting baptised, I-I-I went in there last cause I didn't wanna freeze so badly. I stayed out til last.'

'Very brave of you.'

'Cause I-I can't swim an I h-hate the water an then this friend of mine went in, came out, nothing happens, yeah?'

'John.'

'B-but then this woman went in, when they brought her up she went jumpin round going crazy and cryin an like I was like, "What's goin on here?" and they were like "Oh, she received the holy spirit."'

I'm closing the copy, studying his face, checking to see if he's genuine and he's smiling that big Cheshire Cat smile cause he knows I'm interested and he's going on, 'She was like in her twenties and I was like, "This is gonna be bad," and some people, like teenagers an old people are up – up now like on the path stopping an watching an stuff an I'm just standing there an this other – another girl who goes up to my church, yeah, she went in there and when they brought her out she couldn't stand up,' he's giggling at the memory, 'it was so funny,' he's giddy with the telling, 'she stood up and then she fell down like her legs couldn't like – like her legs wasn't functioning,' his eyes are wide, 'she couldn't stand up – an eh, it had to take two pastors to pull her outta the water cause she couldn't stand up,' and I'm smiling with him, a reluctant laugh escaping and he's saying, 'an then this other woman went in – there's like loads people watchin now an kids, teenagers are shoutin an stuff an some are like, some are throwin stones an stuff in the water an this other woman went in just like started goin crazy, fallin all over the place an talking in tongues an everyone behind us was like laughin an I hate the water. It was crazy sir.' His hands drop to his lap like he's spent. Finished.

'And?' I'm saying, my hands now opened to him, 'what happened you?'

'Oh,' he's smiling, like he forgot, 'when – when I first went in like, to my feet, it was cold sir an your clothes an stuff stick to you an I-I had to go up to my – up to here,' he's bringing a flat hand to his waist, 'an little stones are droppin in the water an kids an stuff are like shoutin an I thought I was gonna freeze so badly and the worst part of ih – yeah – was wh-when they goh my head, an stones are fallin in the water from the teenagers, an I-I-I was scared I was gonna die an I remembered y-you said something like for football about a game we had like, "Five minutes of pain for a lifetime o-of something."'

'Glory,' I'm whispering, embarrassed, surprised, remembering the nonsense I spoke to them for some team talk.

He's smiling, 'Yeah – glory   glory, that's ih, an my head went down in the water, an, an I-I thought I would die cause I like swallowed loadsa water or a stone would hit me, but nothing happens and I came out to glory – j-just like you said – cause you sir – you are always true – an I know, like, to believe you. Nothing happened. J-just glory.' He's drumming on the table, looking somewhere beyond me, 'Ih was greah sir.'

His picture looms over me. The closer I get to the stage the harder it seems to make it there. It's like I'm trying to plough through water and all the happy faces, standing and nodding to me, clapping for me, don't seem to notice. I look up to see the principal's big forced grin and his blank eyes. Trying to look as if he approves. Still the thunderous applause echoes around the gym, next foot up and the water's at my waist and I'm on stage, a big bright light shining on me, blinding me, reminding me of my classroom and there's a flurry of handshakes and ridiculous whispers of 'congratulations' and 'well done son' warming my ear like they're all desperate to have some sort of positive focus, hero, someone to smile about, be happy about. The mayor hands me over this cut glass statue of a boy sitting on a rock reading. It's heavy and there's a cheer – a cheer – from the audience either because they think I've won something or it's a trophy that needs to be celebrated.

The principal pats my shoulder and poses for a stiff photo before the mayor puts out his hand to show me to the microphone with the big afro head on it. I wade over, the massive bright light from the back of the gym making me squint, and with shaking hands, take out a crumpled piece of paper. The claps die out to one or two delayed slaps, all seats screech again as people sit back down, my paper folding is amplified over the speakers, sniffles in front, a cough or two, someone sneezes, a baby coos and I go, 'Ahem,' clear my throat, hear the voice echo around the four walls, out into the corridor and see it float past my blinds, sneak into my room and caress the ears of Andrew.

I fill my lungs and feel that fear John musta been talking about, know when I go under this water, hold my breath and say what needs to be said, everything, absolutely everything will be changed when I resurface.

'Good afternoon everybody,' I say and I'm under and the echoes are muted and the sniffles are muted and the glare is dimmed, everything is submerged and distant and surreal and I realise then how easy it would be to say a simple thank you and emerge washed in this water of admiration and back-slapping and joviality and all that lark.

★

If I drop off between stations – miss a few stops – I sometimes panic, but a quick glance above the door between carriages tells me where I'm heading in smooth left-moving red pixels. At Tara Street young lads are always caught trying to dodge the fare, but sure, you can't get away with that anymore. Things, life has become more certain around them. The small percentages of chance you might've had years ago of getting a free ride on a train have long since been eaten into by the onset of now. The certainty of the future. Years ago you could have slipped in between or manoeuvred around steel tripod barriers, or hopped them. But not now. Now there is no wonder, no room for manoeuvre. For imagination. For hope. Even the bus stops on the quays no longer leave things to chance. They have a timetable system in action on yellow pixels zipping across a board above the shelter. The traffic lights on College Green don't leave anything to chance either. They count down for you from twenty so you know when the green man is going to appear. A massive screen above the entrance to Stephen's Green Shopping Centre tells you what's happening in the city, throws out thousands of mixed colours to inform you what you need to be seeing, where you need to be going. People don't have time, or energy to be hoping they'll come across something that might suit them because life doesn't afford such luxuries anymore. They need certainty. Then there's the orange beacons beside the Luas stop constantly flashing and changing the numbers of car-parking spaces in all the venues around town. Continuous reassurances brought to you by incredibly bright lights. At the bottom of Wexford Street they've even put in a new cinema-screen type advertising board to help you if you're at a loose end, unsure of what to do with your evening, your afternoon, your life. The neon sign above the Camden Deluxe used to just flash and flicker, repeat over and over again the name Camden Deluxe, Camden Deluxe, Camden Deluxe, but now they've added a multicoloured neon wonder show tickertape update of what's going on in the pub today, tomorrow, the day after, the day before, whenever. You are never lost. You have a wealth of information, knowledge to titillate your senses, fill your life. But you don't know, you don't have one inkling – not an iota – as to what you are going to do when you get to the empty apartment and sit down on the silk green couch and really deal with what you're doing. You have no idea what you're really doing or how you will meet tomorrow as a result of it. There is no pixelated tickertape running along the bottom of your mind telling you what's going to happen because nothing is certain anymore. You are horrified by this, excited by this, ready for this.

★

All certainty fades with the first lines on the platform in front of the two hundred spectators, the town's dignitaries, the principal. 'I'm a fraud – Kembo's accidental death is a fraud – the principal's a fraud – this is wrong.' I imagine I'm lighting a little trail of gasoline from the stage while my words enter the void. I begin to explain myself and the trail ignites red and flickers down the steps, zips down the aisle, rounds the corner out of sight.

I'm talking, explaining the beats, the Droogs, the laptop. My eyes are open, my mouth is moving, but I'm underwater, like John, swimming from the harbour wall to the lighthouse and cause of the sand, the oil, the trawlers, the bracken, even though my eyes are open, I can't see a thing, not a thing. I'm being washed in the truest of Balbriggan water, the sea and the canal. Even though I know what words I'm saying, I'm underwater so I can't hear them. But I'm saying them. Believe me. I'm saying them.

I'm telling them I was in the school on the Thursday. I'm telling them I ran out after him and followed him to the estate. I'm no longer struggling to stay under the water. I'm at ease. I'm floating, plenty of air in reserve, face down, just going with it. Three figures at the scaffold. The fall. The panic. The terror. Short of air. I see the fire flicker down its little trail into the corridor, catch hold of the door to my room and set it alight and continue on, the little blaze trailing away from my smoking cell and out towards the entrance to the school.

My words are of the darkness, the ambiguity of the estate, the voices, the fear, and the confusion. The lack of clarity. The cowardice. The gig in London. I'm explaining what the principal said to me, what he wants to do next year with non-Irish-speaking students. The thin line of flame takes a sharp left at the entrance door and races towards the principal's office.

My words tell of a band now using the stolen beats of a dead teenager; the actions of his killer in looking for silence; the indifference of his two other friends in looking for nothing; the silence not only of three local boys, but the culpability of a fourth, local man. Because I am a man. And I take responsibility. If no one else will take responsibility for this, I'm saying, I will.

The little line of fire rounds the corner and returns down the aisle and jumps back onto the stage and everything around us goes up in flames. I emerge from the water with a big whoosh and a single flash from a photographer captures me. It's the only noise in the whole hall. I look over both shoulders to stunned, terrified faces, the fire raging all around us; they're too stunned by how my words reflect on them to notice.

'I'm sorry,' is all I can hear now that I've resurfaced, it's all I can say, 'I'm very sorry,' and I don't bother looking into the crowd cause I know there'll be no friendly faces cause Lauren's gone to London. I step away from the podium, dripping in sweat, into the most pressurised collective emptiness I've ever moved through. The mic's screeching and I'm saying, 'Sorry, I'm sorry,' going down the steps and a baby begins to cry and I can feel the eyes of two hundred people willing me to die, and I'm halfway down the aisle when the sound of another flash-and-capture pierces the stunned nothingness and someone at the front, a distance behind, starts to weep and I'm at the back of the gym, still no reaction, and I'm expecting someone to lunge for me, hit me, grab me. But it doesn't come. My shoes are sounding off the tiles and I get to the corridor and leave the gym and stop outside, feel the sun warming my face, drying my new skin and let my whole body deflate, for a second, two seconds, and I hear chairs scraping, voices mumbling, whispering, talking, shouting and I look back into the gym, see shadows emerging, angry shapes forming, hear the chaos starting up and look to the school's exit gate and take off.

I run. Run like I've never run before, sprint, every muscle in my body focused on moving me further and further from the gym, that school, those memories, that guilt. Away from the consequences of what I've just done, away from the responsibility of the truth. I run, for the effort of running, and only the running. I run, but know, and try to block out the knowing, that the words I spoke on the stage will have to be dealt with when I stop.

★

It's dark. And quiet now. The phone has stopped ringing, the text messages have stopped beeping, asking, insisting I explain myself, return to the town. Numbers I don't know have my number. No one knows where I live. All my school-related post goes to my parents.

I pick up the phone again. The glow from the screen lights the whole room and I scroll down and find her name and begin to text but stop. That's something I would've done days ago, weeks ago, months ago. So I bring up her name. Lauren and Lauren New. I press Lauren New and just go for it, forget everything and get ready to say whatever comes out first, natural. Don't think about it, look into the darkness and get ready to talk.

The dial tone goes weird cause it's England; there's a little click and her phone starts to ring, and ring, and ring. Nothing. And then her voice appears, like a light, and says, 'Hi, this is Lauren, sorry I missed your call, please leave a message and I'll get back to you. Thanks, bye,' and the beep goes and I'm lost.

This mad deep reverberating silence waits to be filled and for a second I bottle it – just a second now – and go, 'Hi Lauren, it's Rob here. Hope you're keeping well. Just seein how you're getting on and how you're fixed for a visitor.' It's a disaster. 'Yeah, I'm eh, well, decided enough's enough here and was hoping you might be interested, ye know, in hooking up – I don't know how soon I'll be over, it depends on a few things, but I, ye know, I'd really like to . . .' and the phone beeps again and the time is up on the message and my screen zaps off and everything seems darker than before I called.

Why she didn't answer begins to needle. Maybe she wasn't near her phone, fair enough, but maybe she was out with friends, or out with someone new. Enjoying London. Enjoying a new start. Enjoying life.

I sit and rest after my running. Sit in the empty darkness and think about what's to come: the uncertainty of the new; the fear of the old; the relief of the truth and the death of my ambition. I'll have to deal with them. But now, darkness. Total darkness. My mind's racing all over it, looking for something in it, when my phone vibrates, the ring tone surprises and the screen lights up the whole room. I'm shocked by the volume of the tone and I jump for the phone and in the jumping knock it to the floor and pick it up and hope, before I turn it round and see the name on the screen, that it'll be her name there so I can answer, and talk, and tell her what I want to tell her and ask her what I want to ask her because for some reason, I dunno, I feel like I can say things I haven't said before.

Acknowledgements

Thanks to: Seán O'Keeffe and everyone at Liberties Press, especially Dan Bolger for his sharp editing, encouragement and belief in this story from the word go; to my early readers, Stephen White, Graham Nolan, Matthew Kilmurry, Colin Troy, Damien Byrne, and as always, my mother; to the lads, John, Ronan and Daniel; to Declan Meade and all the crew at the 'Stinging Fly Novel Writing Workshop', David Butler, Clodagh O'Brien, Michael O'Connor, Phyl O'Leary, Susan Gill, Annette O'Meara, Mary H. Reynolds, Mary Rooney: your insights into the early stages of the first draft were invaluable; of course, to Sean O'Reilly, for his energy and insistence on digging deeper for a better story under the rubble of ideas; everyone at the Irish Writers' Centre, in particular June Caldwell and Carrie King, for giving me the chance to take part in the Novel Fair; and finally, but most importantly, to the love of my life, Helena: your enthusiasm, optimism and understanding made this possible.

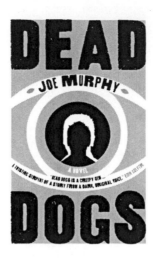

Dead Dogs: A Novel
by Joe Murphy

In rural Wexford, a young teenager is worried about his friend Seán – Seán, you see, has just accidentally killed a pregnant dog and her puppies. Seán's not stupid, but he's definitely not all there – something about his wiring is crossed, misfiring. When the unnamed narrator brings him to Dr Thorpe's house to see about putting him on some new medication, they end up watching through the letterbox as Thorpe beats a woman to death. *Dead Dogs* examines the unnamed narrator and Seán's 'place' as they feel the pressures of rural life; sinister undertones follow the teenagers as they battle their socially prescribed identities and the murderous Dr Thorpe.

This sharp-witted and psychological narrative explores the immediate and more existential troubles facing these teenagers as they move towards a climax that will tear their worlds asunder . . .

€12.99 | ISBN: 978-1-907593-45-1
Available from all good bookshops and from libertiespress.com
Trade Orders to Gill and Macmillan
Telephone: +353 (1) 500 9534 | E-mail: sales@gillmacmillan.ie

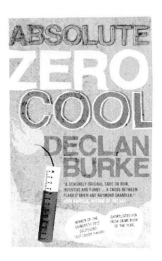

Absolute Zero Cool
by Declan Burke

Absolute Zero Cool is a post-modern take on the crime thriller genre. Adrift in the half-life limbo of an unpublished novel, hospital porter Billy needs to up the stakes. Euthanasia simply isn't shocking anymore; would blowing up his hospital be enough to see Billy published, or be damned? What follows is a gripping tale that subverts the crime genre's grand tradition of liberal sadism, a novel that both excites and disturbs in equal measure. *Absolute Zero Cool* is not only an example of Irish crime writing at its best; it is an innovative, self-reflexive piece that turns every convention of crime fiction on its head. An imaginative story exploring the human mind's ability to both create and destroy, with equally devastating effects.

€12.99 | ISBN: 9781907593314
Available from all good bookshops and from libertiespress.com
Trade Orders to Gill and Macmillan
Telephone: +353 (1) 500 9534 | E-mail: sales@gillmacmillan.ie

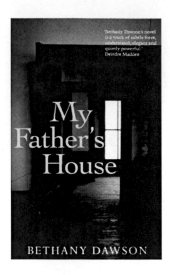

My Father's House
by Bethany Dawson

Robbie Hanright has a normal, settled life in Dublin. With a wife and baby, an undemanding job and a nice home, everything is just as he wants it. However, after an enduring estrangement from the rural landscape of his youth, Robbie receives a phone call from his sister asking him to come home. Left with little choice, Robbie returns once more to County Down, and to Larkscroft Farm, to confront the father who tormented his childhood and face up to a history he wants only to forget.

Set against the backdrop of a decaying farmhouse and fragile family connections, *My Father's House* is a powerful, lyrical story of loss and regret, through which Bethany Dawson reveals an affecting compassion for the profound, and often painful, complexities of family life.

€13.99 | ISBN: 9781907593604
Available from all good bookshops and from libertiespress.com
Trade Orders to Gill and Macmillan
Telephone: +353 (1) 500 9534 | E-mail: sales@gillmacmillan.ie

Lightning Source UK Ltd.
Milton Keynes UK
UKOW03f0207040414

229403UK00002B/27/P